CAPTIVE
OF THE
STOLEN
EMPIRE

MEGAN
VAN DYKE

CAPTIVE OF THE STOLEN EMPIRE

CITY OWL PRESS
www.cityowlpress.com

Cover Design by MiblArt. All stock photos licensed appropriately.

Edited by Heather McCorkle.

For information on subsidiary rights, please contact the publisher at info@cityowlpress.com.

Paperback Edition ISBN: 978-1-64898-365-8

Digital Edition ISBN: 978-1-64898-366-5

Printed in the United States of America

PRAISE FOR MEGAN VAN DYKE

"Van Dyke puts an imaginative spin on "Cinderella" in her second Reimagined Fairy Tales romance, The Ugly Stepsister, which takes place after the traditional tale's happy ever after. Van Dyke keeps readers guessing with a clever, twisty plot that proves stories are always filtered through the point of view of their tellers. The hero and heroine make a swoon-worthy pair, and supporting characters add color, especially rebel Mina and her brothers. This adult fairy tale will captivate fans of fantasy romance." — *Publisher's Weekly*

"A fun, sexy, swashbuckling read. Hook is a swoony, caring, protective surprise of a hero, and he meets his match in the dauntless and sassy Tink, who'll go toe-to-toe with a pirate any day. Magical creatures, seafaring adventures, plot twists and turns, steamy kisses (and more!) await in this exciting, reimagined version of the story of Captain Hook and Tinker Bell." — *Amanda Bouchet, USA Today Bestselling author of The Kingmaker Chronicles*

"A seductive reimagined Neverland fairytale dusted with magic, passion, and adventure that will hook readers from page one!" — *InD'Tale Magazine*

"Such a wonderful retelling. Fast paced, well plotted, full of glorious pirate action and a great enemies to lovers romance at the heart of it." – *The SFFRomCast Podcast*

"Van Dyke's action-packed debut puts a sexy, adult spin on Tinker Bell and Captain Hook. On this daring adventure, mermaids become the least of their problems, as Hook and Tink come under threat from their mutual enemy, Blackbeard. As they spend time together, they learn the complicated truth behind each others' storied pasts—Van Dyke does a good job making Hook and his crew sympathetic—and a fiery passion grows. The steamy scenes, explosive battles, and adventurous treasure hunt make for a gripping tale." — *Publisher's Weekly*

"Packed with steamy romance, adventure, and an unforgettable cast of characters, Megan Van Dyke's clever reimagining of Peter Pan, centering Tinker Bell and Captain Hook, is an absolute treasure. The writing is effortless and draws you in immediately, leaving you fully immersed in a fantastical world that feels both familiar and fresh." — *Paulette Kennedy, International Best-selling Author of Parting The Veil*

"Keep your hands and feet inside the ride at all times. Ladies and Gentlemen we are going to Neverland. But not the Neverland you remember from your childhood. Hook and Tink are amazing in this new twist on a classic." — *Melody Caraballo, author of Unhinged Witch*

"Megan Van Dyke's story resets the balance of Neverland, turning an imaginary playland into a world that lives and breathes through every scene. Highly recommend!" — *K.J. Harrowick, author of Bloodflower*

"A delightful, sexy romp set in a fresh, yet familiar fantasy world. Perfect for anyone who has shipped Tinker Bell and Captain Hook!" — *Jeffe Kennedy, award-winning author of Dark Wizard and The Forgotten Empires*

"A fun read that hooks you from chapter one with vivid characters and a smooth, fluid writing style." — *Desirée Niccoli, author of Called to the Deep*

"Megan Van Dyke just became a one-click author for me." — *Ashley King, Author of Painting the Lines and Forever After*

"A fun and sassy retelling that's impossible to put down." — *Kat Turner, author of Hex, Love, & Rock and Roll*

To all the gamers who couldn't stop thinking about what would happen to the world after the heroes lost and you reached "game over."

CHAPTER 1
ILYA

They conquered my city, but not me.

Our people lay dying. Sorrena burned. The once salt-tinged breeze, turned putrid with the scent of smoke and death, ruffled my hair. Surrender was the only way to cease the carnage, but that didn't mean I had to like it. Not when I'd be taken from the city I was born to lead and made the hostage of a tyrant.

My sandaled foot clicked against the marble floor, sharp staccato beats in time with the fury pumping through my veins.

"Stop that, Ilya," Mother said from her high-backed seat at my side. She cut a hard glance up to me where I stood next to her on the dais, her dark eyes carefully devoid of emotion.

I pressed my lips together but nodded in return. The heiress of Sorrena couldn't appear nervous, furious, vengeful, or any of the other racing emotions churning within me. No, I must be just as severe and resolute as my mother. Her back sat as straight and stiff as the cliffs that plunged into the sea. I tightened my fist, blocked from her view, in a vain attempt to keep my emotions in check.

Thunder rumbled, echoing through the room. The wall across from the throne was open, clinging to the top of the cliffs and providing a view of the sea beyond. Only a handful of marble columns obstructed the sight. Dark clouds hovered low on the horizon, dropping a sheet of rain into the turbulent waters below. We could no more halt the storm than the vastly more threatening and terrible fate we waited for.

Any moment now, Emperor Ryszard's dogs would be shown into the throne room to demand our surrender. To refuse would mean death—a long, bloody, terrible one.

Lightning flashed over the sea. Its light reflected in the twisting silver of Mother's crown, so similar to the streaks painted by age in her brown hair that it was hard to tell where one stopped and the other began. The central sapphire was unmistakable in its brilliance though. My hand found the smaller twin stone around my neck, the Mark of Sorrena, the symbol of the heir of the city.

I swallowed the humorless laugh trying to break free. A failure of an heir who'd been forced to watch from the high tower as our troops were slaughtered. We'd never been fighters. Our small military were more peacekeepers maintaining order in our coastal trading city, the farthest east before the Ocean of Storms, but we'd had to try.

The double doors groaned open. Rain and sea spray splattered onto the polished floors across the room. Men and women in crimson and grey—the emperor's colors—filed in. Blood and dirt marred their uniforms, but otherwise, many looked none the worse for wear. I wish I could have said the same about my people.

Lieutenant Barbarous led the procession of our enemy. It should have been Nyke, our captain of the guard, but he was lost among the dead or dying. Word of his loss still cut me deep. My chest tightened at the lack of his reassuring presence. I'd seen him almost every day of my life, discussing plans with Mother, instructing our troops, or providing me with weapons lessons that I never could quite master. No more.

"Perhaps they'll all slip and fall into the sea," I muttered as they crossed the wet marble to ring the room.

For once, Mother didn't rebuke me.

Terror gripped my limbs as the first of the emperor's captains entered the room. Then another. And another. It was easy to spot the captains with the armor that covered them head to toe, all gleaming metal and polished leather. Five in all, each lethal with both blade and magic. The emperor sent only a handful of his *children* to drive us into submission. Each bore a different helm resembling an animal. No one truly knew the faces of men and women who led the emperor's armies and carried out his every whim.

Mother rose as they came to stand before us.

I glanced at the side of the throne room where my father stood with my little sister and a cluster of nobles and advisors. He nodded to me, offering a tight smile that pulled at the laugh lines around his mouth. The best support he could give, I supposed. He was always the bright spot in our family, calm and soothing in contrast to my mother's sharpness. A small circlet graced his head, the only sign of position that separated him from the other well-dressed courtiers he stood with.

My sister chewed her bottom lip, her attention far away on the stormy horizon. The High Priest of Soliel, God of Light, had kept watch over my sister during the battle, but she was wise for her cycles—she knew far more of what happened than anyone wanted.

My attention fixed on the captain in the center, the one who advanced nearer than the others—Lucien, they called him, with a helm like the great stags of the northern wood. Everyone knew of the emperor's first-in-command. Blessed by Erabus, the God of Darkness, he could craft masterful illusions, force someone to see their worst fear, their greatest desire, or their doom staring them in the face. He didn't use it now, but he didn't need to. His presence struck a horror all its own. My throat dried. I notched my chin higher as I stared him down, infusing my eyes with all the fury simmering under my skin.

We'd lost, but I'd never let them conquer me.

"Lady Astraea Valerious." Captain Lucien's voice rang with power, deep and fluid as the churning seas.

"Captain." Mother gave the briefest of nods in return.

My back stiffened as another captain, one with a helmet resembling a bear, snickered. A glance from Lucien silenced him. Perhaps our pitiful defense was humorous to him, or he enjoyed the thought of my proud mother submitting to them. If I'd been blessed by The Four with magical gifts like each of the emperor's prized captains, I'd have used them at that moment. Burnt them to ash. Stolen the air from their lungs. Graced them with the kiss of death. But no, I wasn't so blessed. Few in our city were. Nor had the Gods and Goddesses heeded my prayers as I'd kneeled in each of their four temples in turn to beg their protection and grace. Perhaps if I'd been more devout, they would have listened.

"In the name of our emperor, I ask you to pardon your people from further death and destruction and kneel. In return, Emperor Ryszard is prepared to let you and all your people"—he gestured to those assembled—"live as long as they follow his edict."

He paused, but Mother did not respond. There would be more. We'd heard enough about the fate of our neighboring city-states to know. The emperor would demand a hostage as a show of our submission to his rule. An *honored guest* he called it—such a joke. Everyone knew one step out of line by the city-state would mean the hostage's head. And it wouldn't be my father's, nor my little sister Justina's. He'd take the person my mother would least want to lose.

Me.

Not because of any great love, but because I was her prized heir. The child she'd trained from birth to follow in her footsteps. *All for Sorrena.* Our motto. I swallowed the bitterness on my tongue. I'd have given my life to ensure Sorrena's future if it would have saved us from this moment.

Lucien's attention slid to me and held.

A shiver rolled across my skin, raising gooseflesh in its wake. I fought the urge to squirm and stared him down, our gazes locking across the space between us. What I wouldn't give to rake my nails across his face or hurl him off the cliffs. His death wouldn't save us, but it might spare the next city-state the emperor eyed.

It could have been a trick of the light or my imagination, but the hint of a grin flashed behind the slim opening at his mouth. My wall of defiance shattered for the briefest of moments. My lips parted. Heat raced to my face. Lucien's attention returned to Mother. The shift in his focus snapped the spell over me, if there'd been one at all. I straightened, my resolve firmly back in place.

"Our emperor also requests a tax be paid to support the greater good of the empire," Lucien said as he looked to another captain, who stepped forward bearing a large scroll, a crimson wax seal face up on its seam. "Failure to meet these requests will result in a consequence of our emperor's choosing."

Greater good. I dug my nails into my palms. I didn't need to read the scroll to know what he'd demand. Food, money, and supplies to support his army and keep us weak. No doubt he'd want any profits from our trade network as well, first access to the goods we imported, and control over the sea trade routes we'd developed to the west and south. It's what I would demand if the roles were reversed.

"Further, members of your household will join him as honored guests in Zhine." Lucien's attention slid back to me. "Your daughters."

Daughters.

Plural.

No. No, no, no.

It was supposed to be me. Just me. But Justina—

Mother spoke.

I didn't hear what she said, nor the words of the captains as I stepped off the low dais and advanced on the enemy in front of me. "Leave my sister out of this!"

"Ilya!"

The heat of Mother's exclamation scalded me, but I didn't back down as I stared up at Captain Lucien, his fierce figure only an arm's length away. He could pull his sword and cut me down before I could retreat, but it didn't matter.

Mirth danced in grey eyes as stormy as the clouds behind him. "Intriguing." His voice was so quiet I nearly missed it over the murmurs and conversation that erupted in the wake of my outburst.

"Take me. Let her stay." My chest rose and fell in quick succession as I braced for his reply. An invisible rope stretched between us, pulling us closer though neither moved.

"Our emperor will want you both."

The rope frayed. I stumbled back as my anger seared brighter than the lightning crackling in the clouds.

"No. He can't, he—"

"Ilya." Mother stood beside me. My name might as well have been a slap in the face. Her look said everything she couldn't. *Be quiet. Don't make this worse.*

Emotion roiled under my skin like the storming seas. First my city, my people, and now my sister. I'd destroy them all. My teeth ground together as I stared Lucien down. Let them take us and use us as pawns against Mother, but I'd make them pay for it. Him. Them. I spread my anger across the allies at his sides. Even the emperor himself.

Mother turned to Lucien. "We accept."

Tears burned at the corners of my eyes as Mother knelt, her violet dress, the same shade as my own, pooled around her on the floor. Her regal head tilted forward. The only sign of subservience she'd ever shown.

The storm reached us then, the rain blowing in sideways from the opening toward the sea. Thunder rumbled through the very ground as the biting wind tossed my hair.

An all-consuming fire spread through my chest and up my neck. My knees wobbled. I knew this was coming. I thought I was ready, but nothing prepared me to see her like this.

All for Sorrena.

She'd give it all, and so would I.

I didn't remember kneeling or bowing my head, but there I was, staring at the boots of the emperor's captains as the sideways rain soaked through my dress and onto my legs. The cool, salty wetness did little to douse the inferno that roared within me.

"In the name of Emperor Ryszard, we accept the fealty of Sorrena and all its people," Captain Lucien said, his voice once again booming and clear despite the raging storm.

"In the name of the emperor," his soldiers echoed.

A single tear escaped to join the puddle. Just like that, Emperor Ryszard added another city-state to his collection.

Mine.

They'd pay. If it took my very life, I'd tear the empire apart one stone at a time.

I craned my head up at Lucien. He stared not at Mother, a ruler on her knees, but at me.

CHAPTER 2
LUCIEN

H onor and duty. They were the foundation of my life, yet they could be cruel mistresses. They were for the armies of Sorrena today. How many died for their ruler's foolishness?

Weariness pressed on my shoulders. Drying sweat and grime clung to me under my armor—it chafed against my senses as much as my skin. Death walked with me long before my first battle. I'd been born with the blessing of the God of Darkness after all, but this one bothered me. So much bloodshed could have been avoided if Lady Astraea had only bent the knee and sworn fealty earlier. Or better yet, if they hadn't blocked the trade routes, perhaps our emperor would have spared them. They weren't a threat to us, not a military one. Their arrogance cost many lives—theirs and ours.

At least we finally had another city-state brought in line and added to the empire. One step closer to my emperor's goal of lasting peace and prosperity for the entire region. Perhaps then death wouldn't be such a constant companion.

My attention shifted to Lady Astraea's daughter, Ilya. A proud spark of defiance flickered in her strong-willed gaze. I could almost admire it. She showed more strength than many of the men on the battlefield. Her look alone would have flayed a lesser man. Yet she'd be trouble, a nuisance that would live under our roof in Zhine and likely try to murder each of us in our sleep.

The young woman notched her chin higher despite the unmistakable wetness on her cheeks that wasn't from the rain. "She's just a child. Don't tear her away from her home, from her fa—"

Her mother latched onto her arm. Ilya grimaced and went silent. I stiffened and fought the urge to step back. Her words had struck a blow worse than any I'd received from their men on the battlefield.

Old memories, ones I'd long ago tried to repress, crept to the surface. A cabin in the resting season. Death. Starvation. My skin prickled as a chill slid down my spine. The deep sorrow of loss still haunted my nightmares.

My emperor had found me there long before he rose to power after his brother's illness and ultimate demise. I was the first of his adopted children, his captains. He gave me life, purpose. All that I'd become was thanks to him. For that, if nothing else, I served him with every waking breath. I stood a little straighter, forcing away the reckless thoughts. I couldn't afford a distraction. Not now. Not here.

"A feisty one." Orson stepped forward. His words anchored me back to the moment. Like me in height and bulk, his armor still bore our enemy's blood that he'd refused to wipe away. He thought it made him more intimidating, like the red paint he applied to the teeth of his bear helm, but it was sloppy, disrespectful. Our emperor didn't raise us that way.

"Maybe she already needs a reminder of who she swore fealty to." Kasida's tone spoke of a threat rather than a question. Her feline helm cocked my way, sharing the sharp glint in her eyes.

They were still jumpy from the battle, bloodlust unquenched despite the terror we wrought. I gripped the pommel of the dagger sheathed at my side. This could get out of hand, and though I'd grown numb to death, any more of it today would complicate this surrender.

Ilya's lips thinned. She held my gaze as I turned back to her, not bothering with the other captains. Wise, she knew where power resided, but her look said much more than that. I rolled my neck to ease the sudden tension there. By The Four, she would be a thorn in my side.

"Rise." I gestured to the women on the ground. Rain pinged onto my armor, the storm at my back just as furious as the women in front of me.

Orson returned to his place behind me with a huff of frustration.

Lady Astraea finally released her daughter. The imprint of her tight grip faded from Ilya's arm as she rose. Wet, purple fabric clung to her legs from the water, accenting a form that would be pleasing if she weren't our captive. A gust of wind tousled her hair, rich as good soil.

"I'll offer you a deal."

"Lucien, we—"

My teeth ground together as I waved Orson silent. He tested my authority more and more lately. We had orders to bring our emperor a guest from Sorrena to reside with him in Zhine—whomever the ruler valued most. Any fool could see that was Ilya. She'd come with us. On that, I wouldn't budge. But he didn't specifically demand *two* from Sorrena. He'd taken Lord Merrin's twins after his oldest had been put to the sword following a failed uprising. I'd planned to bring him two from here as well. Assurance, in case of a similar incident. The foresight would please him, but plans could change.

"I want your vow of obedience, here and now, to our emperor and to me, and I will let the little one stay." I gestured to the young girl still trapped within her father's arms, barely visible beyond the advisors clustered around them.

Ilya's lips parted. Her eyes widened before blinking rapidly.

"You already have my pledge, the pledge of all of Sorrena to serve the emperor."

"*Our* emperor."

She swallowed. "Our emperor."

"By your oath of fealty, you and your mother have spared your people —for now," I said. "This additional pledge is to me. No trouble. No stepping out of line. One offense against our emperor or his rule, and your sister will join us in Zhine." By The Four, I didn't need one more thing to worry about in this sprawling empire. If leaving the younger one behind could ensure her sister's willful allegiance, then so be it. But if Ilya caused as much trouble as I feared, I'd bring the young one too to keep her in line and as an extra guard against misbehavior from their mother. Lady Astraea Valerious might hide her emotions well, but I had no doubt she harbored just as much fire and resentment as her oldest daughter.

Lady Astraea glanced from her daughter to me and back again, her expectation clear.

"I agree." Ilya gave a jerking nod, but I didn't miss the way her fists tightened at her sides. Lightning flashed and thunder boomed as if The Four themselves bound her vow.

"So be it." I nodded to Ilya in return and then to Lady Astraea. A flicker of emotion passed over her face, so dim I nearly missed it behind her granite façade. Perhaps the Lady of Sorrena had a heart after all. The governor our emperor assigned to the city would have a task keeping her in line, even if she was smart enough not to directly defy him for her daughter's sake.

Ilya pulled my attention once more, her scowl still etched in place. Who would have the more difficult charge to watch over—the governor or me?

ILYA IGNORED everyone for the first few days of our return journey to Zhine. She sat still as a statue in the coach we'd brought to bring the emperor's honored guest to him. If we hadn't immediately whisked her away, I would have sworn she traded places with her mother. They had the same emotionless expression, one so unnatural it could only be mastered by years of careful practice. She ate little and said less. Even

Orson's crude remarks at a stop on the second day earned no more than a thinning of her lips.

Had her fire gone out? Or was it simmering and building, waiting to burst forth? The change in her demeanor intrigued me. Most of our hostages were complacent upon their capture, not eager to resume the bloodshed that led to it. Even so, there were plenty of hard looks, muffled curses, and occasional tears. One poor girl sobbed for days. There was no such emotion from Ilya.

Even now, as we took a break to rest and water the horses, she sat in the coach, staring at the wall in front of her rather than the activity around us. This section of the dirt road ran near the river, swollen to its banks from recent rains. But soon it would veer away, leaving the forest behind for a while in favor of grazing land. This time of year, the fields would be lush with wheat ready for harvest and cattle fattened from the abundance of the growing season.

Warren slapped me across the back, jarring me back to the moment. "Still weary from the battle?"

"From that scrimmage outside Sorrena? Never." I *was* tired. I'd drained my magic and worked my muscles to exhaustion outside the walls of the city. It was impossible to rest properly on the journey home, even with our slow pace due to the wounded. But I couldn't let that show. Once we returned to Zhine, then I could rest properly and refill the inner well of my magic as only time and sleep could do.

"Right." Sarcasm dripped from his voice. His fox helm canted to the side.

"You weren't there." I rolled my shoulders, forcing away the tension building there. I'd ordered Warren to stay behind and guard our supplies and our medics during the battle. Our new subjects didn't need to know he never bloodied his sword.

"And whose fault is that?" he asked.

I shot him a level look. "Mine."

Blessed by Vespera, Goddess of Twilight, with the ability to move the very ground beneath our feet, he was one of the strongest among us—magically anyway. But the young man, no more than twenty cycles, suffered from a bad heart. The last battle he'd fought in nearly ended him. I couldn't lose him—I wouldn't. Not like that.

I'd been raised together with my fellow captains at Emperor Ryszard's country manor. There we were trained and tutored in all matters of war and government, but none of us were related by blood, at least not that we knew. As orphans, it was hard to know. Even so, the bonds between Warren and I were as strong as any blood relation. My brother by choice. I couldn't say that about all of them. A few I'd have preferred to see the back of if not for our shared bond of loyalty.

"Anyhow, you seem..." He shrugged. "Distracted."

Distracted by a puzzle I yearn to solve. My attention slid past him to the coach. Midmorning sunlight slanted in through the open window, highlighting the edge of Ilya's face. "It's nothing."

Warren shrugged. "Whatever you say."

Three sharp whistles split the air.

Fuck. I pulled my sword and ran toward the warning from our scouts as another set echoed the first. "To the east."

Warren and a cluster of nearby troops followed.

My grip shifted as we plunged into the heavy green underbrush, weaving between the thick, maroon trunks of the Naya trees. We'd spread out our troops, traveling in a long line through the forest roads. An ill strategy for defense, but I didn't think we'd need it. Not this deep in territory we controlled. *Who would dare?*

"Captain!" A young soldier rushed up to meet us, brushing a branch lush with needle-like pointed leaves out of his path. No visible injuries hampered his movement.

"Report."

"We were fired on from just across the clearing up here. At least ten strong. They fled when we whistled for help."

Fled? So quickly? It wouldn't be easy to do with the heavy overgrowth here, to say nothing of the Naya tree's pointed leaves that could leave quite the sting on the skin if you hit them just right. I toyed with the pommel of the dagger at my side as I ordered the troops near us to spread out through the forest. "See what you can find. Take them alive if you can, dead if you must." They couldn't have gotten far. Turning my attention back to the scout, I addressed him directly. "Injuries?"

He shook his head. "None, sir."

"None?" Warren echoed my thoughts.

The clearing was visible down the slope ahead, an open, grassy plane spotted with shrubs. Any archer with decent skill would have been able to hit a target that far away. With several of them firing, someone should have been injured.

Unless they meant to miss. I stiffened.

"A distraction?" I asked, more to myself than anyone.

The scout's eyes widened.

"The valuables we took are near the back with Orson and Kasida," Warren said. "Why pull us away here? A mistake?"

"Possibly. Unless they're not after the valuables." Was their aim to separate us? Divide the line? My lips pressed thin as I pondered the sudden attack. But to what end? They might take out some of our troops, but they had to have known they'd be outnumbered. Not to mention attacking us would result in our emperor exacting retribution from their respective city-state. Plus, their honored guest would be—

Ilya.

I snapped my head back in the direction we'd come from, suddenly certain of their ploy. "They're after our hostage."

CHAPTER 3
ILYA

Three sharp whistles had called away several guards and two of the captains, including the one I loathed most.

Bastard.

Yes, he'd let Justina stay, but he'd tried to take her away in the first place. Besides, what he'd done to my city, my people, was unforgiveable. Bile burned the back of my throat as memories of leaving Sorrena flashed through my mind. Bodies of the dead being arranged for a mass pyre. Blood leaking over blue and silver armor. Burned buildings. Blackened stone. I shuddered.

The days had blurred into a haze of seething rage. My captors hadn't shackled my wrists or locked me in a prison wagon, but the coach might as well have been one. I ate the rations they offered—flatbread, smelly cheese, and the occasional roasted hare or deer. I couldn't slip out in the night and slit their throats, but that didn't mean I had to talk to them. I'd promised good behavior, not courtesy.

Mother would be dismayed. An heir of Sorrena turning up her nose at anyone who dared approach? Unthinkable. It wasn't how I had been raised to behave in front of company. But these captors were far from pleasant foreign nobles. Without thinking, I slammed my fist into the coach wall, earning me a wince of pain.

Craning my neck out the open window, I watched for returning forms—or lack thereof. A few guards in their crimson and grey uniforms still lingered about, tending to the horses as they looked off into the forest after their comrades. From this vantage I could see little beyond the thick trunks with their maroon bark and their branches laden with needle-like leaves. The guards wouldn't be able to see too much more.

Something was amiss, but what?

The river stretched out in either direction off to my left, the steady rush of water pleasantly calming despite the situation. Some horses drank at the grassy edge of the water, but only a few of the emperor's men lingered there. If I were ever to make a run for it, now would be the time. My skin tingled as I grabbed the door handle. I could do it.

I sighed in defeat, my hand slipping into my lap. Not only would they certainly catch me, but I couldn't risk Justina. Not for something so foolish. Mother would be disappointed that I even entertained the idea. If I were going to act, I'd need to formulate something better.

A horse squealed. A human curse followed.

I glanced back toward the river in time to see an arrow plant into the ground near the horse's hooves. A second one already speared the mud nearby.

"There!" a guard called. "Across the river!"

Movement flickered on the opposite bank. Forms moved among dappled shadows amid the trees. My heart leaped. Allies? I embraced the side of the coach, yearning for a better view.

"Too few," I whispered. I sank my teeth into my bottom lip. What could they hope to accomplish with only a handful?

An arrow crashed into the side of the coach. I yelped and jumped back from the window. A second one whistled through the opening before planting itself in the far wall with a heavy thump.

My heart beat against my ribs as I stared at the fletched end. *By The Four, that could have killed me!*

A strip of paper had been wrapped around its center and tied to the shaft with twine.

I mustered my courage and peeked out the window. An archer in nondescript colors stood near the opposite bank. The figure gave a dramatic nod before hurrying off into the forest. My skin turned clammy. A message? From Mother?

Hurriedly, I untied the twine. My hands shook as they pulled at the knot. My gaze flickered between the arrow and the world outside. If anyone saw... If they knew...

The paper unfurled, dropping to the floor where I retrieved it.

Rebels rise. Help us.

My eyes widened. Could it be? Not the faintest whisper of rebellion had reached my ears in Sorrena. I turned the narrow paper over. Blank. My heart dropped.

Movement caught my attention out the window. The captains.

In a rush, I rolled up the paper and the twine and shoved them the only place I could think of—down my dress and between my breasts.

I threw open the door and stumbled out as Lucien reached me.

"Lady Ilya," he said.

I feigned hiding behind the coach, letting apprehension and worry show on my features. All I really wanted to do was grab the arrow and shove it into his eye socket.

"You're here." He looked me up and down. "Unharmed."

I cocked an eyebrow at him, feigning offense. "Did you expect me not to be?"

His hand toyed with the pommel at his side. "What's this about?" His voice hardened. "Did you plan this? Set up some kind of rescue attempt for yourself?"

I gaped. "You think I know? That arrow could have killed me!" I thrust an accusing finger toward the object in question. It hadn't been meant to harm me, I knew that now, but he didn't.

He stiffened as he looked past me at the coach. "But why would they…" Captain Lucien trailed off, and he glanced toward the forest on the opposite side of the river.

"Exactly." I spat the word in his direction. "Why would I plan my own assassination?"

He whirled on me so fast a gasp lodged in my throat. I stepped backward, retreating from his advance until the side of the coach dug into my back. Too close. Far too close. His nearness swarmed my senses, radiating fury. The sharp gleam in his eyes matched my own.

"If I find out you orchestrated this, then—"

"You'll what? Threaten my sister?" I crossed my arms over my chest and stood a little straighter, staring him down.

Another captain trotted up with a female soldier in tow. He stood shorter than Lucien and bore a helm resembling a fox. Warren. He hadn't been present in the throne room, though I'd identified him from the chatter of the guards on our journey here. His magic remained a mystery. Of all the emperor's captains, we knew the least about him.

"Lucien," Warren said.

"What?" Lucien snapped the question at his companion.

Warren looked between us, silent and calm.

Lucien's shoulders sagged, and his voice was calmer when he turned to his companion and asked, "What have you learned?"

"Same as what our scouts reported," Warren said. "Should I send troops after them?"

Lucien peered at the river. The current ran fast and strong from the recent rains. It would be a tough crossing for man or beast unless they found a bridge nearby.

"Do it, but don't go too far. It might be a trap. See what information you can gather."

Information you can gather.

Of course. Hope glowed within me. I could gather information for these rebels. Who would be better suited and more motivated than a hostage in their midst? I'd wrest out their secrets, find some way to leak the information outside of Zhine, and take them down from within, one step at a time. I didn't know how I'd get the information out—any letters

I wrote, if I were allowed any, would undoubtedly be read—but I had nothing but time to figure that out.

"You look pleased." Lucien stared me down once more. His companions had ventured off to carry out his orders.

"I couldn't help but imagine you drowning in the river with all that armor on." The words were out before I could stop myself.

He blinked, as if shocked by my words.

I notched my chin higher and refused to look down.

"What have I gotten myself into?" He shook his head before turning to walk away.

My lips thinned as I stared at his back. I'd expected a retort, anger, or a spew of accusations. I wanted them—anything to let me vent my fury at the terrible man. Not nothing. Instead, I channeled my frustration into a plan. Sit and play the happy captive? No. Never. I couldn't reverse time, not even the Gods and Goddesses could. But I'd find a way to unlatch the shackles placed upon us.

And I'd do it as far from Lucien's watchful gaze as possible.

I KNEW we approached Zhine when farms and grazing pastures became a regular part of the scenery. We neared the end of the growing season, and the fields were still lush with tall grain and other vegetables waiting to be harvested. The cattle had grown fat and lazed in their pastures. Those sights almost made me smile, until I remembered that this wasn't the outskirts of Sorrena, and any food here likely went to feed the emperor's armies above all.

The city of Zhine was large and old, its buildings of stone and wood occupying both sides of the river that cut through its center. The emperor's castle commanded the largest hillside near the city, where it lorded over the sprawling city in the valley, marring the landscape like a giant barnacle on a rock.

The castle itself was formidable, massive—a relic of an age many cycles ago when only three families had controlled all of eastern

Galanthia's numerous city-states. Not so anymore. Cycles of strife generations ago had resulted in the breakup of the territory into its current parcels. Each city-state had a sizeable city as its capital with the surrounding area towns belonging to its control.

Multiple towers of grey stone speared the sky, with lower levels of the castle barely visible beyond the high wall that ringed the entire thing. We approached along a rutted, cobbled road that split just ahead, one branch veering toward the heart of the city and the other ascending the hillside to the massive iron gate at the castle wall.

We passed through the gate into the castle bailey, where I was let free from my temporary prison. The yard bustled with activity and smelled of horses, sweat, and waste—unsurprising given the number of men and beasts present. I had little time to stretch my legs before I was led inside and promptly searched by a female guard, not that I'd even had the chance to steal a knife or anything of use. Good thing I'd burned the little scroll in a campfire one night.

Lucien led me through the maze of stone hallways. And it truly was a maze, almost like the castle was built in pieces over time without any semblance of a plan. Perhaps it was. Some passages bore colorful tapestries, others were simple and plain. At one point we must have neared the kitchens or dining hall, as the savory scent of roasting vegetables and meats caused my stomach to give an embarrassingly loud rumble. Through it all, Lucien kept a steady watch on me, frequently looking back over his shoulder to make sure I hadn't somehow disappeared despite the guards following just behind me. Too often during our journey, I found his attention lingering on me. Avoiding his notice was difficult, gathering information more so, especially since I spent most of my time alone in that cage of a coach.

At length, we reached a set of guarded double doors. Lucien's fellow captains entered first, with us trailing.

My blood boiled as I caught sight of the man seated at the back of the room.

"My emperor." Power and respect laced Lucien's words as he bowed to the man where he sat in a high-backed chair behind a massive desk. It wasn't a throne, not exactly. The room we entered was more of a private office than a space to hear the pleas of his citizens or hold a formal gathering. Although, much of the room lay barren, as if the emperor was used to having an audience standing in wait of his attention. The far side of the room he occupied, however, was lavishly decorated with wide pieces of art in gilded frames, a plush rug under his feet, and golden candelabras standing near the walls.

"I bring you Lady Ilya Valerious of Sorrena." Lucien gestured to me before stepping aside and leaving me alone.

An odd part of me yearned to have him back, blocking my view of this most loathsome man. Even the captain was preferable to his emperor.

Emperor Ryszard steepled his fingers in front of him as he scrutinized me with his shrewd and narrow gaze. His heavily greyed beard and hair spoke of a man who had seen many cycles, though a hint of strength still clung to his frame below the layers of rich fabrics that draped his skin. Unlike his captains, he didn't bother to hide his face, though I truly wished he would. Then, I wouldn't have to look upon the man who carried an aura of ownership over all he beheld, as if he truly thought himself the rightful ruler over so many he conquered.

"Ilya Valerious." His fingertips drummed against one another.

"Emperor." It took everything I had to keep the fury from my voice. My body shook with rage seeing the man responsible for so much death and destruction. And for what? So he could reign like a god over us and increase his own wealth and power? He promised peace and prosperity for all, but those conquered by him had seen none of it. He started the wars. He weighed taxes on our people that would ensure hungry bellies during the resting season.

The emperor rose from behind his heavy desk of dark wood and stalked my way. The fur cloak around his shoulders brushed the stonework behind his polished boots. "My guest should kneel when greeting her emperor."

My body stiffened, refusing to bend. I had to, I knew that, but kneeling before this monster, with his gleaming captains ringing the room, rebelled against my nature.

"Perhaps some persuasion?" Kasida asked. I recognized her from the journey here. In fact, most of the emperor's captains I knew from rumor and reputation, if not introduction.

She advanced, but Ryszard waved her back as he approached.

I swallowed and forced my knees to bend, lowering my eyes to stare at the boots of the approaching tyrant.

He extended a ring-decked hand. Rubies and garnets shone in their golden settings from the light of the candle-lit chandelier above.

It took everything to lean forward and kiss his rings. Oh, to have a dagger to plunge into his neck. It would cost my life, but that would be a worthy price to end his reign. I'd contemplated it for endless hours during our journey to Zhine. Unfortunately, I'd never had the chance to steal a weapon, and they likely would have discovered it and taken it from me.

"Welcome to Zhine, Lady Ilya. I'm pleased to finally have Sorrena join our empire."

As if we'd chosen to serve him. I fought the urge to wipe my mouth as the emperor turned and strode back to his desk. His every word was poison, just like what he'd used to murder his brother and steal his throne. He claimed illness took him, but rumors said otherwise. We should have seen his lust for power then and acted, but the city-states had mostly tenuous relationships with each other at best. Working together wasn't something we did much at all, certainly not easily, and now it cost us everything.

"Excellent work, my first," the emperor said as he reclaimed his seat.

Lucien bowed to his emperor.

"Captain Warren, see our guest to her room."

A room? Not a cell? I clenched my jaw shut to keep the thought from spilling forth. So quickly the emperor dismissed me, as if I'd brought him tea and not proof of my city-state's fall. He'd regret that. I'd make sure of it.

Warren escorted me through the halls. He wasn't the worst of them, and if I'd had to choose one to escort me, I likely would have picked him. He was kind to those he commanded, from the little I'd seen, and had slipped me a few sweet cakes during our journey here. Because I wasn't eating enough, he'd said. Fair. Though who could eat with the memory of their people's conquest fresh in their thoughts? Perhaps, in another world where Warren wasn't one of the emperor's captains, we could have been friends. In this one, however, he was one monster serving another. Didn't he see the death and destruction he caused?

"I think you'll like Lady Elin. She's kind, though a bit skittish," he said as we traversed the halls. He had a gentle voice, and a young one. This captain could be a teenager for all I knew. It would explain why we knew so little about him. "Perhaps you can share some of your courage with her?" he added.

I looked at him sideways but didn't reply. I'd never met Elin Glaus of Ourelas, one of the northernmost city-states, but there were worse people he could have assigned me to share a room with. She was another woman after all, one only a few cycles younger than me, and rumor held that she was pleasant as Warren described.

We turned a corner down another long hallway. My breath caught. I skidded to a halt. A familiar face stared back.

"Lady Ilya." Gabriel Laril, the heir of Trale, gave me a sad smile. "The rumors are true then. Sorrena has fallen."

More grey colored his sandy hair than I remembered, but there was no mistaking the kind man who had periodically traveled to Sorrena to negotiate trade agreements on his brother's behalf. He'd been my companion, a sort of temporary uncle, when I'd visited Trale with Mother cycles ago. The stories he told made me laugh, and he'd included me in conversation where most overlooked me for my youth.

"Your room will be the first on the left. Your trunks will be delivered soon if not already," Warren said. "I'll leave you."

We weren't truly alone. Guards wandered the halls in silent patrol. Another two stood at the end of the corridor. Of course, we'd be watched at all times.

"It's true," I said once Warren rounded the bend, out of sight.

The fall of Gabriel's city-state was a terrible blow. If we'd helped them then... I grimaced at the thought. We'd have only lost sooner. We weren't outfitted for war. Defending sea-fearing vessels from rogue pirates was the best we could muster, and truthfully, we were not as successful at that as we ought to have been.

"I'm so sorry, Ilya."

We met in a friendly embrace, sharing the sorrow of my news. But we couldn't linger on that. Not for long. We had work to do.

"I bring other news," I whispered in his ear. "Rebels rise, and we can help them."

CHAPTER 4
ILYA

I reclined in the grass under the thick boughs of a tree, savoring the fresh air and the breeze across my skin. It almost felt like a dream, but it wasn't. For the first time in the few weeks since I'd been brought to Zhine, they let us outside. Not just in the inner courtyard garden that we were often allowed to wander, but truly outside, beyond the castle walls.

It was a risk on their part, I knew, but also part of their clever ruse. After all, if we looked like honored guests instead of prisoners, some people might just start to believe it. Sneaking off would be impossible with how many guards were around. Even some of the captains lingered near, but still, it was a pleasant change. If only we could have used the opportunity to pass off information to the rebels somehow—maybe left a note in a tree or something. With the emperor holding us captive, he tied the hands of our respective families, our people. But not us.

"There's a workroom where a scribe copies letters," Lord Fernand

Reis of Nassia whispered when we had a moment where the guards moved out of earshot.

The young man had hidden his pregnant wife in a temple to the Goddess of Dawn when his city had been invaded, keeping her out of sight from Ryszard's men. Even they respected the sanctity of The Four. The ruse had worked, ensuring her safety, but now the two were separated, and he'd missed the birth of his first child.

One more emotional burden. One more separated family. All the more reason he was eager to work with Gabriel and I to smuggle information to the rebellion somehow.

"Locked, I'm sure." Gabriel stretched his arms over his head before reclining back on the soft patch of grass, pretending to relax.

"Not always, from what I overheard," Fernand replied. "And it's not far from the dining hall. We just have to get through the guarded door."

"Oh, that's all," I said, letting the sarcasm drip from my words. The clang of metal rang out as nearby soldiers shifted in their drills and began sparring. I'd hoped that watching the drills might give us some insight into the emperor's plans for his armies, but the drills were basic enough that they told us nothing.

"Maybe we need a distraction?" Gabriel suggested.

A man slipped in his drills and fell to the ground, groaning a curse that carried over to us. "Or we wait for them to slip up." I gestured to the man for emphasis. Green as some of them were, it was possible.

"You could use your feminine wiles on them." Fernand smirked, his eyes hooded with mischief.

I fought the urge to roll my eyes. "Or perhaps you should charm them." With his dark hair, chiseled jaw, flawless golden skin, and confident air, the man certainly had the ability to turn heads with little effort.

"My charms are better used elsewhere," he replied.

Elsewhere? I fought the urge to prod for more information as another set of guards wandered in our direction. Their feigned casual approach wasn't fooling anyone, probably just as our relaxed and casual nature might not either, but it was a careful dance we all played.

Despite the sour note Fernand's suggestion elicited, upon further thought, he did have a decent point. I'd caught a fair share of guards looking my way, like this pair now. I stretched out my legs, baring a little more skin to the light. As expected, one of the guardsmen adjusted his focus ever so slightly. Perhaps it was worth a try.

Elin wandered up, the book she'd been reading clasped tightly in front of her, and sat on the ground next me, spreading the skirts of her dress out around her like a proper young lady. She sat straight-backed and tall with posture even my mother would have praised...unlike my reclined and casual position.

Though only a few cycles my junior, she'd retained an innocent disposition more like my sister's than my own. Perhaps that was part of what made us easy friends. That and sharing a room together. Though I'd been hesitant of the arrangement at first, Elin's presence had become a welcome comfort in this prison of a castle. Much as I was loathe to admit that a captain was right, Captain Warren had been correct that I would like her, though none of my courage seemed to have worn off on her, at least not yet.

"Should they really be doing that, you think?" she asked to none of us in particular before gesturing to Lord Merrin's twins, Titus and Theo, sparring not far from the training ring. Someone had let the boys borrow wooden training swords, and they met in a clumsy clash before springing apart once more.

Elin was always worried about stepping out of line, and she jumped at the slightest odd sound. A surprise, given her father's penchant for trouble. It was no wonder Ryszard had targeted their city-state early on for supposed infractions upon his border—ones Elin fervently denied. She'd awoken in tears from nightmares of that conquest more than once —not that I could blame her for that. We all had memories that haunted us now. Sometimes they woke me too. And the poor girl, she'd witnessed even more than I had, having lost all three of her older brothers in the fighting when their city-state fell.

Gabriel shrugged. "I trained at their age. It could be good for them. Take their mind off things for a while."

The boys had had a difficult time of things as well, particularly once they first arrived. Gabriel mentioned that they had only recently started to calm down, and if training helped that, if the emperor's men would allow it, I supported it wholeheartedly. In fact, part of me yearned for it myself. I'd trained often with Nyke, our captain of the guard, back in Sorrena. Though I'd probably started too late. Perhaps that's why I struggled to master the skills he taught. At only seven cycles, these boys would be better served learning now. I only hoped they had a bright future to learn for—more reason we had to succeed.

As the guards wandered off, I voiced the next part of our plan. "If we do find something, then we need to make use of it. Get it…" I gestured around us. And not just out, but to someone we could trust, someone who could get it to the rebels. Ideally, one of our families, if we could be so lucky.

Elin gave a dramatic sigh. "I should have kept reading…" She supported our plans, though all of it made her nervous. Fair enough. But she was trustworthy and steadfast. Even if we refused to let her get involved in anything dangerous, she was good at listening and gathering information. After all, the guards were not quite so careful around her given her innocent and unsuspecting disposition.

"I've got that handled," Fernand said with entirely too much confidence. He'd claimed as much before, but never shared exactly how he'd accomplish such a feat.

"Care to share?" I asked.

He shrugged. "Best if I don't."

I scowled at him. That lack of trust and cooperation got the city-states into this mess to begin with. If we'd worked together from the start, the emperor wouldn't have been able to pick us off one by one.

Foolish, so foolish.

Though perhaps not a surprise. After all, it was how the city-states came to be. Once, three families ruled the stretch of eastern Galanthia that the city-states now occupied. But their heirs started squabbling among themselves, refusing to support one another, and so the territory splintered off into the various larger cities and their surrounding lands.

"Well, maybe the workroom will have a stack of outgoing letters I can add to. Unless you're willing to talk?" My brows arched high as I tilted my head to the side. *Stubborn man.*

Fernand stared me down, but it was Gabriel, ever the voice of reason, who replied. "If one of us gets caught and interrogated..."

I sighed. They didn't want whatever connections they'd begun to cultivate to potentially be compromised by someone else. It was smart, really, and I admired their determination to help their homelands however they could from within Zhine. After all, it was that spark of defiance that now brought us together. Still, it chafed to know I wasn't privy to all elements of the plan.

"They don't tell me anything either," Elin interjected, opening her book once more and thumbing through its pages.

"Perhaps later," Gabriel whispered before bobbing his head with a significant look past me.

A tingle of unease crawled down my spine, almost like a cloud had covered the sun and promised rain, though no such tufts of white or grey marred the sky. Without even meaning to, I tensed up before I looked over my shoulder, half-knowing what I would find.

Striding our way around the corner of the training area were two more captains: Zurina, with a mask like a great hawk who could control animals, and the one who always seemed to be stalking my shadows, Lucien. Every time I looked at him, I remembered the fall of my city and his threat to bring my sister to this horrible place. Worse, they weren't watching the guards in their drills, but instead stared right at us.

I couldn't see their faces, not with those ridiculous helms covering them, but one doesn't need to see lightning to hear the thunder and know it might strike them.

"Elin, read aloud to us." We needed something so our gathering would look less suspicious.

"Um..." She tucked a loose strand of blonde hair behind her ear. "I'm not sure you'd like it."

"Doesn't matter. Just read. Start at the beginning." I shifted my attention to the captains once more, and this time she followed.

Her eyes widened a fraction before she looked away. Dutiful as ever, Elin flipped the book back to the beginning and started to read, "Once upon a time, in a small village—"

Gabriel groaned and laid back on the grass.

Elin looked to me, her blue eyes round and unsure.

"Ignore him." I shuffled closer to her, half-turning my back on the men. A good story might be just the cure for my irritation, and Elin really did have such a lovely reading voice.

"Right. Well." She smoothed out the page and started again. "Once upon a time..."

Chapter 5
Lucien

The exterior training yard was full of soldiers working their drills, ones they certainly needed based on the sloppy sparring taking place. But the men and women working up a sweat under the blazing end-of-season sun weren't the main reason why I'd chosen to take a walk around the training yard with Zurina.

My gaze fixed on a group of the emperor's honored guests lounging in the tree-dotted grassy expanse nearby. "I still think this is a terrible idea."

"Why?" Zurina replied, catching the direction of my attention. "It's not like they're in any danger."

I halted, leveling her with a hard, flat look. "That's not my concern." Which she likely well knew. Sometimes she seemed to know my thoughts better than I did. Not literally, of course. Her gifts came from Aurora, Goddess of Dawn, and though she could communicate with animals, that did not extend to humans. Any power of the human spirit or mind could only come from Erabus, God of Darkness, who granted my blessing of illusions.

"You worry too much." She smacked me on the shoulder. "The guards have eyes on them at all times. There's no way they could sneak away. Besides, it might be good if they relax a bit, you know?"

"You're not worried about how comfortable some of them have gotten with each other? What they might be plotting together?" Ever since Ilya arrived, the mood of the others had changed. They seemed bolder somehow, encouraged, and it wasn't because she was a blinding ray of sunshine. Oh, she shone, so brightly I often couldn't look away, but it was with a raging fire of fury rather than a pleasant disposition. Somehow she used that passion to galvanize the others, little sparks spreading to them like the start of a wildfire that would consume everything in its path. If I'd seen such heart in one of my soldiers, I'd have admired it, praised it, stoked that fire hotter and seen how it would transform her even more. In Ilya, it spelled trouble. Just like I thought the day I met her.

"What could they plot here?" Zurina asked. "Even if they do, what could come of it? We're better off focusing on real problems, like where we're going to store all that delicious wine you brought back from the last conquest."

She laughed at her own joke, but it only soured my mood. We had plenty of things to worry about, and that was the least of them. Whomever had attacked us on the road still remained a mystery, one that plagued my mind into the late hours of the night.

"Oh, come on," Zurina replied to my silent scowl. "You know I'm kidding."

A heavy sigh slipped through my lips. "I know." She was always the one trying to lighten the mood, which I appreciated, even if it didn't take any of the weight off my shoulders these days.

Perhaps it would be wise to separate them more though—at least for a time. I hadn't thought it would present a problem for Ilya to stay in the same room as another guest, or for all of them to be housed so close together. It saved space and made it easier for us to watch them. Now, doubt nagged at me. I turned back toward the group lounging under a tree some distance away. The men both lay in the grass, seeming to rest. Ilya had slid next to Elin, who sat with a book open in her hands, reading aloud. The soft, high notes of her voice were a muted hum mingling with the grunts and groans of the training soldiers and crack of wood as training staves met over and over.

"See, they're reading," Zurina said. "Not a problem. If you really want to worry about our guests, then spare a moment for those poor boys." She gestured to the twins where they beat at each other with wooden swords. "They'll never learn like that."

I winced as they met in another wild clash, both huffing with exhaustion. No, they certainly wouldn't. The sight pulled at something deep within me. Maybe it was the scars of my own childhood, but seeing the boys struggle always left me with a hollow ache. And how they'd suffered... Their older brother had refused to submit to our emperor's hospitality. His rebellion earned him death and condemned his younger brothers to live here in his stead, far from their family. They were old enough to know exactly what happened, but too young to endure it without a barrel of tears and sorrow-laced fury.

Maybe, just maybe, if I helped them, they'd come to understand and appreciate the peace our emperor worked toward, that their time away from the family served a greater purpose.

"Care to help me give them a lesson?" I asked Zurina.

She shook her head. "Two of us might overwhelm them. You go ahead."

Laughter erupted behind us from a group of soldiers seated at the resting benches near the training area.

"I'm curious what's going on over there," Zurina said, gesturing to the group. "I'll see you later."

As I watched her leave, one of the soldiers moved, revealing the likely source of their enjoyment. Lady Reyna of Alidade, one of the few of the emperor's honored guests who seemed to understand the emperor's vision and embrace their home in the castle, sat among them with a broad smile on her face as she gestured wildly with her hands. The moment she slapped them together in front of her, peals of laughter rang out again. If only all our guests could be so amiable. The same could be said for their respective city-states. Hers was one of the few that wisely submitted to the emperor earlier on and agreed to support his campaign for unification.

When I turned back to the boys, one of them—Theo—fell to the ground, groaning in pain.

The other, Titus, dropped his sword and leaned over him. "I'm sorry! I'm sorry!"

Shit. My chest grew tight. Injuries were always a risk in training, but if I taught them the proper methods, those injuries could be minimalized. It wasn't just that though. Seeing children hurt or upset always dredged up painful memories of when my emperor had found me suffering as a child and saved me from certain death. A nightmare that Ilya had reminded me of all too recently when she begged for her sister to remain. In retrospect, I was glad she did. I probably would have ended up regretting bringing the girl, even if it pleased my emperor. Not that I'd ever admit it.

I raced toward the boys, but someone else beat me there. Ilya dropped to the ground and laid her palm on Theo's head. Calming words spilled from her lips as she tended him like a mother or older sister. Elin lingered just behind her, one hand cupped over her mouth as she stared at the scene, the other clutching her book to her chest.

"Is he alright?" I asked as I reached them.

Titus jumped away from me liked a spooked hare and bolted to Elin's side. She pulled him close, her arms and book a shield. Gabriel arrived then and stared warily between me and the kids as if I might cart them off to the dungeons.

Ridiculous.

I ignored them and knelt next to the injured boy on the opposite side from Ilya. Theo grabbed at his arm, still whimpering and rolling on the ground.

"You have to let me see it," Ilya implored.

"Be still," I said. Theo looked at me and paled, going quiet and still as death.

Ilya glanced at me, so brief I nearly missed her scowl, before she gently pried the boy's hand off his arm and set about feeling the injury. A light touch had him yelping in pain.

"This arm may be broken," she said, her voice calm and even. "He needs to see a healer."

I stood and gave a sharp whistle, commanding the attention of the soldiers nearby. A few of them stopped their drills and climbed over the simple wooden railing around the training area to come to our aid. "Take the boy to the infirmary."

A soldier scooped up Theo off the ground with care, though the child had once again begun to whimper and squirm while clutching his wounded arm.

"Gabriel, go with him," Ilya said. "Make sure he's cared for."

My lips thinned. The way she said it, you'd think she expected us to toss the boy in a room and forget about him rather than provide the appropriate care that such a child, especially one of the emperor's guests, deserved.

"I'm going with my brother." Titus pulled away from Elin and trailed after the others toward the castle.

"Back to your drills," I ordered the remaining soldiers who had come to assist.

Short acknowledgements filled the air as they followed my command. Another figure, Fernand, hurried after the group heading toward the castle, probably to go see after the boy's health as well. That left only Ilya and Elin, the latter of whom shifted uncomfortably and stared at the ground.

"You've become quite the general," I said to Ilya. The others listened to her, followed her orders. If I had any doubt, the last few moments erased it.

She huffed and crossed her arms. "And why are you here? To punish them for sparring?"

I crossed mine as well, staring down the challenge in her brown eyes. "I was going to offer to train them."

Her brows arched.

"Though I suppose that won't be happening today." Maybe not anytime soon if the boy's arm was broken. A shame.

"You would train your enemy?" She bent and picked up the wooden sword off the ground, bringing the false blade up to tap against her palm.

"We're all citizens of the empire." Why couldn't she see that? Things would be so much easier if she could. "Besides, better that than they continue to injure each other."

"A fair point," she acknowledged. Ilya turned the sword this way and that, adjusting her grip. "Would you spar with me?"

"Ilya..." Elin warned.

Something about watching her hold the training sword, especially with annoyance still written in her pressed lips and slightly scrunched brows, had a strange warmth building behind my ribs. "If you're up for the challenge." Let her duel me. Maybe she'd finally release some of that anger she held. I toed my boot under the edge of the other discarded wooden blade and kicked it up to my waiting hand.

"Show off," Ilya grumbled.

The corner of my lips twitched at her comment. "Perhaps you'd like to change first?" I offered. Fighting in a dress wouldn't be to her advantage, though I was curious to see what skills she possessed with a blade.

Ilya settled on her grip, adjusted her stance, and swung the sword through the air. "We can't always choose what we're wearing when battle finds us." Another quick move had the tip pointed in my direction, her arm steady as she held the heavy thing aloft.

My chest swelled in admiration. A wise and true statement.

"But sometimes we do get to choose when to fight or to leverage a different approach." She let the blade drop to her side and adopted a relaxed stance. Ilya shrugged before tossing it at my feet. "Perhaps another time." She turned on her heel and called over one shoulder, "Come on, Elin."

And what approach are you taking? I mused as she retreated back to the tree with Elin trailing after her. Anger was an interesting emotion. In a fool, it could spell their demise, but in someone as clever and influential as this woman appeared to be? That could be a dangerous thing indeed.

CHAPTER 6
ILYA

My time in Zhine had been unproductive thus far. I intended to change that.

I trailed my fingertips along the empty stone wall in one of the many hallways within the emperor's maze of a castle. Casual, bored, unassuming. Or so I pretended to be as the guards passed by, chatting with one another and barely giving me a passing glance.

My heart raced much faster than my slow walk down the hall. A soft breeze carried the last whispers of voices retreating behind me as the guards turned the corner, leaving the short hallway empty if only for a few moments.

All week I'd walked this way, letting them get used to my presence. This pair left their post near the off-limits door early, eager to get to dinner before their fellow guards could take the best morsels. At least, that's what they complained about often enough.

Locked doors and stationed guards kept us contained in limited areas of the castle. Always someone watched the emperor's honored guests. Every meal, each stroll through the gardens. Except for now, when the young guardsmen left their post early. Fortunately for me, they guarded the door I needed to get through, one that led to the room where scribes copied missives and wrote letters to be sent across the empire. An ideal place to potentially find useful information and possibly send an illicit message of our own.

With a quick look either way, I cracked the door open. An empty hall lay beyond. *Thank The Four.*

My body shook as I slipped through the doorway and closed it behind me, my breathing far too loud in the now quiet space. A fool's errand, searching for information we could use against Ryszard and his captains in this labyrinth of a castle.

But...

Each remembered cry of my people as they fell to blade or magic, or mourned the loss of their freedom, stoked the fire within me. It was risky, doing something that could get me in trouble. But leaving them in bondage to a tyrant was something I could never do.

Four doorways lined the torch-lit hall before it took a right turn. Faded tapestries shielded the walls between the doors. I dug my shoulder into the dark wood of the first door, earning me a twinge of pain. Locked.

The second... I gagged at the pungent scent that wafted from the privy chamber as soon as I cracked the door. My eyes stung. They didn't clean this one near so well as the one by our assigned chambers. We'd never let things get so bad in Sorrena. *Disgusting brutes.*

Muffled conversation tickled my ears as I approached the third door. My legs locked up. The end of the hall pulled my attention. No, not there. The sound came from within the room. Chatter. Laughter. Growing louder.

I couldn't be caught in this part of the castle.

In haste, I fled toward the door I'd exited, my sandaled feet slapping across the worn stones. Hinges squeaked behind me. Laughter echoed into the hall, swarming my senses and sending a prickle of dread sliding down my spine. The door loomed just ahead. *A few more steps and—*

The racket quieted before a gruff, male voice took up its place. "What do we have here?"

A cold sweat broke out on the back of my neck. I'd been seen. Running wouldn't help me now. And unfortunately, that voice didn't belong to a random guard.

Swallowing my nerves, I raised my chin and turned toward my fate. Though I knew what to expect, the sight sent a tremor through my bones. Not just one but three of Ryszard's captains filled the narrow hall. Fernand had thought I could potentially seduce my way past the guards. What nonsense. But he had been right about one thing—the guards didn't watch me as closely as they did the men. They didn't expect such treason from a woman. If I got caught, they might be more lenient with me than with Fernand or Gabriel. It's why I volunteered for this. The emperor's captains though? They would be much harder to sway.

"I got lost. My apologies," I replied, taking a step back. I dipped a small bow, my fists clenched at my sides, trying to curry whatever favor might get me out of this mess.

The tallest one, with a helmet bearing a snarling bear, crossed his arms and tapped a boot against the stonework. Orson. An ugly bastard if his attitude and voice were any indication of the man beneath the mask. Some of the things I'd overheard him say on the journey here would make the saltiest sailor blush.

To his left stood Brishon, bearing a mask resembling a fanged fish complete with a fin atop his head. On his right, Kasida, one of only three female captains—that we knew of. Her helm resembled a beastly feline, including metal whiskers that assaulted the air around her head. It fit her personality—arrogant and selfish with a temper that could spring from nowhere.

"A likely story," Orson said as he drummed his gloved fingertips across his arm.

"Ilya, lost? Could the heir of a trading city have such poor navigation? Or such thin lies?"

My cheeks flamed at Kasida's taunt. Directions were not my strong suit. Trade, city planning, economics? Yes. But even getting around the city I'd lived in my whole life proved problematic at times. I bit my tongue, holding in a retort, when the door behind me, the one I'd entered from the hall, crashed open.

"Where are the guards that—"

I turned slowly toward the voice, one whose rank demanded attention from the other captains.

Antlers skewered through the bright torchlight spilling in through the door, silhouetting his form. My back stiffened. The remnants of dinner turned foul in my stomach.

Of all the captains to catch me in a restricted hall, he was the worst. He'd threatened to bring my sister here if I stepped out of line, and now, when I was somewhere I shouldn't be, of course he would show up. The Four really were deaf to my prayers.

"What's going on here?" Lucien asked, joining the other three to encircle me against the wall.

"A mouse out of her cage," Kasida answered, one hand on her hip.

His eyes settled on me as if seeing me for the first time. Standing still under his prying inspection took significant effort. Especially when I yearned to run.

"Did you forget that this hall's off-limits?" The deep timbre of his voice made it as much a statement as a question.

"No." My retort carried more strength than I felt. "I got lost on my way back to my room." A thin excuse at best, but I couldn't very well tell him I'd planned to search for information to use against them. That would damn me—and Justina.

He shifted his weight. "You're too smart for that. What were you really up to?"

Shit.

"A night in the cells might loosen her tongue," Brishon supplied. "Or several."

The captains advanced, closing the distance between us and trapping me in.

"I could think of another way to put her tongue to work." Orson's lewd gibe and the accompanying laughter it evoked boiled my blood.

"There were no guards," I bit out. "I didn't mean to get lost." Really, it was their fault their shoddy patrol hadn't stopped me.

"What do you think, Lucien?" Orson asked as if I hadn't spoken at all.

Unlike the others, Lucien didn't laugh. My body grew taut as a bowstring until he grabbed my chin, forcing my eyes to meet his through the breaks in his mask.

My enemy, the monster who stole my home.

"Lost or not, your behavior is suspicious." He released my chin but did not step back.

"Told you we should have guards escort them," Brishon mumbled.

"Mmm...the cells then, I think," Orson said, advancing. The leer in his voice made my stomach roll. Nothing good would await me in the cells, though it wasn't the damp, cold walls that raised the fine hairs along my skin.

Lucien waved him off. "I have a better idea." His deep voice wrapped around me like a caress, too soft for the monster it came from.

"It was a simple mistake. I meant no harm." A lie—I'd need them all if I had any hope of getting out of this mess.

A shake of his head cut me off. "Perhaps, but perhaps not. Either way, we can't have our guests breaking the rules without consequence."

My heart plummeted. He couldn't force Justina to come here too, not just for this, not when I hadn't been successful.

"She's not worth your time, Lucien." Orson closed the distance until I could practically feel the sliminess of his presence, slick like a sea eel. "Let me take the girl to the cells. We'll see if that doesn't adjust her behavior."

Lucien barely looked at Orson before focusing his attention on me once again. "No. I think I'll take her to my quarters instead."

Whistles split the air, accompanied by a shrill laugh from Kasida. I gripped the material of my dress to prevent myself from smashing my fist into Lucien's face. It would hurt me more than him, but I yearned for it all the same. Relief and fury warred within me. It wasn't the cells, it wasn't Orson, but what he implied was just as disgusting.

He pinched my chin once again. "Some time under my watchful eye will yield the truth, whether this was a case of a poor lost woman or something craftier."

Bastard. I willed the fire racing under my skin into my eyes.

I'd fight him every step of the way. If he thought to teach me a lesson in the same way as Orson, he had something else coming. No one conquered me.

No one.

Orson slapped Lucien on the back, metal ringing in the air. "I'm sure you'll have her crying out all kinds of confessions."

More laughter followed, echoing through the halls that closed in like a cage.

I'd burn them all. Someday. Somehow.

Lucien ignored the laughter of the others and grasped my forearm. "Come on."

A gentle tug, out of place for the man himself, urged me to walk beside him toward the bend in the hall. My body rebelled, unwilling to follow the monster toward his den. Another, firmer jerk had me stumbling into motion.

"Find out where the guards went," he said to his companions. "See that this lapse doesn't happen again."

Laughter subsided as they confirmed their agreement, but that didn't silence their comments. They continued, chased us around the corner until we reached another door.

"This is a mistake. A misunderstanding," I said while Lucien practically dragged me along.

He flung the door shut behind us, cutting off taunts still aimed my way, and turned to face me. I forced myself to stare him down.

Stormy grey eyes, visible through the thin slat in his helm, bore into mine. "I don't know what you're planning, but even one step out of line like this is too many. If you're innocent, then you shouldn't mind being under my watch."

"Is that what we're calling it now?" Keeping me close was one thing. I could be crafty, secretive. He couldn't observe me all the time. But what the others implied was an entirely different matter.

A sound resonated from his mask that may have been a sigh. "I'm calling it what it is."

"I haven't broken my oath to you." It was a risk, reminding him, but I had to know what he planned. "You can't force my sister for this."

"I won't have her brought here. Yet."

The constricting bands of worry around my chest loosened, but only where my sister was concerned. Another tug had us moving down the long hallway. Flickering pools of torchlight illuminated the space along with the glow of the twin moons filtering in through the occasional uncovered window.

Each step brought me closer to my inevitable fate. My thoughts spiraled inward. I'd be strong, I had to be. Though swallowing down the curses and fury rising to the tip of my tongue had never been so difficult.

I thought myself prepared for anything, to give anything. But as Lucien drew me to a halt in front of a set of guarded double doors, my fear surged to the front. The urge to run gripped me tight. Staring down his army in the face of defeat, even bending the knee on that fateful day, had been easier than this. I clenched my necklace in a tight fist, the star sapphire digging into my palm. The Mark of Sorrena had never felt so cold—so heavy—around my neck.

Be strong. Have courage.

All for Sorrena.

CHAPTER 7
LUCIEN

Ilya stopped struggling as if she'd suddenly been turned to stone. Her arm went limp in my grip as her face paled.

She should fear me.

Still, the sight pulled a frown at the corners of my lips. Leaving her to Orson was out of the question. He'd lock her in the cells, carry out his taunts, and worse. The emperor wouldn't want his guests treated in such a way whether they'd been trespassing or not. Orson had a habit of taking things too far, asking for forgiveness instead of permission. Though lately, he'd been pushing his limits even more than usual.

Ilya was certainly up to something. The way her mind worked behind her brown eyes when she assumed no one watched her spoke volumes on their own, to say nothing of the whispered words she managed to utter to her fellow guests as soon the guards turned their backs. Perhaps she assumed no one saw, but I did. Little went on in the castle that escaped my notice.

She beckoned like a warning flame high in the mountains, calling my attention when it should be elsewhere.

I'd never forget the way she looked at me when I entered the throne room of Sorrena. I expected a cowering heir or restrained indifference. Instead, the look of promised revenge stirred my blood in an entirely different way. Her defiance, her fire. It had dimmed only briefly at the beginning of our journey to Zhine weeks ago. But she had a soft side too, one I'd seen in her care for the younger guests. The thought of Orson touching her, breaking her, bothered me more than it should. She was just a curiosity, that was all. And trouble. I couldn't forget that. Keeping her apart from the others was a wise move, one I'd already been contemplating, and this simply provided the catalyst to move that plan into motion.

"Ajax." I waved the guard over where he stood at attention outside my chambers. The crimson and grey of his jacket hung loosely about his shoulders and arms. The young man could do with more time in the training yard—another day.

"Lady Ilya will be staying with me until further notice. Have her things brought here in the morning."

"Yes, Captain." He gave a perfect salute.

Though he lacked physical strength, the boy was loyal. For that reason alone, I'd assigned him to watch my quarters—not that I needed any protection. But Emperor Ryszard had ordered guards stationed at any places off-limits to his guests. A substantial portion of the castle—though much of it they guarded by merely watching the entrances to various wings or staircases.

I'd need the guards outside my door now, to keep an eye on Ilya, if nothing else.

She followed me into my quarters without a word, her lips thin. I studied her as she took in the main room. Her eyes flitted this way and that over the sparse furnishings. I'd never needed more than a simple seating area for a rare discussion with one of the guards or my other captains. Now, I couldn't help but wonder how she saw the worn, brown leather on the long couch, the simple tables, or the thick drapes that barely covered the balcony across the room. Shabby furnishing to an heiress. The stunning gem in her necklace, as blue and brilliant as the seas of her homeland, was proof of that.

"Don't think to leave," I warned as the guard clicked the exterior lock into place. "Not without my permission. That door"—I pointed to the far one on the left wall—"contains a servant's chamber, which will be your room. It's dusty but can be freshened tomorrow. The middle door holds a small privy chamber."

The servant's chamber was an unnecessary relic of the castle's past before Emperor Ryszard claimed the structure as his seat of power. Not once had I used it. I wasn't some prickly noble who required a servant at their beck and call. Better they stay out of my space as much as possible. We'd had no personal servants at the emperor's estate where I was raised. There were instructors, tutors, cooks, maids, and groundsmen aplenty, but they saw to the estate in general, not us specifically. Unlike some of my fellow captains, I didn't see the need for change now.

"What? No more threats?" Her voice dripped contempt, though I didn't miss the little quaver in her tone.

I stalked around her, coming between her and the sitting area until she had no choice but to look at me.

For all her courage and bite, Ilya retreated as I advanced. One step, then another, until the soft material of her odd sleeveless dress pressed against the stone wall near the door. She'd need something warmer soon —thicker. Her scanty attire, while enticing, would be little protection when the bitter winds of the resting season came in full force off the northern mountains. Already the nights cooled in the final days of the living season as farmers brought in the start of their last harvests.

Her throat bobbed as I neared, nor did I miss her flinch. For all her bluster, she was full of fear and wariness. It flickered with a deep unquenchable fire in her eyes. *Good.*

"What did you expect, Ilya?" When she didn't answer, I leaned in closer until the faint scent of olive flower wafted through my armor to tickle my nose. "Did you think I'd be like Orson? Take you screaming against your will?"

To her credit, she didn't look away. "Yes."

The one word hit me like a punch to the chest.

Somehow, some part of me hoped for better, though I couldn't say why.

Measured, deep breaths calmed the sting of her words. Why did I want her regard? She was the emperor's guest. A curiosity. I simply wanted his guests to find contentment in their place. That's all.

"The fear in your eyes right now, the risk of what I or any of the others could do to you if you step out of line again, that's your punishment." I bit the tip of my tongue as the words slipped free, harder and more biting than I'd intended.

The stiffness of her jaw softened. Her face tilting ever so slightly to the side as her brows wrinkled. "Why?"

She looked at me like I'd just declared her free or unclasped invisible shackles on her wrists. She expected me to bring her sister here, had dared to ask about it. Her accusations in Sorrena had dredged up nightmares of my youth—a child's fear and terror that I'd long ago shoved to the back of my mind. Memories of that cabin where I nearly died always came back to chase me, no matter how I pushed them away. To make another child feel that fear...I couldn't bring myself to do it unless I had to.

"I'm not a monster, whatever you think. I saved you from one tonight," I snapped. "Consider that."

I turned away, not bothering to wait for a reaction or response. Hopefully, she'd think on my words. Hopefully, no one would read too much into what happened this night and spread any ill rumors about exactly why I brought Ilya to my quarters. But if they did, I was certain they would fade away in a matter of days. They always did—some new distraction earning the attention of guards and servants alike as they gossiped in the halls.

"You'll find better rest here tonight than in that dusty room," I added, gesturing to the couch draped with heavy furs. Then, I stalked to the nearest door, the only one I hadn't explained to her. "The furs should keep you warm. I'll have your things moved here tomorrow."

Her head tilted to the side. "You don't have a servant who stays with you? Someone to remove your armor? Clean your room?"

"No. I've attended to my own armor since I was a boy. We all do." My room in the emperor's old manor house, where we'd lived before his reign, had been small, not much more than a closet, but it had been mine when nothing else was. At least, as much as a room can belong to anyone. A haven to rest aching muscles and ease the bruises gained from endless days of training.

"I suppose that's a new concept for you," I added. As a noble lady, she'd have had all her needs seen to, until she came here. Had her people not blocked our trade routes and imposed a heavy tax on our conquered vassals, perhaps she still would.

Ilya frowned, her nose wrinkling. "Not entirely."

I turned away to hide the spark of a grin her indignance ignited.

"And how long will I be staying?"

Her near breathless words tugged at me, too feminine for my rooms, especially given the stuffed buck head staring down at her from the right wall. My icon, my symbol, assigned by the emperor long before I'd fought my first battle or had its likeness formed onto my helmet. Craning my neck, I stole another look at her. She reclined against the wall, palms flattened against the surface and eyes guarded.

"Until I decide you're harmless or otherwise."

Truly, I didn't know. I hadn't thought that far along. Perhaps this punishment would bring her into line and smother some of the rebellious spark she ignited in others. Truly, I didn't want to see her punished further. That reaction in and of itself was...dangerous.

Without another word, I flung open the remaining door, savoring the view of the spiral stairs to my private sanctuary beyond. There I could sort out my thoughts.

I didn't spare her another glance as I pulled shut the door between us. The magical lock I'd acquired cycles ago would keep her out of my bedroom. I nearly sagged against the wood, the looming stairs suddenly more intimidating than ever.

The tingling running through my veins didn't cease until I stepped out into the night air on my balcony. The city of Zhine loomed below, candles and oil lamps illuminating some of the windows—far fewer than before Emperor Ryszard started his crusade. We'd make a better life for all at the cost of those who'd died for it.

Peace and prosperity. That's what he promised. Each time we thought it secured, another city-state would step out of line and demand to be conquered.

I flexed my hand, the light of the two moons above glinting off polished metal. We'd never failed, not yet, but so many had been lost. None of my fellow captains. Our magic gave advantages far beyond normal men, not to mention cycles of training. The green recruits taking up arms in our ranks now weren't seasoned soldiers. They needed more training, more weapons practice, more—

Light beckoned below, a dim flicker as Ilya stepped onto the small balcony off the sitting room. She moved with grace across the stone and leaned over the railing, head craning this way and that. Looking for a way down? My lips twitched. There was none, and a fall from there would kill her.

I itched to tell her so, to lure her away from the balcony edge. She didn't need the warning. Her palms slammed onto the stone railing before she spun around and pushed through the heavy drapes into the room.

My magic hummed under my skin, tempting me to use it to weave a pleasant illusion to disguise myself. I could go back down there and—

No. I shook my head. More important work demanded my attention. Perhaps it was a mistake, bringing her here.

You're playing with fire, Lucien.

I huffed a laugh at my thoughts. If only fire burned half so hotly as the woman in my quarters.

CHAPTER 8
ILYA

Two young guardsmen escorted me to breakfast the next morning. They lacked the strength and gristle of seasoned warriors. We'd heard that Ryszard had recruited many young men and women into his ranks—those who wanted to serve and even those of his people who didn't. War required soldiers, and he'd refused to take the armies of his captives, taking the weapons of those who survived battle instead. A smart move. No soldier of Sorrena would have bowed to his command. The governors and spies he left behind in the city-states he conquered saw that local armies were disbanded. No training. No weapons. And certainly no rallying against him. That would earn death for the offending, and quite possibly for the city-state's honored guest.

Lady Elin met us just outside the dining hall.

"Ilya!" She rushed to me, her long, blonde hair fluttering behind her.

"I was so worried when you didn't come back last night. I asked the guards, but they wouldn't tell me much, and I just..." She wrung her hands together.

"I'm fine," I replied. "I just got a little lost after dinner and stumbled into a restricted hallway."

Elin's hand flew to cover her open mouth. Her blue eyes widened. My small offense was something the sheltered girl would never consider.

The two guards behind me waited patiently, or so I assumed from the lack of commands or other comments. However, this wasn't a conversation I wanted to have around prying ears.

"Come on, I'll explain over breakfast." I waved her toward the open double doors just a few steps away.

The scrape of silverware on dinner plates met my ears, along with the scratch of wooden benches on stone. People milled about as they ate, the scent of fatty meats and roasted potatoes heavy in the air.

Ryszard held meals as communal affairs. His captains, advisors, higher-ranking guards, and *guests* all ate together at long tables in the great room. We served ourselves from large dishes passed up and down the tables. The only advantage of the often-rancorous meals was that we could occasionally talk without having every word overheard—just every other.

A few whistles and lewd comments floated my way as soon as we entered. My cheeks flamed hot as the fires burning in the hearths on either side of the large room. Elin looked even more uncomfortable, her face turning pale as we advanced to our traditional table. A few other captives already waited there for us.

Only three people had been present when Lucien ordered me to his quarters the night before. We'd passed some guards in the hall who might have made assumptions, but I had a suspicion about who'd spread rumors. One day I'd gut Orson like a fish for that, if for nothing else.

"Lady Ilya." Gabriel's grey eyes were full of sorrow as I took a seat across from him, Elin at my side. Gabriel had once again donned the role of honorary uncle, both to Elin and me. His brother's sole heir after the loss of his brother's only child, he was well suited to be a presence of calm and reason. Further, he seemed to enjoy his fatherly role, perhaps because of the child-sized hole in his own life—not that Elin and I were children anymore.

"I got lost," I said. He'd know something was wrong already, perceptive as he was. Besides, he'd helped develop my plan and knew what I would attempt last night. He took risks for his people too, as did Fernand at his side. "Unfortunately, I ran into some unexpected company."

Fernand bit back a curse and ran a hand through his wavy, dark hair.

"Then the rumors are true." Gabriel's shoulders hunched. His greying head shook.

"What do they say?" I had to know for certain.

Both men glanced at Elin. I understood their concern. If Orson spread the rumor, as I assumed he did, it likely would make the poor girl faint.

"Never mind. I think I know, and it's not true."

Gabriel breathed an audible sigh of relief. "If that had happened, I wouldn't forgive myself. I should have gone instead."

I dropped my voice to a low whisper and leaned forward on the table. "I chose to involve myself. I know the risks. Anything that happens is not your fault."

"Still..." Gabriel frowned, adding to the fine lines marring his features.

I cut him off with a shake of my head before I slopped a spoonful of what I assumed was an egg and potato mixture onto my plate. "It doesn't matter. We'll have to wait and try again." They'd keep a closer eye on that door, at least for a while, but time and boredom had a way of making people complacent. "Also, I'm to stay in Lucien's quarters until he decides I'm innocent and not up to any mischief."

Elin's spoon clattered onto her plate, her face white as a sheet.

If the worst had happened, she may never have recovered on my behalf.

"He didn't do anything. Barely touched me. Certainly not what they imply." I tilted my head toward the table of men that made the crude remarks. Nearby guards and other hostages eyed us curiously, though nothing we spoke of was a secret. In another day or two, likely everyone would know.

"How long will you stay there?" Elin asked.

I shrugged, finally swallowing a spoonful of the unappetizing food that tasted of soil and grit. Had no one washed the potatoes properly? The food in Zhine simply couldn't compare with the fresh fruits and fish we often ate at home.

"Perhaps..." Gabriel leaned forward. "It could be an insightful stay?"

I frowned, swallowing down the thick breakfast. "Not so far. There's nothing of note outside his personal room." I'd checked. "And I—" A thought struck me like waves in a storm, crashing against my mind.

"What is it?"

I couldn't get in Lucien's room right now, locked as it was, but what if I could? Breaking in might not work. No doubt he'd notice that, and I'd be in worse trouble than now, but if I earned myself an invitation... "What if I made the rumors true?" I whispered. Fernand had suggested as much the day we were outside of the castle, but I'd thought the notion ridiculous. Swaying guards when I saw them for moment? Unlikely. But sharing quarters with someone lent more time and far more possibilities.

Gabriel's fingers drummed on the table as his lips pursed.

Fernand relaxed in his chair, looking me over appraisingly. "See, you liked my idea after all."

I knew the moment Elin caught on. "You can't mean to—" she practically yelled, catching far too much attention before she clamped her hand over her mouth.

"I do." I lowered my voice and leaned in. "It might be just the break we need."

I hated the man. He disgusted me. But, on my terms, it might not be terrible. I'd pay that price to find some weakness, some information we could use to our favor. Who would know Ryszard and his strategies better than his first captain? Besides, I didn't need to go all the way, just far enough to get into his room and get him to let his guard down. And if it took everything...well, then it did.

A wicked grin tugged at my lips as I dug into my breakfast with gusto. "Trust me on this. It will take time, but I can do it." While we waited on the guards outside the workroom to lose their sharp edge, I'd take steps toward a new target.

CHAPTER 9
ILYA

Two evenings later, I reclined on the leather sofa in Lucien's sitting room after dinner. Burnt orange and faded pink light spilled in from the open balcony doors, catching the gold clasps of my thin, sleeveless dress. In Sorrena, I would have worn a tight underdress, something to further disguise and conceal the peaks of my nipples where they poked against the thin material, especially in this cooler climate. A fur cape as well, perhaps. Tonight, I didn't bother. I wanted sultry and seductive. I needed every advantage, even if the cooling air raised gooseflesh across my skin.

I rubbed my bare feet against the smooth leather as I stretched and adjusted the fall of white fabric about my legs. The little dinner I'd eaten rolled uneasily in my stomach.

A lady and future leader of this city should not parade about like a harlot. I could practically hear Mother's criticism of my idea. *A future leader must respect herself if others are to respect her as well.*

Every day had been a lesson. How to lead, to rule, to earn respect, to be balanced and fair. Sorrena must always come first.

All for Sorrena.

Those words had been drilled into me for longer than I could remember.

But Mother wasn't here, nor could she move against Ryszard without signing my death warrant. So, it was up to me to free our city. I was born to rule and lead, after all.

The last rays of sunset trailed out of the room, leaving me in chilly darkness broken only by the flickering wall sconces illuminating the room with a soft glow.

"Where are you?" I grumbled. If he'd returned to his rooms the last two nights, it had been late, long after I'd retired to sleep.

The guards had brought me straight here after dinner again, as Lucien instructed, yet the man himself had yet to make an appearance. Unless I'd missed him and he already hid away in his room? I'd tried the door to his room as I had every night, but as always, it didn't budge.

The lock of the main doors clicked.

I flew into action, assuming my practiced pose with one bare arm draped across the back of the cushion and my legs dangling gracefully from the side. My body reclined at the optimal angle to show off my assets while looking relaxed and inviting. Or so I imagined. This wasn't exactly something I'd practiced before.

"Good evening," I pitched my voice higher, giving a soft lilt to my words, so at odds with the slimy feelings sliding under my skin like seaweed.

At first, he didn't acknowledge me. He crossed the room, head tilted upward as if lost in thought. But after a cursory glance in my direction, he halted mid-step, metal armor locking up with his body. His lips formed a thin line, just visible through the slit in his helm. Only his fingers moved as they toyed with the pommel of the dagger strapped to his waist.

Eternity passed before he responded, words tight as his frame. "Do you need something?"

I bit the inside of my cheek, fighting against the frown aching to break free.

"Perhaps some company?" I stroked the back of the sofa, leaned forward, and scooted my legs back to offer him room.

"So you can stab me in the neck with a knife you've squirreled away from the dining hall?"

"Would you like that?" I teased. I'd considered it. Briefly. If I could manage the act, it would certainly mean my death. Not to mention the steep tax and bloody reprisal that Ryszard would inflict upon my people. One captain's life wouldn't be worth that suffering. Nor was he worth my life. My forced smile stiffened with the effort to keep those thoughts from my face.

"No. I don't think I would." He crossed his arms, his head tilting to the side. "I expected anger. More indifference."

"And you're disappointed?"

"Confused. You've made your disgust of me well known, not to mention that look in your eyes when I brought you here."

I shrugged, all easy limbs and casual airs that I aimed to project. A far cry from the racing of my heart. "What look?" I tilted my head and ran my fingers across my collarbone.

His stance broke as his fingers slid across the golden pommel once more. "And you wonder why I expected aggression."

Then, he'd had me cowering in fear of what I'd thought inevitable. Now, he wouldn't even approach me, as if I were some kind of wild animal that might snap its jaws upon his neck. How easily I'd turned the tables on him.

"Perhaps I can clear up that misunderstanding." I leaned back, one leg sliding ever so slightly to the side. A tease I'd seen noblewomen practice on their would-be lovers when they thought no one else was watching. It wasn't enough to reveal any of my body's secrets, only give him a whisper of possibility.

Lucien coughed and looked away. "You're a grown woman. You can entertain yourself."

I nearly gaped as he turned and headed for his room once more.

"Wait!"

He paused, barely glancing over one shoulder.

Shit. Don't look too desperate, Ilya.

"I thought it might be nice to talk? We spent so much time traveling together, and yet I know nothing about you. Now that we're living in the same room..." I shrugged. "Usually, I'd talk with Elin or some of the others, as permissible, but here I'm alone. They didn't even bring my books when they moved my trunks in here." I rambled, but whatever, he'd stopped and turned my way. It was better than simply being dismissed.

His boot tapped on the ground, four gritty clicks before he responded. "This is a punishment." His deep voice rang through the room, stripping the last bit of heat from my skin. "It's not a change of scenery for your enjoyment." He crossed the space to the door and flung it open with ease without using a key.

"I only wanted—" The door slammed on my words. "Bastard." I smacked the cushion next to me before rising and rushing across the room, barefoot on cool stone. I grasped the handle to his room and pulled with all my might. Nothing. Not even a creak or a slide of wood.

Magic.

It had to be.

Someone gifted by Aurora, the Goddess of Dawn, must have enchanted his door. Only someone with Her blessings could imbue objects with magical properties.

Disappointment pulled me onto the balcony.

Lucien was known to wield the power of Erabus, God of Darkness. Possibly he could have the power of the Goddess of Dawn as well, which might allow him to enchant objects. The two were not opposites, like the God of Darkness and God of Light, though being blessed by more than one deity was exceptionally rare, even among the already limited number of the blessed.

Wagon wheels crunched over cobblestone far below. Darkness swallowed them as they departed the torch-lit gates and continued on the stone road leading down the hills and into the city. Zhine's temples and judicial buildings soared high above the other structures. Farmlands stretched out to the east.

Though vast, these rich lands didn't supply all the food needed for the bulk of Ryzsard's armies. With what I'd seen, however, I'd begun to wonder how massive they truly were. He captured one city-state at a time, wielding the magic of his captains rather than ground troops whenever possible. We'd seen it ourselves and heard it from others. But he didn't leave his forces in a city-state once it fell. A few, yes, to report on any mischief, but he kept the city-states in line by holding their heirs hostage.

One more thing to discover, if I could. If we knew more details on the scope of his forces, it certainly would help.

Even harder, though, would be getting that information out of the castle and into the hands of someone who could put it to good use.

An unexpected groan of wood and rattle of metal had me jumping against the railing. Hard stone bit into my side. I whipped around and froze at what I saw.

Lucien crossed the room to the seating area, a thick tome with worn navy-blue binding gripped in front of him. He gestured my way with the book before setting it on a wooden side table near the seat I'd formerly occupied.

My mind struggled to keep up with the scene playing out before me. He brought a book...for me.

"Thank you," I managed to mumble in return.

He dipped his head, the only acknowledgment before he retreated to his room without a word.

My feet rooted me to the dark grey stones. I remained on the balcony long after his door closed. It did not reopen.

A strong, chill wind finally urged me to move inside, close the heavy curtains, and retreat into the meager warmth of the room. I trailed my hand over the book Lucien had left, savoring the fine leather of the binding. Pressed into the cover was the title, *Archimond's Treatise on War and Strategy*.

A smirk tugged at my lips. At least the topic was appropriate.

GABRIEL and I strolled through the inner gardens together, pretending to share a casual discussion of no consequence. We were allowed to roam the castle during the day, but only certain areas and always under watch. This courtyard was one of our favorites, with winding paths, thick hedges, and grassy expanses. A large fountain gurgled in the center and helped obscure our speech from listening ears.

"Has your new room been illuminating?" he asked.

Gabriel's vague question brought the pain of my failure into the light of day. For three days, I'd tried to get Lucien's attention. Revealing outfits, invitations to talk, to spend time together. Nothing worked. He hadn't spoken more than a handful of words to me since the first night I got his attention, and he avoided my presence as if I were a rabid dog.

Not that I had much experience in the ways of wooing men. Mother strictly warned me off it for cycles, and with all my focus on studies and learning to rule my city, there was little time for anything more than a random tryst. All for Sorrena. Nothing for oneself. That was the way of our people, or at least those of us born to rule.

Father's place at Mother's side was purely for show. They attended formal events together as custom and duty demanded, but otherwise led separate lives. Often Father took long assignments in other cities to expand our trade routes. Whether for the benefit of Sorrena or simply to avoid Mother, I could never tell, but I longed to join him. The stories he told of the places he visited and things he'd seen filled me with wonder. I read endless books about them, studying maps and ships just in case I got the chance to go with him. But no, Mother deemed that unnecessary.

"Not at all," I admitted, returning my focus to Gabriel. "The rumors are far more interesting than anything that's happened."

By now, most of the castle assumed Lucien and I had slept together, likely without my consent. I didn't need to talk to the others to confirm it. I could see the pity in their eyes and the searching looks of the guards, and I could hear the occasional comment whispered when they thought I wasn't listening.

None of that mattered. Not really. If anything, it proved a worthy distraction and a reason to pursue the man for my use. My reputation was already tarnished, so what did I have to lose? Womanly virtues were not high on my list of values anyway.

"Hm..." he mused as we passed near a cluster of guards.

"It doesn't hurt to keep trying." I shrugged. "It's not like anything else has been enlightening, and it doesn't seem that this will be a short change of situation."

Lady Reyna entered the gardens, chatting loudly with a few guardsmen. Her lithe form brushed up against a guardswoman who grinned at her in return. A young man dared to touch a lock of her shining, dark hair when she wasn't looking. I scowled as she flirted and carried on with our enemy. They should have been her enemy too. Her city-state of Alidade, along with Lord Derrin's city-state of Palero, had submitted to Ryszard willingly quite early on. Perhaps they truly thought of themselves as his guests. *Fools.* One more reason we didn't involve either of them in any of our more strategic discussions.

I drew Gabriel to a halt, looking him up and down as an idea came to mind.

"Do I have something on my face?" His brows wrinkled as he cocked his head in my direction.

"No. I just had a thought." I meandered to the nearby bench wrought of wood and deer antlers and patted the space next to me for him to sit. "What do women do to get your attention?"

He laughed as he relaxed into the seat, one booted foot crossed over his knee. "What haven't they done would be the better question." He shook his head and stared across the garden. "Let's see, some of the more inventive ones wrote poems proclaiming their great love or sang a song they'd composed for me. Two I found naked in my bed at night. Another confessed to being pregnant with my child, though I'd never touched her and couldn't even tell you her name."

I sat a little straighter on the bench. No man had tried half so hard for my hand in Sorrena. Mother had discouraged the brave few who showed interest, too worried they'd grab at power or expect more than a simple romp in the sheets.

"I don't recommend trying any of those things, mind you," he said. "They don't work, at least not on reasonable men."

"No lovely ladies have managed to snag your eye?"

He flashed a pleasant smile as he turned to me. "No *women*."

"Oh," I said, a hint of warmth rising to my cheeks. "I didn't know."

He shrugged. "It's hard to find the right person. Now that I'm here, I wonder if I'll have the chance at all," he lamented with a sigh. He stared at everything and nothing, his attention far away with his thoughts.

One more reason for us to reverse the damage of recent cycles and free our cities.

Gabriel clamped a hand on my shoulder. "To answer your question, though, I favored those who didn't try too hard. They knew themselves, and that's a beautiful thing."

Knew themselves, huh?

My hand wandered to the necklace about my neck, the sapphire suddenly cool despite the warmth of the sun above. The Mark of Sorrena had never felt quite so out of place.

I was the heir of Sorrena, Lady of the city. But that had been taken from me, not to mention my dreams of travel. I couldn't be myself. All my plans for Sorrena, my role as heir, my hopes of seeing the world...none of that mattered anymore. Not here.

CHAPTER 10
LUCIEN

Warren sat across the game board from me where we savored a rare moment of peace within my quarters. Cycles ago, before the emperor took power, we'd played all the time. These days, spare moments were harder and harder to come by.

I slid the triangular piece across the wooden board to occupy a free space.

Warren's brows scrunched as he moved a square piece of his own, claiming mine with barely a moment's thought.

"Really, Lucien? Are you letting me win?" A broad grin brightened his features as he moved the stolen piece to the side, adding it to his ever-growing pile.

I frowned at the board. How had I missed such an obvious play? "That wasn't my intent."

"You're usually not so easy to beat. In fact, I don't think you've ever given up so many pieces this early."

He was right. I hadn't. But my mind wasn't on the game or my friend sitting across the table. My thoughts were still with the woman I'd brought to my quarters and what to do with her now. The outfits she'd worn recently, the sudden change of attitude...I'd never seen that coming, and it made me more uneasy than I'd ever admit.

"One more move like that and I'll claim victory," he taunted.

The boy's golden eyes sparkled with mischief in the light of my sitting room. With the guards on watch, we could go without our armor, or at least some of it.

Warren still held a youthful innocence I envied. Such carefree joy had been stripped from me long ago, if I'd ever truly had it at all.

"Don't think I'll give in so easily," I responded, studying the board before me. Victory would be hard-won in this match, but the challenge gave me a thrill. I lived for uneven odds and difficult situations. My ability to work through them earned me the position of Emperor Ryszard's First years ago.

The door banged open. Zurina stormed in, a force to be reckoned with, and pulled free her hawk helmet. Her short, dark hair stuck out around her ears.

"Please tell me the rumors are false." She pinned me to the chair with her sharp stare as she crossed the distance between us with her long-legged stride.

"Nice to see you too," I said.

Zurina's scowl deepened. She'd been off on a mission for the emperor for the last few days. Rumors had picked up about potential rebels rising throughout the city-states. I had a hunch they were the ones who attacked us on our way back from Sorrena, though for what aim I couldn't yet say.

"What do you think?" I asked.

She pursed her lips. "I get back and the first stories I hear are full of filth, and about you no less. I'll kick your ass if even a hint of it's true. To treat a woman that way and—" She cut herself off. Metal groaned as she fisted her armored hand. "You're better than that."

My muscles tensed at the accusation, and the fact that so many believed it. My stomach rolled. I was harsh. Demanding. I had to be for my role, but to imply I'd treat a woman like that was a new low.

Warren glanced between us, but his features lacked surprise. He'd heard the rumors too, but he hadn't mentioned it. Usually, such nonsense passed quickly, but not this time. For whatever reason, residents of the castle seemed to linger over this particular rumor and spread it with gusto.

"I'm glad you think so," I said. "And you're right, I wouldn't do such a thing. Never." I scrubbed a hand down my face. The move I'd been formulating against Warren vanished from thought.

"Good. Don't let the power twist you. Not like some others."

She didn't need to say who. Orson. Kasida. Maybe more. We'd been raised together, though I held no love for them like I did Warren and Zurina. They'd always been the darker sort, willing to lie, cheat, and undermine to get ahead. Power and conquest twisted them until they gave up any pretense of being respectable people beyond their armored façade.

Orson had been trouble from the start. He never held back with training blows. In our youth, he set half the mansion on fire once, just for fun. Another time he cut off Zurina's hair one chunk at a time until she sent a swarm of bees after him.

Zurina skidded a chair across the stonework and threw herself down in it, hooking her legs over the armrest. "You can be a cold bastard sometimes, but I don't think we could be friends if you'd fallen that far."

Where training and war darkened many, it had the opposite effect on Zurina. Or something had. She'd grown protective over our emperor's guests recently, suggesting they be treated with true respect, given minor freedoms, and watched out for, particularly the younger ones.

"I corrected those I've heard, not that many speak out in front of me. I'll see what I can do," I said.

She gave a jerking nod. "Good."

"I can help," Warren offered. "The guards aren't quite so careful around me."

"Please do."

"Though I wonder..." He toyed with one of the discarded pieces, not meeting my eyes. "What do you plan to do with Lady Ilya now that she's staying with you?"

A groan slipped from my lips. "Keep an eye on her. Figure out what she's up to."

Zurina cocked her head, brows raised. "Sticking a knife in your back. That's what she'll be up to if you give her the chance. I've seen the way she looks at you. At all of us, actually."

I couldn't stifle a wince as I reached for my glass of whiskey. I savored the burn as the stiff drink slid down my throat. Once, I'd thought the same. "She's been quite the opposite in here recently, wearing dresses that would make our old tutor blush and sporting a come-hither look. You'd think she actually wants me."

Warren whistled.

Zurina smirked. "Maybe she does."

I shook my head. "Not a chance. I just don't know what she's after." Though I couldn't deny that the sight of Ilya in those outfits caused something dangerous to stir in my chest. She had a lot of traits I would admire if she hadn't been so set on radiating fury toward the empire until recent days.

Zurina patted my head as if I were one of her dogs she could control with her magic. "You'll figure it out."

"Make your move or surrender." Warren swept his hand toward the game board.

I slid a piece up a space, hardly noticing it at all. "Are you going to tell us about your trip or are you saving that for when we're all together?"

"Like I'd keep you two waiting?" She stretched her arms and rose to her feet again, unable to sit still. "We found the remnants of what looks to be a rebel campsite, but no people or evidence of which city-state they belong to. We considered pressing on to the forests near Nassia, but I decided we should circle back here to see if there was any new information." She raised her brows at me in question.

"We've heard nothing new." That worried me more than anything. Some of the guards reported hushed rumors in taverns. Others mentioned flickering campfires in the night where no homes or villages existed. If there were rebels forming warbands, they did an excellent job of covering their tracks and avoiding the conquered cities where our emissaries kept careful watch.

"Do you ever wish we'd just left the city-states alone and held our borders?" She leaned in on the back of the chair she'd occupied, an imposing figure with her tall height.

"Doubting our emperor? That's treason, Zurina." But the words lacked heart as I said them. I tried not to. What kind of First would I be if I doubted the man I served? One who'd adopted me—all of us—put a roof over our heads and saw that we were trained and educated.

She shrugged as if it were nothing, but her eyes told a different story.

"It would be nice to have peace." Warren's reply came as no more than a whisper, the wish of a gentle heart.

His words sat heavily on my chest. We created a better world for everyone. A united front against the vast empires to the west.

"Of course we'll have peace." Zurina perked up, a blinding smile replacing the questions of moments ago. "We've conquered all the city-states that have raised a hand against us. They've stayed in line since that debacle with"—she waved her hand in the air—"whatever his name was. And I'm sure these rebellion rumors are nonsense. Probably just some locals out hunting. You can't blame people for putting food on the table, right?"

Maybe, but that still didn't explain the odd attack in the woods.

"Of course." Warren's smile matched hers as he moved another game piece. "Besides, I'm closing in on a victory here."

The board taunted me. Enemies closing in on all sides, forcing me to move in one direction, right into my defeat. "Damn, you're testing me today." I scrubbed a hand through my hair, trying to find a move that wouldn't sink my chances further.

Warren reclined in his chair, smug. "I don't think you can get out of this one."

CHAPTER 11
LUCIEN

T he lack of findings on the rumored rebels frustrated my
emperor. Today's incident, only two days after Zurina's return
and my game with Warren, set us all on edge.

Torture was dirty work, but no less than treason deserved. If the
maid had only confessed her crimes, she might have saved herself some
pain, though nothing could save her from exile to the western mining
camp.

How did she find out about our troop locations? I sighed. Probably one of
the new recruits. They'd need a reminder to keep private conversations
behind closed doors. Another one. Emperor Ryszard recruited able-
bodied men and women from within the city-state to fill the ranks of
those who'd fallen in battle. But training took time, discipline even
more so.

The maid's cries followed me back to my quarters, echoing in my
head and turning the meager dinner I'd eaten to dust in my belly. I'd

tried to get the information out of her first and save her some pain, but she wouldn't talk. Brishon touched her with his poisoned hands for only a moment before the screeching began. She sounded more like a mortally wounded animal than a traitor.

Worse, if one of the guards hadn't stopped her and searched her pockets before she left the castle with her little letter, she'd have gotten away with it. Information about our green guards and recent movement of our troops could be deadly in the hands of the rumored rebels—if they existed.

I groaned as I sank onto the sofa in my sitting room. The weight of the evening's events sat heavier than the armor gracing my form. *By The Four, I need a drink.* The maid fainted before we'd gotten any information from her. So bravely she defended whomever she'd been sending the letter for, claiming it her own doing. Perhaps she had written it, but intuition told me it wasn't her idea. Regardless, I needed to rule out options and confirm that Ilya hadn't passed it off to her somehow. My fellow captains would be testing our other guests in similar ways.

Time ticked by slower than the coldest of nights in the resting season until the door creaked open.

Finally.

If Ilya wanted to play games, I'd play them with her, but on my terms.

She stumbled into the room as soon as the doors opened.

My brows scrunched together. It wasn't like her to be so clumsy.

The pale fabric of Ilya's dress swished as she jerked to a halt, her eyes going wide. "What are you doing here?"

A smile ached to break free. "It is my room." I'd adopted her customary position on my sofa, legs crossed and a book in my lap—not that I'd read a word of it tonight. Already my plot worked, throwing her off-balance.

I set the book aside and stretched out, one arm on the back of the seat and legs spread in open invitation.

Ilya scowled. Her nose twitched as she stared me down.

"Come, sit with me." I patted the space next to me. A casual request. Almost friendly.

The barest flash of pink tongue peeked out as she licked her lips.

Gods. That one simple act had me aching to pin her to the wall and taste her lips myself. The way she ambled across the room, limbs loose and limber like a warrior preparing for battle, made it hard to concentrate. It wasn't often women showed any interest in my direction, and our emperor strongly discouraged such liaisons. But I was still a man, and no amount of training and discipline could quench all my natural desires.

She was the emperor's guest though. I couldn't want her that way. It was curiosity. A puzzle that ached to be solved. That was all.

"What have I done to deserve this honor?" Ilya practically fell onto the sofa, her hand landing on my leg for support.

My body tensed as her olive flower scent hit my nose.

"Sorry." Her grin said something different.

That glassy look in her eyes and slight slur in her words said much more. "You're drunk."

Ilya with her guard down? The circumstances couldn't be better to learn what I needed to know. She didn't pull away as I grabbed her arms to steady her.

"Not drunk. Just..." She shrugged. "Maybe a little." A sheepish smile leaked out with her words. She curled her legs underneath her—so relaxed, so innocent. Another act?

"Why were you drinking?" I asked.

She scowled. "What else is there to do here?"

A fair statement. So many idle days would have driven me mad.

"It's a pity you indulged tonight." My casual shrug took effort. The longer she sat there, the more her imbibed state became apparent. "I hoped you'd look at something for me."

She frowned. Her delicate fingers trailed down my armored bicep, a gesture too obvious to be misconstrued. "What did you want me to look at? You perhaps?"

By The Four, this woman tested me. My cock twitched, demanding attention, but I couldn't give into my base desires. Not with her. Not now. I coughed, hoping my armor hid my body's reaction as I adjusted my posture, pulling away from her alluring scent and wine-stained lips.

"Not exactly." *Unfortunately*. "First, write something for me." I gestured to the low table in front of us where'd I placed a stack of blank papers, an inkwell, and a fine quill of grey and brown feather.

Her brows pinched together. "What do you want me to write?"

"Anything. Just a few lines should do."

She blinked, her head tilting to the side before she shrugged. Ilya slid her feet to the ground and scooted to the edge of the seat, closer to me. The pale material of her dress slid against my armor. Her leg bumped mine and stayed there.

The feather grazed her cheek as she rubbed the quill between her fingers. Her eyes lit with excitement as she bent over and wrote a line across the top page.

A sinful grin tempted my better judgment as Ilya handed me the paper, that delicious-looking tongue flicking out ever so slightly again to moisten her lips.

Unexpected relief surged as I took in the handwriting. Her drunken scrawl was more looped and flowing than the maid's stiff letters. Although I doubted it to be Ilya's hand, I'd been worried all the same. More than I realized. Far more than I should be. The idea of seeing her punished sat poorly with me, though the idea of anyone suffering such measures was unpleasant.

I squinted at the page, reading the words aloud as I interpreted her scribbles. "Lucien would be...so much more fun if he...drank too." A deep rumble of laughter bubbled up from within as I folded the paper and set it back down. "Perhaps."

Her lips parted as she stared back at me, something like surprise written on her features. She squirmed under my gaze but didn't look away. Brave woman. So much fire and spirit.

"One more request for you." I pulled us back to the task, away from the unhealthy thoughts her brown eyes lured me to. I tugged out a folded and crinkled letter I'd concealed under my armor. "I hoped you might be willing to look at this."

"What is it?" Her legs slid against mine against as she reached for the paper. The faint blush on her cheeks deepened as if the touch affected her too.

"A letter. One someone convinced a maid to send, though the poor girl wouldn't admit who."

Her back straightened, eyes widening, as she glanced at the note still in my hand. "It's not mine."

"No." I gestured to the page she'd written on. "I don't believe it is. But if you want to prove your innocence, then you can tell me whose it is." *Help me, Ilya.* The same stubborn fire that made her my enemy pulled me to her. But if she could be turned? If she would submit to our emperor fully, she could make a valuable ally. It would be worth the effort to try, especially while she stayed in my quarters.

She pulled away. Her lips thinned as she hugged her arms around herself. "If I don't know who wrote it?"

I tapped the paper on my leg. "Then you don't."

"And if I tell you, you'll trust me?"

"If the information is truthful, helpful, then perhaps." *Not a chance.*

I held my breath as she held my gaze.

"Fine, give it to me."

A sigh of relief rose in my chest as I passed over the paper.

Tension fled her form as she read over the words. She didn't recognize the handwriting. Despite her swift relaxation, she continued to study the letter, no doubt reading it over. Most of the information she would know already. Attentive as she was, she'd probably noticed our lack of a strong force stationed near the castle, only the household guards and a few extras. She knew my fellow captains resided within the castle. The letter also contained hints of where the army was encamped, though that information would be inaccurate as soon as my orders to move reached them.

"I don't recognize it. Perhaps the maid wrote it herself," she said, meeting my gaze and thrusting the wrinkled page back to me.

An honest response. I didn't bother to hide the hint of a smile that stretched my features. "I think you may be right. But whom did she write it for, I wonder? And why protect them?"

"I don't know." She bit out each word with a measured space in between.

Her gaze slid away. I reached forward and grabbed her chin, forcing her attention back to me. A soft gasp slipped from her as I closed the space between us, close enough for her scent to tease me once again. "Don't you?"

"No." She held my steady gaze unblinking. Truth.

I released her and refolded the letter, tucking it away out of sight. I expected her to leave. To snap out another retort or berate me. I'd prepared for anything but her delicate fingers sliding down my arm again.

"You don't believe me?" Her voice was soft, sweet like honey.

"Should I?"

Without invitation, she slid into my lap.

Oh, fuck me.

My entire body went rigid. Her soft backside occupied one thigh as her legs draped across the other. Part of her dress rode up, revealing lightly tanned legs and sandaled feet.

"I think you want to."

Gods, did I ever. A muffled growl of desire rumbled in my chest as she trailed those bewitching fingers down my arm again. I couldn't feel her with the armor between us, but watching the act, the thought of how her delicate fingers might feel sent my head spinning. How long had it been since anyone had attempted something similar?

Too long. Far too long.

And even longer since I'd given in to the temptation.

Her eyes hooded. White teeth bit down on her bottom lip, hard.

Who cares if she's your enemy? If she's just trying to use you?

"What do you want, Ilya?"

"Will you take this off?" Her hand shook as she traced the contours of my mask all the way to the tip of one antler.

The thought of those hands tracing another part of me almost had me spilling like an inexperienced lad. *Focus, Lucien.* One breath. Another. My racing pulse slowed as I drowned in her eyes. My hands flexed around her waist, savoring the curves hidden beneath her clothes. When had I grabbed her?

"We don't remove our armor in front of others. Certainly not our *guests*." The thickness of my voice betrayed the controlled words.

"Well, according to the rumors, I've already seen some of you." She glanced downward for emphasis. "It's only fair."

If only I could figure this woman out. "Why? Why do you want to see me?"

"Can I not be curious about the man whose quarters I share?" She leaned closer. "You want to know if you can trust me. Let me keep this secret. Let me prove myself to you."

She offered one of my desires on a platter: to have this headstrong beauty on my side. Not my side—our side, my emperor's. It would serve our greater good. We needed our guests to serve the emperor in truth. Their willful submission could bring their relatives in line and create a smoother transition for the empire. And if she turned, perhaps the others she influenced would as well.

Showing her my face would go against my emperor's orders, and I always obeyed him. He'd saved me, raised me. I owed him my loyalty and my life for all that he'd given me.

"Well?" Ilya ran her hand down my chest.

But if it could aid his reign and help keep the peace within the empire, wasn't it a service to him? I couldn't trust her. Not yet. But I had leverage on my side.

"This would have to stay between us. If you tell anyone, I'd have to reconsider our agreement regarding your sister." A cruel threat, but I needed to hold her to her word.

Her lips thinned, but she nodded.

"A test then." She'd been honest about the letter. Perhaps she could be turned in truth. It was worth the gamble.

Ilya's eyes flew wide as I reached for my helm.

CHAPTER 12
ILYA

Be hideous. Awful. More monster than man.

Time slowed as he lifted the monstrosity of a helmet from his face.

My heart raced. The air grew thin.

Rich, dark brown hair, slightly mussed, fell away from his forehead to curl around his ears. Dark stubble coated a strong jaw, accenting even, balanced features. A faint old scar curved down from one cheek, sliding through the shadow of a beard. Mesmerizing, grey eyes asked a question he'd yet to speak.

He set the helmet to the side, his gaze never leaving my face.

I forgot to breathe, even when his hand slid down my thigh, a gentle whisper through fabric.

"As terrifying as you expected?"

It took a moment for the question to register. For it to slide past my shock and sink in. Impossible thoughts flitted through my mind as I searched for a response. At last—after silence stretched taut between us —I whispered the first truth that came to mind.

"More horrifying than I could have ever imagined."

Suddenly he was too close, too warm. The faint aroma of sandalwood sent my heart spinning and made my mouth go dry as I stared at the man before me. The one whose lap I still sat in.

I leaped away from him, nearly falling over the table with my awkward limbs. Lucien reached for me, but I jerked back, hurrying around the seating area. I didn't spare him a backward glance before I practically ran to my little room, threw open the door, and slammed it behind me.

Breaths came in short gasps as I flung myself down on the narrow, uncomfortable bed.

Not a monster. He's...

My fist slammed into the thin coverings.

Why did I think drinking so much was a good idea? I'd wanted to drown my thoughts, forget my failures and the title I'd lost. But instead of escape, the red wine pulled me further into misery. It was impossible to deny the warm tingling low in my core. But it couldn't be because of *him*, his touch, his fair appearance. *It's the wine. It has to be.*

Or an illusion.

The thought washed over me like a gentle rain. It settled my racing heart and loosened some of the knots that had twisted tight within me.

That's right, he was a master of illusion, of magic. That couldn't be his face. I wouldn't be attracted to someone as awful as him.

The sweet ache between my legs taunted me, refusing to let me deny the truth my body told. Yes, I'd planned to seduce him, but it hadn't been entirely an act. Not tonight.

Magic. It had to be magic.

A faint knock pulled my attention like a thread caught on a nail. No words left my open mouth as I strained my ears listening for the sound to come again, for Lucien to speak, for anything.

When silence stretched, I settled into the bed, convinced my hazy mind created an illusion of its own from my racing thoughts.

Lucien's face haunted my tipsy mind all night as I lay awake, a mess of wine and emotions. He appeared in my dreams too. Instead of the fearsome warrior who demanded our surrender in the throne room of Sorrena, clad head to toe in armor, I saw the man beneath.

Or whatever image he'd projected for me to see.

And it undid me.

He looked like a gentleman with combed hair, tailored clothing, and a jeweled necklace that accented the silver buttons on his jacket. He was regal, refined. Nothing like the man I knew him to be.

With morning came clarity. I had bigger things to think about than the male who held me captive. Namely, the letter and whoever had asked the maid to send it.

After Emperor Ryszard appeared during breakfast to announce a feast for the changing of seasons, I strolled through the gardens with Gabriel, Elin, and Fernand. I only planned to warn them of the letter and possible interrogation, but Fernand's expression spoke volumes. It was easy enough for me to sort out the puzzle of his wide-eyed edginess. He'd coerced the maid into sending the letter.

I didn't reveal his secret to the others. He could do that himself in due time.

Fernand made a grave mistake working on his own without involving us, but he'd slipped the noose—for now. Unfortunately, this would make sending out information more difficult. We'd need a better plan, and Lucien might be the key to that if I could get him to trust me. Judging by the way he'd given in and removed his helm, even if he'd likely shown me an illusion, I was well on my way to achieving that goal.

———

THAT NIGHT, I waited for Lucien.

I paced back and forth near the balcony, trying to distract my thoughts. If he'd beaten me back to his quarters, I'd have to wait another day or hope something pulled him away from his room before I fell asleep—however unlikely that may be.

"Please don't let there be another letter debacle." A cool breeze stole my muttered words and sent a shiver across the exposed skin of my arms. The change of seasons would be upon us soon.

Maybe Lucien could tell me what happened to the maid, though part of me dreaded to know. I'd already whispered two prayers. One to ask Erabus, God of Darkness, to allow her into his halls of rest if the worst had happened. Another to Soliel, God of Light, to help me see past Lucien's magic. Since Lucien's magic belonged to Erabus, only his opposite, Soliel, had any hope of dampening his powers.

On the one hand, I admired Fernand's tenacity and eagerness to get information out of the castle. But I also pitied his wife. It didn't take much creativity to reason out how he'd gotten the maid's staunch loyalty. The thought alone made me cringe. Having someone at home and betraying them that way wouldn't be possible for me. Thankfully, I had no such lover.

The sun had long set by the time the door cracked open to reveal Lucien—shoulders stiff, attention far away.

"Good evening." I crossed to him in long strides. "I have two questions for you."

His stance relaxed, looking almost casual, where he halted behind a chair. "Interrogated as soon as I enter my room. Perhaps I should have locked you in a cell after all."

A flash of teeth through the slit of his mask marked it for a joke, but that didn't stop my frown.

"What happened to the maid? The one with the letter."

His grin disappeared in an instant, a thin press of lips appearing through the slit in his mask. "Why do you want to know?"

I shrugged, though his shift in attitude caused my muscles to tense up, making the movement awkward and stiff instead of casual and easy. "I feel bad for her is all. Unlike the rumors about my mother, I do have a heart." *Sometimes.*

It was hard, so hard, not to squirm under his intrusive gaze. Everything in me urged me to run away, not to ask any more questions of this deadly man, but I held my ground.

"She'll be sent away from Zhine," he said at last.

"Where—"

He cut me off with a jerk of his head. I wouldn't get anything more, but at least she was alive.

"What's the other question?" he asked.

"It's about your magic," I hedged.

He crossed his arms. His boot stamped against the stonework as his posture stiffened.

I pressed ahead despite his reaction. "How do I know when you're using it or when you're not."

"You've seen it?"

I shook my head. I hadn't—not for sure. Not here nor in Sorrena, though I'd heard about it, or rather, its effect. Men turned on each other and themselves. Some fled the battle. A few who escaped were near broken with fear. Whatever they'd seen...I couldn't imagine it.

"Hm..." His fingers drummed against his crossed arms. "Wait here."

I sat in one of the chairs while I waited for him to return. Nerves sloshed in my stomach like rolling waves on the sea during a storm.

What's taking so long?

When he returned, he no longer wore his helmet, though the rest of his armor remained intact. I nearly gaped at the sight. Were we so familiar now that he'd show himself to me regularly? He wore the same guise as the day before, and though part of me dearly wished he'd kept the helmet on, another painted a self-satisfied smile across my lips. *Progress.*

The growing smirk on his lips distracted me so thoroughly that I didn't notice the object he held in his hands until he presented it to me.

I rose to my feet, inching toward him, but didn't take his offering.

Lucien held a large silver bangle. Ornate designs of swirls and dots were inlaid in the metal, making it look like a piece of gaudy but fashionable jewelry. A spring clasp on one side with a slit on the other would allow it to open and close to fit around arms of varying sizes.

"What is it?" I glanced at the piece with unease. Was it an illusion? Would my hand pass right through it?

"This bracelet is enchanted to protect the wearer from magic."

My mouth dropped open. I'd heard of such objects, but they were exceedingly rare. And expensive, even for someone born to wealth like myself.

Those rare few blessed by Aurora, Goddess of Dawn, who could work such magic charged a small fortune for it. Yet they had no lack of customers.

"When you have it on, you won't see my illusions," he said. "But without it..."

I yelped as juniper-colored vines crawled across the now mossy ground near my feet. To my right, a tree blossomed with pink blooms, so real their floral perfume teased my nose with memories of the growing season. My mouth watered, imagining the sweetness of the juicy pears that grew in moments on the branches. A few petals let free and drifted down, blown by the warm breeze that tickled my skin.

Lucien nudged the bracelet in my direction. "Take it. Put it on."

Hesitantly, I took the object he offered. Heavier than I expected and cool to the touch, it dwarfed my slim wrists. I slid it on without opening the clasp.

In a heartbeat, the illusion disappeared. The breeze halted. The sweet floral notes vanished from the air. Nothing remained but the sparse, masculine room I'd grown familiar with.

I slipped the bangle off and the scene returned, complete with chirping birds and a doe that stalked through the other side of the room, peering at us curiously as her pointed ears twitched.

The scene flickered, there and gone, as I slid the bangle off and back on again, gaping at the change around me. In awe, I twisted to look at the man behind me. On or off, he looked the same. The gentle smile that tugged at his lips transformed his features more than any magic. He looked almost...

Don't go there, Ilya.

I slid the bracelet off and held it out to him.

"You're frowning."

Was I?

"I thought you might have enjoyed that illusion."

"I did, it's just...so real." His smile stirred that warm, melty feeling within me again, and I looked away, down to the bangle still in my hand. "How do I know this isn't part of the illusion too? You watched me slide it on and off."

A puff of laughter filled the space between us. "So doubtful." He turned his back to me. "Try again, without me looking."

I did. Once again, the illusion came and went with the bracelet. *Okay, so maybe it does work. But that means his face...*

I swallowed as he turned around. The illusion vanished all at once.

"You believe me now?" Lucien asked.

"I do." I held the enchanted band away from me, offering it back to him.

He shook his head. "Keep it for now."

My eyes flew wide. My heart leaped. "Why would you give me something so precious?"

"It's for you to borrow, not keep. Think of it as another secret between us."

Or another test. My heart sank.

He didn't need to say it. Each action he took was to determine my innocence, or perhaps in a twisted way, my loyalty to him for the perceived favor of saving me from a cell. And Orson. Though it was hard to blame him when each of my actions were to serve my own goals as well.

"Wear it," he added. "Though if anyone asks, say it's a trinket from your city."

I eyed it dubiously. Some people, including Mother, did prefer such large pieces, though I'd never been one of them. "I think it may fall off."

"Here, let me."

I passed him the magical object. My back stiffened as he closed the distance between us. I had to crane my neck to look him in the face. As my heart thundered, he clasped the bangle over my upper arm, lingering too long after the metal ends clicked shut around my skin. His gaze locked with mine. Grey. Deep and swirling as the seas.

"It looks nice with those sleeveless dresses you favor. Though I hope you have something warmer in your trunks come the resting season."

I ignored the small spark of warmth that raced to my cheeks as I switched my attention to the temporary addition to my wardrobe. It was less obtrusive than I expected. One might almost think it fit my sense of fashion. It could work.

For now.

CHAPTER 13
ILYA

Emperor Ryszard stood like a God behind the high table of the dining hall. He proclaimed the beginning of the fading season and gave a lengthy, droning speech about the glories of the empire.

The walls of the room, stuffed with boisterous bodies, closed in around me. Cramped. Claustrophobic. At home, we celebrated the change of seasons on the cliffs above the sea with plenty of wine for drinking and dedication to the Goddess. Did they do that now? The longing to join them ached down to my toes. I'd had the honor of presenting Vespera, Goddess of Twilight, with the first grapes of Her season for as long as I could remember. Who would perform the dedication in my place?

Thank The Four, Ryszard left after his speech. Without his oppressive presence leering over us all, I could breathe again. Roasted meats and sweet cakes made my mouth water despite myself. The food here was edible, if a bit bland and different from what we ate in Sorrena. But tonight the chefs had outdone themselves if the smells were any indication.

"That's quite pretty," Elin said, motioning to Lucien's bangle as she and Gabriel joined me near the edge of the room. Many of the tables had been removed or pushed against the walls to allow space for people to congregate and dance in the center.

"Thank you, it's a recent gift." I winked.

Elin's brows scrunched together, but Gabriel caught on.

"Ah, you've made some progress?" he asked.

"I think so. We'll see what it yields."

"Oh!" Elin exclaimed. "It's from—" She cut herself off before she could spill my news to the nearby guards who'd approached after her exclamation.

A group of musicians arranged across the room tuned their instruments in preparation to play. A few captains resided in high-backed chairs behind the emperor's table, Lucien included. His gaze caught mine across the distance. An unexpected tingle ran under my skin, and I looked away.

Gabriel, Elin, and I chatted about everything and nothing for a few minutes until the guards lost interest. Nearby, Fernand sat alone, sipping at a mug of ale. His dour expression and hunched shoulders kept other revelers at bay. I hadn't shared his secret, though Gabriel had likely caught on from his mood alone. He shook his head with a shudder and downed the rest of his mug in one go.

When I looked back to the high table, Lucien and many of the others had left.

"It turns out your advice was right," I said to Gabriel. "The other night, after we shared that bottle of wine during dinner, I—"

Reyna joined our circle, a blinding smile on her face. Her cheeks were flushed from wine, dancing, or both. "It looks like you all are having a good time."

Hardly. If it weren't for the opportunity to possibly overhear something of use, I'd have found an excuse to miss the feast altogether.

She looked between us. Her smile dimmed. "Did I interrupt something?"

"We, uh…" Elin faltered.

"We were just comparing the traditions in our city-states," Gabriel said.

Reyna looked between us again. The silence was stifling despite the volume of the room. "Uh-huh," she said after a heavy pause. "Well, maybe I can borrow Ilya for a moment?"

Me? "Okay, what do you—"

"There she is." Captain Zurina strode up to fill the gap between Reyna and me.

Reyna's blinding smile returned. There was a reason we didn't trust her, didn't include her in our plans, and it wasn't only because her city-state had submitted willingly to the emperor when his troops advanced on their border. Reyna was far too friendly with our enemy, including the emperor's captains. She genuinely seemed pleased to be an honored guest and wore the title with pride.

My back stiffened. Zurina wasn't referring to Reyna—she stared directly at me. Elin and Gabriel slipped away as Zurina leaned in, her tall figure towering over me.

"Glad to see the rumors were false," she said, just loud enough to be heard by Reyna and me.

I raised my eyebrows in return. "And how do you know they are?"

The hint of a frown teased out from behind her mask. "Because I've seen the scars that leaves on someone." All hint of joy fled her voice. "You don't bare them."

A knot rose in my throat as her gaze bore into mine. The shadows there had me looking away, an unexpected twinge piercing my heart.

"We've told people the rumors are untrue. They should quiet down soon," Reyna said.

So it's we *now?* My lips thinned. Since when did they care about my reputation?

"A good thing too." Zurina's light tone returned, her voice rising in volume as she clapped onto my shoulder. "If they'd been true, I'd have had to cut that one's balls off." She hiked a thumb over her shoulder.

My breath caught as I spied the figure advancing on us. Lucien. Gods, when had he gotten so close?

"You'd have tried," Lucien replied.

"And succeeded," Zurina said.

His attention slid from his fellow captain to me. Unwanted butterflies fluttered in my stomach. Absently, I touched the bangle on my arm before flinging my hands down to my sides and squeezing my dress in clenched fists. "You wouldn't have," I said. "Because I'd have done it myself."

Zurina and Reyna burst into laughter. Lucien straightened, but it wasn't anger that stirred in his eyes. The unmistakable hint of a grin formed in the slit of his helm. My cheeks burned.

"You needed me for something?" I asked, turning to Reyna and trying to banish all thoughts of Lucien from my mind.

"Yes." She pushed a lock of dark hair behind her ears before she grabbed my hand, entirely too familiar. "Come with me."

She waved at Zurina over one shoulder and led us in the opposite direction. I fought the urge to look behind me, hard as it was.

"I wanted to give you something," Reyna whispered. She leaned in close until the floral notes of her perfume overrode the banquet around us, then pulled us to a halt before fishing around in a pocket sewn into the skirts of her crimson dress.

"Here it is." A narrow, glass vial filled with pale green liquid hovered in the air between us, pressed between her thumb and forefinger.

"What—"

"I'll take that." A burly guard with way too much facial hair swiped the vial from Reyna's hand.

She frowned at him. "It won't do you any good."

"No? Passing liquids around suspiciously. What is it? Poison?"

Reyna rolled her eyes. "Really, like I'd carry poison? I'll prove it." She plucked the vial from the guard, unstopped the cork top, and let a drop fall to her outstretched tongue.

The guard frowned.

"It's to help with women's pains. Do you really want it?" She wiggled the vial at him.

"Fine," he grunted. "Forget it."

Reyna replaced the stopper and handed the vial to me.

"What is it really?" I whispered.

She looked both ways before responding. "Contraceptive. Just a few drops after..." She grinned. "You know."

My mouth dropped open. She thought Lucien and I had... "I thought you believed the rumors were false? I don't need it." I tried to give it back, but she closed my hand around it instead.

"Keep it. Just in case." She winked before slipping off into the crowd without a word.

Drink flowed freely as the feast wore on. The crowd grew raucous, full of laughter, wild dancing, and boasts of prowess. Not long after Reyna delivered her gift, I found my way back to Gabriel. He watched over Elin from the side of the dance floor where she partnered with a young guardsman. Her skills and beauty earned her a string of requests from other would-be partners. While the distractions provided us with the occasional opportunity to talk, we learned little new. Gabriel overheard a guard discuss the intricacies of their training drills, ones focused on fighting on horseback. It seemed they planned to target the city-state of Marsali next, renowned for their skilled riders, but that was no surprise. They were the next closest city-state after all, though they had strong allies who might stand with them. It was the likely reason they hadn't been targeted earlier.

At least I managed to avoid Lucien and the other captains since receiving Reyna's odd gift, which I slipped to Gabriel to hold onto for me. He didn't ask about it, nor did I offer to explain.

A few seats down from us at the table, two men started to arm wrestle. A small crowd cheered them on, thumping their mugs on the table and splashing ale over other onlookers who appeared not to notice.

"Should I give it a go?" Gabriel teased.

Elin perked up. "I bet you can beat them."

Gabriel chuckled as he pushed up his sleeves, revealing lightly tanned skin and wiry muscles. A darker splotch, roughly shaped like a star, marked his inner arm.

"What's that?" Elin asked.

"A birthmark," he replied. "All the men in my family are born with it. My father, my brother, and his son had one before he went missing."

My brows scrunched together at his words. "Missing? I heard he died."

Deep sorrow touched his eyes. "About the same, isn't it?" He shook his head and looked away. "We never found his body, so we assumed the worst. A young boy with a distinctive mark like this would have been easy enough to identify, especially with the entire city-state searching for him."

From the grief etched in his features, the loss still hit him hard, even though twenty-something cycles had passed. He must have treasured his nephew very much. Time and prayers to The Four had not produced another for their family.

"I'm exhausted," Elin exclaimed with a sigh.

No doubt, since she'd danced the night away. Had she even bothered to eat?

"Any interesting partners?" I asked. She'd had no lack of them, and with her innocent demeanor they might be more loose-tongued with her than with the rest of us.

Elin tilted her head to the side. "A few guards. They were all gentlemen though. I wouldn't dance with those drunken ruffians."

A pity. The drunken ones might have let something interesting slip. Perhaps I should have danced after all.

Shouts erupted two tables down. Two men locked arms and tried to wrestle each other to the ground, knocking a chair over amid their scuffle.

Elin winced as the game grew raucous. "I think I'm going to go to bed."

"I'll let you know how my duel turns out," Gabriel promised with a wink. That brought the hint of a smile back to her lips.

"I'll go with you. I'm about done with this anyway." Understatement. I'd been done with this for a while. Curfew had been extended for this night only; however, watching others get drunk and forget where they were didn't hold much appeal.

We headed for the doors, dodging dancers and drunks. I no longer spied Lucien amid the crowd. One more trial I'd hoped to avoid. The guards who normally accompanied me were absent tonight as well.

Another test, Lucien?

I barely held back a sigh. *Probably.*

I warred between going straight to his quarters or walking with Elin. A guard I didn't recognize slunk back toward the dining area. His eyes roved all over her before a sharp whistle screeched through the air.

"Disgusting," I murmured in his wake. Elin's frown and pursed lips matched my own. "I'll walk with you."

"Is that alright?" she asked.

I shrugged. "I don't think anyone is sober enough to notice or care."

Mounted torches beckoned us down the grey, stone hallway, shedding light on the lack of routine guard patrols. Perhaps on my way back to Lucien's quarters, I could make a few detours. If they were going to slack on their patrols, I'd make them pay.

One turn of the hallway from her room, another set of whistles and laughter stopped us in our tracks. Fine hairs rose along my arm as I twisted around to find three men headed our way. The crimson and grey of their outfits marked them for castle guards, but the glassy look in their eyes, stumble of their steps, and unkempt appearance told me more about them than anything.

"You ladies lookin' for some company?" the tallest one asked, a slur to his voice.

"No, thank you," I replied, voice firm and edged. My back stiffened as I notched my chin higher.

"Ilya…" Elin's voice quivered as I ushered her behind me.

The men slunk closer. "Come on. The party's not over yet."

"It is for us." Where were the guards who always patrolled these halls?

"Go," I whispered to Elin. "Get in your room and lock it."

"What about you?" Elin's gaze flitted between me and the men inching their way in our direction, one stumble after another.

"I'll be fine." I swallowed the tightness in my throat. Probably a lie, but better one victim than two. "Go. Now!" I commanded with a shove. Elin finally relented, hurrying down the hallway. My heart hammered in my chest. In moments the men would be upon us.

"Where she going?" one man groaned.

"Our emperor's holdin' out on us. Keepin' the beauties locked away." His attention slid past me to Elin's retreating form.

"Leave her alone. Don't you know better than to mess with the emperor's guests?" I settled into a loose stance. Nyke's guidance from our old training sessions flashed through my mind as I stared down the men. He'd trained me for years, and though I was never good with blades, his lessons on self-preservation had stuck well. In just a few moments I could rush the advancing guards, push past the bastards and flee. Too bad I didn't have a knife. Leaving a few bloody gashes in my wake would be the perfect revenge for terrifying my friend.

"Yer pretty 'nough," one man slurred as his attention slid over me like an eel. "Can't wait to hold that hair while ya scream."

He lunged for me. I dodged, landing a kick to his legs that sent him stumbling.

The dark-haired man to his right stepped forward. My fist connected with his nose. He reeled back, roaring in pain.

Before I could turn, something crashed into my cheek, sending me careening into the stone wall. Pain bloomed fierce and bright on the side of my face. Blood trickled down to my chin as I leaned on the wall for support.

"Ilya!" Elin's cry hit me harder than any physical blow.

What was she still doing here? I'd seen her leave. Why did she come back? She didn't have the skills to defend herself let alone me. Dread flowed through my veins as I tried to get a grip on my surroundings. I had to protect her. She was too much like Justina. Sweet. Innocent. I couldn't let them touch her.

The man who'd hit me paled and stumbled back just as a gruff voice full of barely suppressed rage rumbled from somewhere behind me. "That was a mistake."

CHAPTER 14
LUCIEN

Magic leaped and tingled under my skin, responding to my fury and begging to be unleashed. How dare they?

"You know our guests are not to be harmed, especially not by your hand," I said, voice rough and quivering as my control slipped.

The men tripped over themselves as they backed away, stumbling and mumbling.

"We d-didn't—"

"Just having fun."

Ilya twisted against the wall. "Lucien..."

"Take Lady Elin to her room," I ordered Warren. She'd come upon us in the hallway. Her wide-eyed, troubled expression and hurried pace signaled a problem before she spoke. Then I'd heard Ilya cry out in pain. My hand fisted tighter. If only I'd gotten to her sooner.

"See that she's safe," I continued. Firelight danced off the bangle around Ilya's arm. She'd worn it. Thank The Four.

I released the tourniquet on my magic, letting illusions leap forth into the hall—dark, bloody beasts of legend. Black claws scraped against stone. Mouths with double rows of razor-sharp teeth opened wide to keen and bellow. The scent of burned hair and the metallic tang of blood filled the hall. Pus oozed from sores upon the creatures' bodies where they crouched upon the stone, ready to spring.

Ilya's head snapped toward the men as yells filled the hall.

The man who'd hit her fell screaming to the ground, clutching his face as the illusion hound raked its claws across him. Another man attacked his chest and arms, scratching and clawing where the creature's poisonous spittle splashed over him. The third fell into a heap, crying and twitching where he lay.

The scene should have given me satisfaction. An enemy brought to their knees by a simple showing of my powers. But all I could focus on was the injured woman nearby.

In a heartbeat, I was beside her. "Are you alright?"

Her attention was fixed on the men, though I knew the bangle protected her from the illusion I'd crafted. She blinked, only turning when I cupped her uninjured cheek and turned it my way. She'd fought so bravely.

"Ilya?"

Curses and another scream echoed from the end of the hall.

Fuck. Of course others would come running when they heard the cries. I pulled my magic, reining it in until the illusion vanished. Power still hummed under my skin, willing me to use it, to continue what I'd started.

The screaming subsided. Sobs took up their place. One guard retched, voiding his stomach.

"Guards," I called to the new arrivals. "Seize these three." I waved a hand at the offenders. To their credit, the new guards obeyed at once. Four encroached from one direction, two from the other. I committed each face to memory. They'd have my thanks—later.

"Bind their arms. Throw them in a cell for attacking our emperor's guests. We'll sort out what to do with them later." I'd seen those three before, trailing after Orson like loyal dogs. He'd encouraged their disgusting behavior or ignored it. Either was unacceptable. Another problem to deal with.

"R-right away," a blonde woman replied before pulling a length of rope from the pouch at her waist.

I gave barely a passing glance to the three struggling to regain their composure. One's begging only hardened me against him. Had he stopped when Ilya asked? *No.* Another still whimpered in a pool of his own making, praying to The Four. They couldn't save him. Not now.

Ilya still hadn't spoken, her wide eyes taking in the scene.

"Can you stand?" I softened out the edges of my voice. Calm. Controlled.

She swallowed thickly as I held out a hand to her. I had half a mind to pick her up and carry her away, but I had a feeling the fiery woman wouldn't want that. She could stand on her own two feet.

A barely imperceptible nod of her head confirmed my decision as she took my hand, her delicate fingers smeared with blood from the wound on her head.

"Elin..." she mumbled, voice thick. Heavy breaths showed the fear she hid from her eyes.

"Warren is with her. He'll see to her safety." I grazed her face, avoiding the bloody wound. "We should see about this."

She was alert and not too badly injured from what I could see, though all her focus was still on her friend, the one she'd protected. The anger simmering through my blood slowed.

Guards swarmed the halls. Too late. I'd have to increase their training, remind them of the rules. Ilya didn't speak as we traversed the torch-lit halls, nor when we finally reached my quarters.

"Lady Ilya." The guards at the doors gaped at her wound.

"Have breakfast brought to the room tomorrow, and any other meals if Lady Ilya chooses," I said. "She's had a trying night."

"Of course," they echoed in unison.

"Should we alert—"

"No." I didn't want more rumors swirling around Ilya. "I've seen to it and will handle the rest in the morning."

The men nodded, but it was Ilya their eyes clung to.

Pale, bluish streaks of moonlight crept across the floor of my sitting room, shifting like snakes on the ground until they touched puddles of lamplight, which ate them up. A stiff breeze ruffled the heavy drapes on either side of the balcony and caused the flames illuminating the room to wave and dance. The crispness of the cool air invaded the room—a fitting tribute to the change of seasons.

"Have a seat," I said. "I'll be back with something for your face."

I kept a jar of healing salve in my room so that I could avoid the infirmary. Having a healer tend to the rare, odd wound would require the removal of my armor. It was an unnecessary risk when we could attend ourselves or rely on Captain Gaius's blessing of Soliel to heal serious concerns.

"Should I just come with you? It would be faster." Ilya glanced away as if embarrassed. A thin trail of blood ran down her cheek. Another few drops marred the shoulder of her dress. I bore her blood too, a smear across my gauntlets. My fist tightened.

Could I trust her? Let her into the privacy of my chambers? My attention shifted between her and the door. I wanted to, more than I ever should. It was my fault she'd been set upon in the hallway. I'd told my guards to hold off, to let her come back on her own. A test of sorts. I needed to see if she'd obey orders when she wasn't watched. The thought that she'd run into trouble never crossed my mind.

But I still didn't know where her loyalties lay. What would she have done tonight if she thought herself unsupervised? Each warm thought I had toward her left me with a twinge of guilt. Emperor Ryszard would disapprove. He certainly wouldn't want her to linger in my bedroom.

"Wait here," I said before I could change my mind.

I couldn't miss the disappointment that pulled her lips into a small pout. Because she wanted to come with me? Or something else?

You conquered her city. You know what she thinks of you.

I spared her one last glance before my thoughts chased me up the stairs.

CHAPTER 15
ILYA

Alone in the room, the throbbing in my face increased, making itself known anew. I was lucky that Lucien and Warren appeared when they did. If they hadn't, this might have been the first of many wounds—to my body and my soul.

Twice now, Lucien had saved me from a horrible fate. My enemy. Perhaps an ally?

Things were not as black and white as I once assumed. Even within this conqueror's court lay varying shades of grey. Could Lucien be turned? Why would a man who showed his captive mercy support such a ruthless conqueror?

The flames flickered, stirred by a sudden gust, almost as if the night responded to my thoughts.

One step at a time, Ilya. Information first.

My heart stutter-stepped when Lucien returned without his helm, though the rest of his armor was still intact. Within his hands, he held a small pitcher and something wrapped in cloth that fit within his palm.

"You're comfortable showing your face but still not the rest of you?"

His lips quirked up in one corner. "Would you like to see the rest of me?"

My mouth went dry. Damn it all, I did. I wanted to. But I only shrugged. "Just odd that you'd lose one piece and not the rest."

"The helmet's stifling." He set the cloth and pitcher on the low, polished table before where I sat on the sofa. The swatch of tan fabric fell away to reveal a small clay jar painted blue at the bottom and fading up to its natural tan color near the top. A matching lid covered it.

Leather creaked as he took the seat next to me, too close for my racing heart.

I eyed him up and down, my traitor heart imagining the form underneath the armor. "The rest of it looks so much more airy and light."

Deep laughter crawled down my back and burned in my core. It took everything I had not to shudder in something too far from fear for what this man was.

Lucien snatched the cloth from under the jar and dampened it with water from the pitcher. "Turn your cheek toward me."

Heat crept down my neck as my mind slowly processed his request. He intended to clean my wound himself. "I can..."

He shook his head with careful slowness, a tall tree swaying in the breeze. The equally slow upturn of his lips threatened to strip away all thoughts from my mind.

Murderer. Monster. Remember Sorrena.

Flashes of memory doused the uncertain feelings creeping under my skin. Icy stillness embraced my limbs as I turned my head to offer the injured cheek.

"That's better."

I winced, jerking backward as the strip of linen touched the offending area, wiping away traces of drying blood. The material could have been coarse sand for all that it stung.

"Not too bad. It should heal well and quickly. You won't have to worry about any scars on your pretty face."

Pretty face? I bit my lip so as not to gape. I was fair enough, but such a compliment from him...it didn't fit. At least, it didn't fit with the perfectly constructed vision I had of him in my head. Little did these days. Each day stripped away a layer of fury and disgust like the rings of an onion until I feared what I might see once we reached the center.

"Do you treat wounds often?" I asked, a poor attempt to distract myself from my churning thoughts.

He set aside the towel and reached for the jar. "Mostly my own. Working on someone else is significantly easier."

My raised brows tugged the tender skin. "You don't have someone to do that for you? A healer, perhaps?"

Lucien pulled free one gauntlet, then the next. Strong fingers, freed of their shell, flexed before him. Visible calluses marred the otherwise creamy skin.

"One among us has those powers, but like all magic, it takes energy. Best to save that for when it's necessary rather than smaller wounds that can be treated by traditional means."

Pale, bluish goop resided within the jar. The color reminded me of the small flowers that grew near the cliffs of my homeland during the growing season.

"Energy," I mused.

I'd never made a study of magic. As one not blessed by The Four, it didn't affect me. Though as a future leader, I likely ought to have learned about it anyway.

He dipped two fingers into the goo, scooping up a dollop of the concoction. "It's like running or anything else." The goop formed a stiff peak off the bottom of his fingers but did not fall. "The more you do it, the easier it gets. Yet you always have to stop and rest eventually or you'll collapse." He raised the concoction to my face. "Hold still."

I gasped as the mixture touched my skin. A sweet chill instantly soothed the aching flesh. A pleasant fruity scent teased my nose. Strong fingers rubbed the mix into my skin, but the touch didn't hurt. Not anymore.

"Amazing."

He grinned. "Helpful stuff, though costly. Leave it on overnight if you can. It will reduce the swelling and help you heal. By morning, the pain should be gone."

His fingers lingered long after the pain receded. My mouth dried as I stared him down, a thick bubble of silence constricting the air between us. When I could bear it no longer, I spoke again. "Did you learn how to use your magic at a citadel?"

Those blessed with magic were invited to train and hone their skills at one of the citadels consecrated to the God or Goddess whom their magic represented. In the exceptionally rare case that a person was doubly blessed, they chose where to train. Surely, we would have heard if the emperor had plucked his captains from such respected sources, but I couldn't help but ask.

"No." He wiped the excess ointment from his hand using the damp towel and replaced the lid upon the jar. "I learned mostly from trial and error with some instruction from Emperor Ryszard, our master-at-arms, and the other captains. We help each other as much as we are able, though our skills vary greatly."

"Do you ever wish that you would have?" It would have meant a different life. Perhaps one far from war and conquest. Independent of any city or country, the citadels were a people unto themselves.

A hint of sadness touched his eyes, so fleeting I almost missed it. "It's not wise to consider what might have been, only what is and what can be."

"And your master-at-arms?" I didn't know who that could be. One of Ryszard's advisors?

"He died several cycles ago." The sorrow that colored his wounds was unmistakable.

I expected him to leave. He'd tended my wound. The job was done. Instead, he turned back to me, assessing. Those grey eyes dug into my soul, reaching for something. "Do you wish you'd chosen a different path? Not been the heir to your mother's city?"

My brows scrunched. Not have been the heir? But I was. "I was born into it," I mumbled. There was no choice, no other option.

"Then you know how I feel."

Emptiness bloomed within me. I wanted to be the heir...didn't I? My whole life advanced toward that end. Even now, I struggled to regain the title I'd lost despite the odds stacked against me. A touch of sorrow chilled me too. But not for myself. For him. What could he have been if he'd had the chance to study under masters of magic? Now that he'd taken up arms in service of his emperor, he could never go to the citadels to train. They wouldn't take someone who'd pledged themselves to a side in war—it was how they maintained their neutrality. Already Lucien had many skills I could admire: intelligence, strategic thinking, command, and a level of care for others I never expected. If only the emperor didn't claim his service.

Dark terror gripped me as a different image snapped into place. "Are you..." Racing thoughts nearly strangled my words. "Are you related to Ryszard?"

Teeth flashed amid a quick grin. "Is that what had you turning ashen on me?"

I had? I didn't know.

"No," he said after a weighty pause. "But I remember very little before he took me in."

"How did you come to him then?"

"He found me. All of us. Orphans of war, famine, unfortunate circumstance..." He shrugged.

Orphans, all gifted with strong magic. Something was missing, a piece I'd yet to uncover. I needed more, so much more.

"He only took in blessed children?" My back straightened as Lucien cupped my undamaged cheek in his hand. Lightning zipped between us, hot and fierce where his bare skin touched mine. Without the goop between us, his calloused skin rubbed against my delicate flesh, particularly where his thumb traced an almost infinitesimal line up and down.

"So many questions tonight." His steady gaze tugged me toward him like a moth to flame. "What do you want, Ilya?"

To free Sorrena. To take down Ryszard. To learn your secrets. To kiss you.

The truth in my thoughts hit me like a vicious wave. I *couldn't* want that. Not with him. Seducing him was my plan—an easy one when I didn't care, when it only advanced my agenda. Actually wanting him? It couldn't happen. Emotions would ruin everything.

He inched closer, eyes boring into mine, stormier than the seas that crashed against our cliffs, ones I could easily drown in, carried under by a current I never saw coming.

One more tug of the tide, and I'd be a goner. Lost.

"I should get some rest," I said.

The moment vanished faster than a retreating wave. His hand slipped from my face to fiddle with the discarded gauntlets at his side.

"I wouldn't want your good work to go to waste," I continued, pointing to the mark on my face. A poor excuse at best, but the only one my turbulent thoughts could come up with. He'd been kind to me, yes, but I couldn't forget who he was, what he'd done.

"No. We wouldn't." He shoved to his feet, gathering up the jar but leaving the rest.

I rose as well, fighting against the conflicting mess of feelings trying to weigh me down. "Do you need theses?" I gestured to the forgotten pitcher and soiled towel.

"Leave them. I put anything down here that I want the maids to replace."

The comment caught me off guard, halting my steps as I traced to my chamber. "They don't go in your room?" They'd come in mine often enough, straightening the sheets, refilling my basin of washing water.

"No one but me." That look...I couldn't place it. Nor did I have time as he turned and headed for his door.

"Thank you," I said. Now he froze, glancing back over one shoulder, his dark hair hiding part of his face where it fell to brush his strong cheek. "For coming to my aid. And for the ointment."

"It's nothing."

But it wasn't nothing. It should have been. Everything would have been easier if it was.

Once in my room, I slid onto the bed fully clothed, careful to leave my injured cheek pointed toward the ceiling. I should have kissed him. It could have been my opening. The one chance to sink under his skin and learn more of his secrets—and Ryszard's. But at the last moment I'd panicked, thrown off and tripped up by the one thing I never saw coming.

My own foolish heart.

CHAPTER 16
LUCIEN

Racing thoughts woke me long before the sun crested the far hills. Ilya. Her bravery. My failure to protect her. The softness of her skin under my touch.

The last things I should be thinking about.

No amount of training in the yard this morning cleared my head. Even when my emperor summoned me to the war room, I couldn't ponder the reason why. All my rogue thoughts lay with her. Was Ilya awake? Had her face begun to heal?

Sweat slid down my back as I traversed the castle halls, bustling with morning activity. I moved on instinct alone, barely giving thought to the turns I made or the doors I passed through. The castle had become a home, one I knew as well as my own hands.

Two guards saluted as I approached the war room. "Captain," one said.

I nodded my head in his direction and reached for the door.

The guard held up his hand. "Sir, the emperor, he—"

Too late.

I froze at the sight before me. Kasida sat on the map table, her legs wrapped around my emperor. Their lips were locked together as tightly as their arms around one another. Emperor Ryszard pushed away from her, almost knocking her back onto the maps. Table legs screeched against the stone. Figurines warbled from their positions and clattered to the floor.

My fist curled and uncurled, the only part of me that moved. I should have knocked. Normally, I would have, but my thoughts were anywhere but where they should be.

The emperor coughed. "Here already."

Kasida slid off the table, knocking more pieces to the floor as she grabbed her helm. I'd suspected something from the lingering looks she aimed our emperor's way. They went deeper than admiration or fatherly affection—too much heat and desire. But I'd thought it one-sided. How wrong I'd been.

"Apologies, my emperor." I bowed my head in reverence. "You called for me."

"So I did." He straightened the heavy cloak about his shoulders.

When had it progressed this far? Why? Ever since I was a boy, he'd warned us away from romantic relationships. Unnecessary distractions, he called them. *Attachment makes you soft, weak, too easily led astray.* Didn't I know? Ilya pulled at my thoughts, and she wasn't even mine. Emperor Ryszard always focused on a higher calling—uniting the city-states—and trained us to do the same. Committed relationships were not abided. Even passing dalliances were discouraged lest they lead to something more.

Kasida smirked as she passed by me on the way to the door. I followed her with my eyes until she was out of sight but didn't give her the pleasure of turning my head away from our emperor. The doors rattled at my back as she left. Was it just a physical liaison between them? Could anything be so simple for two people tied together as we all were? Or was it—

"My scouts sent word of trouble in the hills." Emperor Ryszard returned a piece to the map, never taking his attention off me.

"What kind of trouble?" I asked. The awkward air of moments ago vanished. This was us. Plotting together. Discussing strategy. Expanding the empire. In a heartbeat, he'd pushed the event away and restored our relationship to its rightful place.

I removed my helm and approached the table. A map of eastern Galanthia stretched across its surface. Carved, wooden pieces painted with exquisite detail marked the current locations of our troops. Well, the ones Kasida had not upended. The black spearmen marked areas of concern—rumors of possible rebels or other troublemakers like the ones we'd encountered on our return from Sorrena. The piece he still toyed with hadn't been there the day before.

"The worst kind." He slammed the piece down. "Traitors."

"They caught them then?"

"No." He relinquished the piece to rub at his temples. "Incompetent men. It's like they try to disappoint me. How can it be so hard to round up a few foolish citizens?"

A few hazy rumors had reached us as we planned the invasion of Sorrena, but we hadn't taken it seriously, not until we were attacked on the way back to Zhine after our conquest weeks ago. The emperor had sent some of my fellow captains to investigate, but so far we'd uncovered little information. Every time the supposed rebels evaded capture. Remnants of their campsites held little information. Even their numbers were obscure at best.

I pondered the placement of the black pieces. None were too close to Zhine, nor to any major city. "A distraction?" They'd used that tactic before, but to what end?

Emperor Ryszard held my gaze across the table. Slowly his pursed lips turned into a frown. "Yes, of course. And who would want our troops heading east more than our enemies to the west?" He gestured to the city-states left unconquered—for now.

I shook my head. "They wouldn't expect us to move our battalions for such a small disturbance." They'd given us no reason to storm their borders, though it was a shame to leave them out of the future of solidarity our emperor envisioned. Perhaps they'd join on their own soon enough. "Nor should we, my emperor. Let me check out this disturbance. I'll get you answers."

He looked from the map to me. "I knew that I could count on you. Let it be done."

My heart swelled, a sense of rightness falling back into place. I needed this. A chance to calm my emperor's worries and clear thoughts of Ilya from my head.

"Argh." He cupped his palm to his forehead, wincing in pain.

"Emperor—" I stepped around the table.

He waved me off. "Blasted headaches."

Those again. He'd had more over the last few years, and they'd only grown in intensity.

"Getting harder to keep them contained," he mumbled. "Slipping free."

My brows wrinkled. "What are—"

A loud knock sounded on the door. "It's Captain Orson."

My jaw stiffened. He was the last of my brethren I wanted to see.

"Come in," the emperor responded, just loud enough to be heard through the door. He walked to a side table, ignoring Orson as he entered.

But I didn't. Orson stormed in with purpose, ripping off his helmet. I barely stifled a grin as his step faltered when his gaze landed on me. He'd thought our emperor was alone.

To his credit, Orson waited while the emperor poured his drink. Amber liquid tumbled into a glass of cut crystal. My brows pinched. No, that couldn't be right. Emperor Ryszard abhorred whiskey. He'd ranted for years about how it dulled the mind and softened the senses.

He raised the glass to his lips and took a small sip before turning to Orson and myself. "What is it?"

Orson's gaze flicked to me before landing back on our emperor. "I... my emperor, I—"

"Spit it out." He scowled in impatience, never one to wait.

"He"—Orson thrust an accusing finger in my direction—"had my men thrown in the cells."

The emperor simply raised his brows and glanced in my direction—a silent request for more information.

Fine, if he wanted to do this now, we would. "*His* men attacked your guests in the hall and injured one of them."

His eyes narrowed as a deep frown pulled at his clean-shaven face. "My guests are not to be harmed." Emperor Ryszard's voice turned hard and flat. "Explain." This command he directed to Orson.

A snarl rippled across Orson's lips. "That whore he keeps in his rooms lured them in, then attacked."

I saw red and crossed the room to him without thought. "She's no whore."

"You can't see straight with that bitch in your bed."

I shoved him. Hard. "She's not—"

"Silence!"

It took everything I had to back down, to step away and turn to my emperor.

He sipped at his glass of whiskey, the deep frown still upon his face. "Fighting like children."

I dropped to one knee before him. "Apologies, my emperor." Orson mumbled the same behind me. What had I been thinking?

I hadn't. And it shook me worse than the emperor's fury or his odd behavior.

"Rise," he said. "I've heard about this, about your command for Lady Ilya to reside with you. You know how I feel about such things."

Do you? Even with Kasida? The traitorous thought surprised me. "I'm keeping her close to keep an eye on her. That's all." No matter that part of me wanted more. "I think she could be a valuable ally."

Orson snorted, but I ignored him.

"She's already my subject. My guest," the emperor said.

"Yes, but someone tried to send that letter through the maids. She might be able to find out who or inform us of other such attempts. She could aid us." All true, even if that wasn't my only reason, not anymore. "Besides, she can't cause any trouble if she's under my watch."

"Tell that to my men," Orson muttered.

I turned on him. "Your men attacked her. I saw it for myself."

"Like I believe that."

The emperor coughed, drawing our attention. "Orson, discipline your men."

He flinched but bowed his head. "Yes, my emperor."

"Lucien..." He looked me up and down. "Do not disappoint me."

My chest burned. "I won't, my emperor. In this, or the other matter we discussed." But his look said I already had by keeping Ilya in my rooms, whatever my purpose. Making it up to him now was the best course of action. I would find these would-be rebels and gather the information our scouts could not. There was no room for failure anymore.

CHAPTER 17
LUCIEN

Tension hung heavy in the air of the emperor's audience chamber when I arrived back in Zhine after my quest. My emperor sent me chasing after whispers of rebellion, yet I'd failed him. His captain. His first-in-command. I even took a few others with me to ensure success. Yet we still couldn't manage to capture, kill, or identify anyone despite spending a week following their traces through the hills.

"If we can't figure out who it is, they'll all suffer!" The emperor banged his hand on the massive wooden desk in front of him. Color reddened his cheeks as his anger boiled to the surface.

Long ago, he'd always been calm and collected. A quiet guardian whose presence lingered even when duty took him from our country manor to advise his brother in Zhine.

The angry outbursts began shortly before the war, a secret he kept hidden from his subjects—other than us. We blamed it on stress from rule and battle. He'd just taken over in his brother's stead after his untimely death, one he blamed on our neighbors to the north. They'd denied poisoning him, but who wouldn't? As our victories grew, so did the private outbursts.

"*All*, my emperor?" Zurina asked, concern flashing in her eyes. "The city-states have already sent us tithes of goods and gold. Any more might hinder their health this resting season. You don't want your loyal subjects to starve."

"My loyal ones, no. But these disloyal ingrates—" He banged his fist on the desk again, causing Zurina to flinch and look away.

Her attention flickered to me briefly, a request for help in her dark eyes. Weariness already pressed down on me from traveling fast over poor dirt roads, sneaking through the woods in the rain to disguise our approach, eating too little food, and getting far too little sleep. I longed to retreat to my chambers and rest. I hadn't seen Ilya since the day after the feast when our emperor ordered this excursion, and he'd demanded a report immediately upon our return. Had she healed? Had there been any more trouble? I'd hoped the assignment would clear her from my mind, but it only proved to do the opposite. During the day, she drifted through my thoughts, distracting as a fly buzzing about my head and just as persistent. At night, she haunted my dreams—and dreams they were. In them, she was the seductress from recent days but with all the fire I'd seen the day I met her, except she didn't burn with rage but with desires that should be forbidden.

Should be...but hadn't our emperor sought pleasure with Kasida? Could it really be so dangerous if it was just physical pleasure? A release?

Now was not the time though.

I shook the thoughts from my head, adjusted the helm tucked under my arm, and stepped forward into the half-circle we'd formed around the emperor's desk. We never wore our helms in front of the emperor unless the guards or others were around. Among our leader and my fellow captains, it would have been a sign of disrespect to do so. We didn't sit either. An unnecessary luxury. A sign of weakness. "We don't know who they are yet," I said. "It's possible they're not from the city-states at all."

"Go on," our emperor grated, his voice rumbling like coarse stones.

As we advanced on the location given by our scouts, we'd seen the glow of campfires illuminating the small valley during the night—too many to be a local hunting party or roving band of traders. By the time we'd reached their location, they'd departed, leaving behind hoof prints and other remnants of recent human presence. Something had tipped them off. Or someone.

"They could be independent wanderers." *Weak, Lucien. Too weak.*

"Spies from the west," Orson said, nearing our emperor's desk on its raised platform of stone. "Or Marsali. Those cunts are as jumpy as their horses."

"Maybe those nasty Northmen," Kasida supplied. "Filthy mongrels."

The Northmen lived in the mountains north of Ourelas. Family units resided together in small villages, not submitting to any one leader. Each stuck mainly to themselves, rarely leaving the cool, rugged terrain they called home. We'd left them alone thus far, as they had us. There would be no reason for them to venture southward and court trouble.

"Unlikely," I said before the idea could sprout. "The remains of the campsites didn't resemble the Northmen." The last thing we needed was a pointless war against a non-threat. This was too organized for the Northmen, too out of character. They shunned our way of life as much as we avoided theirs.

Kasida's lips wrinkled. The dark makeup she painted over her eyes accented her grimace. She batted her lashes at our emperor, the hint of a pout transforming her features. My stomach turned. I could still see her painted lips pressed against our emperor's, her legs around his waist, as clearly as if she embraced him now.

Emperor Ryszard ignored her and focused on Orson. "Marsali..." He drummed his fingers.

Brishon coughed and stepped forward. "We saw a few horse tracks at the campsite, but they were too small to be from the kind bred and prized in Marsali."

"A diversion," Emperor Ryszard replied. "Of course, they wouldn't bring their own here."

"We've had no word from our scouts along the Marsalian border," I said. "They'd have seen something if it were spies from Marsali—or any of the western kingdoms, for that matter."

He pinned me with his sharp gaze, the *rap, rap, rap* of his fingers continuing against the wood. The drumming halted. "My first is wise." He relaxed into his seat with a small sigh and rubbed at his forehead. Another headache? "If not our neighbors to the west or north, then it must be the city-states."

Fuck all. I'd tried to dissuade him of that, but shifting the blame to Marsali or the Northmen would only earn more battles we couldn't afford. And the western kingdoms? By The Four, if we offended them, we'd all be dead. Surely our emperor knew that. The size and scale of their cities dwarfed ours. Even as a combined empire of city-states, their armies would crush us.

"Now that we've settled that. Their punishment—"

"You don't want to do that," Warren said, just loud enough to be heard.

The comment silenced the room. He raised his head a notch as our emperor rose to his feet. The oppressive quiet that settled around him held more barely leashed anger than any words he could shout. Warren rarely spoke in these meetings, preferring to listen and keep the peace. Even so, he seemed unfazed by the heavy tension his comment had unleashed.

"What he means, my emperor, is that acknowledging these would-be rebels could give the city-states ideas or encourage others to join them." I didn't know where the words came from—a blessing from one of The Four? Erabus must have been watching over me. I squared my shoulders and stepped into the center of the half-circle surrounding his imposing desk. "If we acknowledge them, we admit they are a concern. But if we ignore them and take them out quietly, we can snuff out this nuisance before it has the chance to spread."

Emperor Ryszard sat and waved his ring-laden hand, an order to continue.

"We'll squash this annoyance before others learn of it and think to join in or mimic them. Once we have them, we can determine where they're from and punish the responsible party accordingly."

Oppressive silence reigned. I refused to move or blink as he considered my words.

"Let it be done."

Praise The Four.

A few of my fellow captains visibly relaxed. Only Orson frowned. *Bastard.* Did his bloodlust know no end?

I gave a salute and turned to leave.

"Wait."

One word halted all movement in the room. Our emperor's commands carried as much authority as if he wielded magic, forcing us to obey. That wasn't his blessing though. He could sense magic, a gift from my God, Erabus. That ability had allowed him to find us all, to take us in when the world would have otherwise left us to die.

"I don't want this information to leave this room. Relay that to any of the men you took with you as well. No whispers in the halls, no discussions over dinner, and certainly say nothing to our honored guests. Let them...stew over it for a while. A guilty party may yet reveal themselves." He waved his hand again. "That will be all."

Reveal themselves? Unlikely. We read all the letters that went in or out of the castle. Our guests would have no way to know what transpired in our territory or their former homelands, not truly.

Whoever these people were, hopefully they took this near miss as a lesson and went home. Dissuading our emperor again may not be possible, and another war so soon would only result in unnecessary loss of life. Our new troops needed more training. Some of our injured still advanced toward recovery. Acting now could lead to failure—or worse, hinder our ability to maintain the empire. The thought weighed me down, making my legs sluggish.

Only one thing lightened my mood: Ilya. And I knew just where to find her.

CHAPTER 18
ILYA

We finally had information that might aid the rebels. At the feast a week ago, Gabriel cajoled some of the guards he'd warm-wrestled with into divulging their training on horseback in preparation for an upcoming mission. Two days ago, I trailed a particularly chatty man through the gardens and caught wind of a scouting mission to the Marsali border. They'd target that city-state next, I could feel it in my bones. If we could let the rebels know, perhaps they could warn Marsali and stop the emperor's advance.

Lucien left for some unknown venture the day after the feast to mark the change of seasons. Once he returned, I'd see what other tidbits I could pry out of him. He'd already been gone a week. Surely, he would be back sooner than later. During the feast, Emperor Ryszard had announced that we'd be allowed to attend the festival of Vespera. It followed closely after the change of seasons and was one of my favorites of the year, with massive bonfires lit to pay homage to the Goddess and ask her blessing for a bountiful harvest before the resting season.

The festival would be our chance to get out information. We wouldn't need to rely on a maid or someone else to sneak it out of the castle—we could do it ourselves. Gabriel had already found a merchant, one who periodically delivered goods to the castle and who he was certain sympathized with our cause.

I said one last prayer to Vespera to aid our efforts during her festival before I left the prayer room and rejoined Lucien's guards. The same six worked in shifts of two and escorted me everywhere since he'd left the castle. To make sure there was no repeat of the other night's debacle, possibly, but more likely to report on my actions and ensure I stayed in his quarters despite his absence.

"Captain Lucien returned today." At Ajax's comment, my heart leaped. A reaction I still didn't know how to contend with.

I schooled my features into a genial smile. "That's good news."

Finally, I could try to learn the aim of his mission. Since none of us had been led to the gallows, it likely didn't involve an outright rebellion of our homelands.

Or if it did, Ryszard waited to dispatch his punishment at an opportune moment. His eyes roving over us all at lunch today had caused my skin to crawl and the food to turn leaden in my stomach. What did Lucien see in him to follow his lead and wreak so much havoc? What did any of them see?

"He's meeting with some of the others now," Ajax continued. "But I assume he'll be back to his quarters before too late."

"And was it a good venture, wherever he went?"

"He's unharmed, if that's what you're asking."

It wasn't, but that confirmation untwisted the knot I hadn't realized sat deep within me. Ajax didn't seem willing to disperse any useful information, so I let the topic drop. He wasn't a bad guy, and I sensed even the guards were being watched. One step out of line for them could be worse than for us.

Ryszard needed his honored guests alive. But the guards...he had plenty of those.

"The weary traveler returns home," I teased when Lucien entered the room later that day. I set the book of stories I'd been reading on top of the stack I'd finished that week, which included Lucien's book of war.

He grunted, staring me down. "Weary is right. We nearly rode our horses into the ground trying to make it back by nightfall."

Riding in all that armor... What a burden for the poor horse.

"Such a long day," I sympathized. "You must have ridden from very far away." *Tell me where.*

"Indeed."

Ugh.

"What happened to draw you away so urgently?" I tried a new tactic.

"Some questionable activity to the...east. Nothing for you to worry about."

Truth or lie? He wasn't one to stumble over words. I rose to my feet, letting a show of concern flash across my face. "Did someone step out of line?" My hand trailed to my mouth. "Their guest here...are they...will they..."

Though a show, I didn't have to force the worry that colored my words.

As hostages, we'd been lucky to see little punishment, at least in the weeks I'd lived here. However, I'd heard the tale of how Lord Noren Bacher was beheaded after his father rose up with men-at-arms against Ryszard after faking submission. His younger twin brothers resided with us now. The taxes upon their lands had been doubled. No one wanted to suffer Noren's fate or have their people bear an increased burden.

"Your concern for others is admirable, but no one will die tonight." His eyes locked with mine across the room.

"And tomorrow?"

"Tomorrow will depend upon tomorrow."

I wove through the furniture until I stood just before him and craned up to look through the eyeholes of his mask.

"Please, just tell me."

My heart jumped into my throat as he grasped my arms, tugging me closer. Only a handsbreadth remained between our bodies. Heat raced under my skin, threatening to make me forget what I'd asked.

"Who are you worried for, Ilya?" He might as well have asked, *Do you suspect someone?*

"I don't want to see anyone else die."

"Even me?" His hands flexed on my arms.

"Even you."

I swayed on feet. My mouth parted. If Lucien hadn't been holding onto me, I may have lost my balance. The revelation had slipped out without thought, but once I said it, I knew it was true. If Ryszard and most of the others died horribly, I wouldn't mind. But the thought of watching Lucien die didn't sit the same way it had only weeks ago. If Sorrena required it, I could make that sacrifice, but I'd no longer relish it as I once would have despite who he was and what he'd done.

"I actually believe that," he said, almost to himself. His voice rang with quiet awe, an echo of the emotions burrowing into my heart. Weighty silence sat heavy around us until Lucien spoke again. "Can you keep another secret for me?"

"I've kept them all so far." I pressed my lips together.

His arms slipped from mine. "We don't know who caused the mischief, so no one will suffer for it. But our emperor wants to let you all stew over it."

The heavy weight on my shoulders fell away with a sigh from my lips. "Why do you ask me to keep your secrets?"

He glanced at me from the side, stirring up my butterflies within me. "To see if you are trustworthy?" He shrugged. "Should I not trust you, Ilya?"

No. Not at all. "I want you to. I'll prove it to you." *If only so you'll trust me enough to tell me what I need.* My brows furrowed. No, that wasn't entirely true anymore. I didn't only want him for information, for how I could use him against his emperor and revenge for Sorrena. In his absence, the spark of something else that formed between us had ignited into a fire.

"Changing your mind already?" he teased.

I shook my head and smoothed out my features. "No. I just really don't want to be your enemy."

Lucien pushed a stray hair back from my face. His gauntleted hand barely grazed my cheek. "Then don't be."

If only he didn't serve the emperor. He loomed between us like an invisible wall, insurmountable but perhaps not indestructible.

"You have my oath of obedience already—to you and to your emperor. I've kept your secrets. What more can I do?"

I yearned to lean into him, to step into his arms and forget who he was and what he'd done, but I couldn't quite let myself.

"Serve the emperor," he said. "Be one of us in truth. If you learn anything of note—whispers from the guards or your fellow guests —tell me."

My teeth dug into my bottom lip. I glanced away, unable to look at him and the hope in his eyes. He wanted what I could never give. "I'd have to learn something first," I said, dodging his question. I already had, but I certainly wouldn't be telling him what we planned.

"When you do, you know where to find me."

I watched Lucien from the corner of my eye as he left. *Do you really think I would be yours?*

CHAPTER 19
ILYA

For Vespera's feast, we dressed in her colors. I kept the tradition tonight, donning a dress the color of purple grapes, the kind we fermented into sweet red wine. The fabric gathered over either shoulder, clasped with golden pins shaped like birds, before falling down my body. I wore Lucien's bangle on my upper arm as well, even though the metals clashed. Ornate leather sandals laced up my calves. For once, I left the Mark of Sorrena in my room. Somehow my chest felt heavier without the gleaming sapphire around my neck. Lucien wanted me to serve the emperor in truth, to be one of them. While I could never serve him in my heart, leaving behind the symbol of my city might give the impression that I could—assuming he noticed.

Per my request, the guards escorted me to Elin's room. She braided my brown hair in a single ribbon down my back. The loose, pine-green sleeves of her dress brushed against my shoulders as she worked. Afterward, she insisted on loaning me earrings of gold and amethyst similar to the pair she wore. She adored dressing up and had brought an unnecessary amount of jewels with her. She once confided that she longed for a sister to share her things with. The Four had granted her only brothers, and she had lost them in the battle for her city-state's freedom. It warmed my heart how she let me fill that wish in this horrible place.

Guards escorted us to the large lower bailey. The last rays of orange sunlight crept up the higher towers above, leaving the yard shadowed other than flickering torches carried by guards and grooms. Carriages waited with doors open, horses hitched and ready to ride.

Though the festival would be held not far from the city proper, Ryszard intended us to look like the guests he claimed us to be. Perhaps that was his strategy after all. Let the people see us and spread the word of our health and happiness throughout his empire.

"Pick a carriage," one of the guards called. "Any will do."

Gabriel slipped into the carriage with Elin and me. In moments, the horses took off. It would be a short trot to the outskirts of the city where the bonfires would be lit.

"Are you sure about this letter?" I whispered. The short ride provided us with the opportunity to talk, the crunch of wheels and trot of horses along the ground further masking our conversation in addition to the walls around us.

"It's our best chance to get what we've learned to the rebels." Marsali lay to the west, opposite of the direction that Lucien had traveled, if his comment were to be believed. However, that did not dissuade us. We'd learned enough to believe that Marsali was the emperor's next target. Whatever disturbance Lucien investigated was likely something related to the rebels. The fact that he hadn't caught them gave us hope.

"Won't they be expecting that though?" I asked.

"Perhaps, but we'll be quick and careful. What we've seen from the castle confirms the rumors that the fires are being built on the edge of the city. Slipping to the stables near the orchard should be easy enough, even if we're being watched."

"As I'm sure we'll be," I interjected.

Elin nodded.

"You trust this man?" Elin asked. We'd kept her out of the details, for her safety if nothing else, but she caught on quickly.

"I talked to him in passing. Reyna managed to speak with him also."

My brows rose. "We're trusting her now?"

He raised his hands. "I only asked her opinion on the man after I saw her speak with him once during a delivery. He seems reliable enough."

My lips drew together in a thin line. I didn't like it, not at all. It was too big a risk to take on someone we knew practically nothing about. He could take our letter and give it to one of the captains on the same night.

"They're higher than I expected." Elin stared out the window.

Around her head, I caught the edge of what snagged her attention. The last rays of sunset illuminated the tops of tall piles of wood. Their height would soar above the head of a normal man. The three mounds formed a triangle, the Goddess's preferred arrangement and the symbol of her divinity.

The carriage rocked to a stop as the driver called the horses to a halt. People swarmed about as we exited, clamoring to tables stacked with food, large kegs of ale, and the unlit bonfires. Guards were stationed sporadically throughout the crowd and near the wooden and stone buildings that rose up only a few horse's lengths away. They kept an eagle eye on this section of the festival, manning the areas between tents of amusement and stacked crates that made false walls, limiting us to one section near the fire closest to the castle. The city's residents could come and go with approval from the guards. If I hadn't known better, I'd say the guards were there for our protection. It looked that way. But of course, that was part of the show.

WHISPERS TEASED my ears as eyes roved over my skin like little spiders crawling along my arms. My back stiffened as I glanced at the crowd in return, letting my attention float over them without lingering too long on any one person. I'd felt less like a fish out of water my first day in the castle than now. A duo of stringed musicians struck up a tune, inviting dancers to join the revelry near a small fire.

Ryszard planned a beautiful deception for his people, with us as the key players.

There's danger in deception—just possibly, everyone starts to believe it and forgets what's true. If you're the only one clinging to the truth amid illusion, can you still claim to be right?

"Come on, let's find a place near the fires," I said. "They should be lighting them as soon as the sun fully sets." Any minute now, if the festival followed the same schedule as it did in Sorrena.

The green and purple decorations and matching attire worn by the townspeople were a small comfort, a piece of normalcy and celebration amid so much war and grief. The guards still wore their traditional crimson and grey, but a few had pinned ribbons to their chests. Others wore clippings of berries and greenery. In the little ways they were able, they celebrated as well. The few captains mingling in the crowd—ones I did not know well—wore no adornment, but that wasn't surprising.

The high priestess from the city's temple went to each towering pile of wood in turn, bearing a ceremonial torch. Long, wine-colored robes hid the majority of her figure and trailed upon the ground in her wake. The dry wood of the mound nearest us caught quickly, fire licking up one tall branch and then another until sparks took flight into the sky. Prayers were said to Vespera, chanted by the high priestess as loud as her voice would carry and echoed by the rest of us.

Everyone's attention was trained on the fires, but I searched the crowd, looking for the face, or rather, suit of armor that I did not see. Dancing flames from the bonfires as well as lanterns on tall poles provided more than enough light to make out those in the crowd. If Lucien attended, he was far from here. And though I hated to admit it, his absence left me uneasy, unable to relax and focus on the prayers, especially with Orson strolling about. Well, and Gabriel's questionable plan.

Shouts of joy and praise rang out as the prayers concluded. Music wove into the crowd from where a troupe played, encouraging dance and revelry. Elin grinned and strode toward the dancers. Though she was more than happy to go, I slunk away to the side, content to watch rather than participate.

"How much longer?" I asked Gabriel, settling myself on a long wooden bench beside him. The fires still roared high and hot in the background of the festivities. No one could get too close without bursting into a sweat and nearly lighting their hair on fire. Between their blazing radiance, the smaller fires dotting the ground in wide-open spaces, and lanterns and torches, there was no shortage of light—or heat.

He pulled a silver pocket watch from his jacket. "Still a little while."

I nearly groaned out loud. They'd wanted to hold this meeting late enough for everyone to have dropped their guard and hopefully have had a drink or three, but the waiting set my teeth on edge.

He chuckled. "Relax. Go find a nice dance partner like Elin." Gabriel gestured to the crowd.

A young man with sandy hair twirled Elin in a swirl of green skirts. He dressed like a farmhand—heavily scuffed boots, worn and stained shirt—but something about him nagged at the back of my mind. At least she was having a good time.

I slumped against the bench as Gabriel rose, heading off somewhere. He'd be back.

The song concluded. No sooner had the dancers halted their steps and bowed to their partners than the musicians struck up another one. A few dancers left, some changed partners, and others like Elin seemed quite content to stick to their current arrangement.

"May I have this next dance, miss?"

Only after he'd spoken did I realize the words were directed at me. I turned, prepared to reject whatever brave man had gathered the courage to ask me, but the words died in my throat.

CHAPTER 20
ILYA

Lucien stood before me, only not. It was the face I'd come to know behind the mask, the typical mischievous twinkle in his eyes, and he stood at the right height. But this man wore no armor, nor did he dress as a guard or anyone of standing. His outfit—a long-sleeved, green tunic with tan pants, worn boots, and few decorative accents—marked him for a poor merchant at best, a resident of the city out to enjoy the festival.

Hastily, I glanced around, but no one looked our way. They didn't know who stood before me with one, strong arm outstretched.

"Do I have something on my face?" he asked, his lips pulling up in a grin as he cocked his head to the side.

Either the God of Darkness cast an illusion this evening, one the bangle did not protect me from, or Lucien played a game I could only guess at.

My heart raced as I stared into his grey eyes. "You may." I placed my shaking hand in his, allowing him to help me to my feet.

"Why are you—"

"Shh," he whispered as he led me to join the dancers near the fire. "Am I not allowed to enjoy the festival as well?" His palm slid around my waist as he pulled us in step with the people around us.

"But like this?" My eyes raked his form as we moved. His shabby clothing had no chance of hiding the well-toned arms that caged me in. Dark locks brushed his ears. The scar sliding down one cheek added a delicious edge of danger to his handsome face.

He grinned. "It wouldn't be so much fun otherwise."

I tripped up my steps and nearly fell into his arms. "I'm a terrible dancer," I mumbled as I pushed against his chest—a muscular, firm chest that made my throat turn dry.

A deep laugh rumbled into the air between us. "Just relax, follow my lead."

Easier said than done.

My body finally learned the rhythm of the song as it came to an end. Blessedly, the next tune the musicians started was slower, easier to follow. Lucien took advantage of the rhythm and tugged me closer until our bodies were nearly pressed together, an island unto ourselves amid the crowd.

Standing close to him, pretending to be normal people, made it hard to grasp reality. My head swam just trying to process it. No one seemed to know who I danced with. We might as well have been invisible.

"What are you thinking of?" Lucien's voice rolled across me like a soothing wave.

"You," I answered honestly. "And this." I tilted my head around to indicate the dancers. "Can they see what I do?" I wore his bangle, immune to his magic. But could the others see him at all? Or me in his arms? It would explain why no one noticed, not even the guards.

His lips nearly grazed the shell of my ear as he leaned in and whispered, "You think I'm enchanting them? Should we test it?"

The touch of his bare fingers against the skin of my upper arm sent my heart racing faster as he stretched the bangle wide, sliding it down my arm and off into his hand while we moved.

Nothing changed. No one looked nor commented. We were just two people in an ocean of others. His grin widened as he took in my expression and replaced the bangle. But his hand didn't move once he'd finished. Instead, he leaned in until my arm lay against his chest. Another cradled his neck. Dark hair teased my skin.

"Still have your doubts?"

"No." But if Lucien, for all his fearsome reputation, could wander the crowd unnoticed, who else lingered here unbeknown to the rest of us? "Why are you doing this?"

"To keep an eye on you? Because I want to?"

I sighed—likely the former.

"You want to dance? With me?"

"Is that so hard to imagine?" He flashed a grin before his face turned somber. "Tell me, what were you planning to do this evening?"

My steps faltered. "Try not to fall into the fire," I teased as I recovered with Lucien's aid, picking up the pattern again.

Abruptly, he halted mid-dance. "Come with me."

A thread of panic tightened around my neck like a noose. "Where—"

"You'll see."

He took my hand in his and navigated the throng of festivalgoers to the edge of the festival, far from the dancing, where guards watched the perimeter.

Had we been found out? My pulse beat wildly in my throat. He'd been kind, sweet. Was it all a ruse to get me to let my guard down? With my racing thoughts, I hardly noticed who we passed or where we went.

"Our guests are to remain at the party," one guard said, stepping forward with his hand up to stop us.

Lucien made a shape with his free hand, so fast and fluid I completely missed its design.

"Never mind." The guard stepped back into place.

They didn't recognize Lucien, not without his armor, but they knew that symbol.

"Where are we going?" I whispered as Lucien led me past the guards and toward a handful of outbuildings. Festivalgoers cast wavering shadows against the wooden walls of a stable, a storage shed, and other buildings. A shiver of unease raced down my back. The desire to flee back to the party increased with every racing beat of my heart.

"Luc—"

He whipped around in a flash, his hand landing over my mouth. The sudden movement stole my breath. My spine locked up.

"Shh…" he whispered. "Just up here."

My skin turned clammy. Off to where only shadows would witness my doom.

No one else wandered these narrow paths. Darkness prevailed, the structures blocking the blaze of the fires. The last flickering tongues of light trailed along the ground between the guards more than a horse's length behind me.

At the end of the building, Lucien turned, pulling me with him around the corner into deeper shadows. He halted, grasping my waist and pushing me against the building. Smooth wood dug into my back through the material of my dress. "What are you—"

His lips stole my words as they crashed against mine, soft but demanding. His kiss contained no questions, no tentative seeking, only conquest.

And I melted for him.

Fear fled in the wake of desire. I wanted this—*him*, in a way I hadn't realized. My arms laced around his neck, holding on for dear life in the turbulent storm of his kiss. Without the building at my back, I may have very well collapsed into his arms.

"Ilya," he mumbled against me, a soft nip pulling at my bottom lip. My hands slid through his hair. Heat raced under my skin, warming me more than the bonfires. A tight knot twisted in my gut as I parted for him.

His tongue swept inside, stealing the last of my rational thought. There was only he and I, his lips on mine. Where we were, who we were, none of it mattered.

I whimpered as a firm hand slid down to cup my backside and pull me tight against him. Heat and moisture pooled between my legs as an unmistakable hardness pressed into me where our bodies molded together.

I panted, relishing the feel of his warm breath caressing my skin as he broke our kiss.

"I couldn't do that out there." His chest rose and fell as he held me firm. "But I wanted to. I—"

My hand fisted in his hair, tugging him back to me. Our bodies crashed into the building, his arms taking the brunt of the blow where they wrapped around me.

The taste of him, the soft growl rumbling from his chest, threatened to undo me. I shouldn't have wanted him. Couldn't want him. But I did. Every speck of my skin ached to be pressed against his own. In the moment, I didn't care what he was, what he'd done, or what I planned to do to him. I needed this. Passion and heat—enough to burn away rational thought and just let me savor the taste of pleasure I so desperately needed in a wasteland of misery.

"Come back early," he whispered, voice thick and heavy like wet sand.

I nodded, not trusting my words as I stared into eyes that threatened to devour me.

His thumb rubbed across my swollen lips. His eyes hooded as if he might start up our kiss again. "I'll wait for you in my room."

My room. The words echoed in my head long after he said them, stirring up a mess of butterflies in my stomach. Could he possibly mean his bedchamber?

"Do I look okay?" I touched my braid and gave a poor attempt of straightening my dress as he stepped back, cool air rushing in to calm my senses.

"Like Vespera herself."

I searched his face for humor but found none. My core tensed, my thighs pressing together under the skirts of my dress. His hand trailed over my hair, down my back, lingering much longer than necessary. "No one will notice," he promised. "Not if we slip back quickly in case someone is looking for you."

He laced his hand through mine again as we wandered back toward the light, plumes of wood smoke, music, the shouts and whoops of celebration. "How do I get back?" The coaches wouldn't leave again until the end of the festival.

"I'll send a guard to escort you. One you know." He gave me a reassuring squeeze.

The guards who watched us leave didn't look twice as we returned, weaving back into the crowd as if we'd never left. At the edge of the ring of dancers, Lucien halted and raised my hand to his lips. The chaste kiss sent my toes curling. "Thank you for the dances, miss." His eyes glittered with mirth. And promise.

I watched him go as he disappeared into the crowd, navigating between bodies with ease.

Released from the magic of his presence, I could finally think. The fog of my mind started to clear as I looked around for my friends. If Lucien could be here, wandering around like a commoner, would other captains do the same? They always hid their faces, and now I had a suspicion of why. If no one knew what they looked like, they could slip into any place or situation without being spotted.

I'd seen a handful of captains here tonight, but the others...I needed to find Gabriel. The meeting couldn't happen now, not with so many potential eyes on us. Their farmer might be a captain without his disguise.

And I couldn't go to the meeting with them. Not now. I finally had an opportunity to get into Lucien's quarters, to earn his trust and dig for information. But more than that, I wanted to go to him.

Gaze roaming from face to face, I finally spied Elin reclined on the bench I'd long vacated, a young farmer at her side.

She waved to me, a broad smile on her face. Barely a handsbreadth separated her from the young man. Neither moved to increase that distance as I took the open seat next to her.

"Are you alright?" she asked, her pale brow creasing. "You look flushed."

"I got talked into some dancing, though I'm not very good," I admitted, hoping that would explain my look.

"It is exhausting." She brushed a stray hair back from her face. "Especially with the heat of these fires."

"Who is your friend?" I asked, peeking around her to the man at her side. Hints of youth still clung to his features. If I had to guess, I'd say he was about her age. Possibly a cycle or two older. His soft smile and sparkling eyes spoke of a certain enviable innocence.

"Todrick." He dipped his head in greeting. "I live on Balberry Farm just outside the city."

That voice... The fine hairs on the back of my neck rose as I fought to maintain my even features. I recognized it from somewhere, though I still couldn't place it. "A pleasure," I said. "Don't exhaust Lady Elin too much. It wouldn't do for her delicate feet to grow blisters."

"Ilya," she whined.

"I wouldn't dream of it." The young man's smile was only for her.

The hint of a blush rose on her cheeks as she stared back at her companion. They could have been in a world unto themselves, one I was suddenly intruding upon. Their bubble of soft sighs pushed me out, but I couldn't leave, not yet.

"Have you seen Gabriel?" I asked, interrupting their reverie. Elin's attention drifted back to me as she nodded along before I'd even finished. "It's just, I am feeling a little odd, and I asked to go back early."

Her brows wrinkled. The boy's head cocked to the side. Something about him still tugged at the back of my mind, the thread of recognition just out of reach.

"Not in a little while," she said.

"I need to talk to him before..."

My words trailed off as realization slapped me in the face. The man sitting next to Elin, who'd danced with her half the night, wasn't a simple farmer. Warren radiated a gentle warmth so unlike the rest of the captains. I'd caught hints of that through his slitted helm many times on the journey to Zhine and since then. He stiffened ever so slightly as I stared at him.

Lucien wasn't the only captain parading as a commoner. And when there were two...

"Ilya?" Elin asked, reaching for my hand.

I shook my head. "Sorry. I'm really not feeling well."

She had no idea who the man at her side was—she couldn't. What did he hope to learn by getting cozy with my friend? Or by some rare chance, had something sparked between them like between Lucien and me?

"I should leave you two," Warren said, rising to his feet. "Perhaps we can share a dance again later this evening before you leave?"

Elin practically glowed. She truly had no idea who he was. "That would be lovely. I can't wait," she said.

He bowed his head and wandered off into the crowd. Warren knew I'd discovered his secret. I sent a quick prayer to Vespera hoping the information would not come back to hurt me—or worse, us.

"He's so kind," Elin continued once he was out of earshot. "It's such a pity that we don't get to come here more often. I'd really like to...well, I suppose I can't dwell on that." She gave me a sad smile.

"Perhaps you'll see him again after tonight." She would, much sooner than she ever expected.

"Maybe." Her gaze turned wistful as she looked off into the crowd in the direction he'd gone.

"About Gabriel," I prompted.

She shook herself at my words. "Oh yes, when I saw him earlier, he said he'd be back in just a bit. But I'm not sure where he went off to."

"I need to find him. If you see him, tell him—"

"Lady Ilya?" A guard spoke just behind me. I froze, my muscles going stiff all at once. Between the music, the crackle of fire, and din of conversation, I'd never heard him approach.

I twisted around to the voice at my back. Ajax, one of Lucien's guards, stood just a few handsbreadths away. "Yes?"

"I was told you needed an early ride back? We are ready to take you now."

Shit. Terrible timing.

"One moment." I rose and dusted off my dress. "If you see him," I said to Elin, ignoring the guard, "then please tell him...tell him to wait."

Her brows scrunched together as I took her hands in mine. "Be safe tonight. Don't let any pretty faces sway you." *Please understand what I'm trying to say.* With a forced smile, I released her hands. "I'll see you tomorrow."

Two waves of worry—one for my friends and another for what awaited me with Lucien—crashed together. The dice had been rolled, and only time would tell if I'd hit a winning number or a damning one.

CHAPTER 21
ILYA

The ride took ages and no time at all. Part of me yearned to hide in there forever, worrying for my friends and fearing the encounter to come. But another part of me ached to continue what Lucien and I had started at the festival. The latter part finally won out, giving me courage as I exited the carriage and strode through the castle with the guards.

"Thank you, Ajax."

The kindly guard bobbed his head to me, his companion doing the same. The whole walk through the corridors, I'd wondered whether they knew Lucien's unmasked face or if he'd found some other way to instruct them to escort me back here. The question rose to the tip of my tongue over and over, but each time I swallowed it down.

If they didn't know, merely asking might give away the secret and ruin whatever favor I'd garnered thus far.

"Have a good night, miss," he replied before closing the doors behind me.

My breaths seemed to echo in the quiet room. Dim lantern light flickered near the empty seating area. I'd expected Lucien, braced myself to see him here.

My heart sank. He'd drawn me away from the festival, from my friends, but hadn't waited after all. "Lucien, why..."

I froze. The door to his room stood wide open, revealing stairs spiraling upward into darkness.

He waited for me. Up there.

An iron weight tumbled in my gut, making my limbs sluggish and uncertain. My goal was within reach: get into his room, learn what I could. But it would cost me. With nothing to stop us or hold us back, he could ask for everything. And I'd give it to him. Not for my plans or agenda, but because deep within me, I wanted him. I *needed* more of the intoxicating rush that he fueled within me.

Of all the men you could want, Ilya...

Attraction complicated everything. Could I spy on someone if I came to care for him? Use him? If I let myself go to him, I might never be able to separate my heart fully. Even so, I couldn't miss this chance. Not for our mission, nor to slake the seeds of desire he'd sown through unexpected kindness.

Only one way to find out.

A light in the darkness tugged me upward, one step after another.

The landing neared and I hung back, taking in what I could see of the room beyond. Lucien's suit of armor gleamed in the low light of an oil lamp. Weapons and spare pieces were stored on ornate shelves. A large fireplace had been stacked with wood but was currently devoid of life. A desk of polished, dark pine stood to one side, sporting numerous documents and books—my prime target. Many more shelves lined the walls filled with tomes, gathered papers, writing instruments, and trinkets I couldn't quite make out.

But the sight that caused my heart to race and my legs to press tight together under my dress was the massive, four-poster bed whose carved headboard hugged the wall. Dark covers and furs draped over its unmade surface.

Beyond all that, two stone archways opened onto a balcony and let in the night, their heavy, dark curtains pulled wide and tied at the sides with thick cords. Moonlight crept in through the opening, reaching into the room. My throat dried as I spied Lucien with his arms propped against the railing, staring out into the night. His garb still painted him for a merchant, though within this room, no one could mistake him for what he was.

He hadn't seen me—yet. I could turn. Run.

I took the last steps into the room, my heart pounding in my ears.

Lucien and the desk fought a war for my attention, threatening to tear me in two. I edged toward the desk.

"Ilya." His voice wrapped around me like a warm breeze, stirring up the tides of my soul.

The light of the two moons highlighted the planes of his face. His mouth lifted at the corners before his lips parted slightly.

Heat flushed my skin. The desk vanished from thought as if it had never been, as did the rest of the room. I didn't even notice it as I crossed to the balcony.

"You came."

"I did."

He extended a hand to me. "The view is stunning tonight."

That open hand held everything despite being empty. An invitation. A question. An offer. And perhaps even a hope.

I took it, letting him lead me across the deep stone balcony to the edge of the railing. Three large fires flickered in the night below, surrounded by many smaller ones and auras of light from lanterns and candles inside homes and buildings. The number of torches in the bailey had been reduced so as not to overshadow the view on this festive night.

My friends were out there somewhere.

My breath caught in my throat as a strong arm snaked around my waist, pulling my back against the hard planes of Lucien's chest. "Quite the night." His breath teased my ears. Sandalwood and warmth clouded my thoughts.

"Beautiful," I whispered.

"I can think of something better." His arm flexed around me as his thumb rubbed a pattern through my dress.

I turned in his arms, just enough to see his face. "Why me? I'm your hostage."

His lips twitched. "You're our guest."

A frown pulled at my lips before I could stop it.

Lucien grazed my cheek with his fingertips, tilting it ever closer to his own. "Was I mistaken to think you wanted me too?"

I licked my lips. "No. You weren't mistaken." I wouldn't lie about that. What started as a ruse, a plot, had become something earnest. Perhaps it was just his comely appearance, my lack of options, or the need for pleasure after so much heartache, but there was a hint of something else, a terrifying thread I dare not follow. It was easier if it was only lust. Safer.

"But according to you, I'm your captor."

"Conqueror. Captor. Man who stole my future." All true. All reasons to not let this be anything more than a give and take or a part of my ploy.

His brows arched toward the moons. "Then why, Ilya? If you think so harshly of me..."

Only my arm between us kept our chests from pressing together as I turned fully in his embrace. He held me tight, strong arms caging me in as if I might flee at any moment. Heat from his body leaped to mine, as warm and enticing as the fires below.

"Leading Sorrena was all I'd ever known, the thing I'd strived for throughout my life. That's gone." For now. "The way you look at me, even though I've lost what set me apart, makes me think there could be more to me. If there's more to me, perhaps there's something more to you as well, more than I let myself see at first."

"There's so much more to you, Ilya. How can you not see it? Your fierce heart. Your wit. The way you fight—not bad for someone who's not a warrior. The way you protect those you care for." He shook his head. "I can only imagine what goes on inside that head of yours."

You'd hate me if you knew. Certainly never trust me. Lucien brushed a stray hair back behind my ear. My nerves jumped and tingled in the wake of his calloused fingers.

"And you...what is beyond the war and conquest? Your loyal service?" I asked. Hard muscle met my fingertips through the fine linen of his shirt.

"Things you've yet to learn, though I want you to. But one you already know: a man who wants a woman he shouldn't touch."

My throat dried, nearly strangling off my words. "Because I'm your hostage?"

His breath warmed my face as he leaned in. "Because I don't know what's in that head of yours. Can I trust you, Ilya? Or will you stab me in the back?"

"Lucien..." His eyes held me captive, though everything in me wanted to look away from a man who saw too much.

"Say it again."

"What?"

"My name, on your lips." He stroked my bottom lip for emphasis. "The most beautiful sound I've ever heard. Say it again."

"Lucien."

His lips stole the last of his name from my tongue in a gentle press that asked more than it took. This kiss was the opposite of the one at the festival. Tender. Light.

I closed my eyes and lost myself in the feel of him, soft yet firm. His hand tangled under my braid, tugging me closer. His body was firm against mine where I stroked the coarse material of his shirt, lavishing the skin stretched over tight muscle below.

My lips spoke many lies, but not my kiss. It was earnest, yearning, aching to give more than I took. Why couldn't he be just a man? Any other but who he was? He was rough, hard lines to my softness. Darkness to light.

"I want you, Ilya," he whispered.

I cracked open my eyes. My body turned to goo in his arms at the lusty, hooded look he shot my way. He meant it, still not knowing if I'd turn on him. But I...I felt exactly the same way. There was no logic to it, no reason. Only want, need, and desire consuming me from within.

"I'm yours, Lucien."

Our gazes locked. I waited for him to kiss me again, to touch me, but he stood still as a statue. Until he crouched, slipped one strong arm behind my knees, and tilted me into his waiting embrace. I wrapped my arms around his neck, seeking purchase and security. In a heartbeat, I was in his arms, hovering above the stone tile as he carried me into the bedroom. His rapid pulse warred against mine.

"Lucien, where are..." My words trailed off as I eyed the object he advanced toward. The bed. Lightning raced under my skin, moisture grew between my legs.

With infinite care, he set me down upon silken furs, my feet dangling over one edge. But he didn't rise to crawl atop me, he knelt at my feet.

I bit my lip as he inched the hem of my dress up to my knees, exposing my sandaled legs.

His lips twitched. "Intriguing," he said, pulling one long leather strip to release the binding on my calves. "Once the resting season comes, we'll have to find you something warmer."

"We'll?" I questioned, near breathless as he removed one sandal then started on the other.

"I wouldn't be a gentleman if I let you freeze."

"A gentleman now, is it? Not a warlord?"

He tugged the other shoe, tossing it behind him as he gazed up at me with a smirk. "I thought you wanted to discover what I was? Maybe I'm many things other than what the world sees."

"So you say, but what are they?" I slid my legs onto the bed, relishing the tickle of fur across my skin as he worked at the ties on his own boots.

"I love poetry, if that surprises you."

I raised my brows, only partly in show.

"What the sun sees glows, but only shadow knows." A boot thudded away. "What lies in darkest night. Hidden from all pure and bright." The other followed.

My body trembled in anticipation as he rose to his full height, towering above me. Like a predator on the move, he prowled on his hands and knees until I was forced to lay back atop the furs, the beast himself hovering over me, all grinning teeth and gleaming eyes.

His confidence flickered, a question floating across his features. "You'd sully yourself with someone like me?"

I caressed his face, the softness of his skin changing into a prickly, dark stubble along a firm jaw. "In case you forgot, most people believe I already have."

The predator returned in a flash, accompanied by a deep chuckle. "I had forgotten."

"Well, I haven't," I pouted. "You're not even sorry."

"I am." All trace of humor vanished. He closed the distance between us, his hair tickling my face as his forehead pressed against mine. "But I'm not sorry I kept you here with me. This outcome...I never imagined."

I lost myself in his embrace upon the furs, giving way to feeling over thought, pleasure over painful memories. Nothing mattered, not the past, not my goals, only him. The rest could wait.

A moan slipped out between our kisses as a rough and calloused hand slid up my leg to my thigh, pushing aside my dress and silken slip in the process. My skin tingled in his wake, the ache between my legs growing with each touch.

I whined as he pulled away, rising on his knees upon the bed. With a quick move, his shirt was up and over his head, exposing a muscled chest smattered with dark hair. He didn't come back to me immediately. Instead, he tossed the shirt away and displayed himself proudly in the lamplight for my inspection.

And look I did. Firm muscles trailed down his chest, disappearing down below his waistband with a patch of dark hair. I'd felt and fantasized about the chiseled muscles of his arms but never seen them. And there, on the inside of one forearm, was a dark mark shaped like a star.

Cold water doused the inferno within me. I gaped and sputtered like I'd been dumped into the sea.

"Ilya?" He stiffened as his gaze raked over me, searching for injury.

It can't be. It can't.

Deep bells pealed in the distance. Others joined their chorus, multiple notes playing together and ringing through the night.

Lucien went completely rigid above me. "Fuck." His attention flickered between the balcony and me. His lips drew thin as he pulled away. "Fuck! Why now?"

I sat up, tugging the hem of my dress back below my waist. Icy tendrils of fear gripped my heart. "What is it? What do the bells mean?"

Lucien paced, running a hand through his hair. "Trouble."

I flew off the bed, running toward the balcony.

The fires still glowed, smaller now than they were. The whinny of horses and muffled voices echoed up from the bailey, mingling with the tolling bells. I couldn't make out any words, but they didn't sound urgent. No shouts. No clashes of metal. No flares of magic.

Not a battle.

My racing heart slowed as I gazed out into the night, searching for anything amiss. Nothing stood out.

When I turned back to the room, Lucien had donned half his armor and hastily fastened on the rest. Already his arms were covered, hiding the sight I could have sworn I'd glimpsed.

"What's going on?" I rushed to him. "My friends were still at the festival. Are they okay?"

"I don't know. I won't know until I meet the others."

Fear clutched my throat. The bells signaled the captains. To send for them all in the night, a festival night at that...

Nausea churned in my gut. "Take me with you."

"I can't." Another piece of armor strapped into place. "The bells will put the castle on lockdown."

I opened my mouth to protest.

"I'll make sure they are alright and let you know."

I swallowed my retort. His helmet slid on, hiding the man from view and transforming him into the monster who'd stalked into the halls of Sorrena to accept our defeat. How had I fallen into his arms so easily? Disgust, with myself as much as him, dampened the last of my desire.

"Come on," he said, stalking past me.

"I...I can't stay here?" I let a flush rise to my cheeks, pretending to be embarrassed by my request. There would be no better time to search his room. The cold sound of the bells reminded me of my purpose, each ring reinforcing my goal.

Lamplight caught his eyes beyond the helmet, revealing his indecision.

"I may be gone a while." He beckoned me. "Come."

Reluctantly, I followed him down the stairs.

CHAPTER 22
LUCIEN

The night turned from a dream into a nightmare with the toll of a bell. The deep, eerie ring never stood for celebration or praise. Emperor Ryszard rang for only one reason: to summon his captains, urgently.

I'd never considered ignoring a summons. Not once in all my cycles, even when it pulled me from a bath or sleep. Tonight, I would have given much to pretend I didn't hear them. I didn't remember donning my armor, or the long walk to our emperor's audience chamber. Only Ilya... spread out on the bed before me. The way she beckoned with her hooded eyes and parted lips would haunt me forever after.

But it wasn't passion that fueled the speedy return to my quarters. What I'd learned in the emperor's meeting sent my head spinning and my stomach dropping in a way little else had.

My hands fisted at my side as I traversed the quiet halls in the stillness before morning. By The Four, she played me well. I knew her gambit. She'd been so obvious trying to seduce me when she first came to my quarters.

Fool, thinking she could really want you.

I was a master of illusions, and yet it was me who'd been deceived.

Would she be mocking my weakness even now? Emperor Ryszard had been right in his command to avoid romantic attachment. She wasn't even mine and yet she'd gotten under my skin and lulled me into a sense of trust. Minutes more and I would have been deep inside her—making her mine or falling further under her spell? I grunted, ignoring the desire surging to my cock despite the warning in my head.

"Captain." One of the guards outside my room nodded my way as I approached. The other opened the door, letting it swing in on near-silent hinges to reveal my sitting room beyond.

The oil lamp burned low, casting barely a flicker of light into the shadowy gloom of the room. The glow it provided was dimmer than the remnants of burning fire of lust that raged within me only hours ago. The mounted buck head on the wall mocked me. Proud, regal, a king in his domain. I pulled my helm free and tossed it onto the sofa. His mantle was mine to wear, but I'd been tricked by a pretty face.

I cracked open the door to her room. Moonlight spilled across her sleeping form from the window, painting her in soft greys and blues. My chest tightened. A small sigh escaped her lips as she moved under the creamy fur draped across her body.

Fuck.

I still craved her. I toyed with the pommel of the dagger at my waist, unable to hold still.

It took all the little restraint I had left to close the door and go back into the sitting room. She'd been so ready to prove her trust, and I'd wanted it, more than I ever should. My desire was a weakness, one I'd let cloud my judgment. I paced back and forth in the room, unbuckling my armor one piece at a time. The rhythmic routine calmed me...a little. Removing the heavy breastplate should have lightened the load upon me, but the sting of betrayal still wore me down. I needed to talk to her.

Best to get this over with quickly.

Before I could change my mind again, I pulled open the door and entered her sleeping chamber.

"Wake up, Ilya." My words echoed through the room, louder than the bells that drew us apart hours before.

She woke with a start, jerking under the coverings before she twisted toward my voice. Her hand flew to her mouth, then went limp as her shoulders relaxed. "Lucien."

The furs fell away as she sat up in bed, revealing a pale, thin underdress. The one I'd slid up her legs. One I wanted to pull off her even now. I shut my desires in a box and shoved them into the recesses of my mind.

"Tell me, did you think you'd get away with it?"

Her brows drew together as she scooted on the sheets, away from me. "What are you talking about?"

"You should know." My words were bitter like crimson leaf tea. Biting.

"I have no idea. What happened?" Her eyes widened as she sat up straight. "Elin, is she—"

I waved a hand through the air, cutting her off. "She's fine. Safe in her room." Warren confirmed that the girl hadn't been involved. At least some of our honored guests followed the rules.

"Then what happened?"

Gods, she was a good actress. Pretending to be so innocent, just as she'd pretended to want me. "Your friends broke the rules." The words came out sharp, edged, harsher than I intended.

"My friends..." She looked away.

I'd asked for her loyalty, and she denied it. *Of course* she knew. She probably helped develop their plan.

Anger burned under my skin. I lunged across the bed and grasped her chin, forcing her to face me. Her startled *yip* hit me like a punch to the gut. *Hard, too hard.* I loosened my hold but refused to let her go as I settled my weight on the bed beside her.

"Don't think you can fool me," I said. Her olive-flower scent teased me, threatened to steal my focus. "You spend all your free time with them. I'm sure you know what they were up to."

"I don't. I spent the evening with you. At your request." She held my gaze, unflinching.

That look—the same proud, defiant air she'd held the day we met. By The Four, I wanted to believe her. Her words, her actions, that she could want me despite what I'd done... *Don't go there.* A shiver rolled down my skin as I adjusted my grip on her chin.

"Please...Lucien." Pain flickered in her eyes.

I jerked away and stood. I'd hurt her, this woman I wanted to protect. I stared at nothing across the room, trying to sort out the thoughts chasing themselves like hounds after a doe.

A light touch pulled me back to the moment—her hand on my arm. "Honestly," she began, her voice feather soft, "I have no idea what happened."

I read my men like a book, sourcing out their truths and whatever weaknesses they try to hide. It was a daily game, almost like the ones I played with Warren. Who'd been late to their post? Who skipped training? Worse—who might be a spy among us? Cycles of practice honed my skills and told me one truth: Ilya truly did not know what had occurred.

"We caught some of your lot trying to send a letter." I sighed and shook my head. "Brishon saw them himself."

They'd been so foolishly obvious. How could they not expect us to be there without our armor and keeping a close watch on all the emperor's guests?

From the corner of my eye, I glanced at Ilya. She swallowed. Her hand slipped from my arm as she looked away. Her skin paled further under the bright moonlight as she touched her fingers to her lips.

"Who?" she asked, barely a whisper.

"Lord Gabriel Laril and Lord Fernand Reis."

She closed her eyes. Her hand fisted in the covers.

"And what's going to happen?" Her voice cracked. "Or what has?"

Silence reigned. At length, she opened her eyes, their sorrowful, glassy appearance cut me like a blade. Sadness, from fiery Ilya.

"They'll stay in a cell until we decide."

"The rest of us?"

I frowned. Did she think they'd all suffer for the actions of two? Probably. I didn't want to see her in pain, but she'd hurt me too. She'd crawled under my skin and then dug in her nails. They were two of her closest friends here. Allies. So many times, I'd watched them at meals and in the gardens, ever since she'd come to Zhine. She would have known their plan. Known and not told me, which meant she was still my enemy.

She could have planned to stick a knife in my throat tonight after she'd seduced her way into my bed. Sweet words. Soft looks. Bile soured on my tongue.

"You promised to prove yourself to me."

She straightened. "I did. Have I not done all that you asked?"

No, sweet Ilya. I crossed my arms. "You didn't tell me what your friends were up to. All that time when we danced or when we crept into the shadows and—" I cut myself off. My hand slid to the pommel of my blade, grasping tightly for control. "One of my guards overheard you ask Elin to tell Gabriel something on your behalf. Should I interrogate her instead?"

She rose from the bed with a huff and stalked toward me, her attire revealing everything and nothing all at once. I held my ground as she advanced. The fire in her eyes burned as much as my own, two wildfires about to clash.

"Don't touch her." She craned her head up at me. Defiance cloaked her like armor. "She knows nothing."

"But you do, don't you, Ilya?" I crooned. She wielded seduction against me? I'd return that volley.

Color touched her cheeks as her hands fisted. "He wanted to talk to me about something, but I couldn't find him. Something felt off, but I went with you. I chose you!" She shoved my chest. "What more do you want?"

So much fury. Could she possibly be innocent? "Then they trust you, enough to tell you their secrets," I mused.

She flinched. "More than you…"

I unfurled my arms and stepped closer, so near we almost touched. A whiff of her scent soothed the raging fire within like a blizzard. How could she affect me so? "We lost whatever information they planned to pass on," I said, offering her a token of peace. "Burned before we could get it." Without thinking, I grazed her shoulder, the barest touch. She didn't flinch or pull away. "But they might tell you."

"So that I could share it with you?"

I nodded. *Help me, Ilya. Prove yourself to me.*

"They just want to help their people. Is that so wrong?"

"In this castle, it is. Their efforts won't help them or their people. They'd be better off accepting our emperor's rule and making the best of their situation." I touched her shoulder again, savoring the feel of her skin against mine. "You all would."

Ilya jerked away and hugged her arms around herself. "Please. Just tell me now. I can't…I need to know." The flickering lantern light cast jumping shadows across her form.

"Need to know what?"

"What will happen to my fr—er, Emperor Ryszard's honored guests? The ones who disobeyed his rule?"

My attention dipped to the bangle around her upper arm. She wore it even in sleep. Somehow, seeing my gift against her skin acted as a balm to the ache of her likely betrayal.

"Torture," I said.

Ilya gasped.

"By magic."

Her hand flew to cover her mouth. She looked away, eyes glassy.

"Nothing permanent," I continued quickly. "Just enough to send a message. To them and any who would follow their example."

"You can't." She whirled around and latched onto my shirt, tugging on the fabric I wore under my armor. "Whatever it is, talk them out of it. Give them a last warning. Anything."

"It's too late."

She shook her head. "It's never too late, not when it hasn't happened yet."

I'd never seen her like this. So open. Vulnerable. Without thinking, I grazed her arm, the briefest touch. "Emperor Ryszard commanded it. I cannot go against him."

"This is too extreme. Such a punishment for..." Her words trailed off as she caught my meaningful stare.

"We talked him out of worse for the two men," I offered. My emperor asked for death. It took hours to convince him it was an overreaction. "But their people will share the punishment. A higher tax." It was the only way he'd consider sparing them.

Ilya bit her lip, her eyes flittering this way and that.

"Show me your arm." She slid her hand along the loose sleeve of my shirt.

My brows knit together at the odd request. Curiosity convinced me to comply. As I rolled up my sleeve, my birthmark came into view, no more than a dark smudge in the dim light of the room.

Ilya traced a delicate finger down the edge of my mark. My muscles tensed as I let myself savor the touch. "How long have you had this?" she asked.

I smirked. "So curious about my body now?" With her hands on me, I could almost forget the misery of the night. Almost. "As long as I can remember. Does it bother you?"

"No, not at all."

"But?" I grabbed her wrist, letting my thumb rub circles across her smooth skin.

"One of the guests in your cells, Gabriel, shares the same mark."

I jerked back. Another ruse. Another attempt to get under my skin. I should have known. "A coincidence."

She touched my face, soft as a gentle breeze. "It's not. All the men of his line have such a mark."

I frowned and stepped away. Every touch clouded my thoughts, my judgment. "If this is some last effort to talk me into changing their punishment, I can't. And I won't. Drop it, Ilya."

"It's not just that! If this mark runs in his family and you both share it—"

"Then we must be related?" I asked.

"Yes." The word cracked from her throat.

"My parents are dead, Ilya. All my family." The horrible memories of my past, the earliest I knew, flashed through my head. She'd stirred them up more in the past weeks than anyone had in cycles. "The emperor found me alone in a ramshackle cabin, near starved, mourning their bodies."

She stepped back, her shoulders stiffening. "But what if—"

"Did you not hear me? I'm nobody. An orphan plucked out of a village outside Zhine. A weak, sobbing no one!"

Ilya flinched at my outburst, but a determined gleam quickly replaced the sorrow in her gaze. "How old were you?"

"What?" I almost snarled.

"How old were you when the emperor found you?"

My lips thinned. "Five or six cycles? I don't know exactly."

"Gabriel's nephew was almost six when he disappeared. You could—"

"I'm done with this! We'll talk no more of it." No more craftily woven tales to get me to bend. No more pitiful glances to pray on my weaknesses and reopen my old wounds.

"Lucien..." She looked away and shook her head.

Good. I couldn't handle any more of her games. Not tonight. One moment I wanted her, the next I was sure she'd kill me in a heartbeat if she could. I'd gotten nowhere with Ilya and only confused myself more. I needed rest. Clarity. I turned and headed for the door.

"When will it happen?" she asked, her words quiet and far away.

At the threshold, I looked back over my shoulder at the woman who'd pulled in on herself like a beggar huddling for warmth. At least she wouldn't share the punishment of her friends. The briefest thought of having to remove my bangle from her arm and subject her to that sent my stomach rolling and my teeth on edge.

"Two days' time."

CHAPTER 23
LUCIEN

Flames illuminated the fog, jumping like spooked mares in the mist, as I neared the arena. My fingers flexed in anticipation of the magic I would wield in mere moments. Already it tingled under my skin, waiting to be released.

I should have been used to it by now—how many countless humans had fallen victim to my illusions over the cycles? More than I could count or remember. The traitors deserved punishment for their acts, for trying to slip information out of the capital. Such a thing could not slide by without consequences. But it could have been done in private, away from prying eyes. Instead, our emperor demanded a public show.

The wooden arena wasn't enough of a stage. He ordered Orson to ring it in fire. A tactic to further intimidate the accused, as well as those in attendance.

Orange tongues of flame illuminated the somber faces of the audience crammed into the narrow wood stands overlooking the arena.

Emperor Ryszard was impossible to miss, sitting on an armchair positioned in the center and flanked by two of my fellow captains. But it was another face I searched for among the many guards and staff.

She wasn't hard to find, crammed between Elin and the flirtatious Reyna to her right. What little I could see of Ilya's expression didn't bode well—thin lips, squared shoulders. Her eyes locked on me as I neared the arena. Despite the distance separating us, I could feel her piercing gaze full of betrayal and hurt.

I'd warned her, though perhaps not well enough. What would she have said if I'd told her that my emperor ordered me to carry out the prisoners' punishment after we'd talked him out of the more lasting and possibly deadly display he'd initially ordered? Now I'd never know.

Her form wavered through mist and smoke. A spark of pleasure burned in my chest as Ilya traced the silver bangle upon her upper arm. She almost always wore it now, for protection or as some sign to me, I didn't know. Logic told me the former, though my traitor heart hoped for the latter. She wore her necklace again too—a sign of her people, her rank. The night of the festival was the only time I'd seen her without it.

Don't do it, I willed as she slid off the bangle. A humorless huff slipped from my lips as she put it on Elin. No sooner was it in place than she wrapped her arms around the girl and tucked her head into her chest. Of course she'd protect someone else. Better that frail girl than the others, but my stomach clenched when I considered what Ilya would soon witness.

"The one on the left first?" Orson asked, lowering a section of the magical wall of flame for me to step through. The two prisoners had been led into the arena once the audience was seated, one on each side. The guards had bound their tied hands to a length of rope attached to a metal ring driven into the ground. They would have some mobility, but not much. If the rope snapped, they wouldn't make it through the flames or the guards waiting beyond.

"Does it matter?" I replied. It didn't. First or second, both would suffer. What was worse, experiencing the torture unprepared or knowing what was to come?

"Looking forward to this." Orson laughed as he stepped back. The sound grated on my nerves worse than dented armor. Someday, Orson would step out of line far enough for me to put him in his place, perhaps in multiple pieces. He almost had with Ilya the night I first brought her to my quarters—he might have if I hadn't intervened. Saving her from Orson was worth prolonging his comeuppance.

I stepped into the ring toward the unfortunate dark-haired man staring me down: Lord Fernand Reis, heir to the city-state of Nassia. Magic tingled down my arms, collecting in my fingertips as I willed illusion into life. It wouldn't be something simple today, no creation of my imagination. Instead, I directed the magic to Fernand, willing it to dig into his fears and weave a projection based on what it found there. Such a skill was taxing, but significantly more effective than a generic illusion. This would be personal, brutal...effective.

"Fernand?" A beautiful blonde woman in a long, blue dress appeared behind the man. She cradled a bundle of cloth, one that wiggled and cried out.

His child? We hadn't known about the young boy when we conquered their city-state. Fernand hid that secret well. Our governor of Nassia, one the emperor installed to see that their leader followed the emperor's orders, discovered the baby's existence many days after his arrival. Our emperor thought to request that the child reside in Zhine. He still might once the babe grew older.

Fernand whirled toward the woman, bound hands in front of him. So quickly, he dismissed my presence in light of his wife. The rope pulled taut, and he crashed to his knees. Fingers dug into the dirt as he strained to move forward, to reach her.

"Fernand?" she echoed again. The illusion did not see him, but he certainly saw her. And the child.

"Magdalena!" he cried, struggling to reach her.

The sound chafed like soiled cloth. I willed the illusion to continue, but I looked away, searching again for that one face among the masses.

Ilya paled. Reyna grasped her arm in a show of support before wrapping her arms around the twin boys sitting in front of her.

Look away.

Their attention was glued to the scene along with the others in the crowd. All sat in rapt attention as the flawless illusion continued to take shape.

The baby's cries picked up. A building solidified from thin air behind the woman, one with ornate, high windows and painted frescoes. Carved pillars depicting scenes of the growing season. A temple of the Goddess of Dawn from the looks of it.

A piece of the painted temple ceiling broke off, shattering as it landed near the woman's feet. The baby wailed. The woman screeched as she looked around, begging for the man who cried out for her just as ardently. He strained and pulled, crying in earnest as another piece crashed to the ground. Then another.

I steeled myself and swallowed through the dryness in my throat as the horror of the illusion, of memory and fear that I had twisted into a very real nightmare, continued to unfold.

The ceiling continued to fall, crushing the woman and her child as Fernand screamed in agony. The woman's cries halted as remaining chunks of plaster clattered onto the rubble covering her body.

Fernand pressed his face into the dirt, his arms wrapped around himself as he rocked and shook. A slight acid scent burned into the air with the smoke of the flames.

My body shuddered as I willed the magic to retreat, cutting off its flow like tightening the noose at the end of a rope. The man huddled further in on himself, curled like a child in a muddy ball.

One down.

I spit the foul taste from my mouth. This was worse than battle. I'd take the broken, bloodied bodies of fallen warriors over this helpless slaughter of the mind.

I frowned as the line of flame splitting the arena dimmed to ashes in one small section, just wide enough for me to pass through. Orson anticipated my actions, paving the way for me to approach my next unwilling victim.

Unlike Fernand, this man had courage. Lord Gabriel Laril of Trale. Ilya's friend.

Gabriel strained against his bindings, gritting his teeth as I stalked toward him without a word. I had no threats for this captive or any other. I didn't need them. The suffering Gabriel already witnessed, and would shortly endure, was more than enough to inflict a targeted blow. Emperor Ryszard requested this punishment for guests who stepped out of line. While it hurt them the most, it affected the rest of them too. One quick look at the faces of the audience was enough to see them squirm and whisper to one another.

The fire sprang to life behind me as soon as I passed through, the heat rushing up my back and warming my armor. That bastard could have waited a moment longer. Sweat from the fire and the use of complex magic dampened my hair under the heavy armor and ran down my back in a small trickle.

"Get on with it then," Gabriel shouted. He'd seen his friend suffer. He knew what came next.

Good, I wanted to be done with it as well. Magic tingled under my skin before rushing out to the man before me. In moments, an illusion began to appear behind him, stolen from his mind.

A young boy with fair skin and dark hair, no more than six cycles, stood among tree trunks smattered with maroon and green moss. A short-sleeved tunic and dark pants decorated with golden thread hung from his skinny form. Small boots of polished leather hugged his feet, sinking into the loamy ground.

My brows drew together. Gabriel didn't have a son.

The boy's high-pitched voice called out for his father, his uncle. *Ah, that's who he is to Gabriel, a nephew.*

Gabriel twisted around at the voice. "Bastien..." Just as quickly, he turned his back on the boy. "It's not him!" he shouted at me. Despite his denial, his posture stiffened, hands tugging harshly against the ropes. It was him, at least the memory of him.

I glanced past the angry man to the illusion beyond. Familiar grey eyes stared straight back through the man whose thoughts and memories conjured him. Then I saw it. A mark on the boy's right arm. Dark. Shaped like a star. Twin to my own.

The world spun. Breath flew from my chest like a solid punch to the gut, one that sent me stumbling back a step. The illusion wavered, like a ripple over a still pond, before solidifying.

It can't be.

My body shuddered. Heavy breaths heaved in and out of my lungs as I struggled to keep the illusion intact. *A trick. It has to be.* Gabriel had witnessed his friend's torment. Perhaps he'd found a way to summon his own horrific image to counteract my magic. It was the only thing that made sense.

What Ilya had told me... I searched the crowd for her. She sat pale and straight, her eyes glued to me as men and women around her jumped at the sound of wolves howling—more of the illusion.

Had she found a way to communicate with her friend? To thread little bits of information into her interactions with him that could threaten to bring me to my knees?

I shivered despite the fires heating my armor and the sweat rising to the surface of my now clammy skin. I'd consider it later, when so many eyes weren't on me and the scene my magic wrought. The effort of it tugged at my center, a reminder to focus despite the distraction.

A second howl followed the first, shrill and eager. Then a third.

The illusion boy ran through the trees, nearing Gabriel as the man spun around toward the scene.

"Papa! Uncle!" the boy cried, before tripping over a tree branch and falling into a pile of leaves and loamy underbrush.

Gabriel started toward him as the boy rose, scrapes marring his pale arms. "I'm here," he called. The boy rushed ahead, just out of his grasp. The rope jerked tight, drawing Gabriel to a sudden stop that wrenched a cry from his lips as rope bit into his skin.

A wolf bounded into the ring of fire. The boy sprawled backward onto the ground, away from the beast whose grey hair rose along his back as a growl rumbled from its throat. It wasn't just any wolf, but a hulking beast from the mountains north of

Trale. The soiled, matted fur and inflamed jaws marked it a diseased animal—crazed.

Another appeared from behind a tree to pace near the boy.

Gabriel struggled against the bindings, straining toward the child just out of his reach.

It didn't take the blessing of magic to know where this fear would lead. I glanced away, back toward the woman who never failed to draw my attention. She sat stiff as a board watching the illusion play out, arms tight against her sides. My fingers twitched. Something tugged at my chest, urging me to go to her, but I couldn't.

"Please, no more!" Gabriel begged. The cry pulled my attention back to the illusion.

A wolf lunged. High-pitched screams erupted. The other animal paced and snapped before bounding into the fray.

Torn cloth. Blood. Mangy fur.

Screams turned to gargled cries.

Then silence.

I tugged at my magic, willing an end to the gruesome display that turned my stomach.

The scene faded, leaving Gabriel collapsed on his knees, head and shoulders hunched in defeat.

The crowd was deathly silent in the wake of the two vicious scenes. The punishment my emperor dealt affected not only his victims but all in attendance. All except himself, it seemed, as he rose to stand in his box and turned toward the attendees, spreading his arms wide. Emperor Ryszard's frame held no emotion, only cold indifference as he scanned the audience.

The emperor never led his troops on the front lines in battle—that was my task—but he was no coward. No torment I'd ever conjured, real or imagined, moved him. In my youth he'd been different. Supportive. Encouraging. Eager to see our new skills. As the empire grew so did his detachment. Whatever thoughts and feelings floated behind his high cheekbones and fine wrinkles, he kept them locked safely away.

"Let us not forget the terrors we try to put behind us," his voice boomed across the crowd, strong and clear. "And one last reminder for our friends that treason is not without cost."

I retreated through a break in the flames, tasting the bile in my throat as Brishon stepped forward. Mental torment was not enough to please our ruler. He'd requested one more punishment as well, a physical one, though it would fade with time.

Blessed by the God of Light with skills that affected the physical body and donning a helmet like a finned beast of the sea, Brishon could poison another to the point of death with a touch. Death would not fit with the current plan, but a sharp and lasting sting? Our emperor deemed it the perfect closing act.

The men would feel his touch for the next few days—small needles pricking their hands over and over until the poison faded away.

Brishon pulled a short, curved knife from its scabbard and stalked to the first man with a cluster of guards tight on his heels. Fernand had risen shakily to his knees near a pile of vomit, his face marred with sweat and grime. Brishon slashed the rope binding him before removing one glove.

I turned my back on the scene as another scream rent the air. I'd seen and heard enough.

"You're going to miss out on the last bit of fun." Orson stepped in front of me. The hint of a smirk twitched between the slits of his mask, dancing with the last bit of flame glimmering on the metal as he let it die down around the arena.

I grunted and pushed past him.

Orson followed after me. "What? Eager to have that little spitfire wrapped around your cock again so soon?"

I turned on him faster than a striking snake. Magic leaped from my skin, reacting to the fiery pulse of my fury. If I'd had his magic, only a pile of ash would remain. Instead, inky tendrils wrapped around Orson's neck, solidifying into thick ropes, crushing metal and choking off air—at least in his mind.

Orson grasped at his neck, attempting to pry away the illusion.

Gasping rasps slipped from his lips. My magic flowed, tingling with glee, savoring the retribution.

"Lucien?" Zurina stalked toward us out of the mist, confusion ringing in her voice.

I tugged the magic, willing it to recede. "A misunderstanding."

Orson gasped for air, hunching over with his hands on his knees as he recovered from the illusion.

"Orson will be more careful with his words in the future," I finished, with a pointed look to the man in question.

He spit on the ground, daring to meet my gaze before turning and stomping off toward the castle.

Zurina's grieved hand slid to her hip. I could almost picture her raised brows beneath her hawkish mask. "That isn't like you."

"Isn't it?"

"Do you want to talk about it?"

I frowned. "No." My attention glided to my arm, to the birthmark hidden under my armor. I needed answers, but Zurina couldn't provide them. Gabriel wouldn't give them to me either, not after today. But Ilya... Ilya might.

CHAPTER 24
LUCIEN

The sun had long faded beyond the hills before I'd had the chance to seek her out. Not what I'd planned, but it couldn't be helped. No sooner had I stepped into the castle than Zurina had pulled me away to discuss more reports of possible rebel activity.

"Talk to me, Ilya," I called from outside the door to her chamber.

"Go away!"

I nudged the door again. She'd blocked it somehow, determined to keep me away despite her residence in my quarters. Another night I might have offered her space. Not tonight. Not after what happened in the arena. I'd removed my armor, a sign of peace, not that she could see it. Determination overrode caution as I rammed my shoulder into the sturdy door. Wood groaned. The door flew wide to crack against the wall. A chair clattered to a stop on its side. Ilya's wild-eyed stare did nothing to calm my racing heart.

"You tried to keep me out of a room in my chambers?" I eyed the broken chair. She looked as mussed as I felt. Sweat matted my hair and left an unpleasant stench in my wake. I longed to sink into the steaming pools in the castle bathing room, but I had no time for that, not yet.

"Of course, I did! Do you think I wouldn't after today?" She slid across the bed, making it a barricade between us, one I wanted gone. It would stay, for now. She acted too much like a spooked horse that would run or kick when cornered.

I sat on the foot of the bed. "I warned you what was to come."

"But you didn't tell me it'd be you." Her voice cracked at the end. "You tortured my friends."

And I'd hurt her in the process. The betrayal in her words was impossible to miss. Each one stung worse than a physical blow. I didn't bother to hide the emotions that washed across my face, vulnerable and open. So different than with anyone else. "I didn't have a choice."

Ilya crossed her arms and stared me down. "Did someone control your limbs or your words? Physically compel you beyond your own will to do what you did?"

Each accusation stiffened the muscles in my body, drawing me tight as a bowstring. Words rose to the tip of my tongue and died there.

"That's what I thought. The choice was yours," she continued. "Every day we have the choice to do what is right and good, to help others or to harm them. You know what you decided."

"It's not that simple." She didn't understand. How could she?

"It is." She turned away in a flash of dark hair.

"He's my emperor. He took me in, raised me, made me all that I am. How could I go against his direct orders? I pushed it far enough talking him down from something more severe." When she didn't speak, I continued. "Would you go against your mother? Ignore her direct orders or subvert her wishes?"

"I did," she whispered. "You were there."

At the throne room in Sorrena, when she'd begged for her sister to remain there. I ached to cross the space to her, to kiss her hair, wrap my arms around her, and pretend recent days never happened. But they had. The memory of her sister, clasped in the arms of her father when we took their city, brought to mind another child. The boy's face and the mark on his arm had haunted me all day.

"Tell me about the boy," I asked.

Ilya glanced over one shoulder. Her hair hid all but the bare profile of her face, illuminated by the light of the moons filtering through the window. "You don't deserve to know. Or rather, if you really want to know, why not ask Gabriel? It seems your magic has sufficiently pried into his mind."

The words struck me like a blow.

Something coiled tight within me, demanding what I couldn't have —not now. Her words had been daggers, or a brutal defense, but she didn't turn away again. "You didn't wear the bangle I gave you," I said softly.

"I did. But then I slipped it onto Elin, just in case." She'd taken it back at some point, an act that warmed my heart through her current aura of cold indifference.

What wouldn't the woman do for those she cared about? But I couldn't let it go. "We had a deal. No speaking of the bracelet's abilities."

Her jaw worked in her mouth before she gritted her teeth. "I didn't tell her. She hid her face anyway, so she'll never know she couldn't see the magic. Hearing their cries was hard enough. Do you really wish her more pain?"

Another blow. One that nearly took the wind from my lungs. I almost lost the fight against my better judgment. "You saw the other child, the one in the illusion," I said, ignoring her plea. "Gabriel's nephew? The boy called for an uncle."

She turned back to the narrow window. A dismissal if ever there was one. "Go away, Lucien."

The day further unraveled whatever tentative bond had formed between us. She was right—it had been my choices, my doing, even if I'd had no other option but to carry out the emperor's orders.

I'd fix this.

But not tonight.

The weight of my actions pressed on my shoulders as I stood, careful not to stir Ilya's anger further. She'd yet to turn around as I slipped from the room with one last, longing look at the beauty shrouded in sorrow.

CHAPTER 25
ILYA

Gabriel and Fernand did not attend breakfast the next day, though Elin had overheard a guard mention they'd been returned to their quarters sometime the night before. They'd be watched now, more carefully than ever, but still I yearned to speak with them. If nothing else, I needed to assure myself that Lucien's magic had not permanently affected them. Or if it had, to steel my heart against him.

How foolish I'd been to think I saw anything other than the monster he was. I'd have to be careful. I couldn't abandon my plan—it was the best one I had after all—but I couldn't slip up and let down my defenses again.

Elin and a few other guests played a game of rolling round balls across the yellowing grass. At least some of the horror from yesterday had burned off in their minds in the light of day. A smile here. A small laugh there. It was more than I expected, though I couldn't will myself to join in their activity.

A commotion to my left drew my attention. Two nearby guards broke off their conversation. I gasped as I spied Gabriel and Fernand. Clean hair and clothes disguised the events of the day before. If you didn't know better, one would have no idea what they'd suffered.

Unless you looked in their eyes.

Those showed what nothing else did, especially when neither would look at me in return.

I ran to them across the open courtyard. "Gabriel! Fernand!" Their attention flitted to me, then away, but I pressed on undeterred, especially as the guards near them backed away. "Are you..." *Okay* would not be the right word. They weren't. I knew that.

"We've had better days," Gabriel muttered. Fernand said nothing. He wouldn't even look at me as he trailed off to an isolated section of the courtyard beyond waist-high, thorny hedges. Two guards wandered not far behind, keeping him in their sights. Gabriel hissed, clenching his hands at his sides.

"The poison?" I reached for him without thinking but drew my hand back in a flash as he pulled away.

He nodded and rubbed one hand with the other. "It hurts less than yesterday." Yet it still stung enough to wrench a cry from his lips.

Words couldn't reach my tongue as I considered what to say to him. I wanted to explain my absence, that I had tried to warn them, but the guards lingered too close. "Shall we take a walk?" I offered.

He glanced at the nearby guards and shook his head. "Probably best that we don't."

The unexpected rejection tripped me up, but I followed after him as he moved away.

"I thought you'd walk with us the other night," he mumbled as he turned onto a gravel path, barely sparing me a glance.

"Something came up," I whispered in return. Too close. The guards lingered just beyond the near hedge, another pair trailed behind us.

A tingle ran down my back, creeping like little spiders under my clothes. I twisted around. The sight behind me nearly froze me in place. Lucien walked with Warren across the courtyard in the shade of the castle walls, and though his friend nodded along as though they spoke, Lucien's gaze was fixed on me.

Gabriel's eyes had narrowed when I turned back to him. His head tilted to the side. "Something, or someone?"

"It's not what you think." My focus flitted around, searching the locations of the guards. I ached to tell him what I knew. His nephew lived. But after what he endured at Lucien's hands yesterday, he might not believe it—or worse, the knowledge of what he'd become may be more hurtful than thinking him long dead.

"Isn't it?"

I sucked in a sharp breath. "You can't think that I—" My mouth snapped shut, rattling my teeth as several guards glanced in our direction at my outburst.

"I'm not sure anymore." Gabriel's curt dismissal iced my blood as he walked away.

Roots might as well have grown up my legs for all that I could move. The world swayed, or perhaps I did. In a matter of days, all my carefully laid plans had fallen apart. Worse, Gabriel no longer trusted me. I could see it in his eyes, hear it in his voice. Fernand likely felt the same way.

The frayed ends of my plans floated through my head like slimy eels, taunting me.

I jumped as a slender arm looped around mine.

"Come paint with me," Reyna said, her characteristically cheery smile in place.

"Paint?" My forehead creased at the odd request. The imaginary roots anchoring my legs released as she gave me a tug in the opposite direction from Gabriel.

"Of course. It's a lovely day to capture these late-blooming flowers."

An apron was draped across the front of her dress, tan and marred with a few dabs of green and yellow. Her long, dark hair had been tied behind her head with a cream ribbon. The pale color matched the trim around the sleeves of her crimson dress, which fell to just above her elbows.

"I don't know how to paint," I said as we neared an easel set with a partially painted canvas. Another two sets stood propped against a wall nearby, waiting to be used.

"Then I'll teach you. It will be fun. Think of it as a distraction from the trials of doing what's right."

I stiffened, almost stumbling over my feet. "What do you mean?" I whispered.

Reyna just smiled at me before calling out to the guard near her work in progress. "Dion! Can you fetch Lady Ilya an apron like mine? She's going to paint with me, and I'd hate for her lovely dress to get ruined." She winked at him, blinding smile still in place.

"O-of course," the man stammered. "Right away."

He departed faster than if one of the captains had given him the command instead of the hostages under his watch.

She smirked as he hustled off. "If you seem happy and content, they don't watch you quite so closely. In fact, they can be rather helpful." She hefted one of the spare easels and brought it next to her own. The guards did keep their distance here, as if they didn't need to watch this particular woman.

"Grab a canvas," she instructed. "It'll be a bit before he gets back, but we can get you all set up here."

I followed her orders, using the opportunity to ask another question as I set the canvas on the stand she'd just straightened on its grassy footing. "Are you not happy here?" She seemed like it.

Her eyes bore into mine. "Is any fish content in a small bowl?" She smiled again. "You're too obvious, Ilya." She leaned in, pretending to help me settle the canvas. "If you really want to learn their secrets and perhaps earn them to your side, you need to relax. Anyone can tell you'd slit all their throats if you could."

My eyes widened at her observation, heart pounding in my chest.

"So today," she continued, "we are going to paint, and you're going to relax and be happy for once."

"But Gabriel and the others..."

"How did their plans turn out?" She cocked an eyebrow at me as she returned to her canvas.

Not well. If I'd been with them, it would have been a second offense for me. My punishment would have been worse, and Lucien's reprieve would not have kept me from the cells this time.

So, I painted with Reyna that afternoon until my arm cramped from the movement of the brush across canvas. To my surprise, the guards left us mostly alone. More shockingly, I found I enjoyed the craft more than I ever expected.

I didn't notice when Lucien left. Or the fading of the sun as it dipped toward the far hills beyond the lower levels of the castle and painted the sky in hues of brilliant orange growing fainter into the dark blue.

That afternoon, I wasn't the heiress of Sorrena or a woman striving to free her people. I simply was. It calmed my heart, eased my spirit. But mostly, I gained a new twist to my strategy. Relax. Blend in. Don't be a threat.

I'd be the silent snake in the grass until I chose to lash out once again with my fangs.

CHAPTER 26
ILYA

Ajax escorted me back to Lucien's quarters after dinner. He never failed to be kind and courteous. Over the last few days, I'd actually found myself enjoying his company.

"Your painting was delivered earlier this evening," he said. "Quite a lovely piece."

My smile was as much for myself as for his compliment. Artwork managed to disarm and relax the residents of this castle more than several tankards of ale.

"Thank you." I batted my eyelashes. "It's my first piece, but I worked quite hard on it. Hopefully, I can do more in the coming days."

"We'll look forward to it. Perhaps they'll liven this place up a bit," his companion added as she held the door open for me.

My canvas reclined against a side table in full view of the door. It would need a more permanent home, especially if I planned to add to its number. Would Lucien let me hang them in his quarters? The thought of the captain tugged my attention toward his door.

I blinked, barely comprehending the sight before me. The door stood open, revealing the staircase beyond. Fire rushed under my skin as I recalled the last time I'd witnessed such a sight and what it almost led to.

Surely, he can't think I'd leap into his bed now.

I reached for my necklace, aching for the comfort of the solid gemstone, but my fingers touched only smooth skin. I'd removed the Mark of Sorrena before dinner, tucking it away in my trunk. Someone at peace with their new life wouldn't wear the symbol of their old one.

Butterflies warred with eels in my stomach, memories of the past few days churning up the internal battle. I'd be a fool to miss the opportunity to enter his room again. Any little piece of information could change the game. But facing him again in such a setting was bound to be difficult. A shiver racked my body.

Eventually, curiosity conquered fear.

I inched up the stairs, treading on near-silent feet across the smooth stones. With any luck, I'd glimpse Lucien before he saw me, giving me some indication of his intent. Or better yet, I'd be able to garner some information from his room.

The sight that greeted me as I rounded the curve of the ascent shocked me more than anything I'd imagined, including Lucien laying naked upon his sinfully large bed.

Books and papers were strewn about the room, coating the desk, the bed furs, a few gracing the ornate rug on the floor. The man himself hunched over the desk, peering into an open tome, his back to the stairs. No armor hugged his form this evening, only fine, dark clothing.

Like a man possessed, he flipped one page, then the next. The candle near his arm fluttered in the paper breeze, sending a trail of hot wax running down the side to pool on the desk below. Lucien didn't appear to notice the mess or to care.

I cleared my throat where I stood, barely into the edge of his room.

Lucien whirled in his carved, wooden chair. The movement stirred a stack of loose papers whose edges fluttered precariously close to the candle flames before settling back onto his desk.

"Ilya."

His deep voice filled the quiet space, wrapping around me like a shawl.

"You left the door open," I explained. "I assumed you wanted company."

"I do." His back straightened, transforming him from a defeated man to the conqueror I'd become familiar with. "Though I honestly didn't expect you to come, after the other night."

Several responses rose to the tip of my tongue before I swallowed each down in turn. *I didn't expect to come either. You still disgust me. Things cannot be the same as they were.*

None of that would help me.

"What do you want?" I asked.

His brows rose with his body as he left the seat and stalked in my direction. "Tell me about the boy."

"This again?" I shook my head and turned toward the stairwell.

"Please." The plea pierced my side. Somehow that word had a magic of its own that no object of protection could shield me from. "You know who he was and why Gabriel saw that vision."

"I thought you created the illusions?" I forced myself to look up into his eyes as he neared. The room grew warm with his closeness, or at least I did.

"It's much easier if I do, but that one was designed to seek out his fears and project them. It—" He cut himself off briefly before continuing. Lucien edged toward the stairs, blocking any hope of retreat. "Please tell me what you know about the boy."

"You'd trust my words? You didn't before."

He glanced away. Dark circles under his eyes reflected the weariness in his voice.

"I want to," he admitted. He reached for me but stopped as I flinched back. "I remember my past. I can't be related to him as you implied. I can't."

My heart cracked at his words, sending a shiver of pain through me. Why would he not let himself consider this possibility?

"The boy was Gabriel's nephew, as you likely guessed from the illusion. He was Lord Stefan's only living child. Heir of Trale." I wandered away from him as I spoke, moving to the desk with the hopes of glimpsing its contents. "He went missing in his youth. Everyone assumed he died. I suppose..." My fingers trailed across an open book. *Poison Scars* titled the top of the page. "I know Gabriel believes he must have died, and I suppose his mind created that horrible outcome when they could never find him."

I leaned over the desk, my brown hair falling over one shoulder to brush the open book. I ignored the man at my back as I scanned the pages, ones detailing the physical scars of plant-based poison, trying to understand what consumed his thoughts.

My back tingled just before Lucien's hand landed on the desk near mine, splayed across the edge of a book. My breath hitched. He was too close. Far too close.

I hedged toward the chair, but Lucien kicked it away with one leg, sending it clattering and scraping across the stone before he took its place, bracketing me in between his strong form and the desk.

"Not what you expected to see?"

Warm breath tickled my neck. The hard, wooden edge of the desk cut into my hips as I leaned away from him.

"You're trying to understand the boy's scar," I replied, near breathless. "The one like your own."

He captured a lock of my hair, pulling it toward him where he hovered just behind me. "Did you tell him about that, Ilya? Give him a hint to twist my magic?"

I whirled on him, accidentally knocking my leg into his in the cramped space. I might as well have hit a tree for all that he moved, though the impact raced up my leg and sent another flare of heat pooling in my gut.

"How could I have? I didn't see him between the festival to honor the Goddess and your little show in the arena."

He inched closer. I jerked back, knocking into the desk. The wobbly candle tumbled from its stand, splashing wax across the papers and tumbling off into the floor. Lucien grunted and stepped on the still-burning end with a booted foot, snuffing out the last of the flame.

I used the distraction as an opportunity to escape his embrace. My heart pounded in my ears as I forced myself to walk slowly to the balcony, luring him in with crumbs of the information he desired.

Lucien left the mess where it lay and followed me. "You said the mark is a birthmark? That the men in their family all have it?"

"That's right. At least it's what Gabriel told me."

"Then explain to me how I could have the same mark."

Moonlight touched his clothes, accenting the fine fabric but leaving his face shrouded in darkness. Even so, a hint of light glimmered in his grey eyes, begging for knowledge he refused to believe.

"You think I'm his nephew," he whispered into the moon-touched night.

"Yes. And I suppose none of these books have given you any other possibilities?" I gestured to the mess around the room.

He frowned at the strewn handful of tomes on his bed. "No. But I remember my past. I can still feel the hunger, the desperation and deep sorrow in that cabin before Emperor Ryszard found me." He turned away at the end as if the admission embarrassed him. The hard edges of his jaw smoothed out, his eyes turning downward.

Despite the kernel of anger in my heart, I stepped closer, drawn by the aura of sadness that could be felt without any magical touch or power. "And before that?"

His head snapped up. "Before what?"

"Before the cabin. What do you remember?"

His brows wrinkled, and he grit his teeth. "Nothing," he said at last. "I remember nothing."

"What if, before that memory, you were someone else?"

"I was an orphan, Ilya. Poor. Starved. Near death. If he hadn't found me, I would have died in that cabin like my parents had." His voice rose in volume and intensity as the words continued to spill out.

"How did he find you? All of you?" So many powerful magic users.

"Ilya," he warned.

"Tell me. What harm can it possibly do?"

He crept forward, moonlight rolling up his face. "He can sense magic. It's how he found me—most of us. He saved us from death or other horrid fates and trained us from childhood."

Saved...or created his own perfect illusions for each child?

Dawning horror twisted my insides. It was all too convenient. Powerful children in need of a savior. Children who would undoubtedly wish to aid the man who put a roof over their head and food in their bellies. He acted like some kind of noble hero from a storybook, yet the man himself exuded not the slightest hint of mercy or kindness.

"I don't know what happened in that cabin or how you got there, but what if you were someone else somewhere before that? Not an orphan, but a beloved son. An heir. Cherished. Protected." I gasped as he grabbed my shoulders.

"I know what you want me to believe. But I'm the one who led the attack on their city, Ilya. I killed their men—many of them. I crafted illusions for others that likely broke their minds. I stormed their halls and entered their throne room to accept surrender just like I did yours." He pinched my chin, drawing my face closer to his. "I can't be from there. I would have remembered something. *Felt* something." His hand squeezed tighter, almost painfully so.

"Let me go, Lucien."

He jerked me closer instead. "Do you loathe me now?"

"I should hate you. I want to." He released me, but I held my ground. Mere whisps of air separated us. His heavy, heated breaths ghosted over my skin in sharp contrast to the cooling night.

"But?"

I couldn't answer him. To say the words aloud would mean admitting them to myself. I'd said too much already. Instead, I walked away from him onto the balcony and changed the topic. "You were all recruited as children? Before your magic had fully manifested?"

My knowledge on the topic was limited, but from what I knew, magic grew as the person did, reaching its full potential after they reached maturity. A young child of five or six cycles would show little evidence of their power, if any.

He was quiet for so long, I wondered if he wouldn't answer.

"As much as I remember," he said at last.

"But your emperor started to conquer only recently. And even then, he'd only ruled Zhine for the few cycles since after his brother's death. What did you do before then?"

"Trained, mostly. Physical and magical skills. We all lived together in a large manor in the hills, growing up as brothers and sisters."

A family. My chest clenched. I should have known he regarded them that way, with Ryszard as their weird father figure. The truth of it made my goals and wishes so much more impossible. He'd never turn on family, which meant I had no hopes of bringing him to my side, but only using him for whatever knowledge or favor I could garner.

"Brothers and sisters of death," I whispered into the night, so quiet I wasn't sure Lucien could hear me. "That's why you follow him. Even though it means so much war and terror against cities living peacefully."

"Peaceful?" Lucien scoffed. "The city-states have squabbled with each other as long as anyone remembers. The emperor talked about it often. How no one respected his brother's rule in Zhine. Raids on farms. Threats against us."

Now it was my turn to be confused. "A few perhaps, but most lived peacefully, content with their lot and providing the best lives for their people." Sorrena didn't even have a proper army for goodness' sake. How many lies did this man believe? "Emperor Ryszard is the one igniting war."

It was always the northern city-states who squabbled over land and liked to test each other's strength through bloody raids. Mother said the cool air of the mountains made them irritable. How Elin turned out so calm and serene, despite her own father's fiery reputation, was beyond me.

"A temporary inconvenience. If only you all would stop your useless struggling, we'd be one unified country. No more wars or border disputes. No trade embargoes. Everyone can prosper together."

Those words stole the last warmth of the night. He believed it. Oh, by The Four, he believed whatever vision Ryszard spouted for his followers. "And the rest of the city-states? The larger countries to the west and south? You think they'll just leave us all alone?"

A pretty dream. Too impossible to be believed. The various city-states might as well be small villages for how the western countries dwarfed them in size. So many more people. Skilled, truly unified armies with magic users just as powerful as Lucien and his fellow captains. It was a wonder none of them had invaded already. Before, we'd likely only escaped notice since the city-states were too small and weak to be of a threat to anyone. We even gave the large countries better trading terms just to curry their favor and stay within their good graces.

Lucien didn't answer my question. The grimace on his face told me I'd struck a chord. And a truth.

I pressed on. "Do you really think Ryszard will stop? That he'll be content with all of us as his unwilling vassals? He'll set his sights on Marsali next, mark my words. And after that—"

"You speak treason, Ilya," he warned, a hard edge to his voice.

I pressed my lips tight as I wrestled for control of my loose tongue. Reyna's words from earlier in the day slipped through my haze of anger, calming and cool. *Seem content. Blend in.* But oh, how hard that was.

A deep breath calmed some of my anger. Then another.

"You're right. I'm sorry." The words tasted bitter on my tongue, but the vile flavor would be worth it if it defused the situation. I bowed my head, an act of servitude. "I only ask honest questions as a citizen of this new country."

Lucien released his crossed arms and stepped closer. "Could you be one of us? Stay here, by my side?"

My heart hammered at his implication. He'd asked before and I didn't have an answer then. I still didn't. "Do I have a choice?"

Lucien wandered to the balcony edge and leaned on the balustrade. I followed, keeping a respectable distance between us.

"I want to trust you." He glanced over at me. "To not worry you're going to stab me in the back if I leave a knife out on the table."

"I haven't yet," I said.

"No, you haven't." He pushed off the railing. "If I asked you to do something for me, go somewhere…"

I stood a little straighter. "Away from here?" Gods, if I could get out of here it might make my goal of finding and leaking information so much easier.

"Possibly." His attention shifted out to the night before settling back on me. "I can't explain yet. But would you trust me? Do as I ask?"

"I have so far."

His lips quirked into a smirk as he eyed the bangle on my upper arm. "Mostly."

I caught the amusement in his eyes and swallowed through the tightness in my throat before responding. "I'll consider it." It was the best I could offer. Hopefully, it would be enough.

CHAPTER 27
ILYA

Gabriel's mood softened over the next few days, though by no means were we on the easy terms we had been. At least I'd found a few stolen moments to explain my absence and the strides I made elsewhere. Fernand had yet to speak to me, as if somehow all his misfortune were my fault.

"I don't like it," Gabriel admitted as we entered the dining hall for lunch. "Getting close to a man like that..." His eyes followed a guard as he walked away from us. "Nothing good can come of it."

"They weren't this way once. Just orphaned children," I whispered.

"And that's earned your pity? Don't be soft. Whoever they once were is long gone."

His words twisted like a knife in my heart. *Even if he's your nephew? The one you loved?* I needed to tell him...somehow. Fear of his misbelief halted my tongue. Worse, what if it truly convinced him I'd turned sides?

I couldn't lose my ally, not now.

I took my seat as Reyna walked in, accompanied by Captain Zurina. The two talked companionably enough that one would assume them friends—if one were not a hostage and the other her jailer. Reyna broke off the conversation and aimed for the open seat next to mine. She shot me a wink as she settled into her place.

"Pleasant morning?" I inquired.

"Not bad. In fact, I think the day may be quite sunny indeed."

I barely stifled a laugh. It was raining today, pouring buckets from the sky. Unless... My features evened out as her nose wrinkled.

She knew something, though I couldn't hazard a guess at what.

"Let's paint this afternoon. Just the two of us," she continued, reaching for a platter of food. "I've had an inspiring thought that may look beautiful on canvas."

Of all the places Reyna could have picked, she chose the indoor sparring rooms. Soldiers swarmed the area, engaged in practice with several captains who acted as instructors within the large stone room. Windows along one wall showed the rainy gloom beyond. Lit torches and a chandelier sporting wide candles provided what light the sun did not.

"Why here?" I mumbled as a guard set up the easels she'd carried in for us. Another adjusted blank canvases atop them. We'd face the arena, presumably to paint men and women as they trained.

Reyna shuffled through the jars of paint in her basket while the guards finished our setup, seemingly oblivious to my question.

"Thank you so much," she said, gracing them with her broadest smile before they moved off to join the others in training. As they left, she turned to me. "Don't you admire the way their muscles flex and move as they lunge at each other? It's like sex. With clothes."

A soft blush rose to my cheeks. Watching men train would never again feel quite so innocent.

"But honestly," she continued, passing me a jar, "no one pays attention to what's right under their nose."

She had a point. As I glanced around the room, very few people bothered to look at us, much less pay attention to what we did. As if, somehow, we weren't a threat sitting here in the middle of their training. There was a brilliance to it I couldn't help but appreciate.

"So what are we painting?"

"Anything that strikes your fancy. It's different than nature scenes, but..." She shrugged, brush in hand.

I attempted to paint two men sparring with swords, though the first few stokes made it apparent that any talent I had lay in painting nature rather than people. I frowned at my work. "So when do you think the sun will come out?"

One glance proved Reyna lacked my struggles where human proportions were concerned. "Oh, quite soon, I think. Once we go outside, you'll have to ask if the birds are ready to migrate."

I digested her words, searching for a deeper meaning. "How will I know if they are?"

"Listen for their songs. Sometimes they sing quite clearly just before they flee the nest."

"And you think I'll like these birds?"

She grinned but didn't look away from her artwork. "I do. Very much."

My warrior's sword transformed into a grey lightning bolt across the canvas when the people I least expected walked through the doors: Elin and Warren.

My brush hovered above the canvas as I gaped at the sight, especially when I caught the smile pulling at Elin's cheeks. She rushed to the edge of the training circle, eager to watch the soldiers sparring.

"There's worse company she could keep," Reyna whispered.

Still, part of me grew nauseous just watching them. I hadn't spent enough time with her recently, had ignored my friend in favor of pursuing my goals. Against all odds, she seemed happy. Was this not a terrible prison for her too?

"You're right, it could be worse," I replied, sliding my eyes to Orson for emphasis.

She gave a dramatic shiver, the mirror of my thoughts.

"I just didn't expect it." I glanced around, searching for the location of the guards before I continued. "Could it be some kind of trick? A trap?"

Reyna shook her head. "Not with that one. He...well, it seems he retained a sort of innocence."

True, I'd never once heard of him being involved in any of the battles, for whatever that was worth.

He stayed near Elin, speaking with her as they watched the display nearby. He'd been with her at the festival too, the young farmer she'd danced with. Perhaps her charm and innocence had somehow swayed him to her side? Surely, she hadn't planned on that, not with the way she'd paled and shrunk the one time he joined her in the garden. But now...

I could almost picture that farm boy again: the softness in his eyes, the kind smile. How had he come to be under Ryszard's command? What kept him from becoming so corrupt and horrid like Orson?

Unless it was all a ruse.

I shook my head, clearing away my racing thoughts. There were more important things to consider.

"When you say birds..." I hesitated. My teeth bit into my bottom lip. I'd first heard of the rebels on my way to Zhine when they'd shot a letter into my coach. Reyna had been here long before that. Her city-state had been one of the first to submit to the emperor's rule. But what if she'd found a way to get information in and out? Could her birds be the rebels?

Reyna looked at me out of the corner of her eye, one eyebrow raised.

"I wonder if they're the birds I heard chirping on my journey here."

She paused her brushstroke.

"I did enjoy their song. Very much," I continued.

Reyna smiled and added another stroke of yellow to her canvas. "It's such a joy to find someone else who likes their song. Truly it is."

My body hummed with excitement. Reyna knew of the rebels somehow, but we'd hadn't been the ones to tell her. I was fairly certain of that. For so long, we'd believed her an enemy, but if she knew what happened on the way here, she might not be. Unless someone else told her. One of the captains? Maybe Zurina? They seemed close enough. It could be another trick, a ploy to shine a light on my guilt.

Though she had given me the contraceptive, not that I'd had to use it. Whose side was she on?

"You seem...perplexed?" The wooden end of her paintbrush tapped against her lips as she stared me down.

"I don't know anything other than that," I said, spilling the flimsy lie as my defense. "Why tell me this? What can I do?"

She laughed. "Only your arrows can hit the stag. As they say in the stories, the Lord of the Forest influences all the animals within his domain. He's the one we need."

The stag. It had to be Lucien. Whatever plot she had in mind involved him, and thus me as well.

"When you say—" I planned to say *we*, but the word vanished from my tongue as another captain entered across the room.

As if my thought had conjured him from the air, Lucien came to stand near Warren. Elin paled in his presence, stepping away from the new arrival.

Lucien's attention scanned the room before settling on me.

"And look," Reyna added with a blinding grin, "your scent lures him like a hound to the kill."

I forgot all about the painting as he skirted the training circle in my direction.

CHAPTER 28
LUCIEN

O f all the places I'd expected her to be, this was one of the last. If one of the guards hadn't mentioned helping to arrange a painting easel for two of our emperor's guests, I would have searched another hour before finding her.

Ilya's paintbrush hovered in the air, unmoving, as I approached. Her eyes locked on mine, stirring something deep within my chest.

I'd barely seen her the past few days, too preoccupied with my search for truth and Zurina's request for me to carry word of Lord Gabriel's punishment to Trale along with details of his increased tax. Only the fact that the two overlapped had me agreeing to her odd proposition so readily. I could only hope Emperor Ryszard would as well, or we'd both be in for an argument this afternoon.

"What's today's work of art?" I asked, rounding the canvas. I bit the inside of my cheek, hoping she couldn't see the way my lips twitched as I took in her painting.

Ilya's cheeks flushed as she looked up and frowned at me. "You can't tell?"

It took a moment, and some creativity, to puzzle out her interpretation of two people training. Oddly proportioned figures, more animalistic than human, stood on either side of the canvas. Grey rods thrust between them, one impossibly long and spearing toward the sky. Her paintings of plants were much better, including the one of an oak tree colored to reflect the fading season, which I'd secreted away in my room.

"I can now," I replied. "A very interesting duel."

Her lips thinned on the word "interesting," stretching my grin further. The way a blush colored her cheeks when something embarrassed her gave her a girlish charm so at odds with the fiery determination of her spirit.

To her side, Reyna pretended to ignore us, but the careful, brief strokes of her brush across the same section of canvas didn't mask her rapt attention. Lucky for me, my news affected them both. Finding them together saved me another search.

"The painting will have to wait, I'm afraid."

"What's going on?" Ilya set her brush on the thin folding table between them that held their assorted jars of paint and water.

"I need you to come with me. Both of you," I said.

Reyna paused her act and looked at me, placing her brush with Ilya's.

"I can have someone clean this up and store these for you, but I need you to come now."

Ilya stiffened, her mouth gaping ever so slightly, a sharp contrast to Reyna, whose demeanor remained unchanged.

"What's happened?" Ilya asked, not fully hiding the hint of worry in her voice.

"Nothing yet. I can't explain much now, but answer honestly when asked and remember what I asked you the other evening."

Trust me, Ilya. I need you for this.

Reyna placed her hands on her hips. "Lead the way then."

Ilya's brows furrowed, but she followed beside me as I led the women out of the training room. We walked in silence to our destination, only breaking it once Zurina came into view, reclining outside the doorway to the room I aimed for.

"You found them both," she said, pushing off the wall. "Excellent work."

Ilya looked up at me, asking a silent question. I yearned to tell her everything, to explain, but our emperor wouldn't expect her to know the topic to be discussed. Any slip-up on her part could implicate me—or worse, earn her a punishment I couldn't protect her from.

"They were together. Saved me a trip," I replied.

"Well, let's get this over with." She motioned to the two guards standing at attention on either side of the door. Both rushed to comply, pushing the double doors open wide to allow us access to the room beyond.

Zurina entered first, followed by the other two women, with me trailing. Ilya stumbled half a step, but to her credit, she kept her composure and followed Zurina into the center of the audience chamber.

Emperor Ryszard sat at his large, wooden desk carved with animal designs and stained to a deep brown. The circle of heavy chairs on the floor were empty sentinels in a half-moon facing toward the desk on either side of the empty aisle we walked along.

Ilya and Reyna halted as Zurina did.

"There you are, and sooner than I expected." The emperor's ringed fingers drummed on a stack of papers atop his desk.

Zurina placed her hand across her chest and gave a small bow. I swallowed the hint of nerves creeping up my throat and took my place at her side, giving the same show of respect and subservience. Out of the corner of my eye, I caught Ilya's fleeting stare.

"We didn't want to keep you waiting," I replied. "We"—I gestured to Zurina—"have a suggestion regarding the city-states of Trale and Nassia."

He raised his hand, one finger pointed toward the ceiling. His sign for silence. "And these two need to be present as well?" He gestured to the women standing just behind us.

Finally, I was free to glance in her direction. Both Ilya and her friend stood straight as a board, attention fixed on the man who'd just spoken. Ilya's lips had thinned into a tight line, her eyes wide and flickering with emotion.

"Yes." I turned back to my emperor. "What better way to send a message than to have it delivered by your honored guests?" I stepped back to keep both the women and my emperor in view. "Send one of them with each of us to the city-states to discuss the increased tax. It will show that the other city-states are submitting to your rule and encourage their compatriots to do the same. Plus, as you can see, both women are content here, well cared for, healthy. That alone will send a message." I held my breath as the emperor steepled his fingers in front of him.

"Hm..." he mused, before taking a short sip from the glass upon his desk. Drinking again? "Yes, I can see the advantages, but will our guests aid us in this?" He cocked an eyebrow, staring down the women.

"I believe they will," Zurina said.

He waved her silent with a quick slash of his hand. "I'd hear from them themselves. Their oath to convey my message and nothing more. A service to their new country."

I bit the inside of my cheek as Ilya's shoulders squared. *Do it. Tell him yes.* Whatever punishment he would contrive if she outright refused the request—or rather, the order—might not be something I could halt.

Reyna knelt, one knee touching the ground as her head bowed to the other. "I am happy to serve," she answered, voice calm and even.

My eyes narrowed. Too easy, too perfect.

Ilya swallowed visibly before she, too, knelt in a mirror pose of the woman at her side. "I will do as you ask."

Praise The Four. I nearly heaved a sigh of relief. Not so cordial, but it would do.

The emperor gave a shallow nod, his fingers coming apart and rejoining where they remained steepled in front of him. "Very well. I will take your advice. Keep a close eye on them though. I won't have any unnecessary trouble from this journey."

Emperor Ryszard left his desk and advanced on the women still on the ground before him. He halted in front of Ilya, his bejeweled hand outstretched in front of her face, the polished gems and gold reflecting the light of the chandelier above.

Her throat bobbed, but she took the offered hand and kissed his rings. He went to Reyna next, who followed suit.

"I'll take Lady Reyna and visit Nassia. Lucien will go with Lady Ilya to Trale," Zurina said.

Please don't argue this point. I needed Ilya, her insight, her observations. Besides, I longed for her company. Outside the castle walls, maybe she could find it in herself to forgive me. And if she was right about the scar, I needed her wisdom on that front as well.

"Fine. A troupe of soldiers shall accompany you each as well. No detours. No unnecessary stops. If you run into any trouble, well, you know what to do." The emperor waved his hands in dismissal as he traced his steps back to his desk without a word.

"Let's go." I offered a hand to Ilya to help her rise, but she ignored it, her face carefully blank. If I'd learned anything about her in the past few weeks, it was the illusion of that look. She'd be furious when we were finally alone.

I rolled my shoulders, savoring the release of tension that fled my muscles as we exited the room.

"That went well," Zurina said.

Her words echoed my thoughts as we escorted our charges away from the emperor's meeting room. "You were right. It's a good plan. I appreciate you bringing it to me."

"Perhaps one day you'll consider me the clever captain," Zurina replied with a musical laugh.

"I'd be a fool not to. We leave tomorrow morning?"

She nodded.

"Can we finish our paintings?" Reyna glanced between Zurina and me.

"That would be lovely," Ilya echoed, a hint of enthusiasm in her voice.

I stopped and stared between them. Something gave me pause, though I couldn't put my finger on it. "You can finish them once we return," I said.

Reyna frowned. "It'll be several days before we return. Perhaps we can do just a little more?"

Why this insistence? Her words held more than a concern for art. Some secret floated between them, one I couldn't work out. "You'll both want to be well rested. We'll travel hard and fast. Plus, it has been a while since either of you have been on the road. Enjoy a warm meal and bathe while you can."

Ilya's lips thinned, but she didn't argue it further. Nor did Reyna. Zurina shrugged, confused as I was.

"Good. Come along," I said, ushering the women back through the halls.

Silence stretched, heavy as the heat at the peak of the living season. If I played my pieces correctly, this journey might be more insightful than I'd hoped. Perhaps not only could I confirm for Ilya, and for myself, that I had no connection to Trale, but maybe I could gain some insight into her new friendship with Reyna as well. One way or another, I'd get answers only this journey could yield.

CHAPTER 29
LUCIEN

For four days we trekked across the land, covering the distance quickly thanks to strong horses and fair weather. Ilya traveled in the coach, just as she had on the journey from Sorrena to Zhine. The rest of us rode on horseback. I kept my distance, sticking to my role as the emperor's captain as much as I was able.

I half expected her to run, or at least, to test how far she could slip away without being watched. She did neither. At night she slept in the coach rather than join the rest of us near the fires.

During our mid-morning stop on the fifth day, I entered Ilya's transport and stretched out on the cushioned bench. Despite the padding, I still preferred the horse.

The door swung open. Ilya froze halfway in. She swayed where she dipped through the opening.

I tugged at the grey lapel of my borrowed guard uniform, a wry smirk pulling at my lips. "Care to join me, or would you rather walk?"

Ilya gaped, mouth opening and closing. Despite her shock, she joined me and closed the door behind her. "What are you doing?" she asked in a hoarse whisper.

"Acting as your personal guard." I crossed one leg over my knee, reclining into the tanned, cushioned seat. "One guard will look much the same as the next to these people. Regardless of skin tone or gender, all they'll see is the uniform." I knew that well enough from our conquests.

"But won't they expect *you*? And what about the others here?"

My lips twitched. "Worried about me, Ilya?"

She scowled at me. "You were the one who said this needed to go off without any mischief."

"Any mischief on *your* part." Gods, I missed her banter. She'd kept her walls up during our journey so far. It was almost like the journey from Sorrena to Zhine, though with slightly less simmering fury on her part and thankfully no strange attacks or interruptions—yet. Ilya had been upset about me taking her before the emperor without first letting her know and had berated me about it before we'd left. But I couldn't risk her sounding rehearsed. My emperor would not have expected her to know about this journey in advance, so I couldn't tell her.

"I chose these guards for a reason. They won't give me away. Besides, Tiber is about my height and will pose as me in my armor while I wear his clothes." It wasn't the first time I'd swapped outfits with one of them to carry out some covert task, and it likely wouldn't be the last. My boots thumped on the ground as I slid forward, arms on my knees. "You won't give me away, will you?"

She crossed her arms and stared me down. "I promised to carry out this task, though I'm still not sure why you chose me."

"Who among your company can I trust if not you? Besides..." I rubbed my forearm right over the place where my birthmark lay. I wanted her trust, yes, but more than that, I wanted her close to help me understand the illusion my magic had wrought.

Her head tilted to the side. "Are you nervous?"

"Of course not." I jerked my hand away. "Just ready to be done with all this. They won't like the news we bring, or the tax we'll request. It will be up to you to calm their leaders should they cause a scene."

She frowned and looked out the window. "Sounds like so much fun."

I grinned. Whatever awaited us in Trale, at least I had this time with Ilya.

BY MIDAFTERNOON, the dense pine forest gave way to grazing fields turning from green to golden in the early fading season. Stone and wooden homes broke up the horizon, along with the occasional large tree whose limbs sprawled out over the ground, providing a roof of leaves—so at odds from the tall, narrow pines we'd traversed for the last day.

"Is this Trale?" Ilya asked, peering out the window.

"It should be. We've traveled long enough." I soaked in her spark of excitement, willing it to calm my nerves. I wasn't anxious, more apprehensive.

The conveyance of our news and the tax would be fine. Lord Stefan wouldn't like it, not at all, but I'd grown used to unhappy rulers in recent cycles. They'd suffer this and move on, just as they had when they'd been conquered. My personal goals were another matter. Would I be able to sort out the truth of Ilya's words? I rubbed at the mark on my arm, hidden under the fabric of the borrowed uniform. Somehow it was more uncomfortable than my armor.

One glance out the window confirmed my suspicions. "Yes, the terrain looks right. You haven't been here before?"

"Not in quite some time." Ilya slid back from the window, sunlight catching on her hair and giving it extra shine. "I was young the last visit, maybe eight cycles."

Too old to have met the boy from the illusion based on the little I'd learned of when he went missing.

"Mother used to take me on trips with her all the time when I was younger." She glanced back toward the window, the hint of a smile on her lips. "I really enjoyed it. New people. Interesting smells. Strange foods. The first time I saw glow wood, I squealed in delight."

Such wistful, happy memories. I smiled despite myself. With every roll of the carriage's wheels toward Trale, Ilya relaxed. Tension slipped from her shoulders. She looked with wonder out the window. Small smiles teased me across the narrow space between us. I'd never seen her so at peace. So...happy.

"At the time, I didn't know that Ourelas shipped it southward through our port." She shook her head. "I begged Mother to get some for our home, but she refused, calling it an unnecessary expense. Candles and oil are cheaper after all, especially since we make so many in Sorrena."

The rare, glowing wood fetched a hefty price in any market. Ourelas would be broke if they didn't have the only small forest of the stuff on this side of the continent. We'd claimed some of it when we conquered the city, though the emperor sold off most of it to buy horses, metal, and other tools of war. It had been my suggestion.

"You didn't travel with her when you were older?" I asked. Ilya had finally opened up, and I craved the treasure of memories she shared.

She frowned. "No. I wanted to, but Mother insisted I stay in Sorrena and act in her place. Practice, she called it. I think it would have been more helpful to meet with the other city-states, understand their economies, get to know their people..." She shrugged. "I suppose it doesn't matter now."

"You speak a lot about your mother, but you have a father too?"

He'd stood off to the side of Sorrena's throne room when I'd led my men into that grand hall that smelled of salty sea air and olive flower, just like Ilya herself. Grey hair liberally crowned his tanned head that bore only a small circlet to indicate his rank. His wife, Astraea, dominated the raised dais bearing the throne, Ilya at her side. He had been barely discernable from the various other nobles and advisors clustered in the side of the throne room. Their positioning gave away the secret of Lady Astraea's heart, the family member she valued most: Ilya.

"Yes." Her smile returned. "Though he often traveled, especially as I grew older. Negotiating trade deals with faraway ports. Learning about the newest products and demands on the larger countries." Her gaze turned wistful.

"You wanted to travel with him."

She nodded, a delicate, soft movement. "I wanted to travel all over the world, not just to the city-states. But that was the wish of a child. There's no place for such fancies for a Lady of Sorrena." Regal bearing replaced her dreamy look. "Even less for a captive."

Her city, her title...they'd become a cage for her dreams, and she didn't know it. A weight settled in my chest as I watched her expression turn sad. Her body shifted to the side until she gazed out the window once more. I'd added more bars to her cell, trapping her in Zhine to keep her mother in line during this time of transition. Maybe one day, when the war was finished and she truly submitted to the emperor's rule, she could live out those dreams again.

Silence stretched between us as we neared our destination. Dirt roads turned to cobblestones worn smooth in ruts by use and time. Doors slammed closed. Parents ushered their children away from our entourage. No smiles. No cheers. Buildings increased in density as we approached the large manor home near the center of the city. Green awnings arched over the threshold of several places we passed, a signature of the storefronts in this city-state. Though the city was not fully walled—a poor strategic decision on their part—stone encircled this structure on all sides. The tops of the manor's highest floors peeked just beyond the barricade. Banners of green and black hung on either side of the gate we advanced upon.

We were expected. A vague letter had been sent ahead several days ago to announce our arrival. The scent of freshly baked bread wafted into the carriage, eliciting a small sigh from Ilya as she watched the passing buildings.

None of this looked familiar to me, save the memories of when I helped to conquer this city. If I'd grown up here, I should have some memory of this place. The smell of pine drifting down from the nearby hills was familiar, but it wasn't that different than the manor where our emperor had raised us. Nothing else struck a chord or tugged at my memories.

But Ilya gazed at everything with wonder.

"Does it remind you of home?" The way her eyes glittered as she watched the passing scenery, I couldn't help but ask.

She slid back into the seat, away from the window. "Not really. The sights, the smells, even the way they construct their buildings, it's all different. Our buildings are more open. Tall windows. Large sliding doors on storefronts that are often open. Of course, you can never escape the sea while you're there. The crash of waves on the cliff, the hint of salt in the air, the caw of birds and the taint of the day's catch being carted through the streets. Our stone is different too. The color of crusty bread rather than these dull greys." She motioned to the passing buildings.

"The last time I was here, I was so focused on impressing Mother and remembering how to behave like a proper heiress that I barely noticed the city," she continued. "I wish I had."

Funny. I couldn't agree more. In Sorrena, I'd viewed the city from a strategic view. What were its weak points? How best to invade? What positioning gave us advantage? But how much had she and I missed while we each gave everything to our roles? Until Ilya, I hadn't cared to see beyond magic, conquest, and endless days of training.

The carriage rocked to a stop. Tiber rode by the window in my armor, headed to the front. He was responsible for announcing our arrival.

"Should we get out?" Ilya asked.

I shook my head. "In a minute. We're not through the gates yet." As I spoke, the carriage started to move again. A shadow crossed outside as we rolled through the opening in the stone wall, passing the iron bars of a gate that had been opened wide. Men-at-arms stood at attention, dressed in dark green and black with a hint of silver and grey in the buckles of belts and straps holding their swords.

When the carriage stopped again, I made for the door and threw it open. The cobblestone pathway ended near a set of low, wide stairs leading up to the manor proper. This part I remembered, though yellowing grass now covered much of the area that had become a bloody mud slick at the end of the fight for this city. The metallic tang no longer filled the air, but it still filled the minds of the men and women here, judging from the hard looks aimed toward our troupe.

I turned and offered a hand to Ilya. She took a deep breath, evening out her features, before she took my hand and stepped out into the sunlight.

Members of my guard dismounted as grooms rushed into the yard to see to their horses. The beasts would need a good rubdown and rest before they began the return journey in the morning.

Tiber approached the steps that led to a set of double doors at the front of the central building. Before he reached the bottom step, the doors opened to reveal a woman in a long, dark green dress. Her dark brown hair was liberally streaked with grey and partially pinned back. A bejeweled necklace hung from her thin neck and accented her pale face, mostly free of wrinkles despite her hair. The Lady of Trale—Basilla, Lord Stefan's wife.

One of the guards passed me a scroll, bound and sealed with the emperor's stamp in crimson wax.

"They'll be expecting you too," I whispered to Ilya, passing her the document.

She glanced from me to the fake captain before taking the scroll. Like a refined lady, she lifted the hem of her dress and advanced toward the manor with me one step behind her as a dutiful bodyguard.

"Captain," Lady Basilla addressed the armored man, her voice all hard edges, lacking the softness of her features.

"We've come to deliver a message from Emperor Ryszard, as you should be aware." His voice rang clear and strong as he beckoned Ilya forward.

"Lady Basilla." Ilya gave a small curtsey to the woman on the stairs.

The older woman completely dismissed the captain as she took in the emperor's true messenger.

"Lady Ilya. You've grown." Her tone and features softened. She descended the stairs and clasped Ilya's free hand in hers, bracelets chiming as dangling medallions of metal clinked together. "Would that we'd have met again under better circumstance," she continued.

Ilya raised her eyes and met those of the other woman. "I could not agree more."

It took everything to keep my brows from rising. The woman who spoke was not the one I'd grown accustomed to. She was stronger somehow. More confident. This was the heiress of Sorrena standing before me with her raised chin, clear eyes, and squared shoulders, not our emperor's honored guest.

Basilla's gaze floated across the yard, taking in the members of the guard within the walls of her home. When they reached me, the woman's brows scrunched, her head tilting ever so slightly to the side.

I stiffened. She couldn't recognize me. I'd never been here without my armor.

"Will we be meeting with your husband?" Tiber asked, drawing her attention.

Magic tingled under my skin, raising the fine hairs on my arms as I took the opportunity to weave a small illusion over myself—enough to alter the color of my hair and eyes and add a sharper slant to my nose. The effect of my magic should be slight enough not to cause Basilla to question it—or anyone else, for that matter. It'd be an effort to keep it up all day, but worth it, just in case.

"Yes, he's waiting for you all inside," she recovered smoothly. "Please, come with me."

Ilya glanced at me sideways as we followed my double up the stairs. Her eyes asked a silent question, one I interpreted easily.

I shrugged. Whatever the woman saw, or thought she saw, I couldn't say, but my magic would ensure no one else saw the same thing.

CHAPTER 30
ILYA

Lord Stefan Laril waited for us in a narrow reception hall. Light spilled in from tall windows behind his chair, the sun adding its light to oil lamps flickering along the walls. Long, woven tapestries told tales of old battles and the surrounding forest itself. It was so different from my home in Sorrena with its light-colored stone and open, breezy rooms. We might as well have stood within the deep woods that the artwork depicted.

Two lines of wooden chairs—with carved, straight backs whose ridges and swirls would ensure no one rested comfortably—sat facing Stefan's high seat. He'd hold court for his people here, listen to their needs, resolve petty disputes.

The man himself frowned as we filed into the room. The movement pulled at the heavily grey beard that coated the lower portion of his face and grew into a point below his chin. He resembled his brother, Gabriel, in the shape of his face. But the color of his eyes was unique—grey as the stones of his manor.

"Lady Ilya. The spitting image of your mother in her youth." He rose from his chair with a grunt and crossed to greet me before the rest of them. A limp pulled at his left leg. A cane may have helped, but it appeared he refused to use one, at least today. He should have greeted the captain first. It would be a slight not to, but I kept my features neutral as he approached.

"Lord Stefan." I curtsied where I stood next to the fake Captain, Lucien a half-step behind to my other side. As a trio, we presented an intimidating front. The men likely intended it that way.

The emperor's appointed governor stood off to the side of the room, his prominent nose wrinkling as he stared us down. Lord Stefan played as much of a role as ruler of Trale as I did as the emperor's guest. His decisions were not his own anymore, his actions watched at every turn.

"I come on behalf of Emperor Ryszard to deliver a message," I said.

He nodded. "On with it. Let's hear what he has to say."

"Your brother Gabriel is my friend," I began, pausing to swallow the knot of unease that stuck in my throat. He needed to know I was still on their side, despite my role today. "He is alright. However, he was punished by Emperor Ryszard through his Captain Lucien here"—I tilted my head to the left—"for breaking his rules and attempting to undermine his reign."

Stefan's impassive features gave nothing away. He grunted. "And he sent you all the way here just to tell me that?"

"And to ask you to keep his peace," I replied. "He realizes the actions of one may not reflect all of your city-state. Even so, he imposes a one-time tax to remind you that treason does not come without a cost." I stretched out the scroll with the crimson wax seal face up.

"Treason, eh?" Stefan took the scroll and broke the seal.

Tentatively, I looked between Lucien and his double from the corner of my eye as Stefan read Ryszard's words, which would echo the information I'd just presented, if not in so nice a tone.

Lucien bobbed his head ever so slightly to me, keeping his attention focused on the man as well. With them near face-to-face, I couldn't help but notice the resemblance between them. The dark locks of hair on Stefan's head, at least the parts that had not turned grey, matched Lucien's. The men had similar builds. Lucien stood only half a hand higher than the man who might be his father. And then there were the eyes... My breath had hitched when Stefan approached from his throne. I'd know those steely-grey eyes anywhere.

How did no one notice? Especially when they stood so close together?

Stefan waved over one of his household guards and passed off the scroll to him. The older man took it promptly to the governor. He'd ensure the tax was collected—I had no doubt of that.

"Well," Stefan began, "if his imperial highness wants us to suffer during the resting season this year, he'll certainly get his wish. This tax would spell starvation for my people if the harvests weren't promising. Even so, we'll have hungry bellies come mid-resting, mark my word."

I fought down the lump sticking in my throat. I hadn't seen the amount, though it didn't surprise me he'd ask for more than necessary— enough to make sure every person in this city-state felt the consequences of Gabriel's actions.

One step out of line would mean the same for Sorrena. Seeing the flicker of anger and pain across Lord Stefan's features, the true impact of my attempts to aid the rebels sunk home. I didn't just risk myself. I risked everyone I'd been raised to lead and protect.

Yet doing nothing meant leaving them in bondage—an impossible choice.

Reyna hinted that I might hear the friendly tune of the rebels, or birds as she called them, outside the walls of Zhine, but nothing out of the ordinary presented itself on our trip here. She'd known about the journey we'd been asked to go on—a mystery I still couldn't unravel. All the way here, I played her words over and over in my head, waiting on another false raid like the one on our journey from Sorrena. It didn't happen. Nor did anyone creep through the bushes to meet me as I lingered as far from our troupe as I dared during our various breaks and camping stops.

"And you..." He looked between the false captain and the real one at my side. "Do you have a separate message for me, or are you just here to frighten the maids and give them something to chat about once you leave?"

Fake Lucien straightened, armor rattling. "We're here to guard Lady Ilya and make certain our emperor's message is received."

He snorted. "She's more than safe under my roof."

I bit my lip, hiding my smirk at the proclamation that his protection extended only to me.

"I suppose you'll all be wanting a roof over your head tonight and food in your bellies?" No doubt he knew the answer, but he asked anyway, forcing them to spell it out. Based on his scowling face, he'd give them no more than the minimum they asked for.

"Plus fresh supplies for the journey home," fake Lucien added.

He waved a hand. "Of course, of course."

Stefan beckoned another of his household guards forward. "See to rooms for all of our *guests*." He hissed the word. "I assume the guards don't mind sharing?" He glanced back over his shoulder but didn't wait for a reply. "The captain and Lady Ilya will have their own rooms. You will all join us for dinner in the main hall."

DINNER PROVED AN AWKWARD AFFAIR.

Men and women ogled and scrutinized me from their seats as I tried to eat the savory cuts of deer and roasted root vegetables that Lord Stefan heaped upon my plate like a concerned father, convinced I wasn't eating enough. Perhaps I had lost weight. With everything else on my mind, my figure didn't warrant notice.

Stefan sat to my right, his wife on the other side and the emperor's governor next to her. The false Captain Lucien bracketed me between them, comprising the entirety of their high table. Lucien himself sat with other guards as well as many members of Stefan's household at tables near ours.

"We're lucky the weather has been fair," Stefan said at my side. "The grain has done well. The cattle grew fat."

I nodded appreciatively, commenting in return on the farms I'd seen on the ride in. Easy topics. Safe. Whatever information Reyna thought, or hoped, I'd have the opportunity to learn had not presented itself at dinner either. Or if it had, I'd missed it completely.

Invisible spiders raced across my skin. Three women turned away as my head snapped in their direction, hiding their whispers behind raised hands and averted eyes. Did Lucien feel this way in Zhine? Or Ryszard? I huffed a laugh through my nose. The smug bastard probably enjoyed it.

I nearly sighed in relief as dinner came to a close and people started to trail from the room. Maids scurried in their wake to collect empty platters and cups.

"Thank you for dinner, Lord Stefan, Lady Basilla." I curtsied to our hosts as I rose from the table.

"Your hospitality is most appreciated," the captain echoed at my back.

Stefan's lip curled as he stood. He'd deny us, or rather them, hospitality right this moment if he could. But doing so wouldn't earn him any favors.

Basilla remained seated, her eyes trained on the real Lucien as he took to his feet and headed in our direction. "That guard..." Her brows wrinkled as her husband turned in her direction.

What little food I'd eaten turned to butterflies in my stomach. If they learned who he was, even suspected...it might be just the break I needed. "Do you know him?" I asked innocently.

Her fingers trailed to her lips, her attention never wavering.

"Doesn't look familiar," Stefan answered for her with a grunt.

The governor also shook his head before taking another sip of wine from his fourth cup of the night.

Now it was my turn to be confused. If anything should catch their eye, it would be his looks. Unless... The bangle around my arm felt suddenly chill as I considered it. I'd become so used to its presence that I hardly noticed it most times. But if Lucien used magic, it might explain why no one else seemed to recognize him.

My lips pressed together as I examined Basilla's fine jewelry. A golden necklace spotted with small rubies and amethysts graced her slim neck. Matching earrings and rings adorned her. The only piece that didn't match the others was the set of bracelets around her wrists, metal charms hanging from three thin bands. Could it be like mine?

"Lady Ilya will need her rest," the fake captain jumped in. No doubt, he didn't like the sudden change in conversation.

"Of course, we have you all in the east wing. Yours will be the doe room," he said to me. "Fitting spot for a lady. The buck room across the hall is yours." He nodded to the captain.

Stefan called two of his household over with a flick of his wrist. "Escort our guests to the east wing."

Lucien made a beeline for me as the guards huddled around us, ready to be escorted to our rooms. Basilla watched, her lips slightly pursed. She'd yet to move from the high table.

"Magic?" I whispered, just loud enough for his ears.

His answering nod was barely imperceptible. He crossed between the woman and me, nearly brushing my shoulder. Too casual of an act for the role he played, and one that the mix of emotions in my heart could hardly stand.

"She knows."

"What?" he mouthed.

"You. She—" I swallowed the rest of my words as he placed a firm hand on the small of my back.

"We should get you to bed, Lady Ilya," Lucien said, drawing far too much attention.

My hands fisted at my side. "I hoped we could enjoy a drink with our hosts?" I gestured back to Stefan and Basilla. I couldn't sleep. Not when I hadn't accomplished any of my goals.

"Not tonight," the fake captain said. "This way."

The real Lucien nodded. His stare searched me, seeking my aim.

My lips drew thin. *Fine.* Let them take me to my rooms, but I'd find a way out. I couldn't lose this chance.

CHAPTER 31
LUCIEN

Ilya's odd comment at the end of dinner wouldn't leave me alone. *She knows.* Basilla? What did she know?

The moment the hallway cleared of Lord Stefan's men and mine, I slipped into her room.

"What are you doing?" Ilya hissed. She stalked around the bed, eyes wild.

I held a finger over my lips.

"You can't be in here," she said in a harsh whisper as she leaned toward me, all fire and fury.

My lips twitched into a smirk. "No one saw. Besides, how else could your faithful bodyguard keep you safe?"

Something about the room called to me, and it wasn't just the beauty fuming across the rug. An impossible sense of familiarity tingled down my spine. It wasn't the first that evening, despite the lack of such feelings on the way here.

"Keep quiet a moment."

Ilya pursed her lips and crossed her arms but didn't speak. I crept toward a long wall draped with tapestries, meandering past heavy furniture of dark wood. A nagging feeling pulled me to a woven scene. Four does grazed in a glade flush with verdant grass and wildflowers. Tall trees haloed the edges with misty mountains in the far distance. Time had worn away some of the threads, but not the majesty of the scene.

I slipped behind it, rattling the wooden frame. I slid my hands along the planes and grooves of the stone wall. Feeling. Searching. Low on the wall, near my waist, I found the source of my curiosity.

A chill racked my body as my fingers found a circular hole and slipped inside. I'd known what I'd find, and where, though I couldn't remember being in this particular room.

I pulled a soiled handkerchief from my pocket and stuffed it into the hole. A floor-length mirror against the tapestry provided further blockage.

"What are you—"

"Whisper hole," I replied, voice quiet. "Wouldn't do for someone to see me in your room. Or hear us."

Her mouth gaped. "You went right to it... How did you know?"

"Lucky guess." The casualness of the reply and accompanying shrug belied my racing thoughts. I had known. Just as I knew it was the only way to peek in here, or it had been once. The certainty of that thought did nothing to stop me from searching the rest of the room.

Ilya watched me work from the edge of the bed in tense silence.

Magic retreated with a shiver as I let the illusion I'd been wearing all day fall. A small trail of sweat rolled down my back from keeping the precise vision in place for so long. Days on the road and weariness from the use of magic urged me to rest, but I pushed it away. Not yet. Not when Ilya finally let her guard down during the carriage ride.

"I think that's it." I brushed dust off the borrowed uniform. The coarse material still chafed at my skin, urging me to shed the unfamiliar attire. My lips quirked up. What a fit that would send her into.

As I turned to her, I expected anger. An outburst. Another demand for me to leave. Instead, her eyes held something that nearly stole my breath—pity.

"You truly don't remember any of this?" she asked from where she still sat on the edge of the bed, her feet planted on the floor. The softness of her voice echoed the look she cast my way.

Maybe. Maybe not. I couldn't be sure. "A coincidence. Anyone would hide a whisper hole behind a tapestry." I lowered my voice, barely louder than the rush of wind that rattled the windowpane. "Speaking of, we should keep our voices down. Just in case." I looked to the woven scene for emphasis as I crossed the room to her. "I'd imagine many people here would be eager to listen to anything you might say."

Ilya craned her head back to stare at me as I neared. Something about that look, the challenge in her stiff posture, drew me closer until my boots nearly brushed hers. She reclined back, her palms pressing into the mattress to hold her upright. I leaned toward Ilya, narrowing the distance between us. "And even more curious about what you'd say to me," I whispered. "Especially if they learned the name of the guard watching over you."

She gasped as my legs brushed hers, but she didn't move them. I planted my hands on either side of her atop the bed coverings, digging my fingertips in as I fought the urge to push her down and claim her lips with mine. That would earn an outburst for sure, and a knock to the head. The first would attract too much attention and the second... well, I wanted her coming at me with a different emotion. I pulled back, giving her space but never taking my eyes off the woman before me.

"It's not just this room..." Ilya shook her head. "I tried to tell you earlier, but Lady Basilla recognized you. I saw it when we arrived."

"Impossible. She's never seen me without my armor." I swallowed the sudden tightness in my throat.

"She looked at you like someone she knew. You didn't notice her watching you?"

I had. The woman's glances lingered too long and too often. Of course, Ilya with her perceptive gaze would have picked up on it. "That doesn't mean anything."

"Deny it all you want, but you saw Lord Stefan's eyes. I've only seen one other person who shares that rare hue." Ilya shimmied off the edge of the bed and stood before me.

My heart rate picked up as she drew near, barely a handsbreadth away.

She prodded me in the chest with her finger. "You."

So close. By The Four, I barely heard her words with the way the dim, flickering light accented her face and sparkled in her eyes.

A sharp *yip* escaped her lips as I slipped an arm around her waist and pulled her to me. Her hair tickled my skin as I leaned into the side of her face despite her pushing against my chest. Each move and twist of her body had her scent invading my nose, my body thrumming with desire. "I'm not from here, Ilya," I whispered, lips barely grazing her ear. "I told you that. Whatever you're thinking, it can't be true."

"You won't even consider it. If you only took a moment—" She shoved me.

I released her. "And what? Assume all my memories are a lie?"

"Not all of them. But maybe some are missing? You were a child, who knows what illusions your mind created to help you cope with—" She grew silent as I placed a finger over her lips.

The intimate touch sent a shiver down my spine. So soft and delicate.

I leaned in again, body taut with emotion. "My magic creates illusions. Not my mind."

"If you're not going to listen, then why are you here? Go away and let me rest." She didn't hide the bitter edge lacing her voice.

She was still angry with me about her friends, but I couldn't change that now. I could only hope to re-earn her trust and affections. If today were any indication, I'd need them. I wanted them, wanted her.

I stifled a groan as her lips pulled into a frown and her eyes grew cold. Why couldn't I desire a less willful woman? "I'm sleeping in here, just in case you or someone else try something unadvisable."

She crossed her arms, her foot tapping on the woven rug. "Well, I hope you enjoy the floor."

The bitter rejection painted a grin on my face. "The bed is big enough for two."

Her eyes widened. A hint of color rose to her cheeks before she looked away. "I'd sooner sleep with a snake."

"Unfortunately, I don't have any of those available to grace your sheets. At least I don't bite. Unless you ask very nicely."

Her blush deepened, stirring the desire building in my loins. Teasing her pushed away my worries and confusion, let them flee to the recesses of my mind while a more pleasant diversion took center stage.

"We do need rest." I faked a yawn before tugging off the stiff jacket and starting on the row of buttons running down the front of the borrowed shirt. "Do you plan to sleep like that or will you be changing?" I arched a brow at her before eyeing the dressing screen, carved and painted to resemble a pine forest.

"You're impossible." Ilya stomped to the small chest of clothes that had been carted into the room at some point. Her things, packed for this short trip.

I took advantage of Ilya's disappearance behind the screen to shed my clothes. The stiff jacket landed on a chair, followed by the shirt. Boots found a home on the floor. I jerked free the belt and turned for my things.

Fuck. I grimaced toward the door.

I'd forgotten a change of nightclothes when I'd come over here after dinner. They'd be in my trunk, stored in the room across the hall where my double now rested. I could fetch them, but knowing Ilya, she'd slide the dresser in front of the door and lock me out the moment I stepped into the hall.

I could leave her. Give her peace. Part of me wanted her to feel safe, comforted. Another part couldn't pass up this opportunity. I needed to get back in her good graces, and only time with her would grant that. Not to mention seeing Ilya in her nightdress again. *Gods.* The slide of material teased my ears, tempting me with the fulfillment of that wish.

Soft furs caressed my skin as I settled atop the bed in only my pants. At home, I'd have removed those too, but not here. Not yet.

A creamy nightdress hugged Ilya's curves as she stepped from behind the dressing screen, her hair loosely braided down her back. *By The Four.* The pale garment fit her body more divinely than those long, sleeveless dresses she preferred. She crossed her arms and scowled, but I hardly minded when her stance pulled the material tight against her chest.

"We discussed this." She snapped and pointed to the floor as if beckoning a dog.

I smirked and patted the bed. "I won't even touch you."

It would be the hardest thing I'd ever done, but I would—for her.

CHAPTER 32
LUCIEN

Ilya seethed anger, burning brighter than the dim lanterns she snuffed out one by one. Eventually, she settled on the edge of the bed, as far from me as possible. "To have a dagger," she mumbled.

I bit my cheek to hold in a laugh. To see her wield a dagger, or any weapon for that matter, would be a delight. My cock twitched at the thought.

For long moments we lay in silent darkness. I stirred in my thoughts despite my attempts to avoid thinking about the events of the day and the mysteries that plagued me. Ilya tossed and turned, small grumbles filling the silence.

Despite the softness of the sheets and the comfortable mattress underneath me, I couldn't find peace. If I thought of the woman lying on the bed with me, my desire for her rushed to the forefront, tempting me to act on it. Doing so wouldn't earn me any favors. For long minutes I focused on my breathing to tame down the ache I couldn't ease. But as I did so, other thoughts slipped in one by one, the events of the evening and Ilya's thoughts on my origin replaying themselves over and over like a strong current I couldn't escape.

No matter how hard I tried to block out those thoughts and rest, one possibility kept slicing through my thoughts like a cold night wind. "You think they could be my parents?"

I'd been so lost in my head I thought she might have finally drifted into sleep, but then Ilya turned toward me, her face a delicate form of shadow. "I do," she whispered. "I can see the resemblance, even if you refuse to."

I shuffled onto my side under the coverings. My body stiffened as I took in the shape of her face on the pillow next to mine. "I do see it." Admitting it pained me more than exhausting my magic on the battlefield. "But I remember vague flashes of my parents. Similar, but different too. Not regal, nor confident. They were fearful, starving. They had a hint of wildness in their eyes like spooked horses. It's only one memory, but it's all I have of them."

A deep ache settled in my chest, as painful as the time I cracked several ribs falling from a horse. I'd never told anyone about them—at least, not in a very long time.

"You miss them." Her words jumped the space between us, seeping into the cracks in my defenses.

"Yes. It was so long ago, but I can never forget it." It was all I had of them. However painful, however faded at the edges, I clutched that memory near. Truly, the memory was more a feeling now than anything, the details of their faces worn away by time, but it was painful and precious nonetheless.

A soft sigh slipped across the pillow. "We can't change the past, not a one of us, but if these people might be yours too, it could be a second chance."

"At what? They loathe me, Ilya." I scooted closer. Cool blankets chilled my skin as I moved into new territory. "Even if by some chance I am related to them, I'm dead to them now. What do you think of me as? A killer? A monster?"

Heavy breaths filled the silence. *Say something. Anything.*

"Yes."

The word punched the wind from my chest.

Then, so quiet I almost missed it, "But you're more than that too."

Those whispered words healed my aches better than any balm, any magic.

"Ilya." I reached out, cupping her face, and for once, she didn't pull away. "I'm sorry about what happened with your friends. That it was me who delivered their punishment. I've only been one thing for as long as I can remember, but you make me want to be something else, something more."

More than a warrior. More than a killer. Could I be more than Captain Lucien, First of Emperor Ryszard? If he hadn't found me and I hadn't died from starvation, or cold or illness, I'd have been no one. But maybe that no one was someone she could love, even where my someone wasn't.

"Me? I'm just a captive heiress. Worthless." Her voice cracked on the word. "All I ever was is lost."

The pain in her voice wrenched something in my chest. For all the strength and passion she shone with, there was something fragile under the surface. And she shared it with me. The vulnerability, the trust in that wasn't lost on me.

"That's not true," I said. If my words could heal a few of her wounds, I wanted that. "I don't care what you once were. It's not who you are."

Sheets ruffled, but she didn't pull away. Her faint shadow pulled in on itself as if she was hugging her knees to her chest under the sheets. "Who I am? How can you know that if I don't?"

A shiver ran down my arm as her fingertips traced along the back of my hand, barely a tickle across my skin.

"Because I see you every day. I see the fire in your eyes, the way you care for your friends, your sharp wit, your courage. All of those are you. Perhaps..." I swallowed, suddenly nervous as a boy rather than a hardened man. "We could find ourselves together. Not our past, not our titles, but who we are without all that."

Treason. Blasphemous. My fellow captains would laugh at me. Emperor Ryszard would certainly disapprove and remind me of the important role he'd entrusted me with. At the moment, none of that mattered. A glimmer of something greater shone in the darkness, a sense of self I'd never quite considered. A man apart from the role I'd been trained to fill.

"How am I supposed to hate you when you say things like that?"

Laughter rumbled in my chest. "Perhaps one day you won't."

Ilya sighed as her hand dropped away to rest in the narrow space between us.

"You tried to seduce me not long ago. Those dresses...the time you climbed into my lap..." Memories I could never forget. The captain couldn't want those things, couldn't linger over them, but the man within was another matter.

"I was drunk," she whispered. A hint of embarrassment colored her words.

I'd never called out her antics before. I'd hoped to discover her aim before then, though she likely wanted to ingratiate herself with her would-be captor.

"Only once. You're not interested anymore?" Now that the thought was in the air, I couldn't let it go. If anyone listened, hopefully they'd hear only mumbled sounds rather than words.

Ilya sucked in a deep breath and rolled over, away from me. "We need rest," she said to the night.

Her rejection stirred my curiosity further. Why not deny it?

Fuck it. I slid across the sheets and wrapped an arm around her waist.

"Luc—" She cut off her exclamation. "What are you doing?" she hissed. "Let me go."

Bare feet brushed my legs as she moved against me. The thin material of her nightdress tickled my chest, caressed the planes of my stomach, and fed the burning ache below. *Fuck, what was I thinking?* The way she moved, the press of her against me was enough to drive me wild.

"Keep moving on me like that and I never will."

Ilya went utterly still.

I savored the silken feel of her nightdress pressed against my chest and the rapid thump of her heartbeat as I held her close. Her breath hitched and her stomach tightened under my palm as my lips grazed the shell of her ear. "What do you want?"

She shivered. "You."

Oh, fuck me.

My head swam as I rubbed a slow, broad pattern on her stomach, keeping away from the sensitive flesh above and below my fingertips.

My muscles drew taut in anticipation as she turned in my arms. Her soft breaths heated my face where we nearly touched. My hand flexed on her back as I fought the urge to fit the soft curves of her body against me.

Ilya cupped my face, sending my heart racing so loud, she likely heard the rapid thump in the quiet night.

"One kiss."

Her hoarse whisper set my blood on fire. I barely had time to process her words before her soft lips touched mine, tentative and testing.

The gentleness of her kiss compared to her biting words undid me, tearing through barriers. In that moment, it no longer mattered that she was my captive, my charge, or that she'd likely stab me in the back given the opportunity. Who I was, my past, all of it fled. I'd never had a woman affect me that way. It was as if she wielded a magic of her own—a healing balm.

Sweet fire flooded my veins. A gasp slipped between kisses as I pushed Ilya onto her back and slid my bulk over her, careful to keep my weight upon my arms braced on either side of her head. Her lips tasted better than any rich dessert, an exotic flavor I could savor all day and never get enough of. By The Four, I missed this—longed for it since the brief taste of days before.

Stiff nipples pressed against my chest through the thin material of her nightdress, sending another bolt of fire straight to my loins. The thin fabric was too much of a barrier. I wanted it gone.

I settled more of my weight onto Ilya, eliciting a little moan from her soft mouth against mine. My hand fisted in the material of her nightdress near her thighs. A few tugs and it'd be up and out of the way.

"Stop," she gasped, jerking her mouth away.

A command had never been harder to obey. "Did I hurt you?"

Her chest rose and fell against mine. "No, but we can't. I can't."

Poison would have been easier to swallow. *A kiss, she only asked for a kiss. Think of anything else—snow, sharpening a sword, the cabin.*

No thought chilled my veins quite so well as that one. With a groan, I released her and rolled to the side, staring her down in the darkness. My cock still strained against my pants, aching.

"Would you have denied me after the Goddess's festival too?" The thought spilled out into the night unchecked. Was it all just a tease to see how far she could undo me?

"No. I wanted...I..."

Never had Ilya seemed so uncertain, almost innocent. I fisted my hand in the sheets to stop from reaching out and touching her.

Her next words were so quiet I barely heard them. "It's my blooding cycle."

"Oh."

Oh.

I adjusted myself, trying to ease the ache between my legs without success. "If it wasn't?"

A sliver of moonlight shone through the window, sparkling across her blinking eyes. "I might still make you suffer."

I grinned through my agony as she turned away. A witty politician—and a brutal fighter.

CHAPTER 33
ILYA

A haze of exhaustion clouded my thoughts, accompanied by a small headache that grew in intensity as the morning drawled on.

Curse you, Lucien.

He'd thwarted all my plans. Then, his antics kept me awake long after his breathing evened out in sleep. Not only could I not ease the desire he ignited, but his warm presence in the bed had proved impossible to ignore no matter how I tried. All I could think of as I tried to sleep was his lips on mine, the fine smattering of hair on his bare chest, the hardness between his legs when he'd slid atop me.

My nails dug into my palm. I couldn't get him out of my head. I'd wanted him, right then and there, despite what he'd done and despite my blooding cycle.

Wanting him that way made everything more difficult, especially when I needed to focus. Soon, we'd leave. Soon, I'd lose the chance to learn more about the rebels or convince Lucien of what I believed to be his true identity.

And soon, I'd have way too much time to consider last night.

"Sleep well?"

I nearly jumped out of my skin at the sudden gruff voice behind me.

Stefan stalked to my side, a dark fur thrown about his shoulders despite the unseasonal warmth in the air. Horses were led by twos into the yard, freshly brushed and ready to be hitched to the carriage and supply wagon. Others bore saddles, ready to be ridden back to Zhine.

"It was a very comfortable room," I replied, conscious of Ryszard's guards milling about. "I am grateful for your hospitality. I only wish we could enjoy it longer."

Lucien stood in the yard talking with other guards, though his eyes often wandered to where I stood near the main entrance, stirring up far too many memories. The false captain ordered men and grooms around in a show of authority, the governor at his side, as trunks and supplies were loaded for the journey.

"I'd hoped to have the chance to enjoy your company over breakfast," I continued. Our host and his wife had both been absent. Unfortunate, when they were the most likely ones to know something of the rebels.

"Basilla, well, she wasn't feeling well this morning. She might have had too much wine. She started thinking all sorts of mad thoughts last night." He shook his head. "Kept me up far too late, but I'm glad I got to see you off."

Gooseflesh raced up my arms.

"Do you mind if I ask what thoughts she had?" A certain face caught my attention out of the corner of my eye—one looking our way despite the chaotic scene.

"Impossible thoughts, and too long a story for now."

I barely held in a plea for more when two of Stefan's household brushed by carrying sacks of supplies.

"Be careful with those!" he called at their backs. "Always in a hurry." Stefan looked over his shoulder before turning back to me. "The birds are ready to migrate. They only await a sign."

My brow wrinkled. *Birds? Why mention—*

My heart skipped a beat. Stefan's gaze bore into mine as the meaning hit home. Reyna's birds. An army?

"I'm...I'm glad to hear that." Truly, I didn't know what to say, but his curt nod told me I'd done something right.

"Several flocks, in fact. Some headed west recently."

West. Toward Zhine.

"They might roost in the foothills of the Everspelt range if the weather is right."

My heart picked up its pace, pounding away within my chest. I needed to talk to Reyna. She'd know how to get information to the rebels. The certainty of it settled on me like a second skin. I'd become a pawn in someone else's game without knowing it, yet it was one I longed to have a bigger role in. To take down Ryszard, to free Sorrena.

"Your enthusiasm will show to the captain if you're not careful," he mumbled.

Shit. I twisted around, scanning the yard, but the gleaming armor I searched for had vanished.

"The real one," Stefan continued in a hushed voice. "With that cluster near the carriage."

Lucien looked away, pretending to attend the conversation in front of him. "He's just a guard," I said.

Stefan let out a roaring laugh. "I'm not so easily fooled," he said, voice low so only I could hear. "The way he holds himself, his aura of authority over the others...that boy in armor could never pass for a captain. He lacks the commanding presence. I've met Captain Lucien before—a change of clothes can't fool me."

What about a change of face? Lucien gave up any pretense of pretending to be distracted and watched us. Any minute now, he'd invade my discussion with Stefan. I had no doubt of that.

"The way he looks at you..."

My head snapped to Stefan. "What do you mean?"

His beard quirked with his lips. "Like a lover."

Heat rushed to my cheeks. "I'm not..."

He laughed again, a deep rumble that turned into a fit of coughs. Stefan wiped at his mouth, regaining his composure. "I didn't think you'd turn so easily. But could he?" He followed Lucien with his knowing gaze as he headed in our direction.

I swallowed my apprehension.

"Lord Stefan," Lucien bowed before us at the base of the stairs. "Thank you for watching after Lady Ilya, but I should show her to her carriage now."

Stefan took my hand and kissed the back of it, his beard tickling my skin. "It's been a pleasure. Emperor Ryszard can send messages through you any time."

"Likewise," I answered. "And do say farewell to your wife on my behalf." I turned my back to Lucien. "I think she's right."

Stefan's eyes widened as I curtsied before him.

I raised my head and descended the stairs to Lucien, feeling as much like the heir of Sorrena as I had in days. I'd gathered precious knowledge and delivered some of my own.

"What was that about?" Lucien whispered as he walked me to the carriage. He saw too much, but hopefully not enough.

I grinned. "Lady Basilla passed along a comment about how handsome and strong Emperor Ryszard's guards looked this trip." I eyed him up and down. "I merely stated my agreement."

Lucien nearly tripped over himself as I stifled the laughter aching to burst from my lungs.

If nothing else, I'd given him something to stew over on the journey back to Zhine.

CHAPTER 34
LUCIEN

Ilya sprang from the carriage like a buck from the wood as soon as it rocked to a stop inside Zhine's castle. Two guards hustled down from their horses, racing after her toward the large doors exiting the bailey into the castle proper.

Roasted meat from the kitchens teased my senses as I dismounted, hinting at the dinner ready to be served in the main dining area at any moment.

My muscles ached from days on the road in my armor. Though it had been carefully crafted to move like a second skin despite its bulk, the steady movement on horseback never failed to chafe.

"Welcome back." Zurina strode across the bailey yard, the metal of her armor glistening like a flame as the last trails of sunlight spilled across it.

"Zurina. Back already."

"We returned yesterday. More importantly, Emperor Ryszard would like your report. Immediately."

A groan escaped from my lips. I wanted nothing more than to follow the woman who I'd shared lingering glances with the entire ride back, not to mention our whispered words in the dark and stray stolen touches. I'd even take the sharp barbs she loved to fling my way if one of her delightful, wicked grins followed.

I hadn't tried to kiss her. Not after her rejection, but something had softened between us.

"Will you be joining me?"

Zurina swooped her arm in a grand gesture. "Right this way."

"Your journey was a success?" I asked as we traversed the halls.

"I'd say so. Lady Reyna delivered the message we agreed upon, and we encountered no issues. A good thing, since there's been more unrest while we've been gone."

I snapped my head in her direction. "Tell me."

"Some of our watchmen reported suspicious activity in a few city-states, potentially troop movements or something else out of the ordinary. Our emperor has spread his forces in three directions, bent on investigating. A counterpart of ours joined with each group to deal with any threats."

More of this. Something was going on between the city-states. We'd already stretched our territory too wide to control with our meager forces. Our emperor couldn't think to push it further.

"There's more."

"More?" I sighed.

"Scouts have been sent into Marsali. One of our spies reported soldiers gathering, or so Orson said."

Fuck all. "And our emperor thought that was enough to send soldiers across the border to scout them?"

She nodded. "It happened before I got back."

Of course it did. Orson would have waited until we were away to relay that news, if it was true at all. He looked to undermine me at every turn, coveting my title like a hoard of jewels. We couldn't attack

Marsali on a whim, not with our soldiers still recovering from the last battle.

I fisted my hands at my sides as Ilya's words echoed through my mind. What would be enough? When *would* he stop?

"You seem...distracted." Zurina drew us to a halt.

I waved a hand in dismissal. "It's a lot to take in. I assume you'll give me the details later?"

"There's a written report waiting for your attention, but that's not it. You don't seem like yourself." She cocked her head as if she could see through my armor into my soul below. She couldn't, but she knew me well. Too well, sometimes.

The corridors were empty, not a guard in sight. Most of them were in the dining hall at this hour or stationed at the doors that kept this wing off-limits to our guests.

Since we had a brief moment of privacy, I shared the thoughts that kept weighing on me. "Something about Trale felt familiar, and not from when we took the city-state. Something older, more...familial."

Whispers of childhood had seeped to the surface—old memories that shone in a new light. It was as if Ilya's suggestion rolled back a fog I hadn't known lived in my mind.

It was ridiculous. Impossible. Treasonous. I waited for a laugh, a slap on the shoulder. It didn't come. She didn't rebuke me either. Instead, Zurina pinned me with a level look before saying, "Go on."

Something cinched tight in my chest, a warning perhaps, but I ignored it. "I knew the room I stayed in, but I've never been there before. I even knew right where the whisper hole was in the wall."

Her head tilted to the side. "Intuition?"

"Yes and no. Something more, just out of my reach. And then on the ride back..." I shook my head. She was being kind and hearing me out as I would have her. That was all. "You don't want to hear this."

Zurina grasped my shoulder. "I do. Continue, please."

Please. I swallowed the knot in my throat. "I told you about the day Emperor Ryszard found me, starving in that cabin in the woods?"

She nodded.

"It's my earliest memory, and I still remember it, but it's different. Warped. I always felt sadness over the people who died in the cabin. My parents, I assumed. But now the memory feels fearful, and not just from the lack of food or the cold." For so long I'd tried to shut the memory down anytime it would creep up. I shoved it deep within a box in my mind where it couldn't bother me. After all, why should a captain of the emperor be brought low by the ghost of a memory? But after my time in Trale, I couldn't keep it contained anymore. The memory taunted me, over and over, begging me to look at it, to remember. And when I did, when I finally sat against a tree one night and let those haunting moments play over and over, they didn't look quite the same as I'd always thought.

"You wonder what's true." It wasn't a question.

"It's foolish. I never questioned it until recently, but something has changed." *Or Ilya has really gotten under my skin.* The thought that Basilla and Stefan could be my parents tried to drown me again and I shoved it away. Far away with the other jumbled mess of things I couldn't deal with right now.

"Anyhow, we better not keep him waiting." I slid back into my stride down the hall.

Zurina caught up in a hurry. "Indeed. But Lucien..." Her eyes bore into mine from within her mask as she kept pace at my side. "Just because something seems odd or impossible, don't ignore it. We can explore this together, but don't run from your thoughts."

As if I could.

"You'd be wise to listen to Zurina."

I sucked in a breath at the unexpected interruption, my stride coming to an abrupt halt. I'd been so lost in thought I hadn't heard Warren's approach. Thank The Four it was him and not one of the others.

"How much did you hear?"

Warren looked away, trailing the metal of his gloves along the stone wall until a light screech sounded. "Not much," he admitted, finally meeting my gaze. "I was an orphan, but you...I wonder. Memory is a tricky thing, especially ones from so long ago." His whispered voice floated down the corridor, too wise for his cycles, as if a sagely old man spoke instead of my young friend.

"Do you remember anything from before then?" he asked. The look in Warren's blue eyes tingled across my skin and tumbled a stone in my gut.

"Nothing." Yet. But something—a memory almost within reach—taunted me, its frayed edges whipping like a tattered flag in a gale.

Warren nodded as if he expected that answer. Zurina cocked her head, fingers tapping on her arm as if she might ask another question, but she remained silent.

Heavy footsteps approached, invading the silence of the hall.

"We'll talk later," Warren promised.

I ignored the shiver that slid under my skin as Brishon rounded the corner. "Emperor Ryszard is waiting," he said.

Zurina flicked her wrist, urging me on. The strange feeling of the moment before evaporated as if it had never been.

"We're on our way."

CHAPTER 35
ILYA

I ached to check on Elin and my friends. I'd sent up a prayer to each of the four Gods and Goddesses on my return trip, asking for their safety and health while I was gone. And I needed to talk to Reyna. While my trip had been more productive than I'd ever hoped, it would be all for naught if I couldn't leverage the information I'd gathered.

Even so, it was hard to focus on my goals after so many days on the road with Lucien. Warmth raced to my cheeks as I recounted our stolen moments together. It wasn't just my desire for him. I couldn't delude myself about that anymore. He had a sharp mind and way with words that drew me in as few others ever had. Men respected him and he them. He'd shown me concern and care though I was still an enemy. He wouldn't do that if he was truly as vile as I'd once thought. No, there was a surprising amount of genuine kindness lingering within the emperor's master of war.

"Lady Ilya," one of the guards called after me as I opened the heavy wooden doors that exited the bailey into the castle proper.

The bubble of my happiness burst. My teeth ground together as I waited for them to catch up. Of course, I'd still be escorted everywhere. Wasn't I always?

"It should be near dinner time. We can take you straight to the dining hall."

I sighed. "Lead the way."

My heart leaped as I caught sight of Elin and Gabriel outside our destination. "It's good to see you. How are you both?"

I waited for a smile. A hug. Neither happened.

"You're back," Gabriel said. The half-smile he gave me didn't reach his eyes, and he said nothing else before continuing into the room.

Elin winced. "We are glad you're safe." Her kind words did nothing to dull the stab of my friend's curt welcome.

A thread of panic twisted through my heart. "Did something happen?"

Elin glanced between the two of us, a frown pulling at her pink lips. "He...well..." She looked around hesitantly. "He worries you've turned your back on them, and on Sorrena, now that you're serving the emperor and delivering his messages."

My world spun. He thought I'd turned traitor.

"It's not what you think," I whispered.

"I believe you," she said. "Things here are different, so much more than I ever expected." She looked away, her hands twisting in the folds of her dress. "I even...well..." She blushed as her words trailed off, unable to meet my eyes, and followed Gabriel to our usual table.

"Look who's returned," Fernand said as I approached. For all the bitterness in his voice, I could have been Ryszard himself.

I jerked out my chair, letting it clatter across the stone before I took my seat. My elbows dug into the table with enough force to leave a bruise. "Someone tell me what's going on?"

Fernand simply raised his brows as if it should be obvious. Across the table, Gabriel coughed and adjusted his posture before leaning forward.

"Shouldn't we ask you that? We heard you're delivering messages for the emperor now. Was that wrong?"

The doubt in his voice had me sitting a little straighter. "I didn't have a choice. Can anyone truly refuse him?"

He sighed. "Every moment is a choice. Before, I might not have questioned it, but after the festival..." His attention dipped to my neckline, to the empty space where the Mark of Sorrena no longer rested. "You've changed."

Hunger vanished. The savory scents that tempted my stomach to rumble only moments ago turned foul. I had information, details of rebels on the move toward Zhine, yet my allies questioned my allegiance.

"It's not like that. You don't understand." I shook my head. Maybe I had changed, but for the wiser.

"Where's Reyna?" I asked. Perhaps they weren't ready to hear what I'd learned, but she would be.

Fernand leaned back in his chair. "The one who came back all smiles after delivering punishment to my people?" His chin jutted forward. "Seems like the type you'd like these days."

The biting words smacked me in the face, drawing forth a flush from the anger building in my veins. It took everything I had to ignore his jab. I scanned the room in simmering silence, searching for Reyna, who was nowhere to be found. When the nearby guards returned attention to their meals, I sat and leaned in on the table.

"She's on our side," I whispered before glancing each way. "She's looking for what we are. She wants to help."

"Don't you remember who told us about the farmer being on our side?" Gabriel said.

Reyna. She'd said he was a friend, someone we could trust. And yet, Gabriel and Fernand had been caught the moment they tried to pass off information. My skin turned clammy. Wordless noise buzzed in my ears. By The Four, could she have played me? Did she plan to report me to the emperor the moment I told her of my findings?

I grabbed my cup from the table and downed the wine within. My hand shook as I refilled it from a nearby pitcher.

A peal of laughter wove its way into my misery. Reyna entered the dining hall, her arm looped through a guard's as she leaned into him. Her gaze locked with mine, and she gave an enthusiastic wave.

Friend or foe? I turned away, back to the men in front of me.

"Oh look, it's your new friend. Aren't you going to join her?" Fernand twisted his lips into a cruel smile as he raised his brows at me across the table. When I didn't move, he rose and said, "Maybe I'll go find a new seat then."

"Fernand..." He was just hurt. Surely that was all...

He clapped a hand on Gabriel's shoulder. "Care to join me?"

Gabriel gave me a lingering look before shaking his head and starting to rise.

My stomach plummeted as surely as if the chair had been pulled out from under me.

"Wait," I said.

He paused.

"I..." I needed to tell him. Something, anything. But not enough for the guards to understand. "Your brother, he—"

"Don't," he said with a sharp shake of his head.

"But he—"

His throat bobbed before he planted his palms on the table and leaned toward me. "You want to get him in trouble too?"

A hollow opened in my chest. "Never." Of course not. Surely, he couldn't think that.

Gabriel looked away. "I just...don't know what to trust anymore." Without another word, he turned and followed Fernand.

My breaths drew short and quick as I stared at their empty chairs. The rest of the room was a blur, the raucous noise a meaningless hum.

Elin laid a hand on my arm and jolted me back to the moment. "They'll come around," she whispered. "It's just, after all that's happened...." She shook her head and closed her eyes before opening them again and folding in on herself. "They're hurt and hurting, but I believe you."

At least someone did, but I couldn't involve her. She reminded me too much of Justina. Young. Innocent. If I got her tangled up in this mess anymore, I wouldn't forgive myself.

Sorrow mixed with the wine in my stomach. Fernand and Gabriel didn't trust me, and I might not be able to trust Reyna, not if she'd really set the men up to get caught at the festival. The metal cup bit into my skin, fighting back as I took out my frustrations on it.

Until now, I'd always been in control, leading my path, the heir of Sorrena in spirit if no longer in title. Even if things hadn't gone according to plan, at least I had one. But what could I hope to accomplish on my own? Even with the knowledge I'd gained and whatever else I might garner, how could it be of use if I had no one to share it with, no way to get it to the rebels?

I drowned my sorrows until I emptied the cup in front of me. All the hope and excitement I'd stored up during the journey floated away with the last of the bitter red wine down my throat.

The empty cup stared back at me, a mockery of my misery. If I couldn't reclaim my title, free my homeland, then what was I?

Nothing at all.

CHAPTER 36
ILYA

The open doorway beckoned me, tempting me to cross its threshold and ascend the stairs to Lucien's room above.

My shoulders slumped, no longer able to support the weight of the worries that pressed down upon me. My so-called friends wouldn't listen. They thought me a traitor, or worse. I'd lost whatever value I had in their eyes. A useless heir not worthy of the title, if I could still even claim it. I could barely stomach thinking of Reyna either. I enjoyed her company, our painting sessions, her friendly banter. Did she really plan to sell me out?

Wine and weariness urged me to sleep, to curl into a ball upon the narrow bed in my small chamber and surrender my burdens to tomorrow.

But something else, something that almost frightened me, urged me up Lucien's stairs. Alone in my room with my thoughts or upstairs with someone who might make them fade to the back of my mind?

Lucien would be up there. I had no doubt of it. He'd never leave his door open otherwise, and the fact that it remained wide open meant only one thing.

An invitation.

My foot landed on the bottom step, a whisper of sound slipping off the stones. The smooth railing chilled my fingers as I gripped it, hanging on as I sealed my decision. His words from Trale haunted me day and night. Could he really want me? Not the heiress, not the captive, but just the worthless woman who remained?

The room looked much as I remembered, though possibly more books littered the shelves and tables. Lucien hunched over his desk, oblivious to my presence as he studied various pages in flickering candlelight. Pale streaks of moonlight crept across the floor from the open balcony whose curtains had been pulled back to let in the crisp night air. A soft gust raised chill bumps along my arms.

No armor graced his form. He was just himself. A man. Vulnerable.

The emperor's first captain. Murderer. Torturer.

He should be the last person I'd ever go to for anything other than vengeance or my agenda, a knife in my hand to plunge it into his back. Yet at that moment, all I wanted was the man. The companionship. Someone who saw me, wanted me—Ilya. Not my title, my failures, or how they could use me.

I coughed lightly as my toes curled within the boots I'd worn on our journey.

Lucien jerked like a startled animal, head snapping to the side, before he relaxed against the back of his carved, wooden chair. "You came."

His words filled the room, making it suddenly so much smaller than it had been moments ago.

"I did."

Silence stretched, though my feet refused to move, and my thoughts failed to become words.

"Would you like to sit with me? Have a drink?" He hoisted a crystal glass from the table, the amber liquid within shimmering in the dim light.

As if we were friends or amiable companions. I nearly laughed.

Instead, I nodded, not trusting my words. He slid a book atop his papers and rose with fluid grace while gesturing toward a small seating area near a barely smoldering fireplace.

Amber liquid tumbled from a bottle into a fresh glass, one Lucien passed my way before taking the chair opposite the high-backed one I'd settled on.

Nerves tossed the wine already in my stomach like waves on the sea. I'd never been this apprehensive with him before. Not since the first night, when I thought his intentions far more sinister and cruel than they were.

I sipped at the liquid, and fire slid down my throat. Coughs racked me as I struggled to retain a hold upon the glass. A small amount of the vile substance sloshed over the rim onto my hand.

"Ilya, are you—"

"It's terrible," I wheezed.

Lucien's shoulders shook as he fought the grin twitching his mouth. "It's whiskey. They brew it in the small village to the west of here."

"Disgusting. Horrid." Nothing like the sweet wines they aged in Sorrena or the poor excuse for wine they served here. I held the glass at arm's length, scowling as the last of the burning receded.

"Can't let it go to waste." Lucien took the glass. "You know, the first time I tried it, I had a similar response. Though I was only fourteen cycles or so. Our tutor used to talk about retreating into his room with his fiery sweetheart. We thought he'd trapped some poor woman in there, until Brishon snuck in a saw him talking to his whiskey glass. The next day, Zurina convinced him to steal a bottle of it. The three of us kept tasting it in different ways—gargling, sipping it upside down, talking to it like our tutor did—convinced that we must be doing it wrong because it burned so badly." He laughed, the corners of his mouth stretching wide in a wry grin. "Our punishment wasn't half so bad as the hangover."

I forced a smile for his benefit. They really were a family, one that loved and cared for each other. One I aimed to destroy.

"You're not yourself."

"What do you mean?" I blinked, recovering from my spiraling thoughts.

"The fire that lives in your eyes, it's dim."

Not just mine. When I'd walked in, his shoulders had been hunched over his desk like the whole world threatened to crush him. I understood that. Too well. But what could I say? *My friends think I'm a traitor. Reyna may be trying to play me.* Neither of those would work. Lucien would end up asking too many questions that I couldn't answer, not if I still hoped to aid the rebels.

The night pulled my attention. Wooded hills beyond the balcony were dark shadows upon the blanket of night and stars. "I've lost everything I once was. My whole life, I prepared to lead Sorrena and guide my people. But now, I have nothing. I am nothing."

I gasped as Lucien's hand wrapped around mine. When had he risen? Instinctively, I tried to pull away, but he held on, firm but soft.

"You're not nothing. Not to me."

"But I—"

He cut me off with a jerk of his head as he knelt before me, his leg brushing mine through the skirt of my dress.

"You're strong. A fighter. Passionate about your people. Smart. Enchanting. That's all you. Not your title, not how others see you. You'll be those things no matter what name or title you hold, where you go, or what happens, because that's who you are. No title can define that. It didn't make you who you are, and losing it doesn't take away from you either."

His words struck me like a wave crashing against the cliff. Who I am... Not the heiress of Sorrena. Me. The woman who wanted to travel. One who recently learned to paint. Who loves a good glass of Sorrena's best red wine, an interesting tale, and friendly company.

"And you have something else too. You don't have to doubt where you came from, your family, or any of that." A sad smile touched his face, lulling me like no words ever could.

I gripped his hand in mine, still trying to process the impossible—

me, apart from any label. Did he really see all those things in me? For someone to see beyond my title...I'd never known to want it, but now that he mentioned it, I craved that more than anything. My title was just that. Lost, perhaps, but just something people called me. Without it, I still had the most important things. Or many of them. But what he said about my family was painfully true. I didn't have to wonder about where I came from, yet I'd lost them—for the moment—all the same. But maybe, just maybe, in this moment where I was separated from my family, I could help this man find his. "You...you've thought about what I said in Trale?" I asked, turning the conversation away from myself.

"I have."

"And?"

He rose without a word and walked to the balcony. My heart lurched. He'd lifted me up while he crumbled, and I'd only prodded him further. I followed him into the cool night, letting the crisp air raise chill bumps along my skin that did nothing to calm the rapid beat of my heart within my chest.

Lucien stared out into the night, his arms crossed as he reclined against the stone pillar separating the two arches leading onto the balcony. "I've spent my life weaving illusions for others, but now I'm the one who can't figure out what's real."

Oh, Lucien...

"I am." I traced a line down his forearm, savoring the solid muscle just below the skin and the tickle of hair across mine. "I'm real."

"Are you?"

I gasped as he cupped my cheek, drawing me closer into the shelter of his warmth with barely a touch.

"I stole your city, your title. The emperor's command but my actions. I'm a murderer. Your enemy. A tool of war."

Each word sliced at my heart, bleeding me out. Yes. He was all those things, but they were just titles. Labels. Like my own. His eyes widened, his whole form going still as I lay my palm upon his chest. Only the steady thump of his own heart gave him away.

"Yes. You are."

He made to pull back, but I dug my fingers into the fabric of his shirt and stepped closer.

"But if I'm more than my title, then so are you."

CHAPTER 37
LUCIEN

I didn't hear her right. Offering me the words I wanted from her lips...it couldn't be possible.

"Don't toy with me." Not tonight. Not like this. Not with her hands all over me. I held utterly still save for my thumb, which rubbed the soft skin of her cheek where I still held her face in my palm.

Ilya released my shirt, spreading out her fingers until her palm rested against my chest once more. "You suggested we find ourselves together. Was it a joke?"

"No." Never.

It took everything I had not to pull her into my arms as her hand trailed down my shirt. Her lips as she licked them...I'd fight an army just to watch that.

"Then don't push me away." As if to echo her words, she leaned closer, the soft globes of her breasts grazing my chest.

I drew my face closer to hers until her breath tickled my skin and our faces nearly touched. "You want me?"

I had to be sure. There could be no mistakes tonight. Not with her.

"Yes."

That word broke the seal on my control. It still rang in my ears when I pulled her into my arms and claimed her mouth with mine.

Soft. Warm. Sweet.

Something caught between a sigh and a moan slipped between us as her body molded to mine. Her arms wrapped around my neck, her long fingers sliding into my hairline in a way that sent a bolt of desire straight to my cock.

Fuck. None of my imaginings compared.

It didn't matter who she was. A fallen heiress. A captive. My enemy. She saw me, and nothing could stop me from wanting her now.

I spun her around until her back pressed against the narrow wall. Little whimpers teased me as I trailed kisses along her jaw, her earlobe, down into the crook of her neck. Savoring. Tasting. If the feel of her skin against my lips wasn't enough, the scent of olive flower transported me far away. Away from the confusing memories I couldn't understand, from the mystery of my parentage, from Emperor Ryszard's lust for conquest and the movement of rebels seeking to disrupt it.

This night was mine. Mine and Ilya's. If those fucking bells rang this time, I'd ignore them. Consequences be damned.

Daring fingers threaded through my hair and dug into my shoulder. Each touch only fueled my raging desire. My hand slid up her chest, the soft material of her dress silken against my calluses. I swallowed a moan as I claimed her mouth again, my thumb teasing the bottom swell of one full breast. Risking her rejection, I slid higher, taking the sweet globe in my palm. A stiff nipple teased me through the folds of fabric, urging me to continue my pursuit.

And Gods, her taste. Sweet. Better than whiskey, than wine, than cake at a feast. My tongue tangled with hers, teasing, conquering, unwilling to relinquish a moment.

Ilya moaned against me as I toyed with her stiff peaks, her back arching off the wall. When her hips pressed into me, rubbing against my ready cock, I didn't stop myself from bucking into her in return. Each movement of her body against mine nearly had me spilling in my pants.

I grabbed the skirt of her dress, urging the fabric higher despite the friction between us, baring her legs, the start of her thighs...

"Lucien." Her voice was thick and slow as I broke our kiss. Warm breaths tickled my face as I held her hooded gaze.

"May I?" I tugged the dress in emphasis.

She'd stopped me in Trale. She'd had her reasons, but would she again now?

She bit her perfect, pink lip and nodded. "Please."

I nearly groaned as she spread her legs.

Without hesitation, I pushed the bunched material out of the way. My hand slid up her bare thigh until I reached the edge of soft underthings. My muscles tensed; my eyes locked with hers as my thumb slid under the hem.

Delicate skin, soft hairs, and—

"Fuck, Ilya. You're wet." Her body's proof of desire. For me. I nearly crumbled in disbelief.

Her cheeks flushed, matching the pink of her well-kissed lips. "I want you," she replied in a husky whisper. "I don't care where you're from or what you're called. Do you believe me now?"

Her truth. Our truth.

"And I want you. I did even when you would have slit my throat in the night."

It had been pure lust then. And something else I couldn't understand. But the more I watched and learned the woman beyond the title, I couldn't help but fall under her spell, a magic all her own.

She pulled her bottom lip between her teeth before letting it go. "Then what are you waiting for?"

The smolder in her eyes undid me. "Nothing."

Ilya gasped as I adjusted my stance and lifted her off the ground, one arm under her back and the other under her knees. Her arms wove around my neck, muddling my thoughts as I carried her back into my room. I'd never had a woman in this bed. My dalliances had been purely physical. Out of my room, out of my heart.

Not so with Ilya.

Laying her gently atop the bed felt right. Especially as I stepped back to admire her there, face still flushed, dark hair trailing down over her dress of pale violet.

Ilya wasted no time reclining on the soft furs. One boot slid off, followed by the next, thumping onto the stone floor. I stood in rapture as she moved, watching each movement of her body as she worked. She'd lost weight since she'd been here, carving down her lush curves. It didn't weaken my desire, but one day I wanted her healthy, happy.

I swallowed the lump in my throat. I was a reason for her unhappiness. I'd caused it. Could I ever truly make her happy?

"What's wrong?" Ilya frowned, sliding her exposed legs under her on the bed. My bed.

I faked a grin. "Nothing at all." So much, but I'd worry about all that later. My origin, the emperor's plans, Ilya's goals. It could wait.

Her eyes hooded in return. "Good."

She slid off the bed in a swish of silk, bare feet on the worn, woven rug. My breath hitched as she undid the ties of her dress over one shoulder, then the other. It fell to her waist, leaving only the thin underdress that did nothing to hide her pert, dusky nipples.

To taste one. *Both.* I groaned.

Soon. Very soon.

Another tug at the ties on her waist sent the rest of the dress falling to a puddle on the ground. No shy maid after all, Ilya slid back onto the furs and sent me a come-hither look that would haunt every erotic dream for the rest of my days.

I scrubbed a hand down my face. If I went to her now, I'd embarrass myself like a boy. "One moment." I traced back to the balcony, pulling tight the heavy curtains meant to keep out the cold, and tonight, hopefully, keep in any sound. Candles came next, lighting more to make up for the lack of moonlight. All the while, Ilya watched my movement through the room. Each glance toward her reminded me all too well of how clothed I was, and the thin shell of fabric shielding her from me.

Silence had never been so thick, so heavy, so full of possibility and excitement.

Finally, I made my way to the edge of the bed and stood before Ilya where she reclined. "What did you call me the first time you truly laid eyes on me?"

She chewed her bottom lip and looked away as my shirt joined her dress.

"More horrifying than I imagined." Her whispered reply was so quiet I barely heard her.

"And now?" I shucked my boots and reached for the ties on my pants.

"Terrifying. So much so that I—" Ilya licked her lips, her words breaking off abruptly as I shed the rest of my clothes. "I shouldn't want you, but I do."

"Good."

Ilya scooted back across the sheets as I joined her. The bottom hem of the underdress riding up her thighs teased me, barely covering the undergarment below. It had to go. They both did.

"I want to see you, all of you."

Without a word, Ilya came to her knees, the small mirror opposite of my form. The underdress fluttered away, forgotten, as I took in her bared breasts. Her underwear came next, inching down her thighs, revealing dark curls.

Fuck. My cock pulsed. Ready. Needy.

"Lucien," Ilya gasped as I cradled her down onto the sheets.

"My Ilya," I whispered before reclaiming a peaked nipple with my mouth. *Delightful.* Even better than I imagined.

My hand found the juncture between her legs, picking up where I'd left off.

Sliding one finger inside her, I relished the feel of her wrapped around me. My cock prodded her leg, aching to replace my hand. Ilya's fingers slid through my hair, over my skin. Each small whimper and cry I elicited from her were gifts from The Four.

Ilya squirmed under my touch. Soft nails grazed my skin as she rocked against my hand and wrapped her legs around me. She writhed on the sheets, clung to me, practically climbed me like a tree. My head spun, lost in the feel of her and her olive flower scent that invaded my senses like the most skillful invader.

"Please," she whimpered.

I thrust my fingers harder, deeper. "What do you want, Ilya?"

"You. Inside me." She cried out as I teased the taut nub between her legs. "Now!"

Deny her? Never.

I bit my lip, tasting blood as she spread her legs, welcoming me into the embrace of her body. My groan echoed into the room as the top of my cock nudged her entrance, so warm and inviting.

Ilya. The woman who sees the man behind the mask.

She let out a soft moan against my neck as I slid into her. Her legs encircled my waist, holding me tight against her soft body.

Perfection.

All of it.

The way she gripped me. Her warmth. The eager roll of her hips. The way her nipples grazed my chest as she moved. Every speck of my soul demanded I stay lodged within her as long as possible. Any more and I'd lose myself too soon. I stilled my eager thrusts despite her urgings.

"Lucien?" She brushed the strands of hair around my ears as she rolled her hips, sliding along my hard length. Candlelight danced across her skin, illuminating bright, eager eyes.

"I want to savor this. You." I claimed her mouth once more, slowly, gently, relishing the sweet taste of her lips, the delicate flick of her tongue against mine, and the softness of her body.

When I lost myself in her kiss, I dared to move again with slow, deep thrusts, treasuring each slide and pull of her body as we came together.

Ilya bucked her hips when I found that sensitive bud between her legs. I'd never get enough of the way my touch affected her—the careful, controlled woman coming apart in my arms.

Her sheath tightened as she thrashed and whimpered. When I was no longer able to hold back against her wet tightness, a bellow burst from my lungs as I surged into her. Seed spilled in shallow thrusts as her legs held me tight to her, both of us riding out the last of our pleasure.

My forehead pressed against hers. Our heavy breaths mingled as we lay wrapped together. Her arms caressed my back and shoulders. Sweet kisses marked my jaw.

"Ilya." I graced her with little nips in return. My teeth grazed against her earlobe and then down until I licked away the sheen of dewy moisture at the base of her neck. "Stay with me tonight."

"Here?" she asked, breathless.

Wonder shown in her eyes as I raised myself up on my arms and stared down at her flushed cheeks.

I brushed the hair back from her face. My heart pounded anew at the way it splayed across my pillows. "Did you want to leave?"

"No, of course not." Her voice was thick, reminding me of her sweet heat I'd yet to vacate. "I'll stay as long as you'll let me."

Forever.

But I couldn't promise her that. Not now. Not here. Maybe not ever, despite the desire rising in my heart to say just that. She was a treasure, this night a gift, and I'd hoard it as long as I could.

"Good," I replied, cupping her face and bringing my forehead down until it rested against hers, our breaths mingling. "Because I don't intend to let you go."

CHAPTER 38
ILYA

Languid tranquility suffused my limbs as I stretched under soft furs. Darkness and warmth embraced me like a lover, lulling me back into peaceful sleep. Leather with a hint of northern pine filled my nose. Lucien's smell.

Lucien.

I sat bolt upright in the bed. Memories of the night before brought a touch of fire to my cheeks, hotter than the dim embers that burned in the hearth across the room. A sweet ache remained between my legs, one I savored.

Crumbled sheets and furs occupied the bed with me, but nothing else. A quick pan of the room revealed it to be empty as well. Small tendrils of light crept through cracks in heavy curtains, painting lines on the floor. Already morning. Or later.

"Lucien?"

No reply answered my whispered call.

An invisible fist clutched my heart within my chest. Last night was unplanned, unexpected, but I couldn't regret a moment of it. Waking up alone however...

My heart leaped.

He left me alone in his room.

That had been my aim from the start. Finally, it was within my grasp. As much as his absence stung, this opportunity was a balm to all my wounds.

I slid from the bed, shivering as cool air raised gooseflesh along my bare skin. My clothes had been folded and left on a nearby chair, my boots propped together at its base. Warmth from my core chased away the chill. Lucien didn't allow servants up here, which meant he'd taken the time to show care to my things.

A pleasant thought, even if the man himself was missing.

I quickly slipped into my clothes and began a careful search, keeping my ears open for any sign of return.

If I were to keep important information, where would I leave it?

The desk beckoned me like sails on the horizon. Lucien had been hunched over it when I arrived, studying papers that no doubt held some grain of importance.

A thick blue book lay atop an orderly stack of papers. Another pile of books stood off to the side with a quill and ink. I memorized the layout before touching anything.

Satisfied I could restore the desk to order after I searched it, I moved the tome aside and sifted through the papers one by one. Most were benign—training drills, inventories, and the like.

As I scanned the next page, my hand shook.

Reports of possible rebel movement. Activity in multiple city-states, though none of the observed rebels wore state colors. No captures. Little evidence.

Thank The Four.

The news gave me hope. A bright light for all our people and the end of this joke of an empire. This was the type of information I needed. Something to prove to my allies within the castle that I was on their side.

A sudden urgency gripped me. If the rebels were captured and someone could determine which city-state they belonged to, one of us would die—or several of us. I scanned through more pages, reading over notes about troop movements and planned excursions. Another missive confirmed the rumors we'd heard about a possible invasion of Marsali too. This information could be vital to the rebels. We would need to move fast, find a way to alert them. They might win if the city-states worked together for once. Numbers against magic and might.

Near the bottom of the stack, I came across a slightly older missive from a few weeks ago. *This one.* Lucien might notice a recent page missing, but surely he wouldn't go looking for old news.

My heart pounded in my ears as I folded up the paper and tucked it into my boot. The others I placed back upon the desk, the book on top, trying to match their former arrangement as much as I could.

The desk drawers themselves were locked—a pity. And while the bookshelves held a number of interesting titles, none of them appeared to be journals, diaries, or others that might yield information I needed.

Each whisper of leather or parchment set my nerves on edge. Any minute now, Lucien could return. This wouldn't be my only opportunity in his room. Surely not. Though it might if I got caught.

With that thought, I relinquished my search and fled downstairs.

"Hello, friends." My fake smile stretched from ear to ear. I had information to help them, yet they hadn't bothered to look at me as I approached the table for lunch. Only Elin gave me a shy smile.

Fernand looked me up and down, wrinkling his nose as if he inspected a pile of waste. "Someone missed breakfast this morning."

"Overslept." I shrugged.

"Absent, just like all the captains. Convenient."

My lips thinned as I scowled in return, yet the words struck me. No captains occupied the room, and the number of guards appeared less than average. My throat tightened. Something had happened.

"Ilya is not like that," Elin whispered, poking at her plate with a fork.

Warmth stirred in my chest. At least I had one friend here.

Gabriel assessed us each in silence as he prodded a pile of roasted vegetables.

"We can't fight like this. Whatever you think of me, we're in this together," I said.

Elin nodded along.

"How was my brother when you saw him?" Gabriel asked, changing the topic. At least he didn't refute my comment or roll his eyes like Fernand.

I debated lying, complimenting his health and fortitude. But lies wouldn't help any of us. "Honestly, not well."

Gabriel's countenance darkened. He gave a brief nod, willing me to continue.

"He has a limp I don't remember and a cough that's settled deep in his chest. With the resting season approaching and heavier taxes on his people...I don't know."

"It's back then," Gabriel sighed, shaking his head. "He's fought that illness on and off for cycles. We worried it would finish him last time."

His brother could die before he ever saw him again. He likely would if we didn't find a way to end Ryszard's reign. No doubt the emperor would place his wine-loving governor in full control rather than let Basilla take up her husband's place or relinquish Gabriel back to his homeland.

The letter I tucked away in my boot itched against my skin. Every moment it lingered there filled me with more and more uncertainty. I could return it to Lucien's room. Perhaps he would never know what I'd done. He'd trusted me, and I'd stolen from him. My stomach knotted as I considered my actions in the wake of our connection. But...I needed help if I were to aid the rebels. Gabriel and Fernand were my best hope, my true allies—or they had been before.

Reyna chatted loudly with a group of guards, not paying me any mind. I still needed to determine if she was genuine. One mistake would send me to the dungeons, and I couldn't risk that. Not now.

I *accidentally* knocked a fork to the ground, savoring the loud clatter as I got up from my chair to retrieve it. In a quick move, I dug into my boot and slipped the stolen paper into my hand before returning the fork to its original place. No one looked too closely as I circled the table and wrapped Gabriel in a tight hug. I adjusted my embrace and slid my hand over the seam between his vest and shirt. "I'm so sorry to bring sad news, but hopefully good things are in store."

Gabriel's worn fingers rubbed the inner edge of his vest when I returned to my seat. The movement paused. I shot him a meaningful look, which earned a curt nod in return.

For better or worse, there was no going back now.

CHAPTER 39
LUCIEN

We finally had our hands on the rebels. Even so, I couldn't tear my thoughts from the woman whose soft sighs and warm thighs I'd left in my bed, hair strewn out around her, lips slightly parted.

Ilya had still been asleep when I'd dressed in my armor, quietly as I could, and slipped out of the room to request the guards bring us breakfast. I hadn't had a chance to give the order before a different guard rushed up, demanding I come at once. There was no choice but to obey.

What did Ilya think when she woke to find me gone? Nothing good I'd wager.

No wonder Emperor Ryszard frowned upon us taking lovers, no matter how trivial or inconsequential. If he ever found out just how much she occupied my thoughts, or worse, how much she meant to me...

Don't go there, Lucien.

The doors to the emperor's audience chamber groaned open.

"The bastards are more tight-lipped than a mute whore." Orson wiped a smear of blood from his gauntlets as he entered. He didn't bother with the splatter further up his arms.

He relished the torture, an act that turned most of our stomachs. Bile still burned the base of my throat, rising from my empty stomach. I couldn't understand how we'd turned out so differently when we'd been raised together. It wasn't because of our tutor, Nigel, who instructed us in war as well as letters. He was stern but not cruel. Or sagely Florian and his advice on strategy or horses. He'd been a source of laughter before illness took him. Our emperor never praised such behavior when he was around, and the housemaids were far too scared of us to be much influence.

Emperor Ryszard smoldered at his desk, face turning near purple with barely concealed rage. He rose, fingertips drumming on the solid wood. "And you've found nothing to prove where they came from? No symbol or mark?"

He'd asked the same questions of us, his captains, over and over, convinced we must have missed something.

"If I had, I'd have finished the job already," Orson grunted.

Our emperor's lips thinned even more. The drumming stopped. I shot Orson a sharp look, a warning to keep his tongue in check. It was bad enough that he had to pick this, of all days, to return with captives in tow.

"Their attire was plain. Indistinguishable," I said, stepping into the thick tension. "Their appearances were unremarkable. There's no strong dialect that we can detect in their words. Their weapons were simple. No blacksmith markings. No designs or adornment."

Emperor Ryszard nodded, his jaw still stiff.

"I think we have to consider that they may be acting on their own," Zurina said. "Just because they stood in opposition doesn't mean a particular city-state supports them. Their clothing is poor. Their bodies thin. They likely—"

Emperor Ryszard cut her off with a wave of his hand. "All these groups of rebels sneaking around the countryside and undermining my rule are simply poor citizens? I don't believe it. Someone is organizing them, trying to undermine everything I've built. I've given them a unified country, a powerful name that they should be proud of."

"And killed many of their number while taxing them."

Brishon's interruption had my brows reaching skyward. It wasn't like him to contradict our emperor. He'd always been one of his staunchest supporters and had been Orson's ally on more than one mission.

"I've been out there recently, searching for these rebels on your orders," he continued. "The people are unhappy. They rush indoors the moment they see us coming and do not leave. They fear—"

"Enough!" The emperor's palms crashed onto his desk. Heavy breaths shook his chest as he stared us down.

Brishon quieted, but Warren filled the silence. "Perhaps we hold off on our scouting of Marsali. At least until this rebel threat is dealt with and the city-states we've acquired fall more in line."

A reasonable suggestion. One I might have offered if I'd been less distracted. And one I wished for. This constant war and expansion was tiresome. And to what end? The people were unhappy. I'd seen that. It was a wonder the larger countries to the west hadn't risen against us yet to halt the rise of a potential rival power or threat to their territories. I would have if I were them. And this thing with Marsali?

In the days I'd gone to Trale, our emperor had become even more convinced that Marsali was a threat. He claimed they built up troops along their border, but who wouldn't with one of our squadrons stationed nearby to keep an eye on them? Someone must have prodded him, encouraged that thought.

"Stop?" Emperor Ryszard huffed a laugh, crumpling a sheet of paper in a tight fist upon his desk. "No one will respect us if we quit now. Weak. A failure. I won't have it."

Warren glanced my way, sharing a look of unease. He didn't like this either. It was the opposite of wise strategy. Nothing good would come from spreading ourselves thin, chasing rumors, and stirring up trouble.

Cassius Ryszard had been a figure of calm and collected wisdom cycles ago. Before he'd taken over Zhine in the wake of his brother's untimely death. The man before us now was different. Rattled. Erratic. Unstable.

The ever-rising tingle of doubt crept up my spine. Ilya's claim that the emperor would focus on Marsali next, the brief visit to Trale and her claim of my heritage, the wariness in my fellow captain's words. They only fueled the questioning burn that settled against my ribs and never seemed to leave.

"Enough of this," he continued. "If we can't figure out which city-state they belong to, then they'll all suffer until one admits the blame."

A hushed silence filled the room.

"We'll increase taxes. Double what they are now," he continued.

I winced. Cold winds already blew off the northern mountains. This would be a harsh cycle for many, even without the tax.

"And I want children from the city-states sent to the training camps. They'll fall in line if we start young. Five to eight cycles. Pick the strongest-looking ones. Boy or girl."

My throat dried. *Not their children...*

"How many?" I barely heard the question someone posed above the rush of blood in my ears.

"Half."

My heart stuttered. Gasps and murmurs filled the chamber. All the horrible memories from the cabin rushed up to grab at me like a raging river trying to sweep me away. Not the children. Anything but that.

"Half, my emperor?" Brishon's voice shook.

"Half." Our emperor didn't back down. If anything, he stood a little straighter, whiskered jaw stiff and unmoving.

A tingle of magic slid across my scalp, raising the hair on the back of my neck. "I don't like it," Warren said.

I snapped my head toward my friend, though the boy showed no signs of having spoken.

"Face forward, don't react," Zurina said, though her mouth never moved.

A tendril of cold slid down my spine, but it wasn't from the chilling air. The room held no windows to let in a breeze.

"I've linked our minds," Warren added. "Only us three. They can't hear us, but I'll only hold it a moment."

A mind link. A blessing of the God of Darkness. I swore under my breath as the world around me seemed to tilt on its side. Warren, already possibly the most gifted of us all with his ability to move the very ground, was double-blessed, able to wield gifts from Vespera and Erabus.

But I hadn't known, and clearly Zurina had. She wasn't surprised, wasn't caught off guard like I was. The knowledge hit me like a blow.

"I'll explain later," Warren promised.

Could they hear my thoughts?

"It's too extreme, Lucien. Taking their children, their future. It's not who we are," Warren whispered through the link.

"We were to bring peace, prosperity, and comfort to the divided cities," Zurina added. "Not crush their spirits."

Others spoke in the room, but I ignored them, focusing on the mental conversation.

"Someone needs to speak out. Stop this. But you're the only one with the authority," Warren said. "People listen to you. Follow you. If you speak against our emperor, we may have a chance."

"We have your back, Lucien," Zurina said. "In this and other ventures."

"Other ventures..." I mused, barely a whisper. Ilya's face flashed through my mind. The mark on my arm. Trale. The tingling across my skin retreated as Orson's voice rose within the room.

"When do we start? And where do we take them? Our camps can't support such an influx of—"

"Wait." I cut into the conversation, stepping forward to demand attention. "These children have seen war or heard about it from their parents. Why would they become willing soldiers in our army?"

"Children are weak-minded," the emperor replied with a dismissive wave of his hand. "Give them food and purpose and they'll soon stop mewling for their mothers. You'll see."

Conversation erupted in the room in the wake of the emperor's comments, but only a humming buzz filled my ears.

Weak-minded. Like us? Had he thought the same when he took us in? He'd given us food, shelter, purpose, and we followed him.

Memories flashed behind my eyes. The emperor watching us spar or practice our magic. His words of praise and encouragement—all focused on our abilities. The visits became less frequent in the cycle or two before his brother's death. Nor did he stay for long, as he once had. He asked me the same questions each time he was there, almost like a test. What had I learned recently? How far could my illusions reach? There were never any discussions about me beyond my abilities. Nothing about what I liked or might one day want to do.

My stomach rolled. The edges of my vision blurred. Had he ever loved us? Cared? Or were we simply tools to him?

Fuck.

Ilya might be right. About Trale. About Marsali. Everything. The mark on my arm itched, almost like a beacon in and of itself. I couldn't let the emperor steal these children.

"If the city-states are trying to rebel, this won't aid us," I said, raising my voice above the din of the room. "Taking their children will only encourage them to fight back."

The emperor's grey brows reached for the ceiling. "Do you know something we don't, Captain?"

Orson smirked and crossed his arms. It'd been him I interrupted.

"Of course not, but we must consider how they'll react. Show mercy. Give them something to admire and respect." I bit the tip of my tongue as soon as the word slipped free.

His countenance darkened.

Fuck it all. I should have known when he called me captain. Nothing good ever followed that solitary title.

"They'll come in line or I'll enact harsher penalties upon their people. No more rebellions. No more harassment of our troops." His voice rose on each statement, face growing reddish-purple under the salt-and-pepper stubble on his chin. "If they don't listen, I'll show them the meaning of being conquered with blood and magic." He slammed his fist on his desk, the sound echoing throughout the room.

Magic tingled under my skin, yearning to be unleashed in a torrent of fury. This wasn't what I was raised for. It wasn't the vision of a peaceful, united coalition of city-states that he'd fed us for cycles, even before he inherited his brother's throne. Peace. Unity. Prosperity for all once the initial fighting was done.

Fool. I cursed myself. It was too good to be true.

Could I have had a different future? Heir of Trale. Beloved son. A man worthy of Ilya.

Metal clinked as Kasida dipped to one knee. "I'm happy to carry out your commands, my emperor." She placed her feline helm upon the floor at her feet, her bowed head a sign of willing submission.

Her words snapped Emperor Ryszard from his haze of fury. The color receded from his face as he took in the woman on the ground before him. She'd have been a beauty, with her dark hair and bewitching light eyes, if she wasn't so revolting within.

He nodded at her. "You few"—he waved to Kasida, Orson, and others near them—"stay here. The rest of you, out of my sight."

My temper simmered hotter than Orson's flames. I fisted my hands at my sides, holding in my magic.

The odd tingling returned to my scalp. "Not here, not now." The feeling receded with Warren's voice.

He knew me well. Sadly, much more so than I knew him it now seemed.

Have I been blind all my life?

CHAPTER 40
ILYA

G uilt racked me.

I'd stolen information from Lucien, then given it away despite the night we'd shared, despite our promise to be there for each other. It was the opportunity I'd waited for. Longed for. But now...

Gabriel and Fernand sat across the garden from me. The wooden towers they moved around the game board cast long shadows in the afternoon light. A game of cities and conquest. The bitter humor in that wasn't lost on me. Had Gabriel read the information I gave him? Did he care? We'd shared no more than small talk, and Fernand still acted like a hurt child, avoiding me.

Blue skies, crisp breezes—nothing calmed me today. Even the changing colors of the leaves, fading from greens to bright yellows and reds as the season advanced, stirred my frustration.

Bubbly laughter pierced the air, grating on the last of my nerves.

Reyna rounded a bend in the gardens, blinding smile in place, a match for the bright red dress hugging her form. Worse, Elin trailed behind her, looking as happy as I'd seen in days.

I crossed the pathways of moss and stone to them without thought, my body moving of its own accord as I simmered with fury. Pull my innocent friend into her web? Unacceptable.

"We need to talk." One way or another, I'd learn where her allegiance lay.

Laughter cut off abruptly. Nearby guards halted their conversations and looked our way.

Reyna frowned. "I tried the other day, but you were *preoccupied.* Maybe tomorrow we could—"

"Now." I shook my head.

Elin tilted her head in question, but I ignored her. I slipped my arm through Reyna's, a much more companionable gesture than I felt, and pulled her with me toward a side door exiting the gardens. We wouldn't be able to talk out here, not like we needed to.

"Stop right there." One of the guards held up his hand, stepping in front of the doors as we approached. Blessedly, Reyna hadn't put up more of a fight or argument. Instead, she looked as confused as Elin had when we left her behind.

My mind raced, coming up with the best excuse I could think of. "It's my blooding cycle," I mumbled, feigning embarrassment. "I need Lady Reyna's assistance." Bless The Four, the nearby guards were all male.

The guard's brows scrunched as he looked to his companion, a younger man whose cheeks had flushed and wouldn't meet my eyes. He gave a noncommittal shrug.

"Fine, be quick about it," the older one said, throwing open the wooden door behind him. "Second door on the right."

As if we didn't know.

A whiff of human waste perfumed the enclosed room despite the pine branches and dried herbs that hung from the ceiling. Sliding the bolt in the door, I turned on Reyna in the cramped space.

"You're going to get us found out," she said in a harsh whisper.

"Us? You were planning to get me thrown in the cells if I followed your treasonous suggestions."

She reared back, mouth agape. "Why would you think…" She shook her head.

I crossed my arms. "Gabriel and Fernand asked you about a certain farmer. You said he was sympathetic to their goals."

"He was. I'm almost certain."

"And this ally sold them out? Or you did?"

She pursed her lips. "Neither. I didn't know some of the captains were attending without their armor. They didn't decide that until just before, and I didn't find out until it was too late."

"Right, too late or—" My tongue halted as the words sunk in. My arms fell limp. "How do you know they decided just before?" I didn't even know that. Lucien never mentioned it.

Reyna took my hands in hers. "I'm trusting you, Ilya. What I tell you could mean my head. We must be in this together."

I wanted her on my side. Needed it. I nodded.

Her hands tightened on mine. "We have little time, but the quick version: Captain Zurina is my friend."

I sucked in a breath. "How can you be sure?"

"We grew up together. We were best friends when we were young, before she disappeared. I thought she was dead. But when I came here I heard her voice, and I knew it was familiar. It took time to figure out the truth, but once I did, I asked about her past and dropped hints about our childhood. She didn't remember at first, but she said eventually her memories shifted, changed until she could remember the things I'd told her. She even remembered her nickname for me—one I hadn't told her."

My blood iced. Just like Lucien. Lost and missing in his youth. Thought dead.

"Are you alright?" she prompted. "Your face…"

I nodded, blinking rapidly. "Lucien…he might have a similar situation."

"Well now." Reyna grinned. "Does he trust you? He must to tell you so much."

"Yes. I think so."

"And is he sympathetic to our cause?"

An excellent question. "I'm not sure, but he might be..." I ached to tell her his secret, his identity, but I held onto the words.

Reyna drew me closer. "This is great news. Perhaps the turning point we've been waiting on." Her eyes glittered in the dim light of the solitary oil lamp. "We've needed another captain on our side, one with influence over the rest."

Great news for her, and for me. I nearly hugged her. An ally, and not just any—one who'd pulled a captain to her side as well. I'd seen Reyna with Zurina many times. It'd been one of the main reasons I doubted her loyalties. I never thought to suspect one of the emperor's own captains already worked to undermine his reign.

"I knew you might just be the key to landing our stag." Reyna released me. "Zurina thinks Emperor Ryszard may have tampered with some of their memories, making himself into their guardian and savior when really he stole them as children."

"That...it makes sense. But can he do that?" Magic was such an elusive talent. Everyone knew Ryszard had the ability to feel magic—the tool by which he'd found and rescued the orphans who became his captains. But if that wasn't his only blessing, if he could alter memories, it could explain much.

"Who knows?" Reyna whispered, interrupting my thoughts. "However, Zurina has been passing information to the city-states, helping the rebels, and telling them how to avoid patrols. She doesn't like what the emperor's done. His violent approach. Captain Warren is on her side. She thinks Lucien and a few of the others could be turned, but we couldn't risk it. If she revealed herself and was wrong..." She shook her head.

All their plans would come crumbling down, with their heads on pikes as a lesson to any who would follow. I knew the fears that held back their steps. I knew them far too well. She'd revealed far more than I ever expected, and I had more for her as well.

"Lord Stefan confided that birds are migrating west. Perhaps to the Everspelt range just to the north."

She clasped her hands in front of her chest. "I knew he'd trust you. He wouldn't respond to the messages Zurina sent with her birds. Probably thought it was a trap." She shrugged. "Everspelt." She tapped a finger against her lips. "That's close. All the pieces are coming together. If you can get Captain Lucien on our side, it could turn the tide and pull others as well. They look up to him as their leader. Well, most of them. Without his captains, the emperor loses some of his advantage. The people are ready to rise. They only need to know they have a chance, and it won't earn their own deaths."

My body shook with barely contained excitement. The goal I strove for was so much closer than I ever thought possible. Freedom for Sorrena. A return to the days before this bloody empire. Could it be true?

"I can turn him. I will."

Reyna wrapped me in a fierce hug. "I knew you were what we needed."

A hard rap on the door had us jumping apart with a gasp.

"Almost done in there?" The guard's gruff voice seeped through the door.

"One moment!" I called, raising my voice above the bare whispers we'd used.

I counted to ten and opened the door. Both of us smiled innocently at the guard who scowled into the room, as if he expected to find someone or something else.

He flicked his hand toward the gardens. "Come along then."

For once, I didn't mind following the guards' orders or the restrictive way they watched us. I raised my chin, relishing the sunlight as it warmed my skin.

We had a plan. Rebels were moving into place, waiting to rise. We would end this empire, and life would return to the way it had always been. The way it should be. Soon. So very soon.

CHAPTER 41
LUCIEN

I paced across the stone floor, flexing and unflexing my aching hand. Punching the wall had been instinct. Slamming my hand into it repeatedly...

Stupid, Lucien. Just stupid.

It had taken Warren's help to pry the battered gauntlet off my hand. It would take more than that to fix the dents in the metal. The act hadn't distracted my thoughts. If anything, it brought them closer to the surface.

Zurina and Warren had urged me to go back to the emperor's audience chamber after he dismissed us. Confront him. Make him see reason.

That was when I'd hit the wall. Literally. If I'd gone back in there then, I might have attacked him—doomed us all.

"You didn't tell me," I accused Warren as I flexed my freed hand.

Warren stared up at me, blue eyes seeing too much as they always did. "You'd have just told me not to use it."

I scowled at him. He knew me well, but with his weak heart, any outpouring of magic could spell his death. I'd tried to protect him from that as much as I could, keeping him out of battle. But if the rebels closed in, would the emperor hesitate to use his skills to protect himself? Nails bit into my palm, the joints screaming in pain. No. He wouldn't.

The doors creaked open. I froze, muscles pulling tight under my skin.

Ilya strolled into my sitting room, countenance bright, her long hair trailing behind her like rolling hills ready to be planted. Her eyes locked on me.

"I'll leave you. Find me later," Warren said.

As soon as the guards closed the door behind him, I snapped into action, hurrying across the distance to Ilya. She sucked in a short breath as I grasped her bare arm in my damaged hand. Lightning zipped between us where we touched. Her stiff form melted against me as my other arm came around her, pulling her into my armored chest.

My helmet lay on the side table with the damaged article, leaving me room to trail kisses along the top of her head. "About this morning…"

Her brown eyes found mine, flickering with concern and stirring my blood. Her back stiffened under my touch, her whole form going rigid again at the quiet mention.

"I didn't mean to leave you alone after—" The words lodged in my throat. Already I wanted to pull her back upstairs and repeat the events of the night before. "I went to order breakfast brought to my quarters for you and got called away."

Her brows wrinkled, a small smile pulling at her lips as the tension in her body fell away. "That's all?"

I traced her jaw, savoring the simple touch. She wasn't mad? Upset? I expected both.

"I assumed you wouldn't have left me alone up there on purpose." Her cheeks pinked as she glanced away out into the falling night at the last colors of sunset painting the horizon. Ilya bit her bottom lip, eyes flitting about the room. Was she nervous?

With a sigh, I forced myself to let her go, stepping back to give her space. "If you have regrets about what happened between us—"

"No." She whipped around, placing a palm across my chest. "No regrets. Not about that." But she still wouldn't quite look at me.

"Something's bothering you though."

"I..." She shook her head and crossed the room. Leather creaked as she sat heavily upon the sofa, her shoulders slumped.

"Is this about your friends?" Another guess. She'd been upset yesterday, and though she'd burned with her usual fire when she walked through the door, one look at me had extinguished it.

"Something like that."

Not that at all. I took the vacant seat next to her, trying to pry through the thick walls she kept so dutifully fortified.

"Actually, I was thinking about you." She dropped her voice. "Your birthmark." Ilya touched my arm, grazing the armor just above where the odd mark marred my skin.

Her words cracked the dam of my thoughts, ones I'd carefully pushed aside in light of the other revelations of the day. "What about it?"

She shuffled closer. "Do you think some of the others could be like you? Hazy memories. Unsure of where you're from. You were all taken in as orphans, right? That's what we always heard."

It's what I'd always been told and believed. Though Zurina had encouraged me not to discount my memories, and Warren had implied the same. "That's right," I said, but doubt swarmed me. My friends kept secrets. The emperor's actions grew more erratic, his tactics cruel and punishing. I'd always been the emperor's first-in-command, ever since he'd named me so once he came to power. A fighter, a conqueror. So sure of my role, my next victory. I'd had no doubts about my place in life or the friends at my side.

Yet now...

Soft warmth grazed my cheek, and I looked over at Ilya as she dropped her hand back into her lap.

A sad smile painted her lips. "You went somewhere far away."

"I suppose we both have a lot on our minds," I replied with a fake half-smile. I ached to feel her soft curves pressed against me, soothing away all the uncertainty that the day stirred up within me, but it would be only a temporary distraction.

"At least some of the captains are your friends, right?" she asked.

I nodded, but the doubts made it short and jerking.

"Then it's worth talking to them. Trusting them."

"And are we friends, Ilya? Can I trust you?" I needed someone—an anchor in the stormy winds threatening to tear my world apart.

She bit her lip, her cheeks flushing. "I don't have sex with my friends. Only you. So I think we'll need a different title—"

Ilya gasped as I pulled her into my lap. Her thighs hugged my legs through the material of her dress. Her scent swarmed my senses like a marauder at the gates. I didn't give her the chance to continue before I claimed her mouth. I threaded my fingers through her hair, savoring the feel of silken locks against my skin. With Ilya so close, the pain and confusion nearly vanished. Temporarily but needed.

I nipped her bottom lip as I pulled back, a satisfied grin spreading across my features. She soothed my aches faster than healing magic. "No more titles."

"No more." Warm breath ghosted across my face.

My perfect distraction. Too perfect. With a groan, I eased her off my lap. "I have something I need to do."

"Right now?"

The soft pout of her lips nearly changed my mind. It had to be now. Any longer with her and I'd lose myself again. I couldn't afford that tonight, not when I desperately needed to think.

THE FOUNDATIONS of my life shook, crumbling more with each passing day. Only one place beckoned me, offering peace and clarity in the haze of uncertainty—the temple room of Erabus. It would be quiet this time of day, or so I hoped.

Each city and town bore temples consecrated to the four Gods and

Goddesses that oversaw our world, even south of the river Savanet where they considered magic a curse rather than a blessing. Priests and devotees swarmed the halls of the city's temples. Though no priests resided within the castle, the temple rooms offered a place to pray and beseech The Four without traveling into Zhine.

"Can I speak with you?"

The unexpected voice snapped me from my thoughts as I whipped around to find Brishon leaning against a shadowed wall outside the temple rooms—a place he rarely went.

"Sorry to surprise you, brother" he continued, shoving off the stone. "I didn't expect you to seek their wisdom tonight too, but I'm glad you did."

I nodded. I wasn't the only one seeking guidance from The Four. "In here." I wrenched open the door to the prayer room dedicated to Erabus, God of Darkness.

Tall, black candles dripped their wax along the edges of the room. Tonight, the two rows of four chairs facing the altarpiece sat empty.

Brishon locked the door behind him. No one would think twice about a locked door here, not in the space where people came to pray privately to The Four.

We took seats side by side in the front row. Brishon eyed my missing gauntlet but didn't comment on it.

"What did you want to talk about?" I asked.

He hunched in the chair, his fist bunched up under his chin. We'd never been close friends. He often spent time with Orson and his circle, but thankfully, the man lacked his friend's foul disposition.

With a sigh, Brishon pulled off his helmet and ruffled the black hair framing his dark olive face. "I don't like the way things are going for us," he said, barely a whisper in the quiet room. "We were raised to serve and protect, but this..."

I looked at him hard, seeking truth or fallacy in his words. The open, unguarded look in his eyes told me everything. I'd known him too long to be played. His eyes always spoke the truth, even when his words did not.

"I feel the same way."

"I thought you might. It's why I'm glad I ran into you. I don't think I'm the only one either."

I removed my helm with a sigh. "You're not."

"So what do we do?"

I stifled a humorless laugh. They always looked to me, their leader, the one who'd taken charge in adolescence even before I'd earned my title. I'd always enjoyed the honor, relished it. It gave me purpose and direction. Now it weighed on me.

"I'm not sure yet. It's why I came here." I glanced toward the low altar littered with sticks of burning incense and stems of herbs. A painting of one tall, dark tower on a landscape of night and stars was enclosed within a crimson circle along the far wall. The symbols of Erabus.

Though not always the pious sort, I needed divine guidance. Now more than ever.

"Let's meet tomorrow. Midafternoon." Perhaps then I'd have my thoughts in better order. "That big oak by the far training yard."

Brishon nodded and replaced his helmet, preparing to rise.

I halted him with a hand on his arm. "This stays between us. If the emperor knows how much we doubt him...what we plan..."

"I understand."

"Tomorrow then."

Once Brishon left, I replaced my helm and knelt at the foot of the altar. "Erabus, look upon your blessed and guide my path."

For long minutes I prayed in silence upon my knees. Time passed in the flicker of flame and drip of wax. No windows showed the passage of the moons. No sound reached my ears other than the soft, steady thump of my heart.

Silent prayers gave way to memories of youth. I replayed my interactions with the emperor. Memories from cycles ago, and recent ones too. Emptiness ached within my chest. He'd been a father figure, someone I spent every waking moment aiming to impress. But those old memories were no longer quite what I remembered. The gentle smile and encouraging words no longer sounded so genuine. Instead, I saw a blacksmith honing his blades, hammering the edge into lethal perfection. He selected us. Crafted us for his use.

I couldn't let him do the same thing to more children.

When at last I rose, my legs were stiff. My feet tingled from the lack of movement. My spirit, however, thrummed with determination. And a plan.

Zurina and Warren said I could trust them, that they had my back. I'd need them. Brishon too. Four against the empire wouldn't be enough, but we might have a chance if these rebels were truly the force the emperor feared. We knew the emperor's battle strategies. I'd crafted many of them myself. I also knew his weakness, the game piece that the emperor used to keep the city-states in check: his honored guests.

CHAPTER 42
LUCIEN

Bells tolled from the high tower. The mix of high and deep notes cut through the afternoon, spooking horse and man alike. *Fuck.*

I set my jaw, grimacing at the sound. Earlier I'd met with Warren, Zurina, and Brishon near the large oak outside the training yard. If one of them had second thoughts and relayed our discussions to the emperor, it would be my word against theirs.

With the emperor's growing paranoia, I knew who would win that discussion.

Guards and grooms rushed to calm the animals in the bailey, though nothing could ease the racing of my heart. Not after all I'd learned this afternoon.

Several of the city-states banded together, amassing the most skilled and loyal soldiers they had left—in secret. They'd sneak off one by one or in twos to avoid the notice of our guards and spies. No one too well-known or so important that they'd be missed. They wouldn't wear their own colors but common garb, such as the rebels we'd captured. They were careful with the craft of their weapons, using crude farm items.

Zurina had known about it for some time.

She'd helped them.

With the aid of her ability to magically control animals, she sent messages to the rebels, alerting them of our patrols and where our guards were stationed, helping them avoid capture. As the movement grew, it became harder for her to warn them all, hence the recent capture.

One of my best friends worked against me—against all of us.

The wound still bled me out despite her confessions to me now. But that wasn't the worst of it. Not by far.

With a grunt, I slammed the training sword onto the rack. "Keep at your drills. I'll return if I can." Wearing myself into exhaustion hadn't helped.

A few soldiers nodded, but most remained distracted. All the better. They'd seen too few cycles, or too many. Their faces blurred as I headed for the audience chamber. Warren was right, these men and women didn't deserve to die, as they would if the rebels attacked—which they would, soon if Zurina's information was correct.

More war. More death.

Once I believed we could end it, but we'd only made it worse. Me. My doing. The emperor's orders, but I'd carried them out.

My skin turned clammy as I advanced through the hallways. Warren slid into step beside me as I turned a corner.

"What is it?" he asked.

"No idea."

He'd kept secrets from me too. And not just about the rebels.

Zurina hadn't been an orphan. She'd thought so too for many cycles, but Reyna remembered her from youth. She told her the truth and reminded her of the past. Slowly, a little bit each day, it was as if a fog rolled back from her memories. Old memories shifted and changed until the true ones broke free.

Just like mine. Talking with Zurina about it was the final tug on the blanket over my mind. Her truth let me accept mine and see things for how they really were.

It nearly brought me to my knees.

I still recalled the cabin that haunted my memories for as long as I could remember. I still felt the fear, pain, and hunger of that time etched into my soul.

But the sorrow I'd once felt at the death of my so-called parents vanished. Now I knew them for what they were—my captors. I'd caused their deaths. My magic broke free for the very first time. Uncontrolled. Wild. In their fear they caused their own demise, leaving me tied up within the cabin—crying, starving, and begging for help. Cassius Ryszard arrived after two days. I recalled his whispers now too, the way his magic tingled under my skin and wove a new memory. It had held for cycles—until Ilya. She'd started to unwind the threads that held the spell in place as Reyna had for Zurina.

Zurina suspected that was the reason for the emperor's recent headaches. As his magic unraveled, he struggled to maintain his creation. Without success.

If the rebels attacked, the emperor would kill Ilya—and the others. He'd make an example of them for all the city-states. We had to act before then. Find a way to get them out of his grasp.

I toyed with the pommel of my sword. If someone told the emperor of our discussion this afternoon, I'd go down fighting. Maybe I'd take him with me. End this.

Wariness and unease twisted into shock as I shoved past the guards and threw open the doors to the audience chamber. A man knelt on the ground, arms bound behind him. Blood leaked from a cut above his eye, swollen and purple.

Conversation cut off abruptly as I entered the room, Warren quick on my heels. Most of the others had already arrived, standing in a half-circle around the man on the ground and the guard holding the bindings on his wrists. Emperor Ryszard frowned behind his desk, studying a crumpled piece of paper. He didn't spare a glance for us.

Tension slipped from my shoulders. My heart lightened. *Praise The Four.* He didn't know. There was still time to finalize a plan.

"A fight?" I asked, infusing my voice with calm indifference I didn't feel. I recognized the man—Lord Fernand Reis, one of our honored guests and Ilya's friend, the same one who had cried out for his wife amid my illusions in the arena.

Orson spit on the ground.

"A repeat offender." The emperor's flat, even tone disturbed me more than any words or spew of anger he could have uttered. The purple-faced rants I'd grown used to, but this icy calm was new.

Twisting emotions simmered up my chest and threatened to choke me as I took in our emperor. He'd been a father figure once. Someone I respected—loved in a way. But he'd stolen us, stripped us away from a different life in youth, one that may not have been full of war and death. Too many thoughts chased each other through my head, just as they had this afternoon.

With effort, I blocked out my concerns, shifting into the careful role of First Captain I'd worn all these cycles.

Fernand didn't look up as I circled him to take the paper from the emperor's outstretched hand. The man might as well have been a statue if not for the slow drip of blood down his face.

The hint of a smirk painted the emperor's features as I took the letter, but I ignored it. My back stiffened as I recognized the familiar script. Zurina's writing.

And she wasn't here.

Fear surged through my blood, burning its way into my chest. *Why the fuck were you so careless as to—*

The doors opened.

Zurina entered, accompanied by another captain. The last two to arrive. "What's going on here?" she called.

I met her gaze, conveying all the worry simmering under my skin with a single look. Her head tilted to the side, her eyes flickering over me briefly before taking in the rest of the room.

No one stepped in to arrest or accuse her. Nor did anyone attack her with questions as she joined us in front of the emperor.

A tendril of unease wrapped around my throat, pulling my attention back to the paper. This time, I read the words on the page. Zurina's handwriting, but the letter wasn't sent to the rebels or our honored guests. It was sent to me.

My name jumped out at the top, bold and accusing. The paper contained a summary of what we'd learned of the rebels from a few weeks back, the same type Zurina often wrote up and gave to any of us when we missed a meeting.

I kept these pages locked in my desk. But no one entered my room. Had one of my guards—

"Interesting that one of our honored guests tried to pass off information again," the emperor commented, drawing my attention. "Especially information with your name on it."

Zurina flinched before turning to face me, a warning in her eyes, though I didn't know which threat she tried to convey. Warren's connection was silent, offering nothing.

I crossed to the man on the ground and crouched on my heels, metal armor clinking, until I was eye level with the top of his head. "How did you get into my quarters?"

"I didn't," he mumbled.

I jerked his head up by his hair, wrenching a cry from his lips. The emperor wouldn't expect me to be careful, not with a traitor. Besides, I needed answers. This was a wrinkle I hadn't counted on and couldn't afford. "What did you say?"

"I didn't take it."

My grip tightened.

He cried out again. More blood dripped off his face to splatter on the stones.

"And yet you have it, and tried to what? Pass it off?" I flicked my gaze to Emperor Ryszard, who watched me carefully, a small smile on his lips. The emperor wasn't surprised by that comment—he'd already told him.

Fingers of dread tickled the back of my neck as I fixed my attention on the man before me. "If you didn't take it, how did you get it?"

"It was given to me," he groaned.

"By whom?" *Which of my guards had dared—*

"Ilya."

Breath fled my lungs.

Color bled from the world.

My heart twisted so tight it might burst. Voices rose around me, but I didn't hear them. I didn't even see the man who jerked from my slacked grip.

Ilya.

Her name echoed in every recess of my mind.

Ilya.

She'd betrayed me.

I stiffened. No, she couldn't have. She wouldn't. Not after our night together, after what we'd shared.

"Lucien." Warren's calming voice slipped into my mind, barely penetrating the dark pool of betrayal clouding my world. "The emperor asked, 'Isn't that the woman under your watch?'"

The magical tingle faded away as I turned to the man whose question I'd never heard. His brows rose skyward as he drummed his fingers on the desk. No fury, no barks of outrage. He knew the answer but expected me to give it to him anyway.

"Yes," I bit out. "She is."

"Told you we should have thrown that bitch in a cell," Orson said.

Another attempt to rattle me. It worked. The metal of my newly repaired gauntlet flexed in my fist as I tried to hold in my magic surging to get free. Orson had picked his moment to grab for power well.

"It seems you've grown soft. Taking mercy on our guests. Giving them the run of your quarters?" Emperor Ryszard's voice held mockery, bitter amusement.

The tone elicited a high cackle from Kasida. It took everything I had to hold in the surge of magic jumping under my skin.

"Of course not," I replied. My mind raced, searching for words to calm this disaster. "I placed her in the servant's chamber to keep a closer eye on her and separate her further from the rest. Throwing your honored guest in a cell when they did nothing to warrant such punishment did not feel befitting of your hospitality."

I'd believed her. Trusted her. Had everything been a lie? Some ruse to catch me off guard?

Images of her flashed through my mind. Her beguile. Her seduction. The confusion over my true appearance. She'd sought to seduce information from me then, but since...

"My *hospitality* does not extend to traitors. Neither those from outside our walls nor those closest to us." Emperor Ryszard reclined in his chair. The steady *tap, tap, tap* of his fingertips across the wood echoed into the silence as he stared me down. "Tell me, Captain, what punishment would you suggest for the woman who stole from you?" He leaned forward. "Unless you gave her the information?"

My back stiffened as the words wrapped around me like a vise. "I wouldn't." The retort burst from me in a rush. "You know that." Even with all that I'd learned recently, I wouldn't have given Ilya that paper. It wouldn't help any of us.

"Do I?" His brows rose toward the arched ceiling above.

"I've served you since I was a child." And I did now, at least a little bit longer. To have my loyalty questioned when so much rode on it—never.

"Punishment for the woman. What shall it be?"

The question hit me over and over like a hail of fists. The very air in the room seemed to press in on me and strangle my thoughts. I pointed to Fernand, still on his knees. "How do we know he's telling the truth?"

"See," Kasida said, jumping into the conversation. "He defends her still. I told you she'd worked her claws into him."

Orson snorted. "More like she spread her legs and—"

The emperor waved them silent. "It seems, Captain, that you've lost the regard of your peers. And you're quickly losing mine."

Another blow, this one like a rusty knife to my guts. Heads turned my way, including my friends, but I ignored them, staring down the man tightening the reins on my fate. In a matter of hours, my entire world had begun to fray, to balance on a knife's edge.

"Orson shall replace you as First."

A gasp cut through the room. I couldn't say from whom—the buzzing in my head threatened to drown out all sound.

A lifetime of service, respect, and honor stripped away in one moment. Everything I'd worked for was given to the ingrate who smirked at me across the room.

Because of Ilya.

She'd finally stabbed me in the back, just not with the dagger I expected. This pain was much worse. A blow to my pride, my soul, my very being. A physical wound would have been easier to take.

"Now..." The emperor rose to his feet once again. "Determine a suitable punishment, or should I believe that you no longer wish to be one of my captains at all?"

CHAPTER 43
ILYA

Reyna and I set up our easels in the garden with the plan to paint —and seek each other's confidence. I'd yet to tell her about my discussion with Lucien, and there was more, a tension in the air that we didn't quite understand. Fernand's unexplained absence from both meals didn't improve matters. The sick, twisting feeling in my gut alluded to trouble, but what?

I'd only completed a few brush strokes when a troop of unfamiliar guards filed into the garden, stopping in a half-circle around us. The chilly demeanor of the men stripped the warmth from the afternoon sun sliding down the sky overhead. Activity halted. The birds chirping nearby quieted. My chest hollowed out, dread blooming in that empty pit as I looked from one stoic face to the next. Something was wrong, so very wrong.

"Lady Ilya," one of the men said.

"What's this about?" Reyna asked, giving voice to the question taking shape in my head.

"She's to come with us. At once." The lead guard advanced on where I stood.

Elin rose from where she read nearby, concern evident in her features.

I set my brush aside and waved her away. Whatever the guards wanted, involving her wouldn't help us.

Summoning my courage and trying to keep my composure, I asked, "Where to?"

The man ignored my question and beckoned to the others. One frowned, the other showed no emotion as they advanced without a word. I stood a little straighter and stepped back, but they were upon me before I could think, grasping my arms between them. I stumbled forward, tripping over my feet while twisting around for a glance at Reyna. Her wide-eyed stare and white-knuckled grip on her paintbrush told me everything. She knew nothing and was frightened.

That look sent a dagger into my heart. Trouble. Danger. *Gods and Goddesses, help me.*

Another jerk. Another near fall. "I can walk on my own," I grated. Guards closed in around me as the two ruffians loosened their grip, though not quite enough for me to wrench free. Not that I had anywhere to flee if I could.

None of them answered my questions or pleas as I was led into a portion of the castle kept off-limits to us. Only the rhythmic *clack* and *clomp* of boots along stone floors accompanied us as we meandered twisting hallways. Not even the merry chatter of servants reached us here.

Every step increased the invisible ropes around my neck threatening to cinch tight and choke me. Something terrible had happened. If Sorrena rebelled, it would be my head. There'd be no escape, no time to put to use all that I'd learned. My eyes burned with unshed tears.

At last, we came to a halt in front of a guarded set of double doors. The men at attention showed less emotion than those who dragged me here. Despite the anxiety twisting like eels in my gut, I steeled my nerves and raised my chin as they pushed open a door.

I wasn't prepared for the sight that greeted me.

My body locked up, refusing to move into the room, as the squeak and scrape of metal invaded my ears. Captains turned my way, their armor gleaming in the light that filled the room. Not just one, nor two. All of them by the looks of it. Worse was the man sitting behind a large wooden desk on a raised platform, and the bloodied man kneeling on the patterned stonework in the room's center.

On instinct I searched for Lucien. He'd only half-turned in my direction from where he stood to the right of Ryszard's desk.

Look at me. Please.

Whatever this was, he could fix it. He could—

"You may leave us," Ryszard said, dismissing the guards. They shoved me hard toward the center of the room before slamming the door at my back.

Trapped within, the walls of the room closed in around me, tightening their invisible noose. Zurina stepped forward to flank me as the guards had. Like Lucien, her form gave nothing away.

Instead, I looked to Fernand, still crouched unmoving upon the floor. Blood dripped from a wound above his eye and rolled down his chin to splatter upon the stones beneath him. Whimpering sniffles signaled his consciousness, yet he kept his gaze trained on the floor no matter how I willed him to look at me in return.

"Lady Ilya Valerious of Sorrena." Ryszard rose to his feet, a small smile playing about his features. "Care to confess your crimes?"

"My crimes?" I echoed. A scream crawled its way up my throat, one I swallowed down before I spoke again. "What am I accused of?" I notched my chin a bit higher, a show of confidence I didn't feel.

Lucien...

As if my silent plea reached him, the man in question turned to face me. Despite the familiar form and armor, I almost didn't recognize him. The cold, vacant look in his eyes was more haunting than the sight of all the captains together. This wasn't the man I remembered. His chilly demeanor and lack of emotion gutted me, threatened to bleed me out worse than any blade.

"This one"—Lucien pointed to Fernand, who visibly flinched where he knelt—"informs us that you're the one responsible for giving him the information he tried to pass off to a maid."

He clutched a crumbled piece of paper. Though I couldn't read it across the distance, there was only one thing it could be. Dread curled around me. It had to be the page I'd stolen from Lucien and given to Gabriel. How in the name of The Four had Fernand gotten it?

"I do not have such information, and if I did I'd never give it to him." Truth, or as close to it as I could muster. I locked my knees under the skirts of my dress to halt their shaking. Fernand made foolish choices, he'd proven that before, and now he'd dragged me down with him.

Stupid, foolish man.

And foolish me for wanting his and Gabriel's trust and admiration.

"How do we know that's not a lie?" Lucien grated, the sound cutting into me like small knives.

I looked away, unable to handle the harshness of his gaze, and instead focused on Ryszard. A horrible yet preferable alternative. It took everything in me, but I managed to kneel, to pretend subservience.

"I delivered your message to Trale at your request, my emperor." The words tasted like acid on my tongue. "If I'd had such knowledge and wished to pass it off, why would I give it to Fernand when I could have delivered it myself?"

A thin excuse. One Lucien could kick out from under me if he mentioned I'd been alone in his room since then.

The chair scraped as Ryszard pushed it back before coming around the desk. His long fur cape swished about the stonework around his boots. "Such a clever girl. Though how do I know you didn't pass off information to them too? Once a thief..." he drawled.

"I didn't."

"His word against yours then. How do we get to the bottom of this?" Ryszard glanced over to Lucien. Waiting.

"Punish them both. Neither can be trusted."

Lucien's words knocked the breath from me. My mouth gaped, eyes pleaded.

My Ilya. His words taunted me. The memory of his hands on me, his mouth, the way he filled me body and soul. I gagged, unable to hold in the horror that seized me.

I'd stolen from him, and he knew it. And now he turned his back on me. On us. On everything we promised to be and could have been.

"My first, take them to the cells to await their punishment."

Lucien didn't move. Instead, Orson stepped down from the raised platform where he'd stood next to Ryszard's desk. A glimmer of eerie light sparkled in his eyes. Kasida followed.

Orson stepped around Fernand, his leering eyes never leaving me. Screams echoed in my head, my silent voice crying out into the void.

Metal dug into my arm as he wrenched me to my feet and pulled a cry from my lips. "To the cells, where you should have been all along."

No. No, no, no.

Fernand cried out as Kasida hauled him up by his hair, pushing him toward us. None of the other captains intervened as we were led away.

Lucien.

I shoved against Orson, twisting my body until I caught his gaze.

Cold. Uncaring.

My heart cracked as he looked away, all the fight leaving my body in a rush of ice. Tears burned at the corners of my eyes as a wave of pure terror overwhelmed me. Sorrena's hope and future vanished in a moment, all my efforts gone to waste and futility. Watching my city burn and fall had been less painful than this. Slow torture would have been easier. Preferable.

The world crumbled around me until only cold darkness poured into the space left by my shattered heart.

CHAPTER 44
ILYA

The steady *drip, drip, drip* of water and the occasional squeak of a mouse were my staunchest companions within the damp, musty cell. They'd placed Fernand in the one across from me. The whole time I watched him through the metal bars, he didn't move from where he huddled in the corner. Perhaps Kasida had knocked him out when she flung him into the little stone room and locked him in with the echo of her taunts. Not even my attempts to free myself from the cell, useless as they were, roused him.

At least Orson hadn't lingered. Or returned. Yet.

I hugged my arms about me as the damp chill sunk into my skin. What I wouldn't give for a blanket, a bed, or a view of the moons. The low-burning torch down the hallway provided little in the way of light, and if the dim flickers were any indication, soon that, too, would be gone.

I considered countless accusations to fling at Fernand if he were awake to hear them. Not one left my lips. What good would they do now? I'd gambled and lost.

A sharp rock bit into my back as I leaned against the wall. But I deserved the pain. People would suffer and starve for my actions. How much would the emperor tax them? Would they curse my name in the streets for their suffering? They should. And poor Justina... I'd broken my bargain with Lucien. There was no reason left for him not to summon her to Zhine to suffer as a hostage at my side.

Worse than the chill or my despair was the flicker of hope burning in my heart. I huddled against the stone wall, watching the direction of the entrance. I imagined Lucien coming down the hall, keys in hand. He'd apologize, tell me how all of this was part of some greater plan and that he'd never leave me. He wouldn't uphold our bargain and force my sister to come here as punishment for my actions. He'd kiss me like his very life depended on it and steal away all the pain and sorrow of the day.

Anytime now he'd come.

I couldn't allow myself to think of anything else, or what tomorrow or the next day might bring if he didn't. Those days would never come. They couldn't, because then everything would be truly lost.

Without meaning to, I'd fallen for him. Hard. So much more than I realized or ever expected. Much more than I'd told him.

I'd loved him in a way. I knew that now, but he didn't, and now he might never. Even if I told him, would he believe it?

No. Not after today.

He'd meant more to me than he ever should, and still I'd betrayed him—all for a foolish hope that I could make a difference and achieve my goals.

All for Sorrena.

Oh, I'd given it all. More than I thought I had to give. All but my very life, and even that might be slipping away.

The harsh, empty way he'd regarded me in Ryszard's audience chamber haunted me more than the dark, the cold, or my memories of Sorrena's fall. I'd watched men I knew bleed and die. I'd seen flames lick and burn as buildings whose halls I'd walked many times crumbled and fell. I'd been forced to bend the knee to a tyrant and submit to his captivity.

Yet all those things paled in comparison to the empty ache I felt now, the one that threatened to swallow me up in the darkness and hide me from the sun forever.

Time dripped by.

Lucien never came.

CHAPTER 45
ILYA

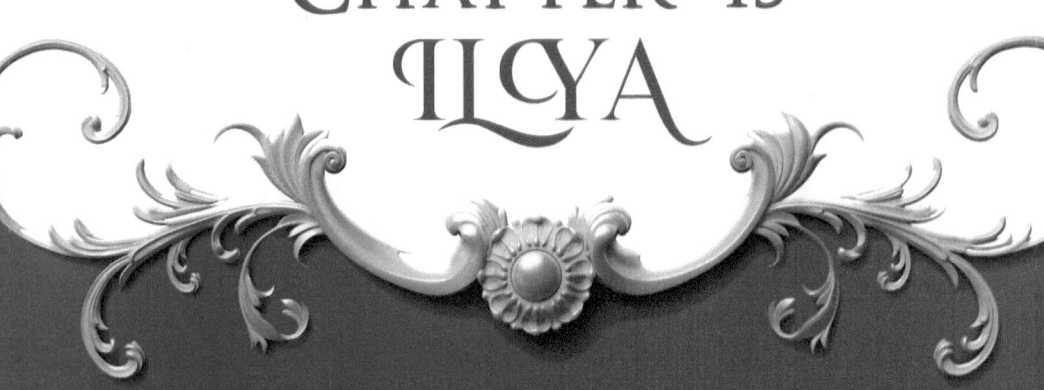

Drizzling rain splattered onto my face as the troop of guards led Fernand and I from the castle the next morning. The dark skies blocked out much of the sun, as if the Gods and Goddesses themselves were displeased with the day's events.

Gooseflesh rose over my skin as a cold wind whipped straight through the damp and dirty dress hanging about my form. I wouldn't look like the heiress of Sorrena today, not with dirt from the cell marring my clothes and skin. I couldn't begin to imagine the mess of my hair, especially as another breeze whipped strands across my face.

Fernand managed to look worse, with his slumped shoulders and head hung in defeat. Did he have no pride left at all?

"Hurry it up," the woman in charge ordered. "They await us already."

With the sun missing, time was near impossible to distinguish, but our destination was not. We'd left through a low, back gate leading to the outer yard. Yellowed stalks of grass fluttered along the worn pathways as we advanced toward the same arena where Ryszard punished Gabriel and Fernand before. But unlike then, I'd be the center of attention.

Would Lucien dole out punishment to me as well? Would he mock me about how he'd drag my sister here to Zhine as further punishment for breaking my oath to him? The thought stole the last of my warmth and sent my teeth chattering despite myself. His bangle still ringed my upper arm—an oversight, surely, one that wouldn't last if he was involved. What would his magic show me? How could any fear be worse than the present?

Figures moved in the stands as we approached, taking their places around the central box, the only section fully shielded from the elements with a covering. Beyond, colorful trees relinquished their leaves to the biting wind and rain.

Each step advanced us toward a destiny I could no longer avoid.

Guards bound my wrists to a metal ring sticking up from the ground in one half of the arena, the one Gabriel had occupied weeks ago. All the while, I searched for the faces I needed to see. They were easy enough to find—so different from the soldiers who occupied most of the stands and the few nobles who crowded near Ryszard within his box, poorly sheltered from the rain.

Reyna and Elin sat side by side, their faces etched with sorrow. Gabriel occupied the space on Elin's other side. His arm wrapped around her for support was likely the only thing preventing a teary collapse. Even Derrin, the smug bastard whose city-state had willingly joined the empire and who always seemed to enjoy his time residing in Zhine, bore a deep frown where he sat between the twins, Theo and Titus, an arm around each one, holding them tight.

The guards retreated as the shackles locked me into place, the twin of Fernand, who'd been similarly leashed on the opposite end of the oval. They hadn't bothered with the ring of fire on this miserable day.

The crowd grew quiet as Ryszard stood. His voice pierced the wind, droning on and on about the world he hoped to create and how terrible we were for disrupting his peace and shunning his hospitality. Another vulgar attempt to show his power and rally those who still followed him.

The words vanished from my mind as soon as they entered. Instead, I focused on the faces in the crowd—all those except for Orson and Kasida, who stood sentinel in front of Ryszard's box. Other captains hovered in my periphery, but not the one the fragments of my traitorous heart still hoped to see.

"Lies! All of it lies!"

The ragged shout pulled me back to the moment. My head whipped to the side just in time to see Fernand jerk at his bonds and spit in the direction of the emperor's box.

"He's a great deceiver. A joke of an emperor who conquers for his own entertainment."

Gasps and murmurs floated on the wind, but none bold enough to drown out his tirade.

Stop. Please stop. Didn't he know his words would do no good? Not here.

"Nothing will be enough to satiate his lusts. Not the next city nor the one after that. How many will die for his pride? Are you all willing to die for him? For nothing?"

Flames licked up in a circle around Fernand. A warning. Steam rose from the fire as it battled against the rain. Metal rang clear through the air as Orson drew a sword and advanced. Kasida freed her twin short swords and slid into a pose resembling a cat ready to pounce.

"Stop."

Ryszard's command was clear. Absolute. But it was not aimed at the man still slinging accusations his way.

I held my breath as he descended the stairs from his box to the ground, ignoring the rain that pelted his crowned head and fur-trimmed clothes. He didn't flinch as his boots and the hem of his heavy cloak settled into the mud.

"He'll bring poverty and death to you all, mark my words," Fernand shouted. "A curse upon us all!"

Fernand... Rope dug into my arms as I tugged against my bindings, unable to move farther than their short stretch allowed.

Ryszard held out his hand to Orson, a look passing between them. The flames vanished. In a breath, Orson flipped his sword into the air, catching the blade in his armored hand. With a bow of his head, he passed the hilt to his emperor.

He took it, showing more strength than I expected from his seasoned form as he entered the arena.

Terror gripped me. For Fernand. For myself. Bile surged up my throat at the certainty of the scene about to unfold. My heart pounded as I looked at my friends in the stands.

Elin buried her face in Gabriel's chest, but he didn't look away from the scene. Nor did Reyna, whose face paled fainter than the twin moons. Derrin actively turned the boys away. I might thank him for that one day, if I got the chance.

Blood dripped from Fernand's wrists as he continued to pull against his own bindings. His hoarse voice turned shrill, raising the hair on the back of my neck. "Rebels rise against him! Join them! End this!"

Metal sliced through the rain as I slammed my eyes shut.

My knees hit the ground.

A scream ended in deadly silence.

Another thump.

A grunt left the emperor as the blade hacked its way home.

Tears stung my eyes and trickled down my face, joining the rain. No one spoke. No sobs. No cheers. Nothing. As if the whole world ceased to breathe and only the cold rain remembered to fall.

Would I be next? A blade in my neck?

Shaking gasps racked my body as I cracked open my eyes.

Ryszard stared down at Fernand's headless corpse. Blood and tissue dripped from the blade at his side as nature attempted to clear away evidence of the brutal execution.

Abruptly, the rain slowed. Even the Gods and Goddesses did not wish to wash away the stain of this event from the ground.

Ryszard jammed the point of the sword into the muddy soil and turned from his deeds. "Clear away this mess."

I gagged as the full scene came into view and I looked away. The emperor's captains rushed to obey. Murmurs picked up again, more audible now that the rain had slowed to a misty drizzle. A few guards rose to their feet and headed for the edge of the stands.

"Take your seats," Ryszard commanded. "We're not done yet."

A shiver racked my body.

He still meant to punish me.

The sound of someone approaching from behind dried my tears in an instant. I wouldn't let them see me cry. I wouldn't—

My breath hitched as I twisted toward the footsteps. I'd have fallen if I wasn't already crouching in the mud.

The last of the rain slid down Lucien's armor as he strode across the arena. When the tips of his boots nearly touched my knees, he finally stopped, staring down at me as I craned my neck toward the grey sky above.

"Have you come to kill me?" The words croaked out rough, almost strangled.

He knelt before me, drawing near until I could practically taste the indifference radiating off him. "Did you take the letter from my room?"

I forced myself to look at him, though I couldn't halt the quivering of my lips. "Yes." What did it matter now?

A flash of something crossed his eyes, too quick to catch.

"But I regret it."

"It's too late for regrets, Ilya."

I dropped my head to stare at the mud. Far too late. Didn't I know it?

"Execution isn't what's proposed for you." His voice was vacant, colder than the rain that chilled my skin.

"Torture then?" I bit my lip, holding in the emotions threatening to rip me apart as I dared to look at him once more.

One quick nod. "Just like last time we were here."

Lucien grasped my arm, right over the bangle he'd gifted me, one I still wore every day. I swallowed, bracing for the metal to be ripped from my arm.

Instead, he stood, drawing me shakily to my feet.

"It's what they expect."

He dropped his arm and stepped back, his gift still in place.

Oh, Lucien.

I wouldn't see his magic, would never know the horrors he'd warp for others to see. New tears sprung to my eyes, but this time I didn't blink them away. These were for Lucien, so he would know what words could not say.

He found it in himself to spare me pain, even with my sins laid bare and confessed for only his ears to hear.

"Get on with it!" Ryszard called from the stands, annoyance clear in his voice.

"It's what they expect," Lucien said again. His gaze locked with mine, still cold and hard but sending a message as clear as he could.

Ryszard expected him to punish me, torture me. I'd need to act accordingly. Somehow.

I lunged backward, widening the distance between us until the ropes around my wrists pulled tight again, digging into my skin. I filled my expression with a mix of real and assumed terror at the magic to come. Whatever reason Lucien had to spare me from the brunt of his power, it didn't mean things were right between us. They might never be again.

Lucien stretched his hand toward me, palm up. "What do you fear?" He raised his voice, loud enough to be heard by others. "Let's see, shall we?"

Give me a sign. Tell me what to do.

"Sorrena's destruction," Lucien said. His voice held a hint of mirth, as it might if he truly wished me to suffer. "Of course."

I thrashed against my bindings, pretending to struggle against the scene I could not see.

Gasps and murmurs of those in attendance let me know that magic flowed before us, painting a scene as real and visceral as if they stood inside it themselves.

"No!" I cried for the benefit of the crowd. "Stop it!" The ropes around my wrists abraded my skin as I pulled against them, struggling to retreat from the imagined scene around me.

Someone in the audience screamed. Others shifted in their seats.

Real memories swamped me like a wave over the bow of a boat. The men dying on the fields had been far from me, seen at a distance rather than up close. But I'd never forget the distant glow of flames and the sickening smoke that even the sea breeze couldn't push away fast enough. On that horrible day, I'd wished to take up a sword and stand with my people—even if I ended up as one of the dead or dying.

My knees wobbled from the memories Lucien stirred up. How much horror would I experience if I could see the illusions he wrought? I thrashed against the ropes again and slipped in the muck. Pain raced up my arm as I fell to the ground. I didn't bother to rise, letting the memories drag me down into the mud.

"Please," I sobbed.

I dug my fingers into the ground, begging as I waited for the torture to end.

"Perhaps you'll think before abusing our emperor's hospitality in the future," Lucien raged. "Or mine."

The last comment had my shoulders hunching further, as if I could sink through the ground away from them all. Retreating footsteps squished through the mud. His magical show must have run its course.

I'd yet to rise when another captain approached from behind. I raised my head just in time to see Brishon circle around and crouch in front of me. His form blocked my view of Ryszard's box and most of the stands on either side.

"Scream when I touch you," he whispered, pulling at his glove.

"What?" My brows scrunched together. Pity from Lucien I could almost understand, but from another captain?

"Scream like you're on fire."

He grabbed my wrist, and I did as he commanded, letting my voice screech like never before, shill and terrible.

Brishon released me and turned without a word, ignoring the

discarded woman he'd supposedly just filled with pain. I made a show of it, gripping my arm where he had and letting myself rock back into the mud. He must have known about the bracelet and its protection, yet he, too, spared me.

As the guards hauled me to my feet and unchained me from the metal ring, Ryszard began to spout more lies. Poison for the ears and the mind.

Before they pulled me away, I hazarded one last look at my friends—and wished I hadn't. Whatever they'd seen told a story on their faces I'd remember long after this day.

CHAPTER 46
LUCIEN

Warren, Zurina, Brishon, and I huddled in a tight circle, a few loyal guards keeping watch nearby. The edge of the forest cloaked us in shadow. Across the training fields, moonlight touched the castle spires, disappearing into the glow emanating from various windows. We'd slipped out one by one before dinner—the first chance we'd had after the events in the arena this afternoon.

"This is getting out of hand," Zurina exclaimed, pacing back and forth. "Killing another of his honored guests? We must act now."

Her words slipped through my mind like water. Ilya consumed my thoughts. She'd stolen from me. Admitted it. But that look in her eyes nearly slew me on the spot. What wouldn't she do to help her people? Nothing. And I knew that, no matter how sharply her betrayal cut.

You didn't tell her you had a plan either. My conscious taunted me.

"Yes, but we must be smart about this." Warren's crossed arms gave away his anxiety despite the level tone of his voice. "They'll send his body back to his people tomorrow. One of us can volunteer for that mission. Use it as a distraction to get the word out."

Ilya must think me a monster now. One who threw her in a cell and condemned her to torture, even if it was less severe than what the emperor believed occurred. The way her body shook when she sobbed in the muck and the crack of her voice wasn't all an act—it couldn't have been.

"You think they'll let us?" Brishon scoffed. "We aren't exactly favorites anymore."

"Then we won't give them a choice," Zurina said, voice fervent. "I'll arrange a troop of guards tonight and leave at first light. Once I'm away from the castle, I can send out my animals to the rebels with messages for them. I need to be somewhere I can focus on the use of my magic without being questioned."

"Can you do so many at once?" Brishon asked.

"I must try. The more time I have to focus and connect with my beasts, the better."

Warren placed a hand on her arm, drawing her to a halt. "We need to think about getting people out first," Warren said. "Any guards loyal to us, servants, and especially the hostages. The emperor will kill them all if he thinks the city-states are in open rebellion. I can't lo—" He dropped his arms, cutting his gaze to the castle. "We can't let that happen."

"Right. Lucien?" Zurina smacked my shoulder.

All eyes were on me as I came back to the moment. The dappled glow of the twin moons glinted off polished armor as I looked from one ally to the next in our tight circle.

"Doubting us now, brother?" Brishon asked.

I shook myself, trying to free the shackles of memory that tried to suck me down into the wooded darkness.

"No. Never." Resolve strengthened me.

"We need you here." Zurina grasped my upper arm. "Only with all of us together do we have a chance."

I nodded. "I'm here." However difficult, I shoved thoughts of Ilya away from my mind.

Zurina gave me another pat and a sharp nod of her head.

"Many of the guards here are uneasy after today," Brishon said, gesturing back toward the castle. "I can send a few loyal to me to our training camp to the west and the scouting teams near the Marsali border. They can spread our truth and the events of today before rumors twist them."

"Send them tonight," I said. "It will give them an extra head start in case their absence is noted."

He nodded. "Hopefully, we can rally some to our cause. Or at least keep them from the battlefield to come."

I turned to Zurina. "These rebels of yours, how long will they take to assemble?"

"A few days to spread the word? It will take my animals time to travel with the message, and I don't know how quickly the rebels can be ready to move. The nearest ones may be able to advance upon the castle here before we'd be expected to return from delivering Fernand's body, but it'll be close."

We planned to bring the rebels to us. Once they arrived, we'd find a way to deliver the emperor to them as a hostage. It wouldn't be clean. Not with Orson and the others still on his side, but it was the fastest way to victory.

No, the fastest would be to assassinate him. Despite all he'd done, I shuddered at the thought of slitting his throat or asking another of us to do it. He'd been the only father we'd known for most of our lives.

The rebels could take him into their custody to await a trial among the city-states. There hadn't been one in generations, but Zurina said it was something the rebels hoped to change. If they'd worked together to begin with, if they'd collaborated, they never would have been so vulnerable to our conquest. If a trial would soothe some of the wounds of war, so be it.

"When the emperor realizes you've left without his authority or the authority of his first, he'll send his troops after you," I said.

"You're still our first, whatever he says," she replied.

Warren nodded along.

A kind sentiment, but not one that helped.

"Besides," she continued, "that'll help us. The fewer soldiers here, the easier it will be for you all and the rebels to seize control. I'll find a place to rest and focus my magic before I circle back to you all."

"And if he grows suspicious of us before the rebels arrive?" Brishon asked.

"We'll think of something." I had no idea, but these few believed in me. Their lives depended on it. I would—

Rustling leaves snagged my attention as a group of guards rushed toward us. Zurina reached for her sword. Magic hummed in the air.

"Wait." I threw out my hand, halting my companions. Ajax, one of the loyal guards who stood watch outside my quarters, led a cluster of men and women.

"Captain." The boy saluted. "Er...Captains," he stammered, face flushed. He swallowed and looked between them, an uneasy, wild look flashing in his eyes.

"What is it?" Brishon demanded.

"It's Captain Orson. A member of our squadron overheard him during dinner. He plans to...well, he hinted that he might..."

"Spit it out," I urged.

"He mentioned paying a visit to Lady Ilya in the cells tonight."

A stillness more absolute than the mirror lake to the north overtook me. All at once, the world rushed back, accompanied by a blazing fire hotter than the Goddess's bonfires those weeks ago. "I'll kill him."

I shoved past the guards, not seeing their faces as I homed in on the castle battlements beyond.

Orson, you'll pay for this one. If one hair on her head is—

"Wait!" Warren grabbed my arm, but I shook him off without a thought.

"Stop!" Brishon circled in front of me, blocking my path and pushing me backward. "She's just one woman. You can't—"

My fist crashed into his jaw, sending the other man reeling. "I can't let him touch her."

Zurina whistled.

Brishon groaned and shook his head. "I know you want her, but this is madness. You don't even know what he plans."

"Nothing good," I fumed, staring at my fellow captains in turn. Whatever Orson had in mind wouldn't be pleasant. He already didn't like Ilya, and he'd likely be even more cruel to her on account of my regard. "I'm saving her. Now. We'll move up our plans. Act tonight. We'll flee. Meet up with the rebels and—"

"I understand, I'll see to it," Zurina promised. Her gaze locked with mine, the sister of my heart who understood me well. "Save her, we'll handle the rest."

"I'll go for the other hostages. They'll suspect me the least," Warren said.

Zurina nodded at me once, solid and sure.

Without another glance, I took off at a run toward the castle, the footsteps of my companions close behind.

Holy Four, let me make it in time.

CHAPTER 47
ILYA

Despair rippled under my skin. I shivered against the rough stone walls of my cell. Though water dripped from my dress and hair to puddle among the stones, my clothing refused to dry.

This section of the dungeon remained empty—except for me. The guards didn't bother to patrol its length, favoring the warmth and light of the central room instead. Those comforts lingered out of reach through the door at the end of the hall.

Only hard bread and water awaited me in my cell, though somewhere nearby a mouse occasionally squeaked and scratched.

Ryszard killed him. He'd actually done it. My heart ached for Fernand and the wife and child who would never see him again. Would the emperor demand they join us soon? A new pair of hostages in their loved one's place?

Most likely, though whether I'd be above ground to see them remained unclear. And Lucien...

You spared me pain to leave me here? My heart twisted.

Hinges groaned, echoing down the hall.

I scooted toward the narrow stretch of metal bars running floor to ceiling beside the similarly wrought door to my cell. Light flooded in as the far door swung open, causing me to squint against the blaze. My breath caught in my throat as a figure took shape in the doorway at the end of the hall—one wearing gleaming armor.

Lucien.

My heart cried out to him.

And then shriveled in terror.

No deer antlers grazed the top of the threshold. Two small bumps rose up on either side of a tall captain's helm—bear ears.

Orson.

The scraps of bread in my stomach rebelled as I lurched back into the darkness of my cell. Oh, to have a knife or to be blessed by one of The Four. How had they seen fit to gift their talents to one such as him while bypassing so many of us completely?

Whistles, like beckons for a hound, snaked down the hallway, accompanied by heavy footsteps. Rock dug into my back as I squirmed into the darkness.

A fruitless effort.

"Where are you little mouse?" Orson laughed as his bulk came into view. The flames of the torch he carried jumped and danced as he settled it into an empty sconce outside my cell. "There you are." His leering gaze raked over my skin. "Must be unpleasant stuck in that cold and dirty cell."

I cocked an eyebrow at him, displaying all the indifferent confidence I didn't feel.

Orson jingled the ring of keys in his hand, holding them up in the dim light. "Want out? I could take you back to my quarters."

"No thank you," I bit out. I'd take the cell over him any day. Rotting away down here would be better than whatever awaited me in his rooms.

"You sure? I'd warm you up real nice."

When I didn't respond, he began thumbing through the keys until he stopped on one and moved toward the door. "My quarters are nicer than Lucien's, you know. He never could appreciate the finer things in life. But I bet you do, don't you, pet?"

"I am not your pet."

"Not yet." The door unlocked with a sickening click.

My blood tingled in my veins as I pushed to my feet against the wall, letting my body go loose and languid like the wrestlers who performed during the growing season games in Sorrena.

He flung the door wide and gestured to the opening he half-occupied. "This is your way out, right here."

"I'm not going anywhere with you." Never. Orson wouldn't have me easily. I'd claw out his eyes, gouge grooves in his armor with my bare fingers—anything to keep his lecherous hands off me.

"You spread those pretty legs for Lucien but not for me?"

These words hit me worse than a slap in the face and had me rocking back on my heels. Would he have told this monster such intimate details?

Orson rushed forward without warning and shoved me against the wall. A sharp rock dug into my back, eliciting a hiss of pain.

"Come on. Be a good little pet."

I kicked at his legs and higher, earning bruises and pain for myself and no more than a whisper of a groan from the brute pinning my shoulders into the stone. My heart raced faster than a horse at full gallop.

With one hand, he yanked off his helm, revealing a face comelier than I expected but tainted by the wretchedness within. No amount of fair features could compensate for the twisted smirk, sick leer, or putrid soul that lay below the surface.

Stinking breath wafted across my face as I clawed ineffectually toward his eyes. The bones in my hand cried out as he crushed them to the wall near my head, grunting his frustration as his body pressed against mine.

But my distraction worked.

I slid my other hand down his side, just far enough to reach the dagger belted around his waist that he'd neglected to remove.

Aurora, Goddess of Dawn, keep my aim true.

In a rush, I pulled the knife and slid the tip up, letting it scrape against his armor until it found a narrow join and slid home.

"Bitch!"

The back of his hand slammed into my cheek. My scream split the air. A myriad of stars and colors swarmed my vision. Breath left me as my body crashed onto the stone floor. Lances of pain radiated up my shoulder, my back, my head.

"You'll pay," he fumed.

The air around me heated in a rush. Flames licked out from his palm, brighter than the dawn as they roared toward me. I screeched and raised an arm to shield my face—a pitiful defense. Fire licked at me in small lashes of pain but did not catch. My hair did not char to ash, nor did my skin blacken to coals. Blood trailed down Orson's side as I stared him down through a wall of rushing orange and yellow.

"Impossible."

His image shifted into a snarl as he spied the bangle upon my upper arm. Flame receded in a heartbeat. Orson grabbed the metal and pulled. The clasp scraped across my skin as he relieved me of Lucien's gift and hurled it behind him.

The clatter and scrape of the bracelet bounding along the stones sealed my fate. Orson stepped back, his palm raised, ready to deliver his flames. I braced for fire. For death, or worse, shutting my eyes against the inevitable fate.

"What? How?" he muttered.

I cracked open my eyes. Instead of flames, a wall of thick tree trunks greeted me, their rough bark and leafy limbs blocking all view of the man beyond. Loamy soil cleansed the air, replacing the acrid, burnt scent of moments ago. My body reclined on leaf-strewn soil instead of stone.

Lucien.

My chin wobbled. Who else could make a forest appear from nowhere?

Metal screeched. Something crashed against and rattled the bars hidden from my view.

"If you've harmed her..."

My traitorous heart leaped at the voice I'd longed to hear. He came. Despite all that happened, he came when I needed him most.

"Come for your whore?" Orson sneered. Metal scraped against stone, setting my teeth on edge. "Don't think our emperor won't hear about this."

A clash of swords rang in the air beyond the illusion, accompanied by grunts, the shuffling of feet, and scrapes on stone.

"Fool! I'll rut her over your corpse," Orson yelled.

Lucien's trees blocked all sight of their scuffle, and the sounds were not enough to discern advantage. *I must do something. If Orson wins this duel...*

I yelped as orange flame licked through the illusion of trees. The heat tickled my skin.

My bruised body ached in protest as I pushed to my feet. I lurched toward the thick trunks surrounding me like a cage, but my mind rebelled, seeing a tree as real as any that grew outdoors. I could almost feel the rough bark under my fingertips. No wonder men went mad from the illusions Lucien wrought on the battlefield.

A heavy thud hit the ground, accompanied by a groan I couldn't distinguish.

My heart constricted in terror.

"No!" I leaped through the trees.

The forest vanished.

Strong arms caught me as I stumbled.

I didn't look, didn't think, as I pulled the thin blade sheathed at the man's side. With a twist of my body, I had the point of the blade under the chin of the captain before me.

"Ilya."

Lucien's voice broke the dam of emotions I'd held back. The knife in my hand wobbled. "Lucien." Tears streamed down my face. Relief, but also hurt. "You...you let them take me."

His chin raised as the point pushed against his helm.

"I did. I couldn't stop them, but I'm here now." His gaze searched me inside and out.

"You came."

"Almost too late. I..."

I dropped the blade. It clattered to the ground near Orson's prone form as Lucien pulled me into his arms. The wounds on my body made themselves known again, throbbing with pain.

I'd betrayed him, and he still came.

"There's so much to tell you, but we must get out of here. Now."

"Is he..."

"With any luck, he will be soon."

My lips thinned. "Where's that dagger, I'll—"

"We have to get out of the castle." Lucien grabbed my hand and tugged me the other way.

I gaped as I followed him down the corridor, ignoring the protests of my body. *Out of the castle.* "We're running?"

A huff of laughter shook his chest. "Or face the execution block."

Because of me. Because of what I'd done. It wasn't just my life I'd risked, but so many more.

His controlled expression broke as he looked back at me over one shoulder. "You're hurt."

"I'm fine," I lied.

"Don't hide your wounds from me." Before I could argue, he lifted me into his arms. Though I sensed he tried to be gentle, sharp pain raced through my chest and arm. Something somewhere might be broken, but I pushed the agony away, concentrating on his words.

"I can't leave my friends behind."

"Warren's getting them now." Lucien strode through the door adjacent the end of the hallway.

His words did little to calm my nerves. "How will we get out of here?"

He halted in the vacant guard room just long enough to snag a heavy blanket. Whatever guards may have been there had been sent away. By Orson or Lucien, I didn't know.

"Trust me," Lucien said, carefully tucking the blanket around my sullied form in his arms. "I'll explain everything. Hopefully, you will too."

My chest tightened. "I was an idiot. A fool." I shook my head. "I didn't mean to hurt you. Never you."

He nodded once—acknowledgement, if not yet forgiveness.

"Tell me once we're free."

CHAPTER 48
LUCIEN

Too late.

I'd almost been too late.

At the barest glimpse of Ilya crumpled on the floor with Orson looming over her, I'd lost it. Magic leaped from my skin, weaving a wall of protection more vivid and real than anything I'd willingly conjured. A quick, clean death would have been too easy for him, though I admired Ilya for her determination to deliver it. Part of me yearned for him to bleed out slowly, painfully—if he regained consciousness at all. Another couldn't forget the boy he'd once been. A thorn in my side, an ass, but a brother too. In the end, I left his fate to The Four.

I stared at Ilya—finally back in my arms—as I carried her through the winding halls of the castle. A bubble of illusion hid us from sight, though sound was another matter. If I went too fast, her eyes closed and her lips thinned in pain; yet no matter how my steps jostled her, she never cried out. I tried to block the noise of my armor with magic, but it was imperfect at best. Quizzical glances crossed the faces of several guards. None of them had discovered us yet, but I didn't expect it to last.

Slow. Careful. *By The Four, let us make it to the stables before someone sounds an alarm.*

I didn't want to fight our way out, to kill these men and women and risk Ilya in the process. My arms ached. Each breath sent a twinge of pain along my ribs, a parting gift from Orson. I nearly sighed as Ajax came into view, waiting by the back entrance near the stables as planned. He paled as I let my illusion fall away.

"The horses? Supplies?" I asked.

"In progress, Captain," Ajax stammered.

"The others?"

Ilya tensed, looking as anxious as I felt.

"They should be back soon." His attention flicked to Ilya. "Can she ride?"

"Of course I can," she insisted, though her voice lacked the bite and fire that normally accompanied it.

"We snagged a few tonics from the storeroom just in case," Ajax said.

"Bring me one," I ordered as we slipped into the dark stables attached to the lower level of the castle. The scent of hay and horses washed over us. As he'd said, the mares were mounted and ready— several bearing saddles, others bearing bags of food and supplies. The men had worked quick, carrying out the instructions I'd barked on our run to the castle with more expert precision than I'd imagined.

Brishon emerged from the shadows to join us. "I sent a few men around to the other side to gather more supplies."

"And if they get caught?" I asked.

"Pray they don't, brother, or we'll be living off this lot until we can find a safe haven." He gestured to the encumbered horses. "I'll join them now and see what I can do to smooth our passage."

"You're all running?" Ilya looked between us, her brows scrunched.

"If it were all of us, we might not need to run," Brishon answered.

No, if we had all the captains on our side, we wouldn't even need the rebels.

Brishon looked toward the door we'd entered through. "Speaking of...Orson?"

"Out of commission." Perhaps I should have killed him, saved him from suffering instead of letting him die the slow death he deserved.

Brishon paused before finally responding, "Nasty business, but it had to be done."

He turned without another word and headed toward the back exit. They'd been close friends once. We all had.

"Tell me what's going on," Ilya insisted.

I settled her on a bale of hay. "No patience at all?" I teased.

She frowned.

"I wish I knew what you planned in that head of yours, but if you were hoping to aid the rebels, you've won."

Her eyes widened. I'd hit the truth, or at least, close to it.

"Though this could have gone a lot smoother if you'd given me time," I confided. "When the emperor handed me that letter you'd stolen—" Gods, it nearly ripped me apart. The sting of her betrayal was worse than the pain of Brishon's poisoned touch.

She opened her mouth, but I halted her words with a finger to her lips.

"It gutted me, Ilya. Not only that I'd lost you, and I thought we'd lost our chance, but for a time I believed I never had you at all." Believing that her passion had been an act was many times worse than her theft. "That is, until the arena."

The tears streaking down her face almost choked me. Everything I'd planned to say vanished.

"I should have told you the truth. I tried to that last night, but if I'd gambled wrong..."

"I know." I crouched in front of her, drawing close. "Or I'm starting to."

Soon. Soon I could get the last of her truth, and clarity on the pieces I assumed but could not fully resolve.

Ajax coughed, drawing my attention as he held out a stoppered stone vial. I took it with thanks.

"You'll need to drink this." I passed it to Ilya. "Two swallows at least, or you won't be fit to ride." With any luck, the tonic would knock her out completely. Grime and dried mud covered her clothes and matted her hair. Bruises bloomed on her skin, and undoubtedly there were numerous wounds I couldn't see. She'd been brave, holding in her pain as we slowly traversed the halls. Even now, she didn't seem to spare a care for her own well-being.

She frowned at the concoction but did not object. "Why flee? Why not just kill him in his sleep? End this?"

He'd raised us, trained us, given us a home—perhaps after taking our first one away. Yet we'd still discussed that. "The emperor has his own means of magical protection. Blindly attempting to break into his quarters wouldn't go over well," I said. "Still, we...when I heard about what Orson planned to do to you..." I shook my head.

"I messed things up again." She looked away.

I took her delicate face in my hands until she finally looked at me. Even with all she'd been through, her beauty shone through. Not outer beauty, but that inner strength that drew me in long before I realized it. "We'll find a way. Join with the—"

The doors flew open again. Noise and commotion rose as bodies filed into the stables, agitating the horses.

Zurina stalked across the enclosed space, nearly tripping over a guard who bolted out of her way. "We need to move."

Her clipped words drew my attention. I skimmed the assembled, looking for signs of trouble and counting the faces present. Warren. The hostages. Guards we trusted. "What's happened?"

She fisted her hand on her hip. "One of our *honored guests*, Lord Derrin, asked too many questions. I couldn't trust him, so I knocked him out and left him. Plus, we had to tell too many lies to get here. It's only a matter of time before someone reports to one of the other captains, or worse, the emperor himself. If that happens before we get out, we're done for." She shook her head.

Fuck. No need to explain to the threats I knew all too well. Derrin wasn't a loss. He liked living in Zhine from what I'd seen. The emperor would likely spare him.

Elin crouched near Ilya. She checked over her wounds, making exclamations of concern.

Zurina stepped between us, demanding my attention once again. "I'm taking Fernand's body now. You all can leave during the distraction."

"Wait!" Reyna latched onto Zurina's arm. "You're not coming with us?"

Zurina's eyes softened; even her form lost some of its rigidity. "Someone must get word to the rebels. I'm in the best position to do that, and they won't come after me once they realize you all are gone."

"And if you run into trouble?" Reyna framed her hands on her hips. "I'm coming with you."

"Not a chance," Zurina replied. "You're going with the others. If anything happens to me, they'll need someone who knows the rebel locations."

Reyna pursed her lips and stared down my companion with the same fire that Ilya often showed me. Zurina mentioned recently that the two were close. I'd had no idea—I'd missed it so thoroughly in the times I'd seen them together. How long had I lived with my fellow captains, guided them, without ever knowing their hearts? Zurina. Warren. Only recently had I learned their secrets, yet I should have known. My role as their first had consumed me. I'd missed a connection with the very people I'd led and loved.

Never again.

I laid a hand on Reyna's shoulder. "Zurina knows what she's doing. She'll find us."

Her gaze flitted between us before she let out a dramatic breath. "And where will she find us?"

"They'll expect us to go to a neighboring city-state, to seek refuge there among allies. That's what I'd expect."

The women nodded.

"Merrowind Manor," Zurina said.

The home of our youth. Where we'd trained, learned, and become the weapons the emperor needed. It had been abandoned long years, but the structure was well-built, the land expansive. It was so clear now. So obvious. I prided myself on games and strategy, yet I'd been so consumed with my role that I missed the moves the emperor played to get me into it.

"There are rebels camped just to the south, or they should be," she continued. "I'll send a bird with a message as soon as I can."

"Do it." I stared at Zurina. "Circle back as soon as you can and join us. Order the other rebel camps to meet there too. We'll end this where it all began."

CHAPTER 49
ILYA

The air grew colder the higher we trekked into the hills. Not even the lined cloak around my shoulders could fully keep the chill at bay, especially once the misty drizzle started up again for the second time since we left Zhine. I hugged my arms around myself as the grey-and-white patched horse followed the old path through the pines.

I'd missed much of our initial flight thanks to the effects of a healing tonic, but the days since had been solemn at best. According to Lucien, our party had split upon leaving the castle, taking different paths to aid in masking our flight. Out here in the wilderness, we kept as quiet as possible, stopping only when necessary to find relief for ourselves or the horses. Nights consisted of cold bread eaten on an equally cold ground, the damp chill seeping into our bones. Fire was too risky.

At least no one had caught up to us. Yet.

I only prayed the others fared as well. The twins rode with our party. Elin, Reyna, and Gabriel travelled with Warren and his group of guards. I yearned to see them, to make sure they were alright. If anything happened to them on our journey, I wouldn't forgive myself. It was my foolish actions that had gotten me thrown into the cells and ignited this hasty flight.

Lucien circled back, passing down our line of horses from his place at the front. "We should be nearing the rebel camp. I believe we can make it before nightfall."

His gaze held mine, a thousand words passing between us other than what he said. We needed to talk, but there was no privacy here, and sneaking away was too risky. Soon. Soon we could discuss it all.

The sun had already begun its slide down the sky. It cast its rays at an angle through the tree branches, creating a haphazard pattern of light and shadow against the underbrush. Suddenly, part of a tree detached from itself. No. Not a tree. A man.

"Lucien!" I cried.

He whirled. The horse reared and startled at the sudden jerk of the reins. More figures moved in the underbrush, crossbows raised toward our party. Fear strangled me like a noose as my grip on the reins tightened.

Before I could take in the look of the attackers, solid stone walls surrounded us. I gasped at the sudden change. Lucien pulled his sword, angling his horse between me and the woods. Metal rang as his guards followed suit.

"Stop or we'll shoot!" called a gruff, male voice.

"We don't want to harm the young ones," another said.

"Name yourselves," Lucien said.

"Cease your magic," the first called back.

Lucien held firm. We'd get nowhere like this.

"Are you friends of Zurina? Her birds?" I asked. If they were the emperor's men, they wouldn't understand my meaning.

The snort of horses filled the heavy silence. I waited for an arrow to whiz by or a man to charge through Lucien's wall of illusions. Instead, a hesitant, female voice called back. "Yes. We are a mighty flock."

Lucien let the illusion fall. At least a dozen men and women stood in a crescent around us. Others occupied spaces between the dense pines and blocked the road ahead. Simple clothes, dyed in browns and greens, adorned their bodies. No official colors or uniforms marked them. The rebels. It had to be. The closest, who advanced on us down the dirt path, wore a leather breastplate covering his chest. Greasy, dark hair hung long around a dirt-smeared face.

"We've come to find you," Lucien replied, clearly coming to the same conclusion I did.

"Kill us, more like." The lead man spit on the ground.

I reared back. "Did you not get Zurina's message?" Had she been unable to send it? Did it not yet arrive?

"Oh, we got it. But that one"—he pointed to Lucien—"turning on the emperor? I think not."

My lips thinned. "I'm Lady Ilya Valerious of Sorrena, and I vouch for him. We come as friends."

The rebel stared us down. A woman, perhaps the one who'd spoken, stepped in front of the man. "Ignore him," she said. "I believe you. Though perhaps you'd lower your weapons?"

Lucien and I shared a look. *Please.*

Though armor concealed much of his features, I could almost read the indecision etched there. We couldn't have a fight out here in the woods, not if we planned to join with the rebels. Not to mention they outnumbered us. At length, he sheathed his sword, the others following suit. The rebels, in turn, lowered their weapons as well.

"Good. I'll lead you to the camp," the woman said.

The man frowned. "If you turn on us, we'll send your head to the emperor with his." He pointed to Lucien.

I held in a sigh. Of course, they wouldn't all forgive Lucien's actions, not with his history, but the open hostility didn't bode well. We might have as much to fear from our would-be friends as our foes.

WE WERE LED FARTHER into the hills. The sky turned from bright blue to bold orange, fading into dark azure. A flicker of flames danced on the ground beyond far trees. Their camp.

Calls like off-tune bird songs rang through the air to join the natural creatures of the forest and the crunch of our trek along the overgrown path. Through a break in the foliage, I spied crude tents arranged in a clearing with the fire. Various people wove around them like fish in the reef. Beyond, a stone structure rose up in the distance. Its woodwork was tinted green with either moss or mold. The last rays of sunset trailed up the building, landing on a roof bearing its own patch of yellowing underbrush.

The whistling calls ceased as men and women flocked our way. Curious glances crawled across my skin. Whispers tickled my ears.

"Let me through!"

I gasped at the familiar voice, scanning for the sight of its owner. Men and women stepped aside as a tanned, dark-haired man pushed through the crowd to us. It was hard to be certain, but that hooked nose, the angle of his chin...

"Nyke!" I cried.

Our captain of the guard in Sorrena.

All at once I was home, his voice ringing in the council chamber as he discussed governance with Mother or critiqued my skill as he provided me secret lessons in combat. We'd thought him dead in the battle, lost in the sea of bodies we'd burned in a mass funeral.

He drew to a halt, stiff and straight. "Lady Ilya?" It was him—not an illusion.

"I'm so glad." I slid from the horse. My vision blurred as I blinked away threatening tears.

He pulled me into his arms in a fatherly embrace. "It's true. We were so concerned it was some kind of trick, that maybe Zurina had been forced to send a false message. But you're here." He released me, his gaze sliding past me to take in the rest of our company. His eyes narrowed.

Nyke turned me away from Lucien. "You really think we can trust that one?" he whispered.

"Yes. I'd stake my life on it."

His brows rose, head tilting to the side.

"And you'll need his help to defeat the emperor," I said.

Nyke nodded slowly. Leave it to a military man to be swayed by battle advantage. "There's more to your words, I think, but tell me later." Turning away, he spoke to the rest of the rebels. "It's true. They've come to join us."

Thank The Four. If Nyke hadn't been here, our reception could've been far worse.

Conversation buzzed around us as Nyke turned back to me. "You need to tell me all you know. Them too." He shook his head, a wry smile on his face. "Can't believe I'll be planning open rebellion with the emperor's first."

For the first time in days, I smiled too.

CHAPTER 50
LUCIEN

Phantoms chased me around every corner of the mansion—my old, abandoned home and now the rebels' temporary hide-out, though they'd chosen to set up most of their camp outside, unwilling to sleep under the enemy's roof. Bad luck, they said. I saw shadows of my fellow captains down each wood-paneled hall. Heard their laughter in the whispers that slipped through closed doors of rooms I knew by heart. My old tutor's gruff voice echoed in the kitchen. The familiar scent of pipe smoke still lingered outside the study.

We'd found the rebels. They'd conceded to let us join them, thanks to Zurina's message and Ilya's quick work, but it was impossible to miss the hard looks and curses tossed my way. How many of them had I fought in battle? Did I kill their friends? Family?

Now I turned my back on my own family—my brothers and sisters, my once father. Despite all I'd learned in recent days, part of me still mourned that broken bond and the hollow wound it left within me.

I shed my armor, storing it away in my old room. The mansion showed more wear than it should, as if The Four had wreaked havoc on it from above.

Perhaps they did. Perhaps we deserved it.

Voices carried up the grand spiral staircase that led down into the main foyer. For a moment, I thought this one was a trick too. Another memory of the past.

"Warren." My steps were light as I descended the stairs. He'd made it. Safely by the sound of things.

Ilya had changed into a fresh outfit and hugged Elin. Her smile, the joy that radiated from her, lifted the heaviness of the mansion pressing down around me.

Warren smiled up at me, his helm tucked under one arm. "Good to see you."

More familiar faces strode through the open door behind him. Ilya ran to Gabriel, throwing her arms around him.

Warren clamped his hand onto my shoulder.

"Brishon?" I asked.

"Let me see if I can reach him now." Warren went utterly still, his eyes glazing over. A few moments later, he returned with a grimace. "Safe for now, they'll be here by lunch tomorrow, but he could see troop movement from the top of Eaglan Ridge earlier today."

"More of the rebels? Did they get Zurina's message?"

He shook his head. "They saw many fires the night before. Large numbers. No attempt to hide their presence."

Fuck. "The emperor."

"Based on what he saw, they're heading this way."

Not good. "Zurina?" We needed her. And the rest of the rebels.

Warren shook his head. "I haven't been able to reach her."

"You." Gabriel's exclamation cut into our conversation.

I turned toward him fully.

He stood next to Ilya, only a few feet away. His brows drew together, a myriad of emotions crossing his face. Anger. Confusion. Disbelief. "You look like…" He gaped as he shook his head.

"I didn't notice it at first either," Ilya said, taking his hand in hers. "Not until we went to Trale."

Gabriel paled. "He can't be."

An invisible hand gripped my throat as I swallowed through the scrutiny of his pinched brows. Would he want to know the truth? His kin attacked his home, took him hostage, and tortured him. It might be better if the nephew he once knew stayed dead.

I looked to Ilya, her unwavering gaze and clear eyes. Solid. True. We'd almost lost each other over lack of trust and hidden secrets. A gap still lingered between us, one I ached to bridge.

Whatever the result, Gabriel deserved to know the truth. Lies wouldn't help us.

"I believe so," I said, rolling up the fabric of my sleeve to show my birthmark—one that marked me as Gabriel's lost nephew. I believed it now that my memories had begun to clear. This close to Gabriel, I could see the familiarity, the shape of a younger face I almost remembered.

"Bastien." He swayed on his feet. "I...we always thought you..."

"I didn't know." My words were heavy, almost difficult to speak. He looked at me with wonder, like family, like a father. In all my years, the emperor had never quite looked at me like that, and it evoked emotions I couldn't begin to sort through in the moment. "Ilya figured it out. The emperor led me to believe I was an orphan. He twisted my memories until I believed it myself."

"Zurina was the same way," Reyna added, sliding into the conversation. She gripped Gabriel's shoulder in a show of support.

"Were you all?" Gabriel's attention shifted to Warren.

"Perhaps. I don't know," Warren admitted. A sad smile touched his lips. "If I had another home once, no one has been able to reveal those memories for me."

Gabriel's face took on a sudden hardness. "And you knew all this before you let them drag Ilya into that arena?"

It would have hurt less if he'd kicked me between the legs.

"I wasn't tortured," Ilya confessed. "Not by him, nor by Brishon. Whatever he showed the crowd, I never saw it."

Gabriel shook his head. "But you were in pain before we left."

My teeth ground together as I fought the urge to punch something. My fault. If only I'd gotten to her sooner.

"Because Orson tried to accost me in the cells, but Lucien arrived just in time." Her eyes captured mine and held them. "If he hadn't..." She looked away.

I'd have never forgiven myself.

"No wonder he dressed you all up in armor." Nyke stood in the doorway. How much had he heard? Dark hair, with a few strands of grey woven in, fell to his tanned ears. His bearing spoke of pride. Not even his worn and dirty clothing could disguise the warrior underneath.

"You know, I received another letter before Zurina's." He pulled a thin missive from a pants pocket and held it in the air. "Sent by Lord Stefan of Trale."

Father. My stomach dropped. My real one, whose people I'd slaughtered.

"Brother," Gabriel said.

Nyke nodded. "He said his wife, Lady Basilla, believed her son alive, and none other than the emperor's first-in-command. Apparently, a visitor confirmed her suspicions." His gaze landed on Ilya.

My attention snapped to her. "When?" And how in the name of The Four had I missed something so significant?

She bit her bottom lip, a hint of color creeping to her cheeks. "Just before we left Trale."

Lady Basilla passed along a comment about how handsome and strong Emperor Ryszard's guards looked this trip. I merely stated my agreement. Ilya's words had caught me so off guard I hadn't questioned them. I smirked. "Clever."

"Is there more?" Gabriel asked.

Nyke looked to me. His weighty silence stole the brief joy of moments ago. There was more, something I wouldn't like. I'd lost one father by my choices, but somehow, losing another suddenly felt so much worse. Of course he wouldn't want a son who'd raised arms against him.

"He asked me to spare you if we met on the battlefield," Nyke said. "To bring you to him alive."

Resignation chilled me. "For what purpose?"

"He did not say."

Ilya stepped to my side and took my hand in hers. The simple touch gave me strength I didn't know I needed.

"As touching as all this is," Nyke said into the quiet of the room, "we have work to do."

Yes, we'd meant to meet as soon as possible to get started on a strategy to take Zhine. But now we had a more pressing matter. I rolled my shoulders, letting the shroud of my feelings fall away. "The emperor's troops are advancing this way."

His features remained neutral, unsurprised. "It's an outcome I started planning for when I received Zurina's message. Let's get to it."

A strategist. I could respect that.

"Thank you for telling him," Ilya whispered as she released my hand.

"Later we..." There was so much to say to her.

She smiled. "Yes."

WHEN I FOUND ILYA LATER, she was reading a small book by the low, flickering flame of a candle, the windows drawn tight and covered to keep the meager light inside.

This room had been mine once. Simple. Militaristic. The room of the emperor's first. But no longer was I his captain. Now I was simply Lucien. A man. A rebel. The bed on which she reclined wasn't meant for two, but it would have to do. The nightstand holding the candle still had a tilt to it, though not enough to dislodge the carefully placed flame.

Watching Ilya sitting alone on my old bed, enthralled with the words on the page, stirred my desire. All I'd wanted to do since I carried her from the cells was draw her into my arms and taste her lips again. Concentrating on the trek here had been a monumental challenge. But now, with a plan in place with the rebels and the late guard shift finally giving us rest for the night, I had a chance.

My legs had been heavy climbing the stairs. Seeing her there, so peaceful despite our situation, rejuvenated me, gave me life.

"What are you reading?" I asked, interrupting her reverie.

"Lucien." She licked her lips and flicked her hair back from where it had fallen across her shoulder.

I closed the door behind me, sealing us in the small space together.

She lifted the small book in her lap. "I found it under a loose board when I was helping Elin upstairs. It's Ryszard's diary...one he must have kept when you all lived here." She looked down at the page and began to read: *"I'll do anything to set us on the right path. To free our people from the burden of poor leadership and ill-fated decision. Can he not see it? That he makes us appear weak? Feeble? My brother doesn't realize how much he needs my help. Only I can set us on the path to glory. And we'll have it. The respect. Our place in this world. Each season my charges grow stronger in magic, wit, and might. Soon, so very soon, I'll have more power than he can stand against."*

"He plotted this for cycles," she continued, scanning the book in her lap. "He even talks about his ability to sense magic and using it to find you all. There are pages about the cycles of training and trying to push his plans through his older brother. When that didn't work, he's the one who set him up to be poisoned and—" Her words halted as soon as her attention landed on me again.

I swallowed the bitterness in my mouth. I'd known his plans—a few of them. Others I'd suspected, though I could never prove them. Our past had been his greatest secret, what gave him power over us. We'd never questioned it. "Another night perhaps," I managed. Tonight, I didn't want to hear any more about the emperor, his plans, or the role I'd played in them.

Ilya snapped the book closed and slid it across the bed. "Another time," she agreed. "It scares me though, how much dedication to a cause, a dream, can twist a person." She looked away toward the covered windows. "That steadfast determination to country...what if I became like that? If my goals—"

"You're nothing like him," I promised. How could she possibly think that? "Even if your title was once the most important thing to you, you have a heart. Compassion. You wouldn't start needless wars all for the sake of securing your name and a place in history."

"But I almost destroyed everything. Fernand's death is my fault. If I hadn't taken that letter from you..." She hung her head in her hands.

The bed sagged under my weight as I took the space next to her and pulled her into my arms. Soft warmth pressed against my chest. She tortured herself over one mistake when I'd made so many. If anyone deserved pain and regret, it was me.

"The emperor swung the blade, not you. Fernand made his own choices. Although..." I cupped her face, forcing her glassy eyes to catch mine. "I hope you won't go behind my back again."

"Never. I was an idiot. I didn't think through the consequences, and once I did, I wanted to tell you. So badly."

"But you didn't trust me yet?"

Her lips pursed. "I think I did, but if I was wrong..." She shook her head. "I couldn't risk it."

Just as I could have told her I had a plan but didn't. How different things might have turned out if we'd chosen to trust.

"No more secrets between us," I whispered, savoring the hint of olive flower that always clung to her.

"None." She stroked my cheek. "Was Warren successful with his magic?"

A hint of bitterness soured on my tongue. "Yes," I sighed. Warren had turned up the ground in portions of the forest, creating natural barriers to provide us with a stronger defensive position. I couldn't use my magic to help, not yet. Illusions wouldn't aid us unless the enemy tracked us down. I'd had only my physical strength and mind to lend to our planning tonight.

Her brows creased. "You're worried about Warren?"

That too. I nodded. I'd never seen him use so much magic at once. He was wobbling on his feet by the time I'd helped him to his room. He insisted he was fine, of course, but I wondered.

"He seems to be doing well, though Elin was worried."

My lips twitched. Elin. Warren had found himself an admirer. "Did she tell you how she reacted when she found out her farm boy was a captain?"

Ilya's gaze darted away before she bit her lip and nodded. "She cried."

"What?" I nearly laughed. "Warren said when he took off his mask after leaving Zhine, she berated him and stomped off."

Ilya smiled. "Oh, she knew before then. She didn't tell me until tonight, but she figured it out when we were still in Zhine."

I raised my brows as Ilya continued.

"She's more perceptive than I've given her credit for."

Both of us. A wry smile tugged at my lips.

Ilya sighed. "I hope Zurina was right about the rebel positions and they can close in quickly. If Ryszard finds us before they do, we'll have little chance."

The weight of so many lives crushed down on me. "We'll do the best we can to prepare."

"And if he comes with the other captains?"

Ilya plucked out my greatest worry, the one I'd hoped to not tell her. "We'll fight if we can't run. Hopefully, it will make enough difference to grant the rebels success."

Her nose twitched. "You don't sound optimistic."

How could she see me so well?

"We'll worry about that tomorrow. Tonight, there's something I want to show you."

CHAPTER 51
ILYA

Lucien stood, all rippling, carved muscle as he pulled his shirt over his head. I watched in rapture as he moved, savoring the sight I thought I might never see again. Dark hair brushed his ears. Stubble coated his strong jaw. A dusting of hair trailed down his chest, disappearing below the waistband riding low on his hips. Old scars marred his skin. The muscles there teased me, angling down toward regions still hidden. All elements of the man I loved.

He was alive. We both were. And he'd forgiven me.

Whatever came with the dawn, we'd face it together.

"You wanted to show me yourself?" I teased.

He smirked. "Yes, but something else too." He returned to the edge of the bed, the warmth from his skin leaping the narrow distance between us. "I want to erase the sadness in your eyes. To show you something beautiful."

"With magic," I whispered. "But you might need it." If Ryszard's forces closed in on us, if they found us before the rest of the rebels could gather and march on Zhine, he would need every bit of strength and power he could muster.

"I can spare a little. For you. Let me do this, Ilya." He stroked my face, sending up a mess of butterflies within me.

My bare toes dug into the sand. Waves crashed. Water lapped at my feet. Sun kissed my skin.

I gasped and pulled away from Lucien to look out over the sparkling blue sea. We no longer sat in the small, musty room in the dilapidated mansion of his youth. Instead, I was home, sitting with Lucien on a smooth rock on Sorrena's shores. The air held the taste of salt. A bird cried above.

"I remember some of what this looked like," Lucien said, his arm sliding around me to hold me close. "I'm sure it's not exactly right, but—"

"It's perfect." I turned to him, sun glinting off his chestnut hair and the stubble across his jaw. In this setting, without his armor, he almost looked like a poor fisherman relaxing in the afternoon sun after a long morning at sea.

"One day soon, you'll get to go back here. To real sand and waves. To your people."

It should have been all I ever wanted. Once it was. But without the man at my side, the vision would be incomplete.

"Only if I can take you with me."

His features morphed into a sad smile. "They'd never welcome me there. Not after all I've done."

I took his hand in mine, squeezing tight. "Then we'll go somewhere else. Together."

He looked at me aghast. "Your home. Your title. It's what you wanted."

"I did." I smiled in return. "It's all I ever wanted. Until you. You saw the woman beyond the title and responsibilities when I couldn't see her myself. We promised we'd find ourselves together, right? I can't do that without you." I paused, savoring the crash of waves and call of birds. "In the arena, you showed everyone my city falling."

His hand slid away, as did his attention. "Yes. The emperor expected me to show your greatest fear or your darkest memory like I had done with the others before. It's what they needed to see."

"Well, you may have messed up. That wasn't it."

He looked at me from the corner of his eye, his attention still downcast. "It wasn't?"

I shook my head. "When I was in that cell, I thought I'd lost you. I thought you'd turned your back on me for good. It crushed me—more than losing my city, more than the death I witnessed. Feeling like I'd found my other half only to shatter the ties between us was worse than anything else."

"Ilya." Lucien pulled me tight. The heat from his body cocooned me, chasing away the remembered darkness of the cell more than the fake sun above. "I felt the same way when they brought you before the emperor," he whispered against my hair. "My best chance was for him not to understand what you meant to me and to get you out later. I was almost too late."

"But you came. When I needed you the most, you came."

Lucien released me, leaving only a handsbreadth between us.

"I don't want to go back to all this without you," I said. "Somehow, I think I fell in love with you." I bit my lip, watching his expression as the words sank in. My skin tingled as his wide-eyed gape transformed into a wolfish smile.

"You think?" His brows rose.

Impossibly, more heat rushed to my face, my chest, even lower. "I know." I traced the muscular planes of his chest, debating whether to continue. "It took losing you for me to be sure, but you're my future. What I want."

Lucien stroked my cheek, drawing my face a breath away from his. "I love you too, Ilya."

His kiss lit up my soul, more scorching than the fake sun on my shoulders and more enticing than the waves still teasing my feet.

My arms slid around his neck, pulling him into a deep embrace that reflected all the joyful emotion threatening to burst from my heart.

He loved me. And I loved him.

We might have to face an army come the morning, but none of that mattered. Not with his lips on mine, his breath in my lungs, and his arms holding me tight.

Lucien's tongue teased my lips. I opened for him without question, meeting him in a dance of passion and forgiveness. My hands tangled in his hair, then slid down his back, a vain attempt to feel all of him as I pressed against him, my body practically in his lap.

His fingers dug into my skin, possessive but not painful. Everywhere our bodies touched came alight from an inner fire.

I panted for breath when Lucien pulled away. The soul-deep, hooded gaze he shot my way sent me squirming in desire. At some point, his illusion had faded. A wood and stone roof replaced the sun. My feet touched the cool floor. Our rock had become the dingy, narrow bed once more. Must and mold replaced with sweet, salty air. Yet none of that mattered. He was my sun, heating me from within and sending waves of desire crashing through me.

I ached for him, deep in my core. Evidence of my desire grew between my legs, slick and eager.

A tug on his waistband signaled my wishes. His grin was the only answer I needed.

His thumb slid across my breast, teasing the stiff peaks under my dress as I licked my lips and took in his form. "My turn," he said, voice husky.

While he watched, I stood and tugged the dress free, letting it fall away to the floor in a heap. The tight shift covering my breasts came next. Gooseflesh rose across my skin as the cool air tickled it.

Lucien wasted no time, rising to his feet to meet me and cupping my breasts in his calloused hands. Each slow taunt and tease unburdened my worries, leaving me loose and free. Just he and I.

Though he'd been eager to join me, he took his time now, as did I, feeling and anticipating, burning up from within. At length, he lifted me onto the bed, setting me down as if I were a fragile vase about to break. Before he joined me, he hooked two fingers under the last of my underthings and pulled, baring me to him until the thin material cleared my legs and was tossed away.

I parted for him, willing him to join me.

He scrubbed a hand down his face. "You undo me."

I grinned in return, wiggling my hips. "Come see what you've done to me."

"I only wish we had somewhere more..." He trailed off, glancing about the room. "We might break the bed."

His sheepish grin made me giggle. "I hope we do."

Our first time together had been all fire and thunder. A hot, fast, burning inferno that neither could deny or back away from.

Tonight, we had no lack of desire between us, but it wasn't about sating our lusts and longing for one another. This coming together was a confirmation, two counterpoints finding their missing half and vowing to find a way forward together.

Slow, sensual, heart-melding. Everything we weren't but could be —together.

I gave my heart as I gave my body, willing them to the man who satisfied the deep longing within my soul. In the worst possible place, I'd found the one thing I never knew I needed and now could never live without.

Lucien.

CHAPTER 52
LUCIEN

The past few days were some of the happiest of my life.

Hard labor and the imminent threat of death filled my time from sunrise to twilight, but Ilya filled my nights, all our secrets lain bare and nothing hovering between us. She'd shared the emperor's journal with the others, only confirming for all present that we'd made the right decision to run, to take a stand against him, even if he had raised some of us.

We aided the rebels in laying traps, setting defensive posts, and crafting potential strategies until my muscles ached and the sun dipped into the tree line. Night was still many hours away, and my short break for lunch was almost over. Already I daydreamed of Ilya's dark hair spread out across the pillow and the soft moans that would slip from her lips when we came together. My cock grew hard again in an instant.

I turned away from the room to hide the evidence and joined Gabriel near a large window. Light spilled in, catching the grey in his hair. He peered out into the garden where Warren, dressed in an old tunic and pants a size too big, sat on a bench with Elin.

"In the end, we're all just people with the same hope and desires," he said. A small grin pulled at the corner of his lips.

Elin's golden hair shown in the sunlight, but not near so brilliantly as the smile that lit her face when Warren handed her a late-blooming wildflower. Its purple petals spiraled out over the thin, green stem.

Together they looked like a happy, young couple in any city within the empire, oblivious to the cares of the world. The image of them on the bench in the calm day could have been a famous tapestry or painting, overgrown garden and all.

I grinned. He wasn't the only one who'd fallen for the charms of a captive they were supposed to guard.

"They look good together," I replied. "In a different situation, they'd be a perfect match."

"Not this one?" Gabriel asked.

"Maybe." A dark shadow clouded my thoughts. "If we can get out of this mess. They deserve some happiness."

Gabriel gripped my shoulder. "I hope you'll come back to Trale before you run off with Ilya."

I looked at him from the corner of my eye, brows raised.

"Don't think we don't all see it," he continued. "But it would do your father well to see you before the God of Darkness claims his spirit. I know what it means to me, so to him..." He trailed off, his look far away.

It wasn't the first time he'd brought this up. I couldn't shake the feeling that Lord Stefan would loathe what became of his only child. A servant of the emperor. A dealer of death with magic and sword. How many of his people—my people—did I kill? I couldn't begin to count them. Yes, he'd sent a letter asking for me to be taken alive and brought to Trale, but I doubted it was for a touching family reunion. He had no reason to want someone like me around.

"You really think that?" I asked.

Gabriel patted my shoulder. "A bond of blood is not so easily broken. We'll see once he learns your whole story."

His confidence was the counterpoint to my doubt. At least Gabriel had forgiven me. That alone was more of a blessing than I dared to hope for, and much more than I deserved. Words were not easy between us yet, but they flowed more naturally with each passing day.

Outside the window, Warren stiffened and pulled away from Elin before rising to his feet. My muscles tensed as the girl's hand flew to her mouth.

"Shit."

Muffled noise grew outside as I raced through the manor. I burst through the front doors, the crack of the wood against stone still ringing in the air as I caught sight of what Warren must have seen.

Dread turned my skin clammy.

A group of rebels carried Zurina on a makeshift stretcher, an arrow shaft protruding from her shoulder. Blood marred her dented and stained armor. Other rebels ran this way and that, their conversations blurred by my spiraling thoughts.

If she died alone out there...

I rushed to the group, falling into pace opposite Warren as they hauled her toward the manor.

"Zurina. Speak to me. What happened?"

Her helm had been removed. Sweat-dampened hair clung to her face. Her olive complexion had paled.

She groaned and cracked open one eye. "Nice to see you too."

Praise The Four.

"They're coming," one of the rebels said. His grim expression told me who.

Fuck. Shit. "Where—"

A loud screech grated across my frayed nerves.

"Zurina!" Reyna slid past me, her dark hair flying behind her just as wild as the look in her eyes.

"Where?" I implored.

Zurina ignored Reyna, who pelted her with exclamations of concern. "Down the hills. Near the river. The others won't make it. Not in time. I had to sneak by."

Fuck all. They must have spotted our lookouts and taken them out. "You risked too much."

She groaned in pain. "Glad I made it."

Rebels settled Zurina into their makeshift infirmary in the dining hall. It had seen minor injuries so far, but soon the empty pallets would bear much worse.

Reyna slid onto a bench beside her. "I've got you," she said, taking Zurina's hand in hers. "We'll fix you up."

"Anything worse than the arrow?" a healer asked, examining the wound.

A sharp jerk of her head was Zurina's only response. We'd earned a reprieve on that score, but we couldn't wait around to see her bandaged and treated.

"Armor now," I gestured to Warren, who nodded in return.

Brishon rushed in, armor on and helmet in hand. "Is she?"

"I'll live," Zurina called, fake humor lacing her voice.

He looked to her and nodded. "Are we under siege?"

"We will be," I answered.

His clear eyes gave no hint of fear, only solid determination. "I'll see what I can do." Without another word, he fled the room, gesturing to the others to join him.

"There's something else," Zurina said. "Orson's alive. He leads the men."

My chest constricted. Orson lived. Another regret. How many could I have? I should have stabbed him through the eye and ended him when I'd had the chance. Something at the time held me back, a sense of loyalty to the man I'd grown up with, however much I loathed him. Sparing him wouldn't bring back the boy of our youth. Only the corrupt man he'd become remained, and it might cost us now. Dearly. He could set the woods aflame in an instant. Destroy our work, our traps.

A soft hand grabbed my arm, pulling my attention.

"Tell me," Ilya said. Though she wore an old, cream-colored dress scavenged from somewhere in the mansion, it did nothing to dampen her regal bearing or the sharpness of her authority.

I'd have given anything to share better news, to be able to promise everything was fine. But I couldn't. And every moment I delayed was one more that the emperor's forces drew closer to our hiding place. "Come with me."

I relayed what little we knew to Ilya as we retreated to my room, where I strapped on one piece of armor and the next. I'd need it all, everything, if we planned to halt this advance. If we couldn't take them all out—a lofty goal—we needed to hold them until rebel backups arrived.

Ilya paced, fiddling with her braided hair. "Give me a sword. I'll come with you."

"No." Fuck if I'd let her walk into death like that.

She froze. "I can't just sit here and—"

"You're not." Gods, of all the times for her to be stubborn. I pointed to the short sword on the table. A hardened iron blade, its leather-wrapped grip worn by use and time. Better it serve her here than me in the woods. I had enough blades tucked away already. "Use it to protect the people here. Zurina will stay, she's barely conscious as it is, but we can't spare any of the warriors. I need you here in case any of the emperor's troops get through."

Emotion fled her face. "Can you stop them?"

I held her gaze, unable to form the lies I yearned to tell her. "We have to try."

Her eyes turned glassy as she looked away.

That momentary look threatened to rend my heart. I dropped my helmet on the bed and pulled her into my arms, savoring her scent, her warmth, perhaps for the last time.

"If we can't stop them, you have to stay alive," I whispered against her hair. "Take the best horses, try to flee to the other rebels."

"And you?" she whispered, looking up at me.

I'd die before I let them take her back. It was my fault her kingdom fell, that she ended up a captive to begin with. If only I'd seen the truths she showed me long ago.

"I love you. Don't forget that."

Her eyes flew wide. "Luc—"

I crushed her mouth to mine, stealing away her words. We'd found each other too late, but no army could take this moment for me. If I went to my grave, it'd be with the memory of her lips against mine, her taste in my mouth.

A hint of salt mingled into our kiss. A wet track remained on her cheek when I pulled away. How many times would I make this strong woman cry?

"Don't forget. Don't lose that fire in your heart."

With difficulty, I released her and grabbed my helm, snapping it down over my head before I could delay any further.

"I'll see you again," she said. A promise.

I nodded.

I'd find her, even in the After.

CHAPTER 53
ILYA

Gabriel thrust the battered, short sword into an enemy only he could see as he practiced across the grand entry room. He moved with a skill and ease that I envied. We'd been left the worst of the weapons, the ones not taken by those fighting outside.

Chaos raged around us, fueled by distant shouts, Zurina's wounds, and worries that I couldn't fully shutter.

"They're slipping through on the west," Zurina said. Her eyes glazed as she watched the unfolding battle through the animals of the forest and the birds circling above it.

Reyna held her head and bandaged upper body in her lap, stroking her short hair back from her forehead like a mother seeing to a sick child. Warren stood nearby, relaying silent messages between Zurina and the squadron leaders in the field. A tactical advantage.

We'd need every one.

He'd argued to go with the others out into the field, but Lucien ordered him to stay and relay Zurina's sight. Mostly, I knew he worried for the young man and what the real use of his powers could do to him. One battle had almost finished him, Lucien had said, and he'd never engaged the enemy in physical combat. The use of his magic alone took a toll on his weak heart, sending him into fits and nearly ending him. Too much physical exertion could do the same, though he trained daily in limited amounts, as evidenced by the lean muscle that formed his frame.

I paced nearby, unable to sit still. Lucien was out there fighting for all our lives, and yet here I was, stuck, waiting like some damsel in distress. My grip tightened on the leather handle of the sword he'd given me.

"They're battling hard. The west flank might be falling. Retreating, at least. He hasn't engaged the other captains yet," Warren said. "Where are they?"

"I can't see," Zurina replied. "Too much smoke."

Orson's flames consumed one section of the forest at a time, destroying the constructs that the rebels had created in the forest and clearing the way for the emperor's forces to advance upon us. Already a smoky haze spread over the gardens outside the windows.

The fires grew close. Too close.

I should have killed him in that dungeon. Someone must have found him before he could bleed out and healed him. If only we'd made sure of his demise, we'd have much more of an advantage now.

"And Lucien?" The question burst from my lips before I could stop myself. I couldn't keep quiet anymore.

Warren's cool gaze slid to me. "Fine. Holding his own."

My lips thinned. *Fine?* Would he tell me if he was badly injured? Worse?

Zurina gasped, her body jerking in Reyna's arms. "They're here. Kasida. Others. Outside—"

My heart skipped a beat. The sword trembled in my grip.

"Get back to the infirmary," I ordered the few healers who waited near the entry for the injured to be brought in.

"You too," I yelled to Elin. We'd hid the twins there, along with others too sick or injured to fight.

The rebel healers rushed to obey, but Elin shook her head. "I can fight."

"But—"

She notched her chin higher and gestured to the bow and quiver slung over her back. "If you can, so can I."

The resolve in her eyes cut off my further protest despite the shiver that racked her form. She'd grown, and I'd missed it. Or perhaps she'd held onto that glimmer of inner strength the entire time and I'd never been able to see it.

"I told them, but—" Another crash cut off Warren's words.

"Help me up," Zurina ordered, scrambling to gain her feet.

"You're in no condition to fight," Reyna said.

Something heavy smashed into the doors, sending them bowing inward with a loud groan. Glass shattered.

"I have to," she replied, pushing away from Reyna despite her protests. She grabbed her sword and positioned her body toward the door and in front of Reyna, a hard grimace marring the lines of her face.

Gabriel, Elin, and I backed toward the stairs. Warren shifted in front of us, sword out and ready.

The main doors bowed inward once again. Wood cracked and splintered.

My grip tightened as my throat dried. Whatever came through that door, it would not bode well for us. Not with so few, even if two were skilled fighters and talented wielders of magic.

Another crash sent the doors rushing inward. Kasida followed in their wake. Her high-pitched laugh caused my teeth to grind together, so much so that I almost missed the soft whoosh of air that zipped past my cheek.

Elin's arrow struck Kasida's mask just below her eye, sending her laughter into a growl of outrage. A touch higher and she'd have killed her with one blow.

"Little bitch!" Kasida spewed, charging into the room.

Another arrow zipped past, but this one Kasida saw coming and knocked away with a flick of one of her twin short swords. Swords wreathed in fire.

"Her magic?" I asked.

"She channeled Orson's fire onto their weapons," Warren answered, never taking his eyes off the woman across the room or the cluster of Ryszard's men slinking in behind her, each with blades exposed and alight.

"And a broken bird, how quaint," Kasida sneered as she caught sight of Zurina, edging toward her.

Zurina pushed Reyna toward the wall at her back as she advanced on her former comrade, drawing her attention. Kasida and Zurina faced off, metal ringing as their blades connected.

Elin felled one soldier with an arrow to the neck. His weapon clattered to the ground, burning where it lay.

I'd never felt more useless, watching my young friend fight while I stood to the side. I adjusted my grip on the sword, trying to recall my lessons from Nyke cycles ago, but the panic coursing through my veins kept the memories just out of reach.

"Hold on to something!"

Warren's warning didn't have time to sink in before the ground rumbled beneath our feet. A great crack opened outside the doors like a gaping mouth. Several of the emperor's men tumbled into the pit with screams that died as suddenly as they began.

The manor rumbled. Dust rained down to mix with the smoke from the flaming swords. Wood groaned. Small chunks of the ceiling thumped to the ground across the room.

"You'll bring the place down!" Zurina yelled.

The chasm outside closed like a wave crashing to the shore, leaving a dirty scar behind. The shaking stopped, though it had been enough to throw off our attackers. Warren drew his sword and engaged the four remaining soldiers.

Kasida's furious blows sent Zurina stumbling backward. A particularly nasty stroke drew a line of red across her exposed shoulder.

Reyna jumped into the fray, wielding a narrow blade with more speed and precision than I would have expected. Between the two, they kept her distracted—for the moment.

Elin shot another arrow but missed her mark. "Almost out!"

I swallowed my fear. "Let's go." I shot Gabriel a look and gestured toward Warren. We couldn't be the only ones doing nothing. Gabriel rushed ahead, drawing the attention of a middle-aged man with dark hair.

"Filthy traitors," the man spat. He swung his flaming sword toward me.

Heat buffeted me as the arcing blow whispered far too near my middle. A surge of energy rushed through my veins. *Focus, Ilya.*

Gabriel engaged the man, swords clashing.

Patience. Careful. Strike!

I lashed out with my blade, the tip pulling heavily against the man's chainmail armor and earning a grunt of frustration.

He whirled on me, striking out with his blade again. I barely raised my own in time to block the downward swing. My arms cried out from the impact. A whimper slipped through my lips as I braced my feet and held back the sharp point edging toward my face. A fetid odor filled my nose as flames from the blade singed loose strands of hair near my face.

All at once, the pressure fled. The man gurgled and spat blood as Gabriel pulled his sword free from the man's back.

Gabriel kicked the body off his sword, sending the fallen soldier tumbling to the floor. Blood dripped from his blade as I stared at the sight, unable to move. A buzzing hum filled my ears. I'd seen blood and death, more than I cared to remember. But never so close, and not one I'd had a direct hand in.

"Snap out of it!" He grabbed my arm, shaking me back to my senses.

Another soldier lay bloody at Warren's feet. He engaged the last two, deflecting blows with practiced precision while keeping the women he faced on their heels. His blade caught one, sending her stumbling back as he focused on the other.

Gabriel exchanged his sword for one of the flaming ones and rushed for the injured soldier. My heart pounded in my ears, drowning out the battle around me as I followed him. The woman bellowed her pain and frustration as she swung at Gabriel. Her sword crashed into his, sending it flying to clatter across the floor.

No.

Time slowed. The woman pulled back, readying for the killing blow.

I wouldn't make it. Not in time.

"No!" My scream split the air as the woman's body jerked, halting in her backswing. The point of an arrow stuck out the front of her throat. Blood bubbled from her lips as she fell limp to the ground. Behind her, Elin lowered her bow.

Praise The Four.

I slid to a stop near Gabriel. "Are you okay?"

He stared at me wide-eyed, panting for breath.

Alive. He was alive.

Warren spun, slicing the last of his opponents to the ground in a brutal move, but the victory was short-lived.

My chest clenched at the sight beyond him. Blood marred Reyna's side through a burned hole in her dress. Zurina panted heavily, rocking slightly on her feet. Kasida had discarded her helm, smirking at her victims as she circled with her twin blades, ready to strike.

Zurina bellowed as Kasida's blade sank into her injury, bringing her to her knees as blood dripped from the wound onto the floor. Reyna rushed forward, swinging her own light blade, but Kasida knocked it from her hands with ease and sent it clattering across the floor.

Kasida jerked her weapon free. Zurina gripped her wound, blood running around her fingers as she slumped toward the ground.

With blades pointed at both women, she cackled, "Anyone moves and they die."

Eerie quiet reigned, punctuated by the occasional crackle of flame as the room lit from fallen weapons. The tang of blood and burned flesh filled the air. Distant shouts and screams echoed outside the broken door.

"Drop your weapons and walk over here. No mischief," Kasida ordered.

My scalp tingled. The hair rose on my arms.

"Do it." Warren's voice whispered into my mind.

Magic. The odd sensation vanished as quickly as it came.

A cold sweat broke out on the back of my neck as I walked with the others toward Kasida. Zurina's blood dripped onto the ruined rug where she crouched. Reyna's, too, painted lines down her side, though she refused to cry or cower. Instead, she stared at Kasida, her chin raised and teeth gritted. I took my cue from her, summoning the last of my courage. If I died, it wouldn't be sobbing or cowering in fear.

"Kneel, all of you. Hands on the ground."

Elin's pale form shivered as she knelt next to Warren, so close they nearly touched.

"That's right, like good dogs," Kasida taunted.

I knelt next to Elin, Gabriel to my side. "Let's talk ab—"

Kasida cackled again as she slid her sword forward, the tip nearly digging into Reyna's neck. "I think not. Now..." Kasida looked between Zurina and Reyna. "Which one should I start with?"

Fire blazed outside the windows, hitting us with a wave of sudden heat. Another form stepped through the ruined doorway, one that sent a surge of bile crawling up my throat.

"The fools and the whores," Orson grunted. "Don't you know you've lost?"

An icy chill locked around my heart. *Lucien. Where was Lucien?*

He looked to Kasida. "Starting without me?" Lines of flame raced across floorboards like fish along the seafloor, cutting off any retreat to the hall or the kitchens should we try to run for it. Orson's lecherous gaze locked onto me. "You, I'll kill last."

"I'll decide who lives and dies."

I gasped as Emperor Ryszard stepped into the wrecked room. Elaborate metal armor, decorated with gemstones of his signature crimson and grey, guarded his form. His traditional fur cloak hung down his back, dragging along the ground. Though sweat stuck the hair to his face, he still wore his thin crown and jewels about his neck. A hint of mud marred him, but no blood colored his attire. He hadn't seen battle, not the thick of it. And yet, he'd made it here...

"My emperor?" Kasida stiffened but kept her blades aimed at her targets.

My arms shook. I cut a glance to Warren but could deduce nothing. Was Lucien dead already? His body cooling somewhere in the forest? I bit my lip, holding in the scream threatening to tear its way to the surface.

"I desire to deal with these traitors myself. Hearing a report would simply be..." One ring-decked hand toyed with the pommel of the ornate dagger at his side. "Unsatisfying."

My world spiraled into darkness deeper than any I'd known. My arms shook, but I couldn't feel them anymore, nor the heat of the fires cooking the room.

"Put out those flames before you burn us all alive," Ryszard ordered, waving a weathered hand at Orson.

Orson extinguished his flames and the enchanted swords. Only trails of smoke remained. Some spilled out the shattered windows, others clouded the room and burned my lungs.

"What do you plan to do with us?" I demanded. The question took all my courage, all my cycles of training to be calm in the face of disaster.

Ryszard turned, his cold gaze sliding over me as if I were dirt under his horse's hooves rather than the *honored guest* he'd once called me. His fingers drummed along the hilt of the blade sheathed at his side just inside the long fall of his cloak. "You'll see."

A wicked light glinted in his eyes, unlike any expression I'd seen him show. In a move I almost missed, he slid the blade free, twisted around, and tossed it end over end. No one had time to move before the tip sunk into Kasida's eye and she tumbled to the ground.

CHAPTER 54
LUCIEN

Magic pulled at my energy, wearing down my strength and consciousness.

I'd used too much in the forest. Keeping up this disguise, the face of the man who'd raised me, took everything I had left. Sweat dripped down my back. My legs shook. In a moment it wouldn't matter.

My friends were alive, if barely. I'd made it in time. And Ilya...my heart flushed with pride over her courage. Chin up, eyes clear in the heat of battle. I'd expect nothing less.

"What do you plan to do with us?" she demanded.

Oh, that spit of fire. That brightly burning soul that entranced me from the moment she'd stared me down after I conquered Sorrena. Her look was much the same then as it was now. Scathing. Proud. I loved her for it.

A grin pulled at my lips, and I let the illusion slip just the briefest bit for her to see it. She hadn't figured me out, none of them had, and now that I'd moved the pieces to my advantage on this playing board, it was time for the final act.

I gripped the dagger sheathed at my side, a real one I'd wrapped in illusion to mimic the emperor's. *Training don't fail me now.* I sent the blade twisting end over end until it lodged in Kasida's eye.

She didn't scream, didn't even drop her smirk before her body went still and tumbled to the ground.

A child's error removing her helm in battle.

The remorse I expected didn't come. I didn't wait for it as I turned to Orson and let my magic slip away.

"You—" he gaped.

Gasps and exclamations poured out behind me, including a strangled squeal in Ilya's mesmerizing tones.

"Should have killed you before." I pulled the sword from the scabbard across my back and charged. Orson didn't suspect a thing when his emperor rode out to meet him on the edge of the battlefield. He'd barely questioned why Emperor Ryszard—who rarely took the field —would choose to join him unexpectedly today.

A sharp keening sounded as my blade slid against his, the tip scraping against his armor where he barely blocked me in time. His physical strength outmatched mine. He moved without the hindrance of injury. He'd been fully healed by magic. How unfortunate.

Warren edged closer in my periphery as Orson's blade rang against mine once more. The blow pushed me back a step. My muscles waned from overuse. The ache echoed through my body no matter how I pushed it away. Alone, I wouldn't win.

The moment magic tingled on my skin, I ordered through our bond, "Keep him moving. Don't let his magic free." The bond had slipped away earlier when Warren had engaged Kasida and her guards, but not before he'd given me enough information to put my plan into action and follow Orson into the mansion.

If we could keep Orson distracted, he wouldn't have the chance to unleash his magic and burn us all alive.

Reyna cried out, yelling for Zurina, but I couldn't turn from the battle.

"Unconscious." Warren's panic echoed through the mental bond before he adjusted his stance and struck out toward Orson. "I can no longer reach her."

Fear turned to anger, giving strength to my weakened form.

Blow followed blow in a dance of life and death as Warren and I backed Orson toward the doorway. The frame would block him in and restrict his movements. Victory hummed through my veins until Warren doubled over, his sword arm stiffening before going limp.

He grunted in pain as his knees hit the ground.

His heart. Fuck it all.

Elin screamed and ran to his side. Orson knocked me back with a powerful blow that stung my arm, followed by a kick to the gut that had me seeing stars.

Fire licked out across the ground, hot and furious as Orson bolted for the door.

Ilya's scream stole my attention. Flickers of red and orange trailed up her skirts, leaving ash in their wake as she furiously beat against the magic. Reyna and Gabriel did the same, beating back the fire where it crept toward Zurina's limp form upon the ground.

The floorboards beneath my feet shook with the violence of a quake. Lumber cracked and split.

"Warren!"

I snapped my head toward my friend, who gritted his teeth in pain where he lay crumpled upon the ground, Elin's arms around him as her tears fell upon his armor.

I lost my footing as Orson tumbled into me, spewing grunts of hatred as we both rolled across the still moving floor, metal crashing and grating against wood. Pain lanced through my back. Smoke invaded my lungs. The tang of burning skin and hair rolled even my solid stomach. My palms slipped against the hilt of my blade as I struggled to adjust my grip and rise.

Orson gained his footing as I did mine. Beyond him, the front doors had collapsed, the debris meeting a pillar of sharp rock that skewered between broken boards.

Warren's magic stilled.

My armor grew stifling as the heat rose.

"I'll burn you all," Orson fumed.

He needed to die. Now.

I leaped forward with my sword, feeling the familiar weight slice through the air as I aimed for his neck. He blocked. A burst of flame seared my leg through the armor, sending me off-balance. He swung.

I moved too slowly. His blade slid off mine, the sharp edge grating against the metal before scouring my side between sections of plate armor. A burn worse than flame raced across my skin, but that pain was nothing compared to the sharp stab of worry at what I witnessed.

Ilya crept up behind Orson with the blade I'd given her. One twist of his weapon in her direction, one blast of his flames, and he'd kill her.

Never. I'd never let that happen.

"Is that all?" I grated.

My magic yearned to break free, to be unleashed. It called to me from within, begging me to use it. But drawing it forth now, in my weakened state, might give Orson the chance to end me. Or worse, end the woman I loved.

Instead, I summoned mortal strength, all I had left, and pointed my blade at him as I forced my grimace into a taunting smirk.

One foot in front of the other, I charged. Our blades met in a clash and grind of metal as I pressed forward. My legs ached, my arms more so, but none of it mattered as I stared into his eyes through the slits in his mask.

I knew the moment Ilya stuck. His eyes flew wide. His strength wavered, giving me an edge. Blood bubbled to his lips.

With one last burst of strength, he shoved me back, splaying his arms wide as blood and spittle dribbled down his armor.

Ilya screamed, tossed back into the wall with a heavy thud.

My woman—mine—crumpled on the ground near the broken remnants of the door.

I shoved Orson's dying corpse aside, Ilya's blade still sticking from his neck, before falling to my knees at her side.

Burns marred her lower legs and arms. Blood trickled from a mark on her face. A knife to the gut would have been less painful and easier to take.

"Ilya, love." I brushed the hair back from her face, some of the ends short and crinkled where flame had claimed their length. "Speak to me." If she died, all was for naught.

She didn't move.

I twisted around, searching for aid. My heart lurched. Elin whimpered over Warren, who lay barely conscious in her lap. Reyna and Gabriel, both burned and bleeding, used strips of fabric to staunch the flow of Zurina's wounds.

"She's still breathing, but she—" Reyna was near hysterical with worry.

Panic crept up my spine. Ilya. My friends. I couldn't let them die. Not now.

I sheathed my sword before cradling Ilya in my arms. My legs wobbled as I stood. Blood ran down my side, and my body barked and screamed in protest. Each step sent a flare of pain burning down to my bones as I limped over and around debris until we were just outside the manor.

"We need help!" I yelled to any who could hear.

Holy Four, let them live. Ilya's head lolled to the side, resting against my dented armor. Distant shouts and the crash of wood rang through the ruined gardens. Smoke still clouded the air, obscuring the woods beyond.

"Anyone!" The plea rasped from my lungs.

"Luc..." Ilya's stirred.

"Come back to me. Please. I can't lose you."

"Lucien?" My name cracked from her throat.

"Ilya, I'm here." I shook with relief as I knelt, laying her gently on the ground. I pulled off my glove and placed my palm against her face, skin to blessed skin.

Her hand covered mine. "We're alive."

The wonder in her eyes stole my words and my pain. All I could do was nod and hold her close. Voices reached us through the smoke. I followed Ilya's gaze as she looked to the forest. Hazy forms took shape between the trees, drawing closer.

No. The emperor wouldn't have her back. I'd give my dying breath to ensure her freedom.

I rose, nearly stumbling back to the ground. "Can you walk?"

"I...maybe."

"I'll hold them off as long as I can." I pulled my sword with a groan. "Go. Make a run for it."

"I'm not leaving you. Not again." She pushed to her feet, the burned and bloodied dress hanging from her shoulders.

"Ilya—"

"I won't."

Of all the times for her to be stubborn. "Get behind me." I adjusted my stance, holding in the roar of pain that threatened to break free. Soldiers reached the edge of the gardens. Muted browns and greens. Worn clothes. Leather armor cobbled together in haphazard pieces.

"Rebels," Ilya gasped.

My body sagged. Pain and weariness washed over me. I fell to my knees, no longer able to support myself.

"Lucien!" Ilya grabbed me. Her face blurred before me. "You're hurt," she sobbed. "Why didn't you tell me?"

"Had to," I groaned, "make sure you were alright."

"Idiot." She sniffled.

I smiled through the pain.

"Secure the building." Nyke's commanding voice rang through the clearing.

"Injured inside," I managed to say. "Allies."

"Get a healer!" he yelled.

My vision blurred. Exhaustion threatened to pull me under.

"Stay with me, Lucien." Ilya's calming voice embraced me.

I leaned into her. *Always.*

CHAPTER 55
LUCIEN

Other rebels had received Zurina's word. They listened. They came.

Just in time.

Two of the closest groups had banded together and followed the path of the emperor's forces, coming up behind them in the heat of battle and crushing them between our struggling group and their line. With the element of surprise on their side, and Orson and Kasida distracted coming after those in the manor, they'd turned the tide of battle.

Warren was weakened but alive. Healers saw to Zurina, though her condition was still severe. Brishon was taken alive by the arriving rebels with only minor injuries. Their wise leader had given an order to take prisoners where possible and sort them out later. A kind, if difficult, plan. One I was thankful for, since their confusion of Brishon's allegiance meant his life, not his death. Nyke's men saw to the rest of us as well, healing wounds and tending to the injured.

Our fallen, and there were many, would be buried with honor in a place of their families' choosing. Their bodies would be carried back by the rebels as a sign of peace and respect to all people of the city-states, including the emperor's.

Another captain was hauled up to the mansion through the forest, bound in ropes and chains. I recognized him at once, especially with the helmet pulled free from his sweaty face. Our healer, wielder of the God of Light's blessings.

"What should we do with him?" Nyke asked as the man was shoved to his knees in a grunt of pain.

"Gaius." My lips thinned. We'd grown up together. Trained together. And though he wasn't Orson, he'd still come to fight against us.

"Captain." Gaius bowed his dark head before meeting my flat gaze. "I chose wrongly. Let me help now."

I cocked an eyebrow at him. "You seek forgiveness? A reprieve?"

He'd healed Orson sometime before the battle. Nothing else explained how he could move so swiftly or wield magic the way he did today, not with the injuries I'd given him only a few days ago. Because of him, many had died. But also because of me. I should have slaughtered that bastard when I'd had the chance, no matter our history or our past together. My side hurt just thinking about him, the wound he'd given me still raw and aching despite the salve Nyke's men had applied or the quick stitches they'd finished only minutes ago. I'd made them start before the numbing cream took effect. No time to waste.

"No." Gaius hung his head again. His shoulders slumped. "My choices cannot be forgiven, but I can make different ones now. At least, as long as my magic holds out." He looked up at me. "Soliel blessed me to heal others. Not kill them."

"Zurina." Her name came unbidden to my lips. "And anyone else who is critical," I added.

Nyke flicked his hand toward some of his men. "Keep a watch on him at all times."

The rebels led Gaius off into the mansion. Despite the havoc wreaked by Orson's flames and Warren's quakes, they'd deemed portions of it stable enough to keep the infirmary in the dining hall and kitchens, which remained mostly untouched. Though we'd won today, the battle was far from over. The emperor may have lost some of his captains, but he still had others, not to mention the guards at his command. We'd need to take Zhine, minimize the loss of life where possible.

A delicate hand touched my shoulder. Ilya smiled up at me, calm and reassuring despite the burned and stained dress that still hugged her form. At least she'd accepted a cloak about her shoulders to ward off the chill, even if she refused to take time to clean or rest.

I cupped her cheek, letting her hair slide between my fingertips until I reached a short section that had been partially lost to flame. She was alive. Safe. Nyke and the others could take her and her sister home. Back to Sorrena. A sad smile touched my lips. I wanted that for her—for all whom the emperor had taken hostage, including my friends whom he'd raised and trained like me. Now they could have it. But the thought pained me. To be separated from them all—from her. No matter what she said, they'd never accept me in Sorrena. Even if I changed my name, my identity.

"What's wrong?" she asked.

Her voice. That voice I could never get enough of. How could I give her up? But how could I not? My fingertips traced her lips as they slid into a frown.

"Nothing. It's...there's much to think about with retaking Zhine. Like what to do about the emperor and the other captains."

"Oh." Her disappointment was impossible to miss. "I was just thinking that once we leave here..." She shrugged and looked away.

"You'll go back to Sorrena."

She winced.

I was right. She couldn't stay. Not with me. No matter how much I loved and wanted her. She had somewhere she belonged. A people to lead, a role to fulfill. That had been her goal all along, and now all that prevented her from returning to the past she longed for was a ride home.

And then she'd be gone.

Back to unreachable heights on the throne of Sorrena, glaring down at me as she'd done the day I took her future away. I deserved the pain that tore my heart in two.

"And you promised to go with Gabriel." Her words were a death knell. The final dagger.

My teeth ground together. "He's most insistent that I at least pay a visit." It might be my last trip anywhere if they put my head on a spike.

Ilya simply nodded. "Your parents will be happy to see you. To know you're alive."

I doubt it.

A rider galloped up, dropping from her horse in front of Nyke with expert skill. "Sir." She leaned in and whispered something in urgent tones.

Nyke's brows rose. The woman remounted and turned her horse as soon as the command left his lips.

"What is it?" Ilya asked.

"A few more captives caught fleeing the battle," he answered. "Gather the others. We'll need to decide what to do with them once they arrive and plot our next steps."

Next steps...away from Ilya and the future I craved.

Would Warren and Zurina leave with Elin and Reyna too once the fighting was done and Zhine taken? In winning this war, I might lose everything that mattered.

CHAPTER 56
ILYA

Reyna gathered the heirs of the city-states together outside the damaged manor home. Her plans for after the war involved all of us.

"A tribunal?" Gabriel asked.

"Exactly, a trial among all the city-states. We'll take the emperor into custody, and he will answer to all of us for the crimes he's committed," Reyna said.

"There hasn't been one of those in an age," Elin said in awe. Warren stepped up next to her, taking her hand in his. He'd nearly died today, and he still walked slowly from the bruises on his body and the seizure of his heart, but he looked like the happiest man alive. He was the opposite of Lucien, who despite our victory today wore a shroud of defeat.

"Let's not get too far ahead of ourselves. I doubt he'll just surrender." My attention slid past him to the group standing in the charred remains of the front gardens. Zurina was up and moving—healed, thanks to Gaius's magic. Thank The Four for that blessing.

"Perhaps not," Reyna said. "But the emperor can no longer use us to hinder our homelands from acting. If we rise up and work together, anything is possible." With the return of Zurina's health had come Reyna's joy and optimism. Even now she talked in broad hand movements and high-pitched exclamations. "Our city-states can imprison the governors and the paltry troops Ryszard left in our homelands to watch over things. Then they can join up with us as one combined force."

Horses galloped into view. Their riders came to halt on the yellowed grasses spreading between the gardens and the forest. Behind them came a horse-drawn cart. No, a prison wagon. A large, wooden cage had been constructed on top of a supply cart and now carried a jumble of prisoners, their clothing giving them away as the emperor's soldiers.

Lucien and Zurina headed in their direction. More hostages of war to sort through, to decide who'd stay locked up for now and who might be willing to join our cause.

"Traitors," one man spat. "The emperor will mount your heads on spikes!"

The words cut through our conversation, but that wasn't what caused fury to simmer under my skin. He aimed the words at Lucien. I could see his form stiffen from here as the accusations slammed into him.

I crossed the garden and slid my arm through Lucien's—the best support I could think to offer at that moment. Tension pulled his muscles tight. I might as well have hugged a tree for how stiff he was.

The man's attention slid to me like a snake through the grass. "And now you've taken up with some rebel whore?"

Lucien stiffened more before relaxing all at once. His fingers intertwined with mine. Solid. Strong. Warm. "Call her that again and they'll be nothing left of you to imprison."

"Imprison!" he fumed. "Like some criminal? The emperor will never—"

"You'd rather the noose?" Lucien adjusted his stance and pulled me further into his arms. "Your emperor won't be there to save you. He'll have his own tribunal to attend."

"The city-states will never accomplish it," the seasoned man continued to spout. Though I didn't know him, Lucien seemed to, which would make him a high-ranking member of the emperor's forces. "They've never been aligned, not until we brought them together."

I leaned into Lucien, showing our unity. Unwittingly, the emperor had brought more than just the city-states together.

"You did unite us," Reyna confirmed, sliding into place at my side. "Though I'm sure that's not what the emperor intended."

"We're allies now." Or we would be soon enough. I took her hand in mine, a show of unity. "You've given common cause to the city-states for the first time in an age. Cause against the emperor. We won't soon forget what happens when we're divided, each looking out for ourselves. You can be sure of that. Our friends here"—I gestured to Nyke and the other rebels—"are proof of what we can do when we work together and trust one another."

"It doesn't look like this one plans to repent," Nyke said. His tanned features hardened. "I think we've had enough of this pig splatter. Lock him in the stables with the other animals."

The man continued to spew his fury as they led him away with the others they'd taken captive.

We'd won. The shock of it zipped through my body like a living season storm. I knew it, but until this moment, I hadn't felt it.

"We can rely on your support and that of Sorrena?" Reyna asked. A formality. From her blinding smile, she already knew my answer.

"Of course. It seems our cities already have a good bit of experience working together." I nodded toward Nyke. "More than I knew." If we'd worked together like this cycles ago, Ryszard would never have had the chance to conquer us. Not if we'd been unified. Allied.

"Good. I thought we might hold the trial in Zhine as a new neutral site of sorts? Something to consider." She waved her hand through the air.

"Someone will need to take on the mantle of leadership there, but I'm getting ahead of things. We have much to do yet. Just don't run off on us, you two." Reyna winked before walking away. She really was optimistic, already planning far down the road, but there was still much to do before then.

The others moved on as well. Alone with Lucien, my throat suddenly tightened.

Lucien... I'd wanted to ask him to come with me. Or at least, to let me stay with him.

How could I go back to Sorrena now? To step back into my role as heir? All politics and service to my city. Mother would never accept Lucien at my side. Not after what he'd done, and maybe not even if he was just some random man I'd fallen in love with. In her mind, leaders had no time for petty distractions like love and romance.

And then there was Basilla and Stefan. They deserved to know their son lived and to see him again. Would they accept him, knowing what he'd become? Somehow, I felt they would.

Lucien loosened his embrace and stepped away. "It sounds like you have a lot of work ahead of you in Sorrena rallying your people to the cause." He tried to smile, but it didn't reach his eyes. "When will you be leaving?"

The question pierced my heart, aching worse than the burns on my legs. "We still need to bring Zhine back into the fold, not to mention any supporters of the emperor lingering in the city-states," I hedged.

"You're not a fighter, Ilya. Politics and planning are your specialty. The rebels can handle the battles to come with me and the others. It'd be better if you're safe. Out of harm's way."

It didn't matter that his words were true, they stung like bees all the same. I looked away. "You want me gone so badly?"

"No!" He took my hands in his. "No. Never. If I had my way..." He shook his head. "But you're the heir of Sorrena. They'll need you to rebuild, to help them organize and join us for a march on Zhine, for the tribunal to come, and whatever other plans Reyna has up her sleeve for the future. You have a role to fill. People to lead."

I looked up into his stormy eyes. "Aren't you the one who said I'm more than my title?"

"Of course." His voice grew thick as his hands tightened on mine. "You're so much more."

"Then stay with me." I held my breath as I waited for him to respond. Each moment lasted far too long. "Unless you don't want that anymore," I continued when the silence stretched.

"I want that more than anything." He released my hands, cupping my face instead. "Anything. But in Sorrena, they—"

I shook my head. "Anywhere."

"But your people—"

"I will make sure they join our cause. As for leading them after the war, they can wait," I replied with a smile. "Mother is still strong. I doubt she'll relinquish the title anytime soon. And besides, I'm not their only heir. If they don't want to wait for me to find myself with you, or if they don't accept you, then Justina can rule." She was young yet, but Mother had plenty of time to train another successor if she needed to.

His mouth dropped open.

"It was all I wanted once, but no longer. There's more to life than a title. I choose love. I choose you. Whatever future that brings us, I want it." Weeks ago, I would have laughed at myself for such a statement, but it was true, every word of it. "Besides, if your parents do welcome you with open arms, as I think they might, you could have your own city to rule one day. You might need someone with experience. Someone trained to rule?" My whole body burned up from within, aching for him, trembling with the passion of my words and worry for his response.

Lucien dropped his arms as his chest shook with laughter. "Had your eye on a different title, huh?"

I swatted his shoulder, the heat rushing to my cheeks. "It's not like that."

"I know." He grinned. "And whatever the future holds, I know one thing for certain."

"That is?" I raised one brow as I slid closer to him.

"I want it to be with you."

Joy burst within me, crashing like the waves of a storm against the cliffs of my home and sending a ridiculous smile pulling at my cheeks.

"I've spent my whole life being the emperor's weapon," he continued. "Whatever comes next, I won't be that anymore, and I think you can help me figure out the man I'm supposed to be. The man I can only be with you at my side."

My lips quivered.

He drew me closer, leaning in until his forehead nearly pressed against mine. "I love you, Ilya. Only you. And I'd follow you anywhere, but I don't want you to be an outcast because of me, because of what I am."

I reached up on my toes and pressed my lips to his. A delicate kiss. A promise. "You're Lucien. The man I love. If they don't accept us in Sorrena or Trale, we'll forge our own path." I grinned as my whole body hummed. "You know, I've always been curious about the western kingdoms and their great cities."

His eyes hooded. "Planning our next adventure already? I think we'll be busy here for a while."

"True. We have our work cut out for us, but whatever comes after that, promise me we'll do it together, no matter what obstacles are put in our path. Just Ilya and Lucien. No titles. No past."

Lucien pulled me into his arms, knocking some of the wind from my lungs. "You make it sound so easy."

I leaned against his chest, looking up into his eyes. "I never promised easy, only that we'd do it together."

My throat tightened as tears pricked the corners of my eyes. He didn't give me time to recover, just took my lips with his, drawing me into a soul-deep kiss. I melted for him. My legs shook as I wrapped my arms around his neck and gave myself over to feeling and emotion.

Lucien broke our kiss and took a deep breath. "If you'll have me, if you truly want me for all that I am and all that I lack, then I'm yours. Whatever comes."

"I love you, Lucien. Whatever comes, we'll face it together."

Thank you for reading! Did you enjoy? Please add your review because nothing helps an author more and encourages readers to take a chance on a book than a review.

And don't miss more from Megan Van Dyke with SECOND STAR TO THE LEFT, available now. Turn the page for a sneak peek!

You can also sign up for the City Owl Press newsletter to receive notice of all book releases!

SNEAK PEEK OF SECOND STAR TO THE LEFT

Nothing attracted attention like free booze. The Lazy Mule wasn't usually this popular, or so the locals said, but the promise of free drinks lured every shopkeeper and down-on-their-luck sailor into the dirty, ramshackle building near the docks. Tropical air, thick with humidity and the promise of rain, filled the bar as tightly as the patrons crammed into every nook and cranny.

Tink pulled her braid over one shoulder, careful not to dislodge the sections covering her pointed ears. She rubbed the loose ends between her fingertips, feigning nervousness as she glanced over her shoulder.

Men and women alike clamored toward the far table where a large, blond man regaled the crowd with tales of his crew's success. He was attractive, with bulging muscles, towering height, and a chiseled jaw. But if he made one more crude joke about plundering something, Tink was going to toss her drink at him. *Stupid pirate*. Soon enough he'd stumble and fall, or the rotting table would finally give way. She grinned. That alone would be worth the cost of the trip.

But the blustering first mate of the *Jolly Roger* wasn't her target. No, to get what she needed, only the captain would do. Tink licked her lips as her gaze caught on the equally tall but leaner man with one shining black boot propped on the seat of a nearby chair. He shouted colorful additions to the first mate's tale and called for another round of drinks for all his "friends."

The poor ale Tink sipped turned sour on her tongue before she forced it down. The captain's arrogance knew no end. He traveled from one pirate-friendly port to the next so he and his crew could rave of their accomplishments. At least it made them easy to track.

Tonight, they bragged about their theft of the Heart of Fire, a stunning ruby set in gold. A half-grin pulled at her lips. What would they say when she stole it from them?

Captain Hook, so named for the distinctive metal weapon that replaced one hand, raised a pint in the air. Dark ale splashed over the side. Mugs clinked, rising with cheers from the crowd who joined in the toast.

Finally, *finally*, the captain glanced her way.

Her heart gave an involuntary leap as sinful lips twitched on a strong face. Or perhaps it was his coal-dark eyes that twisted her up inside. He raised his mug, taking a long swig, but his attention never left her.

Perfect.

One look and she'd hooked Hook. A small laugh burst from her lips that she covered by biting her bottom lip in feigned embarrassment.

Before he lowered his drink, Tink twisted around back to her mug warming on the bar. Warm ale and filthy pirates. Every girl's dream night.

She snorted. *Sure.*

Her stomach turned as she rubbed the mug between her palms. This wouldn't be her life. Not anymore, not after tonight.

A woman squealed as a drunkard yanked her onto his lap, nearly sending them both tumbling to the ale-soaked floor. How did she ever enjoy these horrid human bars? She and her cousin Lily used to slip through the pixie doors—the circles of trees, stones, mushrooms, or whatever the elders of old selected—for a little fun in the human world all the time. They'd drink, dance, flirt with whichever handsome human caught their eye, then sneak back home before the elders were ever the wiser. They'd done everything together for as long as she could remember. The elders frowned on such elicit exploits. But really, only allowing them out to trade and gather goods not available in their homeland was, well, boring.

Her chest grew tight. *Had Lily made it home? Was she okay?* The bracelet around her wrist with its broken gem weighed her down. Tink had committed an unforgivable sin—selling her pixie dust—to save Lily from that wretched Captain Blackbeard and his crew. A nastier man never drew breath. *Filthy pirate bastard.* That act got her banned from her homeland, Sylvanna Vale, rendering her unable to pass through the magical doorways. Pretending to be human and hiding her wings was a pain. *By Durin's beard, binding them hurts!* Without the cloak around her shoulders, someone would notice where she'd lashed them to her back, and that...well, best they didn't.

"Hey there, lovely lady." A man brushed against her at the bar, smelling of sweat and sour ale—or something even fouler.

"Hello." *And please go away*, she added silently, barely giving the man half a glance. If he had any wits, he'd leave.

"You here with anyone?"

Somehow his breath was worse than the stench clinging to him. Hanks of greasy hair lay against dirty skin. When was the last time he bathed? Humans were disgusting in general, but this one was something extra.

Tink glanced back at the pirates and stiffened. The captain was gone. *Shit. Where did he—*

The intruder slid in front of her. "I'll put the wind in yer sails if ya raise my mast."

Tink gaped. He did *not* just say that to her.

A burning flush rose from her chest to the tips of her ears. Her lips thinned. She needed to ditch this slob and quick. If she lost her chance to get the Heart of Fire because of this fool, she'd... Her nails dug into her palm. She didn't even know, but something horrible.

His filthy hand latched onto her arm. "Come on." Grime-crusted nails dug into her skin. "I can pay ya."

With one quick move, Tink *accidentally* knocked her drink over. Ale splashed across the man, some of it splattering her as well.

"You bitch!" He stumbled back. The man behind him barked in outrage.

Tink slid off her barstool, aiming to flee, but the man grabbed her arm again. She wrenched it back, her other hand sliding under her cloak, searching for her hidden dagger.

"I'll—" The man paled as a hand closed over his forearm. Clean, black cloth and fine stitching caught her eye.

"You'll leave the lady alone," the velvet voice rumbled just behind her.

Unexpected heat raced up her stiff spine. Captain Hook pushed the man away and wedged himself between them.

"You...you're..." the man stammered before turning and shoving his way through the crowd in haste.

"Good riddance." Hook faced her, glancing over the splatter of ale on the billowing tan shirt tucked into her tight breeches. "You all right, love?"

"I can take care of myself."

His eyes widened.

Shit. She was supposed to seduce him, not brush him off. "But..." She licked her lips before glancing away, then back. "I really appreciate the help."

He tipped an invisible hat, the motion as natural as if he rarely went around without one. "Always happy to help a lady in distress."

"How very gallant of you." It took everything she had to keep the sarcasm out of her voice.

"Can I buy you another drink..." He cocked his head, waiting for her name.

"Tinker Bell." *Oh, Beryl's wings.* She hadn't planned to give him her real one. She grinned through her error and slid closer. "And I do believe you already ordered another round for everyone."

His fingertips, with nails painted a midnight black, grazed the edge of her shoulder before he pulled back. The touch, so brief and fleeting, sent a thrill down to her toes. It shouldn't have. He was a pirate—a notorious one. Worse, her target. But if he was interested, it made her job so much easier. Stealing the ruby was a test, and she couldn't fail, not if she wanted the merfolk's queen, Titania, to trust her. She needed her trust before the queen would even discuss a trade for the black pearl—the only object known to fix anything broken, even her bracelet.

"Tinker Bell." He took his time with her name, and the way he drew out the words melted her more than any drink.

"Just Tink is fine," she added, suddenly warm.

"Aye. Not that swill, Tink." He gestured to the nearby drinks. "The barkeep has a few more pleasurable options."

"Well..." Tink ran her hand down his sleeve. "I think I might enjoy that."

Don't stop now. Keep reading with your copy of SECOND STAR TO THE LEFT

Don't miss more from Megan Van Dyke with SECOND STAR TO THE LEFT, available now, and discover all her books at www.authormeganvandyke.com

---

Tinker Bell, banished from her homeland for doing the unthinkable, selling the hottest drug in Neverland—pixie dust—wants absolution.

Determined to find a way home, Tink doesn't hesitate to follow the one lead she has, even if that means seducing a filthy pirate to steal precious gems out from under his...hook.

Captain Hook believes he's found a real treasure in Tink. That is, until he recovers from her pixie dust laced kiss with a curse that turns the seas against him. With his ship and reputation at the mercy of raging storms, he tracks down the little minx and demands she remove the curse. Too bad she can't.

However, the mermaid queen has a solution to both of their problems, if Tink and Hook will work together to retrieve a magical item for her.

As they venture to the mysterious Shrouded Isles to find the priceless treasure, their shared nemesis closes in. However, his wrath is nothing compared to the realization that achieving their goal may mean losing something they never expected to find—each other.

The swagger and adventure of Pirates of the Caribbean meets the sexy banter of The Hating Game with a healthy dose of steam in this retelling of Peter Pan that's far from the Neverland you know.

Please sign up for the City Owl Press newsletter for chances to win special subscriber-only contests and giveaways as well as receiving information on upcoming releases and special excerpts.

All reviews are **welcome** and **appreciated**. Please consider leaving one on your favorite social media and book buying sites.

Escape Your World. Get Lost in Ours! City Owl Press at www. cityowlpress.com.

ACKNOWLEDGMENTS

Thank you to my family for always loving and supporting me. You're the best thing in my life and I could not do this all without you. A special thanks to my kids who, without knowing it, played a special part in bringing this story to life. I wrote the first draft of it while pregnant with my son, and made the final revisions several years later, shortly after the birth of my daughter.

A huge thank you to my critique partners, writer friends, and Street Team for your constant support and encouragement, especially all of you who've been with me through the many ups and downs and years that this book was a work in progress.

Thank you to my editor Tee Tate for your incredible feedback and pushing me to consider changes that made this book even stronger.

To Maxym Martineau, thank you for mentoring me on this book years ago when it went by a completely different name. Your suggestions really helped this book grow and gave me encouragement during a time when I desperately needed it.

To the editor who gave me the most encouraging rejection ever: thank you for finding this book worthwhile and giving me the push I needed to keep going with it.

Finally, to my readers, thank you for letting me live my dreams by sharing my stories with you. Each time one of you reaches out to tell me how much you loved a story, or you post about it on social media, or leave a review, it completely makes my day. I am so grateful and wouldn't be able to keep putting out stories without your support.

About the Author

MEGAN VAN DYKE is a fantasy romance author with a love for all things magical and romantic, especially fairytales and anything with a happily ever after. Many of her stories include themes of family (whether born into or found) and a sense of home and belonging, which are important aspects of her life as well. When not writing, Megan loves to spend time with her family, cook, play video games, and explore the great  outdoors. Megan currently lives with her family in Florida. Be sure to sign up for her newsletter so you never miss a minute!

www.authormeganvandyke.com

instagram.com/authormeganvandyke
facebook.com/AuthorMeganVanDyke
x.com/AuthorMeganVD
tiktok.com/@authormeganvandyke
bookbub.com/authors/megan-van-dyke

About the Publisher

City Owl Press is a cutting edge indie publishing company, bringing the world of romance and speculative fiction to discerning readers.

Escape Your World. Get Lost in Ours!

www.cityowlpress.com

facebook.com/CityOwlPress

x.com/cityowlpress

instagram.com/cityowlbooks

pinterest.com/cityowlpress

tiktok.com/@cityowlpress

www.ingramcontent.com/pod-product-compliance
Lightning Source LLC
Chambersburg PA
CBHW030630020726
47493CB00006B/1651